Tales of a Traveller

Tales of a Traveller

Washington Irving

MINT EDITIONS

Tales of a Traveller was first published in 1824.

This edition published by Mint Editions 2021.

ISBN 9781513269672 | E-ISBN 9781513274676

Published by Mint Editions®

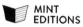
MINT
EDITIONS

minteditionbooks.com

Publishing Director: Jennifer Newens
Design & Production: Rachel Lopez Metzger
Typesetting: Westchester Publishing Services

Contents

PART FIRST

STRANGE STORIES BY A
NERVOUS GENTLEMAN

I'll tell you more; there was a fish taken,
A monstrous fish, with, a sword by's side, a long sword,
A pike in's neck, and a gun in's nose, a huge gun,
And letters of mart in's mouth, from the Duke of Florence.
Cleanthes. This is a monstrous lie.
Tony. I do confess it.
Do you think I'd tell you truths!

—Fletcher's Wife for a Month

[The following adventures were related to me by the same nervous gentleman who told me the romantic tale of The Stout Gentleman, published in Bracebridge Hall.

It is very singular, that although I expressly stated that story to have been told to me, and described the very person who told it, still it has been received as an adventure that happened to myself. Now, I protest I never met with any adventure of the kind. I should not have grieved at this, had it not been intimated by the author of Waverley, in an introduction to his romance of Peveril of the Peak, that he was himself the Stout Gentleman alluded to. I have ever since been importuned by letters and questions from gentlemen, and particularly from ladies without number, touching what I had seen of the great unknown.

Now, all this is extremely tantalizing. It is like being congratulated on the high prize when one has drawn a blank; for I have just as great a desire as any one of the public to penetrate the mystery of that very singular personage, whose voice fills every corner of the world, without any one being able to tell from whence it comes. He who keeps up such a wonderful and whimsical incognito: whom nobody knows, and yet whom every body thinks he can swear to.

My friend, the nervous gentleman, also, who is a man of very shy, Retired habits, complains that he has been excessively annoyed in consequence of its getting about in his neighborhood that he is the fortunate personage. Insomuch, that he has become a character of considerable notoriety in two or three country towns; and has been repeatedly teased to exhibit himself at blue-stocking parties, for no other reason than that of being "the gentleman who has had a glimpse of the author of Waverley."

Indeed, the poor man has grown ten times as nervous as ever, since he has discovered, on such good authority, who the stout gentleman was; and will never forgive himself for not having made a more resolute effort to get a full sight of him. He has anxiously endeavored to call up a recollection of what he saw of that portly personage; and has ever since kept a curious eye on all gentlemen of more than ordinary dimensions, whom he has seen getting into stage coaches. All in vain! The features he had caught a glimpse of seem common to the whole race of stout gentlemen; and the great unknown remains as great an unknown as ever.]

A Hunting Dinner

I was once at a hunting dinner, given by a worthy fox-hunting old Baronet, who kept Bachelor's Hall in jovial style, in an ancient rook-haunted family mansion, in one of the middle counties. He had been a devoted admirer of the fair sex in his young days; but having travelled much, studied the sex in various countries with distinguished success, and returned home profoundly instructed, as he supposed, in the ways of woman, and a perfect master of the art of pleasing, he had the mortification of being jilted by a little boarding school girl, who was scarcely versed in the accidence of love.

The Baronet was completely overcome by such an incredible defeat; retired from the world in disgust, put himself under the government of his housekeeper, and took to fox-hunting like a perfect Jehu. Whatever poets may say to the contrary, a man will grow out of love as he grows old; and a pack of fox hounds may chase out of his heart even the memory of a boarding-school goddess. The Baronet was when I saw him as merry and mellow an old bachelor as ever followed a hound; and the love he had once felt for one woman had spread itself over the whole sex; so that there was not a pretty face in the whole country round, but came in for a share.

The dinner was prolonged till a late hour; for our host having no ladies in his household to summon us to the drawing-room, the bottle maintained its true bachelor sway, unrivalled by its potent enemy the tea-kettle. The old hall in which we dined echoed to bursts of robustious fox-hunting merriment, that made the ancient antlers shake on the walls. By degrees, however, the wine and wassail of mine host began to operate upon bodies already a little jaded by the chase. The choice spirits that flashed up at the beginning of the dinner, sparkled for a time, then gradually went out one after another, or only emitted now and then a faint gleam from the socket.

Some of the briskest talkers, who had given tongue so bravely at the first burst, fell fast asleep; and none kept on their way but certain of those long-winded prosers, who, like short-legged hounds, worry on unnoticed at the bottom of conversation, but are sure to be in at the death. Even these at length subsided into silence; and scarcely any thing was heard but the nasal communications of two or three veteran masticators, who, having been silent while awake, were indemnifying the company in their sleep.

At length the announcement of tea and coffee in the cedar parlor roused all hands from this temporary torpor. Every one awoke marvellously renovated, and while sipping the refreshing beverage out of the Baronet's old-fashioned hereditary china, began to think of departing for their several homes. But here a sudden difficulty arose. While we had been prolonging our repast, a heavy winter storm had set in, with snow, rain, and sleet, driven by such bitter blasts of wind, that they threatened to penetrate to the very bone.

"It's all in vain," said our hospitable host, "to think of putting one's head out of doors in such weather. So, gentlemen, I hold you my guests for this night at least, and will have your quarters prepared accordingly."

The unruly weather, which became more and more tempestuous, rendered The hospitable suggestion unanswerable. The only question was, whether such an unexpected accession of company, to an already crowded house, would not put the housekeeper to her trumps to accommodate them.

"Pshaw," cried mine host, "did you ever know of a Bachelor's Hall that was not elastic, and able to accommodate twice as many as it could hold?" So out of a good-humored pique the housekeeper was summoned to consultation before us all. The old lady appeared, in her gala suit of faded brocade, which rustled with flurry and agitation, for in spite of mine host's bravado, she was a little perplexed. But in a bachelor's house, and with bachelor guests, these matters are readily managed. There is no lady of the house to stand upon squeamish points about lodging guests in odd holes and corners, and exposing the shabby parts of the establishment. A bachelor's housekeeper is used to shifts and emergencies. After much worrying to and fro, and divers consultations about the red room, and the blue room, and the chintz room, and the damask room, and the little room with the bow window, the matter was finally arranged.

When all this was done, we were once more summoned to the standing Rural amusement of eating. The time that had been consumed in dozing after dinner, and in the refreshment and consultation of the cedar parlor, was sufficient, in the opinion of the rosy-faced butler, to engender a reasonable appetite for supper. A slight repast had therefore been tricked up from the residue of dinner, consisting of cold sirloin of beef; hashed venison; a devilled leg of a turkey or so, and a few other of those light articles taken by country gentlemen to ensure sound sleep and heavy snoring.

The nap after dinner had brightened up every one's wit; and a great deal of excellent humor was expended upon the perplexities of mine host and his housekeeper, by certain married gentlemen of the company, who considered themselves privileged in joking with a bachelor's establishment. From this the banter turned as to what quarters each would find, on being thus suddenly billeted in so antiquated a mansion.

"By my soul," said an Irish captain of dragoons, one of the most merry and boisterous of the party—"by my soul, but I should not be surprised if some of those good-looking gentlefolks that hang along the walls, should walk about the rooms of this stormy night; or if I should find the ghost of one of these long-waisted ladies turning into my bed in mistake for her grave in the church-yard.

"Do you believe in ghosts, then?" said a thin, hatchet-faced gentleman, with projecting eyes like a lobster.

I had remarked this last personage throughout dinner-time for one of Those incessant questioners, who seem to have a craving, unhealthy appetite in conversation. He never seemed satisfied with the whole of a story; never laughed when others laughed; but always put the joke to the question. He could never enjoy the kernel of the nut, but pestered himself to get more out of the shell.

"Do you believe in ghosts, then?" said the inquisitive gentleman.

"Faith, but I do," replied the jovial Irishman; "I was brought up in the fear and belief of them; we had a Benshee in our own family, honey."

"A Benshee—and what's that?" cried the questioner.

"Why an old lady ghost that tends upon your real Milesian families, and wails at their window to let them know when some of them are to die."

"A mighty pleasant piece of information," cried an elderly gentleman, with a knowing look and a flexible nose, to which he could give a whimsical twist when he wished to be waggish.

"By my soul, but I'd have you know it's a piece of distinction to be waited upon by a Benshee. It's a proof that one has pure blood in one's veins. But, egad, now we're talking of ghosts, there never was a house or a night better fitted than the present for a ghost adventure. Faith, Sir John, haven't you such a thing as a haunted chamber to put a guest in?"

"Perhaps," said the Baronet, smiling, "I might accommodate you even on that point."

"Oh, I should like it of all things, my jewel. Some dark oaken room, with ugly wo-begone portraits that stare dismally at one, and about which the housekeeper has a power of delightful stories of love and murder. And then a dim lamp, a table with a rusty sword across it, and a spectre all in white to draw aside one's curtains at midnight—"

"In truth," said an old gentleman at one end of the table, "you put me in mind of an anecdote—"

"Oh, a ghost story! a ghost story!" was vociferated round the board, every one edging his chair a little nearer.

The attention of the whole company was now turned upon the speaker. He was an old gentleman, one side of whose face was no match for the other. The eyelid drooped and hung down like an unhinged window shutter. Indeed, the whole side of his head was dilapidated, and seemed like the wing of a house shut up and haunted. I'll warrant that side was well stuffed with ghost stories.

There was a universal demand for the tale.

"Nay," said the old gentleman, "it's a mere anecdote—and a very commonplace one; but such as it is you shall have it. It is a story that I once heard my uncle tell when I was a boy. But whether as having happened to himself or to another, I cannot recollect. But no matter, it's very likely it happened to himself, for he was a man very apt to meet with strange adventures. I have heard him tell of others much more singular. At any rate, we will suppose it happened to himself."

"What kind of man was your uncle?" said the questioning gentleman.

"Why, he was rather a dry, shrewd kind of body; a great traveller, and fond of telling his adventures."

"Pray, how old might he have been when this happened?"

"When what happened?" cried the gentleman with the flexible nose, impatiently—"Egad, you have not given any thing a chance to happen —come, never mind our uncle's age; let us have his adventures."

The inquisitive gentleman being for the moment silenced, the old gentleman with the haunted head proceeded.

The Adventure of My Uncle

Many years since, a long time before the French revolution, my uncle had passed several months at Paris. The English and French were on better terms, in those days, than at present, and mingled cordially together in society. The English went abroad to spend money then, and the French were always ready to help them: they go abroad to save money at present, and that they can do without French assistance. Perhaps the travelling English were fewer and choicer then, than at present, when the whole nation has broke loose, and inundated the continent. At any rate, they circulated more readily and currently in foreign society, and my uncle, during his residence in Paris, made many very intimate acquaintances among the French noblesse.

Some time afterwards, he was making a journey in the winter-time, in that part of Normandy called the Pays de Caux, when, as evening was closing in, he perceived the turrets of an ancient chateau rising out of the trees of its walled park, each turret with its high conical roof of gray slate, like a candle with an extinguisher on it.

"To whom does that chateau belong, friend?" cried my uncle to a meager, but fiery postillion, who, with tremendous jack boots and cocked hat, was floundering on before him.

"To Monseigneur the Marquis de ——," said the postillion, touching his hat, partly out of respect to my uncle, and partly out of reverence to the noble name pronounced. My uncle recollected the Marquis for a particular friend in Paris, who had often expressed a wish to see him at his paternal chateau. My uncle was an old traveller, one that knew how to turn things to account. He revolved for a few moments in his mind how agreeable it would be to his friend the Marquis to be surprised in this sociable way by a pop visit; and how much more agreeable to himself to get into snug quarters in a chateau, and have a relish of the Marquis's well-known kitchen, and a smack of his superior champagne and burgundy; rather than take up with the miserable lodgment, and miserable fare of a country inn. In a few minutes, therefore, the meager postillion was cracking his whip like a very devil, or like a true Frenchman, up the long straight avenue that led to the chateau.

You have no doubt all seen French chateaus, as every body travels in France nowadays. This was one of the oldest; standing naked and alone, in the midst of a desert of gravel walks and cold stone terraces; with a cold-looking formal garden, cut into angles and rhomboids; and a cold leafless park, divided geometrically by straight alleys; and two or three noseless, cold-looking statues without any clothing; and fountains spouting cold water enough to make one's teeth chatter. At least, such was the feeling they imparted on the wintry day of my uncle's visit; though, in hot summer weather, I'll warrant there was glare enough to scorch one's eyes out.

The smacking of the postillion's whip, which grew more and more intense the nearer they approached, frightened a flight of pigeons out of the dove-cote, and rooks out of the roofs; and finally a crew of servants out of the chateau, with the Marquis at their head. He was enchanted to see my uncle; for his chateau, like the house of our worthy host, had not many more guests at the time than it could accommodate. So he kissed my uncle on each cheek, after the French fashion, and ushered him into the castle.

The Marquis did the honors of his house with the urbanity of his country. In fact, he was proud of his old family chateau; for part of it was extremely old. There was a tower and chapel that had been built almost before the memory of man; but the rest was more modern; the castle having been nearly demolished during the wars of the League. The Marquis dwelt upon this event with great satisfaction, and seemed really to entertain a grateful feeling towards Henry IV., for having thought his paternal mansion worth battering down. He had many stories to tell of the prowess of his ancestors, and several skull-caps, helmets, and cross-bows to show; and divers huge boots and buff jerkins, that had been worn by the Leaguers. Above all, there was a two-handled sword, which he could hardly wield; but which he displayed as a proof that there had been giants in his family.

In truth, he was but a small descendant from such great warriors. When you looked at their bluff visages and brawny limbs, as depicted in their portraits, and then at the little Marquis, with his spindle shanks; his sallow lanthern visage, flanked with a pair of powdered ear-locks, or *ailes de pigeon*, that seemed ready to fly away with it; you would hardly believe him to be of the same race. But when you looked at the eyes that sparkled out like a beetle's from each side of his hooked nose, you saw at once that he inherited all the fiery spirit of his forefathers. In fact, a Frenchman's spirit never exhales, however his body may dwindle. It rather rarefies, and grows more inflammable, as the earthly particles diminish; and I have seen valor enough in a little fiery-hearted French dwarf, to have furnished out a tolerable giant.

When once the Marquis, as he was wont, put on one of the old helmets that were stuck up in his hall; though his head no more filled it than a dry pea its pease cod; yet his eyes sparkled from the bottom of the iron cavern with the brilliancy of carbuncles, and when he poised the ponderous two-handled sword of his ancestors, you would have thought you saw the doughty little David wielding the sword of Goliath, which was unto him like a weaver's beam.

However, gentlemen, I am dwelling too long on this description of the Marquis and his chateau; but you must excuse me; he was an old friend of my uncle's, and whenever my uncle told the story, he was always fond of talking a great deal about his host.—Poor little Marquis! He was one of that handful of gallant courtiers, who made such a devoted, but hopeless stand in the cause of their sovereign, in the chateau of the Tuilleries, against the irruption of the mob, on the sad tenth of August.

He displayed the valor of a preux French chevalier to the last; flourished feebly his little court sword with a sa-sa! in face of a whole legion of *sans-culottes*; but was pinned to the wall like a butterfly, by the pike of a poissarde, and his heroic soul was borne up to heaven on his *ailes de pigeon*.

But all this has nothing to do with my story; to the point then:—

When the hour arrived for retiring for the night, my uncle was shown to his room, in a venerable old tower. It was the oldest part of the chateau, and had in ancient times been the Donjon or stronghold; of course the chamber was none of the best. The Marquis had put him there, however, because he knew him to be a traveller of taste, and fond of antiquities; and also because the better apartments were already occupied. Indeed, he perfectly reconciled my uncle to his quarters by mentioning the great personages who had once inhabited them, all of whom were in some way or other connected with the family. If you would take his word for it, John Baliol, or, as he called him, Jean de Bailleul, had died of chagrin in this very chamber on hearing of the success of his rival, Robert the Bruce, at the battle of Bannockburn; and when he added that the Duke de Guise had slept in it during the wars of the League, my uncle was fain to felicitate himself upon being honored with such distinguished quarters.

The night was shrewd and windy, and the chamber none of the warmest. An old, long-faced, long-bodied servant in quaint livery, who attended upon my uncle, threw down an armful of wood beside the fire-place, gave a queer look about the room, and then wished him *bon repos*, with a grimace and a shrug that would have been suspicious from any other than an old French servant. The chamber had indeed a wild, crazy look, enough to strike any one who had read romances with apprehension and foreboding. The windows were high and narrow, and had once been loop-holes, but had been rudely enlarged, as well as the extreme thickness of the walls would permit; and the ill-fitted casements rattled to every breeze. You would have thought, on a windy night, some of the old Leaguers were tramping and clanking about the apartment in their huge boots and rattling spurs. A door which stood ajar, and like a true French door would stand ajar, in spite of every reason and effort to the contrary, opened upon a long, dark corridor, that led the Lord knows whither, and seemed just made for ghosts to air themselves in, when they turned out of their graves at midnight. The wind would spring up into a hoarse murmur through this passage, and creak the door to and fro, as if some dubious ghost were balancing in its mind whether to come in or not. In a word, it was precisely the kind of comfortless apartment that a ghost, if ghost there were in the chateau, would single out for its favourite lounge.

My uncle, however, though a man accustomed to meet with strange adventures, apprehended none at the time. He made several attempts to shut the door, but in vain. Not that he apprehended any thing, for he was too old a traveller to be daunted by a wild-looking apartment; but the night, as I have said, was cold and gusty, something like the present, and the wind howled about the old turret, pretty much as it does round this old mansion at this moment; and the breeze from the long dark corridor came in as damp and chilly as if from a dungeon. My uncle, therefore, since he could not close the door, threw a quantity of wood on the fire, which soon sent up a flame in the great wide-mouthed chimney that illumined the whole chamber, and made the shadow of the tongs on the opposite wall, look like a long-legged giant. My uncle now clambered on top of the half score of mattresses which form a French bed, and which stood in a deep recess; then tucking himself snugly in, and burying himself up to the chin in the bed-clothes, he lay looking at the fire, and listening to the wind, and chuckling to think how knowingly he had come over his friend the Marquis for a night's lodgings: and so he fell asleep.

He had not taken above half of his first nap, when he was awakened by the clock of the chateau, in the turret over his chamber, which struck

WASHINGTON IRVING

midnight. It was just such an old clock as ghosts are fond of. It had a deep, dismal tone, and struck so slowly and tediously that my uncle thought it would never have done. He counted and counted till he was confident he counted thirteen, and then it stopped.

The fire had burnt low, and the blaze of the last faggot was almost expiring, burning in small blue flames, which now and then lengthened up into little white gleams. My uncle lay with his eyes half closed, and his nightcap drawn almost down to his nose. His fancy was already wandering, and began to mingle up the present scene with the crater of Vesuvius, the French opera, the Coliseum at Rome, Dolly's chop-house in London, and all the farrago of noted places with which the brain of a traveller is crammed—in a word, he was just falling asleep.

Suddenly he was aroused by the sound of foot-steps that appeared to be slowly pacing along the corridor. My uncle, as I have often heard him say himself, was a man not easily frightened; so he lay quiet, supposing that this might be some other guest; or some servant on his way to bed. The footsteps, however, approached the door; the door gently opened; whether of its own accord, or whether pushed open, my uncle could not distinguish:—a figure all in white glided in. It was a female, tall and stately in person, and of a most commanding air. Her dress was of an ancient fashion, ample in volume and sweeping the floor. She walked up to the fire-place without regarding my uncle; who raised his nightcap with one hand, and stared earnestly at her. She remained for some time standing by the fire, which flashing up at intervals cast blue and white gleams of light that enabled my uncle to remark her appearance minutely.

Her face was ghastly pale, and perhaps rendered still more so by the Blueish light of the fire. It possessed beauty, but its beauty was saddened by care and anxiety. There was the look of one accustomed to trouble, but of one whom trouble could not cast down nor subdue; for there was still the predominating air of proud, unconquerable resolution. Such, at least, was the opinion formed by my uncle, and he considered himself a great physiognomist.

The figure remained, as I said, for some time by the fire, putting out first one hand, then the other, then each foot, alternately, as if warming itself; for your ghosts, if ghost it really was, are apt to be cold. My uncle furthermore remarked that it wore high-heeled shoes, after an ancient fashion, with paste or diamond buckles, that sparkled as though they were alive. At length the figure turned gently round, casting a glassy look about the apartment, which, as it passed over my uncle, made his blood run cold, and chilled the very marrow in his bones. It then stretched its arms toward heaven, clasped its hands, and wringing them in a supplicating manner, glided slowly out of the room.

My uncle lay for some time meditating on this visitation, for (as he Remarked when he told me the story) though a man of firmness, he was also a man of reflection, and did not reject a thing because it was out of the regular course of events. However, being, as I have before said, a great traveller, and accustomed to strange adventures, he drew his nightcap resolutely over his eyes, turned his back to the door, hoisted the bedclothes high over his shoulders, and gradually fell asleep.

How long he slept he could not say, when he was awakened by the voice of some one at his bed-side. He turned round and beheld the old French servant, with his ear-locks in tight buckles on each side of a long, lanthorn face, on which habit had deeply wrinkled an everlasting smile. He made a thousand grimaces and asked a thousand pardons for disturbing Monsieur, but the morning was considerably advanced. While my uncle was dressing, he called vaguely to mind the visitor of the preceding night. He asked the ancient domestic what lady was in the habit of rambling about this part of the chateau at night. The old valet shrugged his shoulders as high as his head, laid one hand on his bosom, threw open the other with every finger extended; made a most whimsical grimace, which he meant to be complimentary:

"It was not for him to know any thing of *les braves fortunes* of Monsieur."

My uncle saw there was nothing satisfactory to be learnt in this quarter. After breakfast he was walking with the Marquis through the modern apartments of the chateau; sliding over the well-waxed floors of silken saloons, amidst furniture rich in gilding and brocade; until they came to a long picture gallery, containing many portraits, some in oil and some in chalks.

Here was an ample field for the eloquence of his host, who had all the family pride of a nobleman of the *ancient regime*. There was not a grand name in Normandy, and hardly one in France, that was not, in some way or other, connected with his house. My uncle stood listening with inward impatience, resting sometimes on one leg, sometimes on the other, as the little Marquis descanted, with his usual fire and vivacity, on the achievements of his ancestors, whose portraits hung along the wall; from the martial deeds of the stern warriors in steel, to the gallantries and intrigues of the blue-eyed gentlemen, with fair smiling faces, powdered ear-locks, laced ruffles, and pink and blue silk coats and breeches; not forgetting the conquests of the lovely shepherdesses, with hoop petticoats and waists no thicker than an hour glass, who appeared ruling over their sheep and their swains with dainty crooks decorated with fluttering ribbands.

In the midst of his friend's discourse my uncle's eyes rested on a full-length portrait, which struck him as being the very counterpart of his visitor of the preceding night.

"Methinks," said he, pointing to it, "I have seen the original of this portrait."

"*Pardonnez moi*," replied the Marquis politely, "that can hardly be, as the lady has been dead more than a hundred years. That was the beautiful Duchess de Longueville, who figured during the minority of Louis the Fourteenth."

"And was there any thing remarkable in her history."

Never was question more unlucky. The little Marquis immediately threw himself into the attitude of a man about to tell a long story. In fact, my uncle had pulled upon himself the whole history of the civil war of the Fronde, in which the beautiful Duchess had played so distinguished a part. Turenne, Coligni, Mazarin, were called up from their graves to grace his narration; nor were the affairs of the Barricadoes, nor the chivalry of the Pertcocheres forgotten. My uncle began to wish himself a thousand leagues off from the Marquis and his merciless memory, when suddenly the little man's recollections took a more interesting turn. He was relating the imprisonment of the Duke de Longueville, with the Princes Condé and Conti, in the chateau of Vincennes, and the ineffectual efforts of the Duchess to rouse the sturdy Normans to their rescue. He had come to that part where she was invested by the royal forces in the chateau of Dieppe, and in imminent danger of falling into their hands.

"The spirit of the Duchess," proceeded the Marquis, "rose with her trials. It was astonishing to see so delicate and beautiful a being buffet so resolutely with hardships. She determined on a desperate means of escape. One dark unruly night, she issued secretly out of a small postern gate of the castle, which the enemy had neglected to guard. She was followed by her female attendants, a few domestics, and some gallant cavaliers who still remained faithful to her fortunes. Her object was to gain a small port about two leagues distant, where she had privately provided a vessel for her escape in case of emergency.

"The little band of fugitives were obliged to perform the distance on foot. When they arrived at the port the wind was high and stormy, the tide contrary, the vessel anchored far off in the road, and no means of getting on board, but by a fishing shallop that lay tossing like a cockle shell on the edge of the surf. The Duchess determined to risk the attempt. The seamen endeavored to dissuade her, but the imminence of her danger on shore, and the magnanimity of her spirit urged her on. She had to be borne to the shallop in the arms of a mariner. Such was the violence of the wind and waves, that he faltered, lost his foothold, and let his precious burden fall into the sea.

"The Duchess was nearly drowned; but partly through her own struggles, partly by the exertions of the seamen, she got to land. As soon as she had a little recovered strength, she insisted on renewing the attempt. The storm, however, had by this time become so violent as to set all efforts at defiance. To delay, was to be discovered and taken prisoner. As the only resource left, she procured horses; mounted with her female attendants *en croupe* behind the gallant gentlemen who accompanied her; and scoured the country to seek some temporary asylum.

"While the Duchess," continued the Marquis, laying his forefinger on my uncle's breast to arouse his flagging attention, "while the Duchess, poor lady, was wandering amid the tempest in this disconsolate manner, she arrived at this chateau. Her approach caused some uneasiness; for the clattering of a troop of horse, at dead of night, up the avenue of a lonely chateau, in those unsettled times, and in a troubled part of the country, was enough to occasion alarm.

"A tall, broad-shouldered chasseur, armed to the teeth, galloped ahead, and announced the name of the visitor. All uneasiness was dispelled. The household turned out with flambeaux to receive her, and never did torches gleam on a more weather-beaten, travel-stained band than came tramping into the court. Such pale, care-worn faces, such bedraggled dresses, as the poor Duchess and her females presented, each seated behind her cavalier; while half drenched, half drowsy pages and attendants seemed ready to fall from their horses with sleep and fatigue.

"The Duchess was received with a hearty welcome by my ancestors. She was ushered into the Hall of the chateau, and the fires soon crackled and blazed to cheer herself and her train; and every spit and stewpan was put in requisition to prepare ample refreshments for the wayfarers.

"She had a right to our hospitalities," continued the little Marquis, drawing himself up with a slight degree of stateliness, "for she was related to our family. I'll tell you how it was: Her father, Henry de Bourbon, Prince of Condé—"

"But did the Duchess pass the night in the chateau?" said my uncle rather abruptly, terrified at the idea of getting involved in one of the Marquis's genealogical discussions.

"Oh, as to the Duchess, she was put into the apartment you occupied last night; which, at that time, was a kind of state apartment. Her followers were quartered in the chambers opening upon the neighboring corridor, and her favorite page slept in an adjoining closet. Up and down the corridor walked the great chasseur, who had announced her arrival, and who acted as a kind of sentinel or guard. He was a dark, stern, powerful-looking fellow, and as the light of a lamp in the corridor fell upon his deeply-marked face and sinewy form, he seemed capable of defending the castle with his single arm.

"It was a rough, rude night; about this time of the year.—*Apropos*— now I think of it, last night was the anniversary of her visit. I may well remember the precise date, for it was a night not to be forgotten by our house. There is a singular tradition concerning it in our family." Here the Marquis hesitated, and a cloud seemed to gather about his bushy eyebrows. "There is a tradition—that a strange occurrence took place that night—a strange, mysterious, inexplicable occurrence."

Here he checked himself and paused.

"Did it relate to that lady?" inquired my uncle, eagerly.

"It was past the hour of midnight," resumed the Marquis—"when the whole chateau—"

Here he paused again—my uncle made a movement of anxious curiosity.

"Excuse me," said the Marquis—a slight blush streaking his sullen visage. "There are some circumstances connected with our family history which I do not like to relate. That was a rude period. A time of great crimes among great men: for you know high blood, when it runs wrong, will not run tamely like blood of the *canaille*—poor lady!—But I have a little family pride, that—excuse me—we will change the subject if you please."—

My uncle's curiosity was piqued. The pompous and magnificent introduction had led him to expect something wonderful in the story to which it served as a kind of avenue. He had no idea of being cheated out of it by a sudden fit of unreasonable squeamishness. Besides, being a traveller, in quest of information, considered it his duty to inquire into every thing.

The Marquis, however, evaded every question.

"Well," said my uncle, a little petulantly, "whatever you may think of it, I saw that lady last night."

The Marquis stepped back and gazed at him with surprise.

"She paid me a visit in my bed-chamber."

The Marquis pulled out his snuff-box with a shrug and a smile; taking it no doubt for an awkward piece of English pleasantry, which politeness required him to be charmed with. My uncle went on gravely, however, and related the whole circumstance. The Marquis heard him through with profound attention, holding his snuff-box unopened in his hand. When the story was finished he tapped on the lid of his box deliberately; took a long sonorous pinch of snuff—

"Bah!" said the Marquis, and walked toward the other end of the gallery.—

HERE THE NARRATOR PAUSED. THE company waited for some time for him to resume his narrative; but he continued silent.

"Well," said the inquisitive gentleman, "and what did your uncle say then?"

"Nothing," replied the other.

"And what did the Marquis say farther?"

"Nothing."

"And is that all?"

"That is all," said the narrator, filling a glass of wine.

"I surmise," said the shrewd old gentleman with the waggish nose— "I surmise it was the old housekeeper walking her rounds to see that all was right."

"Bah!" said the narrator, "my uncle was too much accustomed to strange sights not to know a ghost from a housekeeper!"

There was a murmur round the table half of merriment, half of disappointment. I was inclined to think the old gentleman had really an afterpart of his story in reserve; but he sipped his wine and said nothing more; and there was an odd expression about his dilapidated countenance that left me in doubt whether he were in drollery or earnest.

"Egad," said the knowing gentleman with the flexible nose, "this story of your uncle puts me in mind of one that used to be told of an aunt of mine, by the mother's side; though I don't know that it will bear a comparison; as the good lady was not quite so prone to meet with strange adventures. But at any rate, you shall have it."

THE ADVENTURE OF MY AUNT

My aunt was a lady of large frame, strong mind, and great resolution; she was what might be termed a very manly woman. My uncle was a thin, puny little man, very meek and acquiescent, and no match for my aunt. It was observed that he dwindled and dwindled gradually away, from the day of his marriage. His wife's powerful mind was too much for him; it wore him out. My aunt, however, took all possible care of him, had half the doctors in town to prescribe for him, made him take all their prescriptions, *willy nilly*, and dosed him with physic enough to cure a whole hospital. All was in vain. My uncle grew worse and worse the more dosing and nursing he underwent, until in the end he added another to the long list of matrimonial victims, who have been killed with kindness.

"And was it his ghost that appeared to her?" asked the inquisitive gentleman, who had questioned the former storyteller.

"You shall hear," replied the narrator:—My aunt took on mightily for the death of her poor dear husband! Perhaps she felt some compunction at having given him so much physic, and nursed him into his grave. At any rate, she did all that a widow could do to honor his memory. She spared no expense in either the quantity or quality of her mourning weeds; she wore a miniature of him about her neck, as large as a little sun dial; and she had a full-length portrait of him always hanging in her bed chamber. All the world extolled her conduct to the skies; and it was determined, that a woman who behaved so well to the memory of one husband, deserved soon to get another.

It was not long after this that she went to take up her residence in an old country seat in Derbyshire, which had long been in the care of merely a steward and housekeeper. She took most of her servants with her, intending to make it her principal abode. The house stood in a lonely, wild part of the country among the gray Derbyshire hills; with a murderer hanging in chains on a bleak height in full view.

The servants from town were half frightened out of their wits, at the idea of living in such a dismal, pagan-looking place; especially when they got together in the servants' hall in the evening, and compared notes on all the hobgoblin stories they had picked up in the course of the day. They were afraid to venture alone about the forlorn black-looking chambers. My ladies' maid, who was troubled with nerves,

WASHINGTON IRVING

declared she could never sleep alone in such a "gashly, rummaging old building;" and the footman, who was a kind-hearted young fellow, did all in his power to cheer her up.

My aunt, herself, seemed to be struck with the lonely appearance of the house. Before she went to bed, therefore, she examined well the fastenings of the doors and windows, locked up the plate with her own hands, and carried the keys, together with a little box of money and jewels, to her own room; for she was a notable woman, and always saw to all things herself. Having put the keys under her pillow, and dismissed her maid, she sat by her toilet arranging her hair; for, being, in spite of her grief for my uncle, rather a buxom widow, she was a little particular about her person. She sat for a little while looking at her face in the glass, first on one side, then on the other, as ladies are apt to do, when they would ascertain if they have been in good looks; for a roystering country squire of the neighborhood, with whom she had flirted when a girl, had called that day to welcome her to the country.

All of a sudden she thought she heard something move behind her. She Looked hastily round, but there was nothing to be seen. Nothing but the grimly painted portrait of her poor dear man, which had been hung against the wall. She gave a heavy sigh to his memory, as she was accustomed to do, whenever she spoke of him in company; and went on adjusting her nightdress. Her sigh was re-echoed; or answered by a long-drawn breath. She looked round again, but no one was to be seen. She ascribed these sounds to the wind, oozing through the rat holes of the old mansion; and proceeded leisurely to put her hair in papers, when, all at once, she thought she perceived one of the eyes of the portrait move.

"The back of her head being towards it!" said the story-teller with the ruined head, giving a knowing wink on the sound side of his visage— "good!"

"Yes, sir!" replied drily the narrator, "her back being towards the portrait, but her eye fixed on its reflection in the glass."

Well, as I was saying, she perceived one of the eyes of the portrait move. So strange a circumstance, as you may well suppose, gave her a sudden shock. To assure herself cautiously of the fact, she put one hand to her forehead, as if rubbing it; peeped through her fingers, and moved the candle with the other hand. The light of the taper gleamed on the eye, and was reflected from it. She was sure it moved. Nay, more, it seemed to give her a wink, as she had sometimes known her husband to do when living! It struck a momentary chill to her heart; for she was a lone woman, and felt herself fearfully situated.

The chill was but transient. My aunt, who was almost as resolute a personage as your uncle, sir, (turning to the old story-teller,) became instantly calm and collected. She went on adjusting her dress. She even hummed a favorite air, and did not make a single false note. She casually overturned a dressing box; took a candle and picked up the articles leisurely, one by one, from the floor, pursued a rolling pin-cushion that was making the best of its way under the bed; then opened the door; looked for an instant into the corridor, as if in doubt whether to go; and then walked quietly out.

She hastened down-stairs, ordered the servants to arm themselves with the first weapons that came to hand, placed herself at their head, and returned almost immediately.

Her hastily levied army presented a formidable force. The steward had a rusty blunderbuss; the coachman a loaded whip; the footman a pair of horse pistols; the cook a huge chopping knife, and the butler a bottle in each hand. My aunt led the van with a red-hot poker; and, in my opinion, she was the most formidable of the party. The waiting maid brought up the rear, dreading to stay alone in the servants' hall, smelling to a broken bottle of volatile salts, and expressing her terror of the ghosteses.

"Ghosts!" said my aunt resolutely, "I'll singe their whiskers for them!"

They entered the chamber. All was still and undisturbed as when she left it. They approached the portrait of my uncle.

"Pull me down that picture!" cried my aunt.

A heavy groan, and a sound like the chattering of teeth, was heard from the portrait. The servants shrunk back. The maid uttered a faint shriek, and clung to the footman.

"Instantly!" added my aunt, with a stamp of the foot.

The picture was pulled down, and from a recess behind it, in which had formerly stood a clock, they hauled forth a round-shouldered, black-bearded varlet, with a knife as long as my arm, but trembling all over like an aspen leaf.

"Well, and who was he? No ghost, I suppose!" said the inquisitive gentleman.

"A knight of the post," replied the narrator, "who had been smitten with the worth of the wealthy widow; or rather a marauding Tarquin, who had stolen into her chamber to violate her purse and rifle her strong box when all the house should be asleep. In plain terms," continued he, "the vagabond was a loose idle fellow of the neighborhood, who had once been a servant in the house, and had been employed to assist in arranging it for the reception of its mistress. He confessed that he had contrived his hiding-place for his nefarious purposes, and had borrowed an eye from the portrait by way of a reconnoitering hole."

"And what did they do with him—did they hang him?" resumed the questioner.

"Hang him?—how could they?" exclaimed a beetle-browed barrister, with a hawk's nose—"the offence was not capital—no robbery nor assault had been committed—no forcible entry or breaking into the premises—"

"My aunt," said the narrator, "was a woman of spirit, and apt to take the law into her own hands. She had her own notions of cleanliness also. She ordered the fellow to be drawn through the horsepond to cleanse away all offences, and then to be well rubbed down with an oaken towel."

"And what became of him afterwards?" said the inquisitive gentleman.

"I do not exactly know—I believe he was sent on a voyage of improvement to Botany Bay."

"And your aunt—" said the inquisitive gentleman—"I'll warrant she took care to make her maid sleep in the room with her after that."

"No, sir, she did better—she gave her hand shortly after to the roystering squire; for she used to observe it was a dismal thing for a woman to sleep alone in the country."

"She was right," observed the inquisitive gentleman, nodding his head sagaciously—"but I am sorry they did not hang that fellow."

It was agreed on all hands that the last narrator had brought his tale to the most satisfactory conclusion; though a country clergyman present regretted that the uncle and aunt, who figured in the different stories, had not been married together. They certainly would have been well matched.

"But I don't see, after all," said the inquisitive gentleman, "that there was any ghost in this last story."

"Oh, if it's ghosts you want, honey," cried the Irish captain of dragoons, "if it's ghosts you want, you shall have a whole regiment of them. And since these gentlemen have been giving the adventures of their uncles and aunts, faith and I'll e'en give you a chapter too, out of my own family history."

THE BOLD DRAGOON; OR THE ADVENTURE
OF MY GRANDFATHER

My grandfather was a bold dragoon, for it's a profession, d'ye see, that has run in the family. All my forefathers have been dragoons and died upon the field of honor except myself, and I hope my posterity may be able to say the same; however, I don't mean to be vainglorious. Well, my grandfather, as I said, was a bold dragoon, and had served in the Low Countries. In fact, he was one of that very army, which, according to my uncle Toby, "swore so terribly in Flanders." He could swear a good stick himself; and, moreover, was the very man that introduced the doctrine Corporal Trim mentions, of radical heat and radical moisture; or, in other words, the mode of keeping out the damps of ditch water by burnt brandy. Be that as it may, it's nothing to the purport of my story. I only tell it to show you that my grandfather was a man not easily to be humbugged. He had seen service; or, according to his own phrase, "he had seen the devil"—and that's saying everything.

Well, gentlemen, my grandfather was on his way to England, for which he intended to embark at Ostend;—bad luck to the place for one where I was kept by storms and head winds for three long days, and the divil of a jolly companion or pretty face to comfort me. Well, as I was saying, my grandfather was on his way to England, or rather to Ostend—no matter which, it's all the same. So one evening, towards nightfall, he rode jollily into Bruges. Very like you all know Bruges, gentlemen, a queer, old-fashioned Flemish town, once they say a great place for trade and money-making, in old times, when the Mynheers were in their glory; but almost as large and as empty as an Irishman's pocket at the present day.

Well, gentlemen, it was the time of the annual fair. All Bruges was crowded; and the canals swarmed with Dutch boats, and the streets swarmed with Dutch merchants; and there was hardly any getting along for goods, wares, and merchandises, and peasants in big breeches, and women in half a score of petticoats.

My grandfather rode jollily along in his easy, slashing way, for he was a saucy, sunshiny fellow—staring about him at the motley crowd, and the old houses with gable ends to the street and storks' nests on the chimneys; winking at the ya vrouws who showed their faces at the windows, and joking the women right and left in the street; all of whom laughed and took it in amazing good part; for though he did not know a word of their language, yet he always had a knack of making himself understood among the women.

Well, gentlemen, it being the time of the annual fair, all the town was crowded; every inn and tavern full, and my grandfather applied in vain from one to the other for admittance. At length he rode up to an old rackety inn that looked ready to fall to pieces, and which all the rats would have run away from, if they could have found room in any other house to put their heads. It was just such a queer building as you see in Dutch pictures, with a tall roof that reached up into the clouds; and as many garrets, one over the other, as the seven heavens of Mahomet. Nothing had saved it from tumbling down but a stork's nest on the chimney, which always brings good luck to a house in the Low Countries; and at the very time of my grandfather's arrival, there were two of these long-legged birds of grace, standing like ghosts on the chimney top. Faith, but they've kept the house on its legs to this very day; for you may see it any time you pass through Bruges, as it stands there yet; only it is turned into a brewery—a brewery of strong Flemish beer; at least it was so when I came that way after the battle of Waterloo.

My grandfather eyed the house curiously as he approached. It might Not altogether have struck his fancy, had he not seen in large letters over the door,

HEER VERKOOPT MAN GOEDEN DRANK.

MY GRANDFATHER HAD LEARNT ENOUGH of the language to know that the sign promised good liquor. "This is the house for me," said he, stopping short before the door.

The sudden appearance of a dashing dragoon was an event in an old inn, frequented only by the peaceful sons of traffic. A rich burgher of Antwerp, a stately ample man, in a broad Flemish hat, and who was the great man and great patron of the establishment, sat smoking a clean long pipe on one side of the door; a fat little distiller of Geneva from Schiedam, sat smoking on the other, and the bottle-nosed host stood in the door, and the comely hostess, in crimped cap, beside him; and the hostess' daughter, a plump Flanders lass, with long gold pendants in her ears, was at a side window.

"Humph!" said the rich burgher of Antwerp, with a sulky glance at the stranger.

"Der duyvel!" said the fat little distiller of Schiedam.

The landlord saw with the quick glance of a publican that the new guest was not at all, at all, to the taste of the old ones; and to tell the truth, he did not himself like my grandfather's saucy eye.

He shook his head—"Not a garret in the house but was full."

"Not a garret!" echoed the landlady.

"Not a garret!" echoed the daughter.

The burgher of Antwerp and the little distiller of Schiedam continued to smoke their pipes sullenly, eyed the enemy askance from under their broad hats, but said nothing.

My grandfather was not a man to be browbeaten. He threw the reins on his horse's neck, cocked his hat on one side, stuck one arm akimbo, slapped his broad thigh with the other hand—

"Faith and troth!" said he, "but I'll sleep in this house this very night!"

My grandfather had on a tight pair of buckskins—the slap went to the landlady's heart.

He followed up the vow by jumping off his horse, and making his way past the staring Mynheers into the public room. May be you've been in the barroom of an old Flemish inn—faith, but a handsome chamber it was as you'd wish to see; with a brick floor, a great fire-place, with the whole Bible history in glazed tiles; and then the mantel-piece, pitching itself head foremost out of the wall, with a whole regiment of cracked tea-pots and earthen jugs paraded on it; not to mention half a dozen great Delft platters hung about the room by way of pictures; and the little bar in one corner, and the bouncing bar-maid inside of it with a red calico cap and yellow ear-drops.

My grandfather snapped his fingers over his head, as he cast an eye round the room: "Faith, this is the very house I've been looking after," said he.

There was some farther show of resistance on the part of the garrison, but my grandfather was an old soldier, and an Irishman to boot, and not easily repulsed, especially after he had got into the fortress. So he blarney'd the landlord, kissed the landlord's wife, tickled the landlord's daughter, chucked the bar-maid under the chin; and it was agreed on all hands that it would be a thousand pities, and a burning shame into the bargain, to turn such a bold dragoon into the streets. So they laid their heads together, that is to say, my grandfather and the landlady, and it was at length agreed to accommodate him with an old chamber that had for some time been shut up.

"Some say it's haunted!" whispered the landlord's daughter, "but you're a bold dragoon, and I dare say you don't fear ghosts."

"The divil a bit!" said my grandfather, pinching her plump cheek; "but if I should be troubled by ghosts, I've been to the Red Sea in my time, and have a pleasant way of laying them, my darling!"

And then he whispered something to the girl which made her laugh, and give him a good-humored box on the ear. In short, there was nobody knew better how to make his way among the petticoats than my grandfather.

In a little while, as was his usual way, he took complete possession of the house: swaggering all over it;—into the stable to look after his horse; into the kitchen to look after his supper. He had something to say or do with every one; smoked with the Dutchmen; drank with the Germans; slapped the men on the shoulders, tickled the women under the ribs:—never since the days of Ally Croaker had such a rattling blade been seen. The landlord stared at him with astonishment; the landlord's daughter hung her head and giggled whenever he came near; and as he turned his back and swaggered along, his tight jacket setting off his broad shoulders and plump buckskins, and his long sword trailing by his side, the maids whispered to one another—"What a proper man!"

At supper my grandfather took command of the table d'hôte as though he had been at home; helped everybody, not forgetting himself; talked with every one, whether he understood their language or not; and made his way into the intimacy of the rich burgher of Antwerp, who had never been known to be sociable with any one during his life. In fact, he revolutionized the whole establishment, and gave it such a rouse, that the very house reeled with it. He outsat every one at table excepting the little fat distiller of Schiedam, who had sat soaking for a long time before he broke forth; but when he did, he was a very devil incarnate. He took a violent affection for my grandfather; so they sat drinking, and smoking, and telling stories, and singing Dutch and Irish songs, without understanding a word each other said, until the little Hollander was fairly swampt with his own gin and water, and carried off to bed, whooping and hiccuping, and trolling the burthen of a Low Dutch love song.

Well, gentlemen, my grandfather was shown to his quarters, up a huge staircase composed of loads of hewn timber; and through long rigmarole passages, hung with blackened paintings of fruit, and fish, and game, and country frollics, and huge kitchens, and portly burgomasters, such as you see about old-fashioned Flemish inns, till at length he arrived at his room.

An old-times chamber it was, sure enough, and crowded with all kinds of trumpery. It looked like an infirmary for decayed and superannuated furniture; where everything diseased and disabled was sent to nurse, or to be forgotten. Or rather, it might have been taken for a general congress of old legitimate moveables, where every kind and country had a representative. No two chairs were alike: such high backs and low backs, and leather bottoms and worsted bottoms, and straw bottoms, and no bottoms; and cracked marble tables with curiously carved legs, holding balls in their claws, as though they were going to play at ninepins.

My grandfather made a bow to the motley assemblage as he entered, and having undressed himself, placed his light in the fire-place, asking pardon of the tongs, which seemed to be making love to the shovel in the chimney corner, and whispering soft nonsense in its ear.

The rest of the guests were by this time sound asleep; for your Mynheers are huge sleepers. The house maids, one by one, crept up yawning to their attics, and not a female head in the inn was laid on a pillow that night without dreaming of the Bold Dragoon.

My grandfather, for his part, got into bed, and drew over him one of those great bags of down, under which they smother a man in the Low Countries; and there he lay, melting between, two feather beds, like an anchovy sandwich between two slices of toast and butter. He was a warm-complexioned man, and this smothering played the very deuce with him. So, sure enough, in a little while it seemed as if a legion of imps were twitching at him and all the blood in his veins was in fever heat.

He lay still, however, until all the house was quiet, excepting the snoring of the Mynheers from the different chambers; who answered one another in all kinds of tones and cadences, like so many bull-frogs in a swamp. The quieter the house became, the more unquiet became my grandfather. He waxed warmer and warmer, until at length the bed became too hot to hold him.

"May be the maid had warmed it too much?" said the curious gentleman, inquiringly.

"I rather think the contrary," replied the Irishman. "But be that as it may, it grew too hot for my grandfather."

"Faith there's no standing this any longer," says he; so he jumped out of bed and went strolling about the house.

"What for?" said the inquisitive gentleman.

"Why, to cool himself to be sure," replied the other, "or perhaps to find a more comfortable bed—or perhaps—but no matter what he went for—he never mentioned; and there's no use in taking up our time in conjecturing."

Well, my grandfather had been for some time absent from his room, and was returning, perfectly cool, when just as he reached the door he heard a strange noise within. He paused and listened. It seemed as if some one was trying to hum a tune in defiance of the asthma. He recollected the report of the room's being haunted; but he was no believer in ghosts. So he pushed the door gently ajar, and peeped in.

Egad, gentlemen, there was a gambol carrying on within enough to have astonished St. Anthony.

By the light of the fire he saw a pale weazen-faced fellow in a long Flannel gown and a tall white night-cap with a tassel to it, who sat by the fire, with a bellows under his arm by way of bagpipe, from which he forced the asthmatical music that had bothered my grandfather. As he played, too, he kept twitching about with a thousand queer contortions; nodding his head and bobbing about his tasselled night-cap.

My grandfather thought this very odd, and mighty presumptuous, and was about to demand what business he had to play his wind instruments in another gentleman's quarters, when a new cause of astonishment met his eye. From the opposite side of the room a long-backed, bandy-legged chair, covered with leather, and studded all over in a coxcomical fashion with little brass nails, got suddenly into motion; thrust out first a claw foot, then a crooked arm, and at length, making a leg, slided gracefully up to an easy chair, of tarnished brocade, with a hole in its bottom, and led it gallantly out in a ghostly minuet about the floor.

The musician now played fiercer and fiercer, and bobbed his head and His nightcap about like mad. By degrees the dancing mania seemed to seize upon all the other pieces of furniture. The antique, long-bodied chairs paired off in couples and led down a country dance; a three-legged stool danced a hornpipe, though horribly puzzled by its supernumerary leg; while the amorous tongs seized the shovel round the waist, and whirled it about the room in a German waltz. In short, all the moveables got in motion, capering about; pirouetting, hands across, right and left, like so many devils, all except a great clothes-press, which kept curtseying and curtseying, like a dowager, in one corner, in exquisite time to the music;—being either too corpulent to dance, or perhaps at a loss for a partner.

My grandfather concluded the latter to be the reason; so, being, like a true Irishman, devoted to the sex, and at all times ready for a frolic, he bounced into the room, calling to the musician to strike up "Paddy O'Rafferty," capered up to the clothes-press and seized upon two handles to lead her out:—When, whizz!—the whole revel was at an end. The chairs, tables, tongs, and shovel slunk in an instant as quietly into their places as if nothing had happened; and the musician vanished up the chimney, leaving the bellows behind him in his hurry. My grandfather found himself seated in the middle of the floor, with the clothes-press sprawling before him, and the two handles jerked off and in his hands.

"Then after all, this was a mere dream!" said the inquisitive gentleman.

"The divil a bit of a dream!" replied the Irishman: "there never was a truer fact in this world. Faith, I should have liked to see any man tell my grandfather it was a dream."

Well, gentlemen, as the clothes-press was a mighty heavy body, and my grandfather likewise, particularly in rear, you may easily suppose two such heavy bodies coming to the ground would make a bit of a noise. Faith, the old mansion shook as though it had mistaken it for an earthquake. The whole garrison was alarmed. The landlord, who slept just below, hurried up with a candle to inquire the cause, but with all his haste his daughter had hurried to the scene of uproar before him. The landlord was followed by the landlady, who was followed by the bouncing bar-maid, who was followed by the simpering chambermaids all holding together, as well as they could, such garments as they had first lain hands on; but all in a terrible hurry to see what the devil was to pay in the chamber of the bold dragoon.

My grandfather related the marvellous scene he had witnessed, and the prostrate clothes-press, and the broken handles, bore testimony to the fact. There was no contesting such evidence; particularly with a lad of my grandfather's complexion, who seemed able to make good every word either with sword or shillelah. So the landlord scratched his head and looked silly, as he was apt to do when puzzled. The landlady scratched—no, she did not scratch her head,—but she knit her brow, and did not seem half pleased with the explanation. But the landlady's daughter corroborated it by recollecting that the last person who had dwelt in that chamber was a famous juggler who had died of St. Vitus's dance, and no doubt had infected all the furniture.

This set all things to rights, particularly when the chambermaids declared that they had all witnessed strange carryings on in that room;— and as they declared this "upon their honors," there could not remain a doubt upon the subject.

"And did your grandfather go to bed again in that room?" said the inquisitive gentleman.

"That's more than I can tell. Where he passed the rest of the night was a secret he never disclosed. In fact, though he had seen much service, he was but indifferently acquainted with geography, and apt to make blunders in his travels about inns at night, that it would have puzzled him sadly to account for in the morning."

"Was he ever apt to walk in his sleep?" said the knowing old gentleman.

"Never that I heard of."

The Adventure of the German Student

On a stormy night, in the tempestuous times of the French revolution, a young German was returning to his lodgings, at a late hour, across the old part of Paris. The lightning gleamed, and the loud claps of thunder rattled through the lofty, narrow streets—but I should first tell you something about this young German.

Gottfried Wolfgang was a young man of good family. He had studied for some time at Göttingen, but being of a visionary and enthusiastic character, he had wandered into those wild and speculative doctrines which have so often bewildered German students. His secluded life, his intense application, and the singular nature of his studies, had an effect on both mind and body. His health was impaired; his imagination diseased. He had been indulging in fanciful speculations on spiritual essences until, like Swedenborg, he had an ideal world of his own around him. He took up a notion, I do not know from what cause, that there was an evil influence hanging over him; an evil genius or spirit seeking to ensnare him and ensure his perdition. Such an idea working on his melancholy temperament produced the most gloomy effects. He became haggard and desponding. His friends discovered the mental malady preying upon him, and determined that the best cure was a change of scene; he was sent, therefore, to finish his studies amidst the splendours and gaieties of Paris.

Wolfgang arrived at Paris at the breaking out of the revolution. The popular delirium at first caught his enthusiastic mind, and he was captivated by the political and philosophical theories of the day: but the scenes of blood which followed shocked his sensitive nature; disgusted him with society and the world, and made him more than ever a recluse. He shut himself up in a solitary apartment in the *Pays Latin*, the quarter of students. There in a gloomy street not far from the monastic walls of the Sorbonne, he pursued his favourite speculations. Sometimes he spent hours together in the great libraries of Paris, those catacombs of departed authors, rummaging among their hoards of dusty and obsolete works in quest of food for his unhealthy appetite. He was, in a manner, a literary goul, feeding in the charnel house of decayed literature.

Wolfgang, though solitary and recluse, was of an ardent temperament, but for a time it operated merely upon his imagination. He was too shy and ignorant of the world to make any advances to the fair, but he was a passionate admirer of female beauty, and in his lonely chamber would often lose himself in reveries on forms and faces which he had seen, and his fancy would deck out images of loveliness far surpassing the reality.

While his mind was in this excited and sublimated state, a dream produced an extraordinary effect upon him. It was of a female face of transcendent beauty. So strong was the impression made, that he dreamt of it again and again. It haunted his thoughts by day, his slumbers by night; in fine, he became passionately enamoured of this shadow of a dream. This lasted so long, that it became one of those fixed ideas which haunt the minds of melancholy men, and are at times mistaken for madness.

Such was Gottfried Wolfgang, and such his situation at the time I mentioned. He was returning home late one stormy night, through some of the old and gloomy streets of the *Marais*, the ancient part of Paris. The loud claps of thunder rattled among the high houses of the narrow streets. He came to the Place de Grève, the square where public executions are performed. The lightning quivered about the pinnacles of the ancient Hôtel de Ville, and shed flickering gleams over the open space in front. As Wolfgang was crossing the square, he shrank back with horror at finding himself close by the guillotine. It was the height of the reign of terror, when this dreadful instrument of death stood ever ready, and its scaffold was continually running with the blood of the virtuous and the brave. It had that very day been actively employed in the work of carnage, and there it stood in grim array amidst a silent and sleeping city, waiting for fresh victims.

Wolfgang's heart sickened within him, and he was turning shuddering from the horrible engine, when he beheld a shadowy form cowering as it were at the foot of the steps which led up to the scaffold. A succession of vivid flashes of lightning revealed it more distinctly. It was a female figure, dressed in black. She was seated on one of the lower steps of the scaffold, leaning forward, her face hid in her lap, and her long dishevelled tresses hanging to the ground, streaming with the rain which fell in torrents. Wolfgang paused. There was something awful in this solitary monument of wo. The female had the appearance of being above the common order. He knew the times to be full of vicissitude, and that many a fair head, which had once been pillowed on down, now wandered houseless. Perhaps this was some poor mourner whom the dreadful axe had rendered desolate, and who sat here heartbroken on the strand of existence, from which all that was dear to her had been launched into eternity.

He approached, and addressed her in the accents of sympathy. She raised her head and gazed wildly at him. What was his astonishment at beholding, by the bright glare of the lightning, the very face which had haunted him in his dreams. It was pale and disconsolate, but ravishingly beautiful.

Trembling with violent and conflicting emotions, Wolfgang again accosted her. He spoke something of her being exposed at such an hour of the night, and to the fury of such a storm, and offered to conduct her to her friends. She pointed to the guillotine with a gesture of dreadful signification.

"I have no friend on earth!" said she.

"But you have a home," said Wolfgang.

"Yes—in the grave!"

The heart of the student melted at the words.

"If a stranger dare make an offer," said he, "without danger of being misunderstood, I would offer my humble dwelling as a shelter; myself as a devoted friend. I am friendless myself in Paris, and a stranger in the land; but if my life could be of service, it is at your disposal, and should be sacrificed before harm or indignity should come to you."

There was an honest earnestness in the young man's manner that had its effect. His foreign accent, too, was in his favour; it showed him not to be a hackneyed inhabitant of Paris. Indeed there is an eloquence in true enthusiasm that is not to be doubted. The homeless stranger confided herself implicitly to the protection of the student.

He supported her faltering steps across the Pont Neuf, and by the place where the statue of Henry the Fourth had been overthrown by the populace. The storm had abated, and the thunder rumbled at a distance. All Paris was quiet; that great volcano of human passion slumbered for a while, to gather fresh strength for the next day's eruption. The student conducted his charge through the ancient streets of the *Pays Latin*, and by the dusky walls of the Sorbonne to the great, dingy hotel which he inhabited. The old portress who admitted them stared with surprise at the unusual sight of the melancholy Wolfgang with a female companion.

On entering his apartment, the student, for the first time, blushed at the scantiness and indifference of his dwelling. He had but one chamber—an old fashioned saloon—heavily carved and fantastically furnished with the remains of former magnificence, for it was one of those hotels in the quarter of the Luxembourg palace which had once belonged to nobility. It was lumbered with books and papers, and all the usual apparatus of a student, and his bed stood in a recess at one end.

When lights were brought, and Wolfgang had a better opportunity of contemplating the stranger, he was more than ever intoxicated by her beauty. Her face was pale, but of a dazzling fairness, set off by a profusion of raven hair that hung clustering about it. Her eyes were large and brilliant, with a singular expression approaching almostto wildness.Asfar as her black dress permitted her shape to be seen, it was of perfect symmetry. Her whole appearance was highly striking, though she was dressed in the simplest style. The only thing approaching to an ornament which she wore was a broad, black band round her neck, clasped by diamonds.

The perplexity now commenced with the student how to dispose of the helpless being thus thrown upon his protection. He thought of abandoning his chamber to her, and seeking shelter for himself elsewhere. Still he was so fascinated by her charms, there seemed to be such a spell upon his thoughts and senses, that he could not tear himself from her presence. Her manner, too, was singular and unaccountable. She spoke no more of the guillotine. Her grief had abated. The attentions of the student had first won her confidence, and then, apparently, her heart. She was evidently an enthusiast like himself, and enthusiasts soon understand each other.

In the infatuation of the moment Wolfgang avowed his passion for her. He told her the story of his mysterious dream, and how she had possessed his heart before he had even seen her. She was strangely affected by his recital, and acknowledged to have felt an impulse towards him equally unaccountable. It was the time for wild theory and wild actions. Old prejudices and superstitions were done away; every thing was under the sway of the "Goddess of Reason." Among other rubbish of the old times, the forms and ceremonies of marriage began to be considered superfluous bonds for honourable minds. Social compacts were the vogue. Wolfgang was too much of a theorist not to be tainted by the liberal doctrines of the day.

"Why should we separate?" said he: "our hearts are united; in the eye of reason and honour we are as one. What need is there of sordid forms to bind high souls together?"

The stranger listened with emotion: she had evidently received illumination at the same school.

"You have no home nor family," continued he; "let me be every thing to you, or rather let us be every thing to one another. If form is necessary, form shall be observed—there is my hand. I pledge myself to you for ever."

"For ever?" said the stranger, solemnly.

"For ever!" repeated Wolfgang.

The stranger clasped the hand extended to her: "Then I am yours," murmured she, and sank upon his bosom.

The next morning the student left his bride sleeping, and sallied forth at an early hour to seek more spacious apartments, suitable to the change in his situation. When he returned, he found the stranger lying with her head hanging over the bed, and one arm thrown over it. He spoke to her, but received no reply. He advanced to awaken her from her uneasy posture. On taking her hand, it was cold—there was no pulsation—her face was pallid and ghastly.—In a word—she was a corpse.

Horrified and frantic, he alarmed the house. A scene of confusion ensued. The police was summoned. As the officer of police entered the room, he started back on beholding the corpse.

"Great heaven!" cried he, "how did this woman come here?"

"Do you know any thing about her?" said Wolfgang, eagerly.

"Do I?" exclaimed the police officer: "she was guillotined yesterday!"

He stepped forward; undid the black collar round the neck of the corpse, and the head rolled on the floor!

The student burst into a frenzy. "The fiend! the fiend has gained possession of me!" shrieked he: "I am lost for ever!"

They tried to soothe him, but in vain. He was possessed with the frightful belief that an evil spirit had reanimated the dead body to ensnare him. He went distracted, and died in a madhouse.

Here the old gentleman with the haunted head finished his narrative.

"And is this really a fact?" said the inquisitive gentleman.

"A fact not to be doubted," replied the other. "I had it from the best authority. The student told it me himself. I saw him in a madhouse at Paris."

THE ADVENTURE OF THE
MYSTERIOUS PICTURE

As one story of the kind produces another, and as all the company seemed fully engrossed by the topic, and disposed to bring their relatives and ancestors upon the scene, there is no knowing how many more ghost adventures we might have heard, had not a corpulent old fox-hunter, who had slept soundly through the whole, now suddenly awakened, with a loud and long-drawn yawn. The sound broke the charm; the ghosts took to flight as though it had been cock-crowing, and there was a universal move for bed.

"And now for the haunted chamber," said the Irish captain, taking his candle.

"Aye, who's to be the hero of the night?" said the gentleman with the ruined head.

"That we shall see in the morning," said the old gentleman with the nose: "whoever looks pale and grizzly will have seen the ghost."

"Well, gentlemen," said the Baronet, "there's many a true thing said in jest. In fact, one of you will sleep in a room tonight—"

"What—a haunted room? a haunted room? I claim the adventure—and I—and I—and I," cried a dozen guests, talking and laughing at the same time.

"No—no," said mine host, "there is a secret about one of my rooms on which I feel disposed to try an experiment. So, gentlemen, none of you shall know who has the haunted chamber, until circumstances reveal it. I will not even know it myself, but will leave it to chance and the allotment of the housekeeper. At the same time, if it will be any satisfaction to you, I will observe, for the honor of my paternal mansion, that there's scarcely a chamber in it but is well worthy of being haunted."

We now separated for the night, and each went to his allotted room. Mine was in one wing of the building, and I could not but smile at its resemblance in style to those eventful apartments described in the tales of the supper table. It was spacious and gloomy, decorated with lamp-black portraits, a bed of ancient damask, with a tester sufficiently lofty to grace a couch of state, and a number of massive pieces of old-fashioned furniture. I drew a great claw-footed arm-chair before the wide fire-place; stirred up the fire; sat looking into it, and musing upon the odd stories I had heard; until, partly overcome by the fatigue of the day's hunting, and partly by the wine and wassail of mine host, I fell asleep in my chair.

The uneasiness of my position made my slumber troubled, and laid me at the mercy of all kinds of wild and fearful dreams; now it was that my perfidious dinner and supper rose in rebellion against my peace. I was hag-ridden by a fat saddle of mutton; a plum pudding weighed like lead upon my conscience; the merry thought of a capon filled me with horrible suggestions; and a devilled leg of a turkey stalked in all kinds of diabolical shapes through my imagination. In short, I had a violent fit of the nightmare. Some strange indefinite evil seemed hanging over me that I could not avert; something terrible and loathsome oppressed me that I could not shake off. I was conscious of being asleep, and strove to rouse myself, but every effort redoubled the evil; until gasping, struggling, almost strangling, I suddenly sprang bolt upright in my chair, and awoke.

The light on the mantel-piece had burnt low, and the wick was divided; there was a great winding sheet made by the dripping wax, on the side towards me. The disordered taper emitted a broad flaring flame, and threw a strong light on a painting over the fire-place, which I had not hitherto observed.

It consisted merely of a head, or rather a face, that appeared to be staring full upon me, and with an expression that was startling. It was without a frame, and at the first glance I could hardly persuade myself that it was not a real face, thrusting itself out of the dark oaken pannel. I sat in my chair gazing at it, and the more I gazed the more it disquieted me. I had never before been affected in the same way by any painting. The emotions it caused were strange and indefinite. They were something like what I have heard ascribed to the eyes of the basilisk; or like that mysterious influence in reptiles termed fascination. I passed my hand over my eyes several times, as if seeking instinctively to brush away this allusion—in vain—they instantly reverted to the picture, and its chilling, creeping influence over my flesh was redoubled.

I looked around the room on other pictures, either to divert my attention, or to see whether the same effect would be produced by them. Some of them were grim enough to produce the effect, if the mere grimness of the painting produced it—no such thing. My eye passed over them all with perfect indifference, but the moment it reverted to this visage over the fire-place, it was as if an electric shock darted through me. The other pictures were dim and faded; but this one protruded from a plain black ground in the strongest relief, and with wonderful truth of coloring. The expression was that of agony—the agony of intense bodily pain; but a menace scowled upon the brow, and a few sprinklings of blood added to its ghastliness. Yet it was not all these characteristics—it was some horror of the mind, some inscrutable antipathy awakened by this picture, which harrowed up my feelings.

I tried to persuade myself that this was chimerical; that my brain was confused by the fumes of mine host's good cheer, and, in some measure, by the odd stories about paintings which had been told at supper. I determined to shake off these vapors of the mind; rose from my chair, and walked about the room; snapped my fingers; rallied myself; laughed aloud. It was a forced laugh, and the echo of it in the old chamber jarred upon my ear. I walked to the window; tried to discern the landscape through the glass. It was pitch darkness, and howling storm without; and as I heard the wind moan among the trees, I caught a reflection of this accursed visage in the pane of glass, as though it were staring through the window at me. Even the reflection of it was thrilling.

How was this vile nervous fit, for such I now persuaded myself it was, to be conquered? I determined to force myself not to look at the painting but to undress quickly and get into bed. I began to undress, but in spite of every effort I could not keep myself from stealing a glance every now and then at the picture; and a glance was now sufficient to distress me. Even when my back was turned to it, the idea of this strange face behind me, peering over my shoulder, was insufferable. I threw off my clothes and hurried into bed; but still this visage gazed upon me. I had a full view of it from my bed, and for some time could not take my eyes from it. I had grown nervous to a dismal degree.

I put out the light, and tried to force myself to sleep;—all in vain! The fire gleaming up a little, threw an uncertain light about the room, leaving, however, the region of the picture in deep shadow. What, thought I, if this be the chamber about which mine host spoke as having a mystery reigning over it?—I had taken his words merely as spoken in jest; might they have a real import? I looked around. The faintly lighted apartment had all the qualifications requisite for a haunted chamber. It began in my infected imagination to assume strange appearances. The old portraits turned paler and paler, and blacker and blacker; the streaks of light and shadow thrown among the quaint old articles of furniture, gave them singular shapes and characters. There was a huge dark clothes-press of antique form, gorgeous in brass and lustrous with wax, that began to grow oppressive to me.

Am I then, thought I, indeed, the hero of the haunted room? Is there really a spell laid upon me, or is this all some contrivance of mine host, to raise a laugh at my expense? The idea of being hag-ridden by my own fancy all night, and then bantered on my haggard looks the next day was intolerable; but the very idea was sufficient to produce the effect, and to render me still more nervous. Pish, said I, it can be no such thing. How could my worthy host imagine that I, or any man would be so worried by a mere picture? It is my own diseased imagination that torments me. I turned in my bed, and shifted from side to side, to try to fall asleep; but all in vain. When one cannot get asleep by lying quiet, it is seldom that tossing about will effect the purpose. The fire gradually went out and left the room in darkness. Still I had the idea of this inexplicable countenance gazing and keeping watch upon me through the darkness. Nay, what was worse, the very darkness seemed to give it additional power, and to multiply its terrors. It was like having an unseen enemy hovering about one in the night. Instead of having one picture now to worry me, I had a hundred. I fancied it in every direction. And there it is, thought I,—and there, and there,—with its horrible and mysterious expression, still gazing and gazing on me. No if I must suffer this strange and dismal influence, it were better face a single foe, than thus be haunted by a thousand images of it.

Whoever has been in such a state of nervous agitation must know that the longer it continues, the more uncontrollable it grows; the very air of the chamber seemed at length infected by the baleful presence of this picture. I fancied it hovering over me. I almost felt the fearful visage from the wall approaching my face,—it seemed breathing upon me. This is not to be borne, said I, at length, springing out of bed. I can stand this no longer. I shall only tumble and toss about here all night; make a very spectre of myself, and become the hero of the haunted chamber in good earnest. Whatever be the consequence. I'll quit this cursed room, and seek a night's rest elsewhere. They can but laugh at me at all events, and they'll be sure to have the laugh upon me if I pass a sleepless night and show them a haggard and wo-begone visage in the morning.

All this was half muttered to myself, as I hastily slipped on my clothes; which having done, I groped my way out of the room, and down-stairs to the drawing-room. Here, after tumbling over two or three pieces of furniture, I made out to reach a sofa, and stretching myself upon it determined to bivouac there for the night.

The moment I found myself out of the neighborhood of that strange picture, it seemed as if the charm were broken. All its influence was at an end. I felt assured that it was confined to its own dreary chamber, for I had, with a sort of instinctive caution, turned the key when I closed the door. I soon calmed down, therefore, into a state of tranquillity; from that into a drowsiness, and finally into a deep sleep; out of which I did not awake, until the housemaid, with her besom and her matin song, came to put the room in order. She stared at finding me stretched upon the sofa; but I presume circumstances of the kind were not uncommon after hunting dinners, in her master's bachelor establishment; for she went on with her song and her work, and took no farther heed of me.

I had an unconquerable repugnance to return to my chamber; so I found my way to the butler's quarters, made my toilet in the best way circumstances would permit, and was among the first to appear at the breakfast table. Our breakfast was a substantial fox-hunter's repast, and the company were generally assembled at it. When ample justice had been done to the tea, coffee, cold meats, and humming ale, for all these were furnished in abundance, according to the tastes of the different guests, the conversation began to break out, with all the liveliness and freshness of morning mirth.

"But who is the hero of the haunted chamber?—Who has seen the ghost last night?" said the inquisitive gentleman, rolling his lobster eyes about the table.

The question set every tongue in motion; a vast deal of bantering; criticising of countenances; of mutual accusation and retort took place. Some had drunk deep, and some were unshaven, so that there were suspicious faces enough in the assembly. I alone could not enter with ease and vivacity into the joke. I felt tongue-tied—embarrassed. A recollection of what I had seen and felt the preceding night still haunted my mind.

It seemed as if the mysterious picture still held a thrall upon me. I thought also that our host's eye was turned on me with an air of curiosity. In short, I was conscious that I was the hero of the night, and felt as if every one might read it in my looks.

The jokes, however, passed over, and no suspicion seemed to attach to me. I was just congratulating myself on my escape, when a servant came in, saying, that the gentleman who had slept on the sofa in the drawing-room, had left his watch under one of the pillows. My repeater was in his hand.

"What!" said the inquisitive gentleman, "did any gentleman sleep on the sofa?"

"Soho! soho! a hare—a hare!" cried the old gentleman with the flexible nose.

I could not avoid acknowledging the watch, and was rising in great confusion, when a boisterous old squire who sat beside me, exclaimed, slapping me on the shoulder, "'Sblood, lad! thou'rt the man as has seen the ghost!"

The attention of the company was immediately turned to me; if my face had been pale the moment before, it now glowed almost to burning. I tried to laugh, but could only make a grimace; and found all the muscles of my face twitching at sixes and sevens, and totally out of all control.

It takes but little to raise a laugh among a set of fox-hunters. There was a world of merriment and joking at my expense; and as I never relished a joke overmuch when it was at my own expense, I began to feel a little nettled. I tried to look cool and calm and to restrain my pique; but the coolness and calmness of a man in a passion are confounded treacherous.

Gentlemen, said I, with a slight cocking of the chin, and a bad attempt at a smile, this is all very pleasant—ha! ha!—very pleasant—but I'd have you know I am as little superstitious as any of you—ha! ha!—and as to anything like timidity—you may smile, gentlemen—but I trust there is no one here means to insinuate that.—As to a room's being haunted, I repeat, gentlemen—(growing a little warm at seeing a cursed grin breaking out round me)—as to a room's being haunted, I have as little faith in such silly stories as any one. But, since you put the matter home to me, I will say that I have met with something in my room strange and inexplicable to me—(a shout of laughter). Gentlemen, I am serious—I know well what I am saying—I am calm, gentlemen, (striking my flat upon the table)—by heaven I am calm. I am neither trifling, nor do I wish to be trifled with—(the laughter of the company suppressed with ludicrous attempts at gravity). There is a picture in the room in which I was put last night, that has had an effect upon me the most singular and incomprehensible.

"A picture!" said the old gentleman with the haunted head. "A picture!" cried the narrator with the waggish nose. "A picture! a picture!" echoed several voices. Here there was an ungovernable peal of laughter.

I could not contain myself. I started up from my seat—looked round on the company with fiery indignation—thrust both my hands into my pockets, and strode up to one of the windows, as though I would have walked through it. I stopped short; looked out upon the landscape without distinguishing a feature of it; and felt my gorge rising almost to suffocation.

Mine host saw it was time to interfere. He had maintained an air of Gravity through the whole of the scene, and now stepped forth as if to shelter me from the overwhelming merriment of my companions.

"Gentlemen," said he, "I dislike to spoil sport, but you have had your laugh, and the joke of the haunted chamber has been enjoyed. I must now take the part of my guest. I must not only vindicate him from your pleasantries, but I must reconcile him to himself, for I suspect he is a little out of humor with his own feelings; and above all, I must crave his pardon for having made him the subject of a kind of experiment.

"Yes, gentlemen, there is something strange and peculiar in the chamber to which our friend was shown last night. There is a picture which possesses a singular and mysterious influence; and with which there is connected a very curious story. It is a picture to which I attach a value from a variety of circumstances; and though I have often been tempted to destroy it from the odd and uncomfortable sensations it produces in every one that beholds it; yet I have never been able to prevail upon myself to make the sacrifice. It is a picture I never like to look upon myself; and which is held in awe by all my servants. I have, therefore, banished it to a room but rarely used; and should have had it covered last night, had not the nature of our conversation, and the whimsical talk about a haunted chamber tempted me to let it remain, by way of experiment, whether a stranger, totally unacquainted with its story, would be affected by it."

The words of the Baronet had turned every thought into a different channel: all were anxious to hear the story of the mysterious picture; and for myself, so strongly were my feelings interested, that I forgot to feel piqued at the experiment which my host had made upon my nerves, and joined eagerly in the general entreaty.

As the morning was stormy, and precluded all egress, my host was glad of any means of entertaining his company; so drawing his arm-chair beside the fire, he began—

The Adventure of the
Mysterious Stranger

Many years since, when I was a young man, and had just left Oxford, I was sent on the grand tour to finish my education. I believe my parents had tried in vain to inoculate me with wisdom; so they sent me to mingle with society, in hopes I might take it the natural way. Such, at least, appears to be the reason for which nine-tenths of our youngsters are sent abroad.

In the course of my tour I remained some time at Venice. The romantic character of the place delighted me; I was very much amused by the air of adventure and intrigue that prevailed in this region of masks and gondolas; and I was exceedingly smitten by a pair of languishing black eyes, that played upon my heart from under an Italian mantle. So I persuaded myself that I was lingering at Venice to study men and manners. At least I persuaded my friends so, and that answered all my purpose. Indeed, I was a little prone to be struck by peculiarities in character and conduct, and my imagination was so full of romantic associations with Italy, that I was always on the lookout for adventure.

Every thing chimed in with such a humor in this old mermaid of a city. My suite of apartments were in a proud, melancholy palace on the grand canal, formerly the residence of a Magnifico, and sumptuous with the traces of decayed grandeur. My gondolier was one of the shrewdest of his class, active, merry, intelligent, and, like his brethren, secret as the grave; that is to say, secret to all the world except his master. I had not had him a week before he put me behind all the curtains in Venice. I liked the silence and mystery of the place, and when I sometimes saw from my window a black gondola gliding mysteriously along in the dusk of the evening, with nothing visible but its little glimmering lantern, I would jump into my own zenduletto, and give a signal for pursuit. But I am running away from my subject with the recollection of youthful follies, said the Baronet, checking himself; "let me come to the point."

Among my familiar resorts was a Cassino under the Arcades on one side of the grand square of St. Mark. Here I used frequently to lounge and take my ice on those warm summer nights when in Italy every body lives abroad until morning. I was seated here one evening, when a group of Italians took seat at a table on the opposite side of the saloon. Their conversation was gay and animated, and carried on with Italian vivacity and gesticulation.

I remarked among them one young man, however, who appeared to take no share, and find no enjoyment in the conversation; though he seemed to force himself to attend to it. He was tall and slender, and of extremely prepossessing appearance. His features were fine, though emaciated. He had a profusion of black glossy hair that curled lightly about his head, and contrasted with the extreme paleness of his countenance. His brow was haggard; deep furrows seemed to have been ploughed into his visage by care, not by age, for he was evidently in the prime of youth. His eye was full of expression and fire, but wild and unsteady. He seemed to be tormented by some strange fancy or apprehension. In spite of every effort to fix his attention on the conversation of his companions, I noticed that every now and then he would turn his head slowly round, give a glance over his shoulder, and then withdraw it with a sudden jerk, as if something painful had met his eye. This was repeated at intervals of about a minute, and he appeared hardly to have got over one shock, before I saw him slowly preparing to encounter another.

After sitting some time in the Cassino, the party paid for the refreshments they had taken, and departed. The young man was the last to leave the saloon, and I remarked him glancing behind him in the same way, just as he passed out at the door. I could not resist the impulse to rise and follow him; for I was at an age when a romantic feeling of curiosity is easily awakened. The party walked slowly down the Arcades, talking and laughing as they went. They crossed the Piazzetta, but paused in the middle of it to enjoy the scene. It was one of those moonlight nights so brilliant and clear in the pure atmosphere of Italy. The moon-beams streamed on the tall tower of St. Mark, and lighted up the magnificent front and swelling domes of the Cathedral. The party expressed their delight in animated terms. I kept my eye upon the young man. He alone seemed abstracted and self-occupied. I noticed the same singular, and, as it were, furtive glance over the shoulder that had attracted my attention in the Cassino. The party moved on, and I followed; they passed along the walks called the Broglio; turned the corner of the Ducal palace, and getting into a gondola, glided swiftly away.

The countenance and conduct of this young man dwelt upon my mind. There was something in his appearance that interested me exceedingly. I met him a day or two after in a gallery of paintings. He was evidently a connoisseur, for he always singled out the most masterly productions, and the few remarks drawn from him by his companions showed an intimate acquaintance with the art. His own taste, however, ran on singular extremes. On Salvator Rosa in his most savage and solitary scenes; on Raphael, Titian, and Corregio in their softest delineations of female beauty. On these he would occasionally gaze with transient enthusiasm. But this seemed only a momentary forgetfulness. Still would recur that cautious glance behind, and always quickly withdrawn, as though something terrible had met his view.

I encountered him frequently afterwards. At the theatre, at balls, at concerts; at the promenades in the gardens of San Georgio; at the grotesque exhibitions in the square of St. Mark; among the throng of merchants on the Exchange by the Rialto. He seemed, in fact, to seek crowds; to hunt after bustle and amusement; yet never to take any interest in either the business or gayety of the scene. Ever an air of painful thought, of wretched abstraction; and ever that strange and recurring movement, of glancing fearfully over the shoulder. I did not know at first but this might be caused by apprehension of arrest; or perhaps from dread of assassination. But, if so, why should he go thus continually abroad; why expose himself at all times and in all places?

I became anxious to know this stranger. I was drawn to him by that Romantic sympathy that sometimes draws young men towards each other. His melancholy threw a charm about him in my eyes, which was no doubt heightened by the touching expression of his countenance, and the manly graces of his person; for manly beauty has its effect even upon man. I had an Englishman's habitual diffidence and awkwardness of address to contend with; but I subdued it, and from frequently meeting him in the Cassino, gradually edged myself into his acquaintance. I had no reserve on his part to contend with. He seemed on the contrary to court society; and in fact to seek anything rather than be alone.

When he found I really took an interest in him he threw himself entirely upon my friendship. He clung to me like a drowning man. He would walk with me for hours up and down the place of St. Mark—or he would sit until night was far advanced in my apartment; he took rooms under the same roof with me; and his constant request was, that I would permit him, when it did not incommode me, to sit by me in my saloon. It was not that he seemed to take a particular delight in my conversation; but rather that he craved the vicinity of a human being;

and above all, of a being that sympathized with him. "I have often heard," said he, "of the sincerity of Englishmen—thank God I have one at length for a friend!"

Yet he never seemed disposed to avail himself of my sympathy other than by mere companionship. He never sought to unbosom himself to me; there appeared to be a settled corroding anguish in his bosom that neither could be soothed "by silence nor by speaking." A devouring melancholy preyed upon his heart, and seemed to be drying up the very blood in his veins. It was not a soft melancholy—the disease of the affections; but a parching, withering agony. I could see at times that his mouth was dry and feverish; he almost panted rather than breathed; his eyes were bloodshot; his cheeks pale and livid; with now and then faint streaks athwart them—baleful gleams of the fire that was consuming his heart. As my arm was within his, I felt him press it at times with a convulsive motion to his side; his hands would clinch themselves involuntarily, and a kind of shudder would run through his frame. I reasoned with him about his melancholy, and sought to draw from him the cause—he shrunk from all confiding. "Do not seek to know it," said he, "you could not relieve it if you knew it; you would not even seek to relieve it—on the contrary, I should lose your sympathy; and that," said he, pressing my hand convulsively, "that I feel has become too dear to me to risk."

I endeavored to awaken hope within him. He was young; life had a thousand pleasures in store for him; there is a healthy reaction in the youthful heart; it medicines its own wounds—

"Come, come," said I, "there is no grief so great that youth cannot outgrow it."—"No! no!" said he, clinching his teeth, and striking repeatedly, with the energy of despair, upon his bosom—"It is here—here—deep-rooted; draining my heart's blood. It grows and grows, while my heart withers and withers! I have a dreadful monitor that gives me no repose—that follows me step by step; and will follow me step by step, until it pushes me into my grave!"

As he said this he gave involuntarily one of those fearful glances over his shoulder, and shrunk back with more than usual horror. I could not resist the temptation to allude to this movement, which I supposed to be some mere malady of the nerves. The moment I mentioned it his face became crimsoned and convulsed—he grasped me by both hands: "For God's sake," exclaimed he, with a piercing agony of voice—"never allude to that again; let us avoid this subject, my friend; you cannot relieve me, indeed you cannot relieve me; but you may add to the torments I suffer;—at some future day you shall know all."

I never resumed the subject; for however much my curiosity might be aroused, I felt too true compassion for his sufferings to increase them by my intrusion. I sought various ways to divert his mind, and to arouse him from the constant meditations in which he was plunged. He saw my efforts, and seconded them as far as in his power, for there was nothing moody or wayward in his nature; on the contrary, there was something frank, generous, unassuming, in his whole deportment. All the sentiments that he uttered were noble and lofty. He claimed no indulgence; he asked no toleration. He seemed content to carry his load of misery in silence, and only sought to carry it by my side. There was a mute beseeching manner about him, as if he craved companionship as a charitable boon; and a tacit thankfulness in his looks, as if he felt grateful to me for not repulsing him.

I felt this melancholy to be infectious. It stole over my spirits; Interfered with all my gay pursuits, and gradually saddened my life; yet I could not prevail upon myself to shake off a being who seemed to hang upon me for support. In truth, the generous traits of character that beamed through all this gloom had penetrated to my heart. His bounty was lavish and open-handed. His charity melting and spontaneous. Not confined to mere donations, which often humiliate as much as they relieve. The tone of his voice, the beam of his eye, enhanced every gift, and surprised the poor suppliant with that rarest and sweetest of charities, the charity not merely of the hand, but of the heart. Indeed, his liberality seemed to have something in it of self-abasement and expiation. He humbled himself, in a manner, before the mendicant. "What right have I to ease and affluence," would he murmur to himself, "when innocence wanders in misery and rags?"

The Carnival time arrived. I had hoped that the gay scenes which then Presented themselves might have some cheering effect. I mingled with him in the motley throng that crowded the place of St. Mark. We frequented operas, masquerades, balls. All in vain. The evil kept growing on him; he became more and more haggard and agitated. Often, after we had returned from one of these scenes of revelry, I have entered his room, and found him lying on his face on the sofa: his hands clinched in his fine hair, and his whole countenance bearing traces of the convulsions of his mind.

The Carnival passed away; the season of Lent succeeded; Passion week arrived. We attended one evening a solemn service in one of the churches; in the course of which a grand piece of vocal and instrumental music was performed relating to the death of our Saviour.

I had remarked that he was always powerfully affected by music; on this occasion he was so in an extraordinary degree. As the peeling notes swelled through the lofty aisles, he seemed to kindle up with fervor. His eyes rolled upwards, until nothing but the whites were visible; his hands were clasped together, until the fingers were deeply imprinted in the flesh. When the music expressed the dying agony, his face gradually sunk upon his knees; and at the touching words resounding through the church, "*Jesu mori*," sobs burst from him uncontrolled. I had never seen him weep before; his had always been agony rather than sorrow. I augured well from the circumstance. I let him weep on uninterrupted. When the service was ended we left the church. He hung on my arm as we walked homewards, with something of a softer and more subdued manner; instead of that nervous agitation I had been accustomed to witness. He alluded to the service we had heard. "Music," said he, "is indeed the voice of heaven; never before have I felt more impressed by the story of the atonement of our Saviour. Yes, my friend," said he, clasping his hands with a kind of transport, "I know that my Redeemer liveth."

We parted for the night. His room was not far from mine, and I heard him for some time busied in it. I fell asleep, but was awakened before daylight. The young man stood by my bed-side, dressed for travelling. He held a sealed packet and a large parcel in his hand, which he laid on the table. "Farewell, my friend," said he, "I am about to set forth on a long journey; but, before I go, I leave with you these remembrances. In this packet you will find the particulars of my story. When you read them, I shall be far away; do not remember me with aversion. You have been, indeed, a friend to me. You have poured oil into a broken heart,— but you could not heal it.—Farewell—let me kiss your hand—I am unworthy to embrace you." He sunk on his knees, seized my hand in despite of my efforts to the contrary, and covered it with kisses. I was so surprised by all this scene that I had not been able to say a word.

But we shall meet again, said I, hastily, as I saw him hurrying towards the door.

"Never—never in this world!" said he, solemnly. He sprang once more to my bed-side—seized my hand, pressed it to his heart and to his lips, and rushed out of the room.

Here the Baronet paused. He seemed lost in thought, and sat looking upon the floor and drumming with his fingers on the arm of his chair.

"And did this mysterious personage return?" said the inquisitive gentleman. "Never!" replied the Baronet, with a pensive shake of the head: "I never saw him again." "And pray what has all this to do with the picture?" inquired the old gentleman with the nose—"True!" said the questioner—"Is it the portrait of this crack-brained Italian?" "No!" said the Baronet drily, not half liking the appellation given to his hero; "but this picture was inclosed in the parcel he left with me. The sealed packet contained its explanation. There was a request on the outside that I would not open it until six months had elapsed. I kept my promise, in spite of my curiosity. I have a translation of it by me, and had meant to read it, by way of accounting for the mystery of the chamber, but I fear I have already detained the company too long."

Here there was a general wish expressed to have the manuscript read; particularly on the part of the inquisitive gentleman. So the worthy Baronet drew out a fairly written manuscript, and wiping his spectacles, read aloud the following story:

THE STORY OF THE YOUNG ITALIAN

I was born at Naples. My parents, though of noble rank, were limited in fortune, or rather my father was ostentatious beyond his means, and expended so much in his palace, his equipage, and his retinue, that he was continually straitened in his pecuniary circumstances. I was a younger son, and looked upon with indifference by my father, who, from a principle of family pride, wished to leave all his property to my elder brother.

I showed, when quite a child, an extreme sensibility. Every thing affected me violently. While yet an infant in my mother's arms, and before I had learnt to talk, I could be wrought upon to a wonderful degree of anguish or delight by the power of music. As I grew older my feelings remained equally acute, and I was easily transported into paroxysms of pleasure or rage. It was the amusement of my relatives and of the domestics to play upon this irritable temperament. I was moved to tears, tickled to laughter, provoked to fury, for the entertainment of company, who were amused by such a tempest of mighty passion in a pigmy frame. They little thought, or perhaps little heeded the dangerous sensibilities they were fostering. I thus became a little creature of passion, before reason was developed. In a short time I grew too old to be a plaything, and then I became a torment. The tricks and passions I had been teased into became irksome, and I was disliked by my teachers for the very lessons they had taught me.

My mother died; and my power as a spoiled child was at an end. There was no longer any necessity to humor or tolerate me, for there was nothing to be gained by it, as I was no favorite of my father. I therefore experienced the fate of a spoiled child in such situation, and was neglected or noticed only to be crossed and contradicted. Such was the early treatment of a heart, which, if I am judge of it at all, was naturally disposed to the extremes of tenderness and affection.

My father, as I have already said, never liked me—in fact, he never Understood me; he looked upon me as wilful and wayward, as deficient in natural affection:—it was the stateliness of his own manner; the loftiness and grandeur of his own look that had repelled me from his arms. I always pictured him to myself as I had seen him clad in his senatorial robes, rustling with pomp and pride. The magnificence of his person had daunted my strong imagination. I could never approach him with the confiding affection of a child.

My father's feelings were wrapped up in my elder brother. He was to be the inheritor of the family title and the family dignity, and every thing was sacrificed to him—I, as well as every thing else. It was determined to devote me to the church, that so my humors and myself might be removed out of the way, either of tasking my father's time and trouble, or interfering with the interests of my brother. At an early age, therefore, before my mind had dawned upon the world and its delights, or known any thing of it beyond the precincts of my father's palace, I was sent to a convent, the superior of which was my uncle, and was confided entirely to his care.

My uncle was a man totally estranged from the world; he had never relished, for he had never tasted its pleasures; and he deemed rigid self-denial as the great basis of Christian virtue. He considered every one's temperament like his own; or at least he made them conform to it. His character and habits had an influence over the fraternity of which he was superior. A more gloomy, saturnine set of beings were never assembled together. The convent, too, was calculated to awaken sad and solitary thoughts. It was situated in a gloomy gorge of those mountains away south of Vesuvius. All distant views were shut out by sterile volcanic heights. A mountain stream raved beneath its walls, and eagles screamed about its turrets.

I had been sent to this place at so tender an age as soon to lose all Distinct recollection of the scenes I had left behind. As my mind expanded, therefore, it formed its idea of the world from the convent and its vicinity, and a dreary world it appeared to me. An early tinge of melancholy was thus infused into my character; and the dismal stories of the monks, about devils and evil spirits, with which they affrighted my young imagination, gave me a tendency to superstition, which I could never effectually shake off. They took the same delight to work upon my ardent feelings that had been so mischievously exercised by my father's household.

I can recollect the horrors with which they fed my heated fancy during an eruption of Vesuvius. We were distant from that volcano, with mountains between us; but its convulsive throes shook the solid foundations of nature. Earthquakes threatened to topple down our convent towers. A lurid, baleful light hung in the heavens at night, and showers of ashes, borne by the wind, fell in our narrow valley. The monks talked of the earth being honey-combed beneath us; of Streams of molten lava raging through its veins; of caverns of sulphurous flames roaring in the centre, the abodes of demons and the damned; of fiery gulfs ready to yawn beneath our feet. All these tales were told to the doleful accompaniment of the mountain's thunders, whose low bellowing made the walls of our convent vibrate.

One of the monks had been a painter, but had retired from the world, and embraced this dismal life in expiation of some crime. He was a melancholy man, who pursued his art in the solitude of his cell, but made it a source of penance to him. His employment was to portray, either on canvas or in waxen models, the human face and human form, in the agonies of death and in all the stages of dissolution and decay. The fearful mysteries of the charnel house were unfolded in his labors—the loathsome banquet of the beetle and the worm.—I turn with shuddering even from the recollection of his works. Yet, at that time, my strong, but ill-directed imagination seized with ardor upon his instructions in his art. Any thing was a variety from the dry studies and monotonous duties of the cloister. In a little while I became expert with my pencil, and my gloomy productions were thought worthy of decorating some of the altars of the chapel.

In this dismal way was a creature of feeling and fancy brought up. Every thing genial and amiable in my nature was repressed and nothing brought out but what was unprofitable and ungracious. I was ardent in my temperament; quick, mercurial, impetuous, formed to be a creature all love and adoration; but a leaden hand was laid on all my finer qualities. I was taught nothing but fear and hatred. I hated my uncle, I hated the monks, I hated the convent in which I was immured. I hated the world, and I almost hated myself, for being, as I supposed, so hating and hateful an animal.

When I had nearly attained the age of sixteen, I was suffered, on one occasion, to accompany one of the brethren on a mission to a distant part of the country. We soon left behind us the gloomy valley in which I had been pent up for so many years, and after a short journey among the mountains, emerged upon the voluptuous landscape that spreads itself about the Bay of Naples. Heavens! How transported was I, when I stretched my gaze over a vast reach of delicious sunny country, gay with groves and vineyards; with Vesuvius rearing its forked summit to my right; the blue Mediterranean to my left, with its enchanting coast, studded with shining towns and sumptuous villas; and Naples, my native Naples, gleaming far, far in the distance.

Good God! was this the lovely world from which I had been excluded! I Had reached that age when the sensibilities are in all their bloom and freshness. Mine had been checked and chilled. They now burst forth with the suddenness of a retarded spring. My heart, hitherto unnaturally shrunk up, expanded into a riot of vague, but delicious emotions. The beauty of nature intoxicated, bewildered me. The song of the peasants; their cheerful looks; their happy avocations; the picturesque gayety of their dresses; their rustic music; their dances; all broke upon me like witchcraft. My soul responded to the music; my heart danced in my bosom. All the men appeared amiable, all the women lovely.

I returned to the convent, that is to say, my body returned but my heart and soul never entered there again. I could not forget this glimpse of a beautiful and a happy world; a world so suited to my natural character. I had felt so happy while in it; so different a being from what I felt myself while in the convent—that tomb of the living. I contrasted the countenances of the beings I had seen, full of fire and freshness and enjoyment, with the pallid, leaden, lack-lustre visages of the monks; the music of the dance, with the droning chant of the chapel. I had before found the exercises of the cloister wearisome; they now became intolerable. The dull round of duties wore away my spirit; my nerves became irritated by the fretful tinkling of the convent bell; evermore dinging among the mountain echoes; evermore calling me from my repose at night, my pencil by day, to attend to some tedious and mechanical ceremony of devotion.

I was not of a nature to meditate long, without putting my thoughts into action. My spirit had been suddenly aroused, and was now all awake within me. I watched my opportunity, fled from the convent, and made my way on foot to Naples. As I entered its gay and crowded streets, and beheld the variety and stir of life around me, the luxury of palaces, the splendor of equipages, and the pantomimic animation of the motley populace, I seemed as if awakened to a world of enchantment, and solemnly vowed that nothing should force me back to the monotony of the cloister.

I had to inquire my way to my father's palace, for I had been so young on leaving it, that I knew not its situation. I found some difficulty in getting admitted to my father's presence, for the domestics scarcely knew that there was such a being as myself in existence, and my monastic dress did not operate in my favor. Even my father entertained no recollection of my person. I told him my name, threw myself at his feet, implored his forgiveness, and entreated that I might not be sent back to the convent.

He received me with the condescension of a patron rather than the kindness of a parent. He listened patiently, but coldly, to my tale of monastic grievances and disgusts, and promised to think what else could be done for me. This coldness blighted and drove back all the frank affection of my nature that was ready to spring forth at the least warmth of parental kindness. All my early feelings towards my father revived; I again looked up to him as the stately magnificent being that had daunted my childish imagination, and felt as if I had no pretensions to his sympathies. My brother engrossed all his care and love; he inherited his nature, and carried himself towards me with a protecting rather than a fraternal air. It wounded my pride, which was great. I could brook condescension from my father, for I looked up to him with awe as a superior being, but I could not brook patronage from a brother, who, I felt, was intellectually my inferior. The servants perceived that I was an unwelcome intruder in the paternal mansion, and, menial-like, they treated me with neglect. Thus baffled at every point; my affections outraged wherever they would attach themselves, I became sullen, silent, and despondent. My feelings driven back upon myself, entered and preyed upon my own heart. I remained for some days an unwelcome guest rather than a restored son in my father's house. I was doomed never to be properly known there. I was made, by wrong treatment, strange even to myself; and they judged of me from my strangeness.

I was startled one day at the sight of one of the monks of my convent, gliding out of my father's room. He saw me, but pretended not to notice me; and this very hypocrisy made me suspect something. I had become sore and susceptible in my feelings; every thing inflicted a wound on them. In this state of mind I was treated with marked disrespect by a pampered minion, the favorite servant of my father. All the pride and passion of my nature rose in an instant, and I struck him to the earth.

My father was passing by; he stopped not to inquire the reason, nor indeed could he read the long course of mental sufferings which were the real cause. He rebuked me with anger and scorn; he summoned all the haughtiness of his nature, and grandeur of his look, to give weight to the contumely with which he treated me. I felt I had not deserved it—I felt that I was not appreciated—I felt that I had that within me which merited better treatment; my heart swelled against a father's injustice. I broke through my habitual awe of him. I replied to him with impatience; my hot spirit flushed in my cheek and kindled in my eye, but my sensitive heart swelled as quickly, and before I had half vented my passion I felt it suffocated and quenched in my tears. My father was astonished and incensed at this turning of the worm, and ordered me to my chamber. I retired in silence, choking with contending emotions.

I had not been long there when I overheard voices in an adjoining apartment. It was a consultation between my father and the monk, about the means of getting me back quietly to the convent. My resolution was taken. I had no longer a home nor a father. That very night I left the paternal roof. I got on board a vessel about making sail from the harbor, and abandoned myself to the wide world. No matter to what port she steered; any part of so beautiful a world was better than my convent. No matter where I was cast by fortune; any place would be more a home to me than the home I had left behind. The vessel was bound to Genoa. We arrived there after a voyage of a few days.

As I entered the harbor, between the moles which embrace it, and beheld the amphitheatre of palaces and churches and splendid gardens, rising one above another, I felt at once its title to the appellation of Genoa the Superb. I landed on the mole an utter stranger, without knowing what to do, or whither to direct my steps. No matter; I was released from the thraldom of the convent and the humiliations of home! When I traversed the Strada Balbi and the Strada Nuova, those streets of palaces, and gazed at the wonders of architecture around me; when I wandered at close of day, amid a gay throng of the brilliant and the beautiful, through the green alleys of the Aqua Verdi, or among the colonnades and terraces of the magnificent Doria Gardens, I thought it impossible to be ever otherwise than happy in Genoa.

A few days sufficed to show me my mistake. My scanty purse was exhausted, and for the first time in my life I experienced the sordid distress of penury. I had never known the want of money, and had never adverted to the possibility of such an evil. I was ignorant of the world and all its ways; and when first the idea of destitution came over my mind its effect was withering. I was wandering pensively through the streets which no longer delighted my eyes, when chance led my stops into the magnificent church of the Annunciata.

A celebrated painter of the day was at that moment superintending the placing of one of his pictures over an altar. The proficiency which I had acquired in his art during my residence in the convent had made me an enthusiastic amateur. I was struck, at the first glance, with the painting. It was the face of a Madonna. So innocent, so lovely, such a divine expression of maternal tenderness! I lost for the moment all recollection of myself in the enthusiasm of my art. I clasped my hands together, and uttered an exclamation of delight. The painter perceived my emotion. He was flattered and gratified by it. My air and manner pleased him, and he accosted me. I felt too much the want of friendship to repel the advances of a stranger, and there was something in this one so benevolent and winning that in a moment he gained my confidence.

I told him my story and my situation, concealing only my name and rank. He appeared strongly interested by my recital; invited me to his house, and from that time I became his favorite pupil. He thought he perceived in me extraordinary talents for the art, and his encomiums awakened all my ardor. What a blissful period of my existence was it that I passed beneath his roof. Another being seemed created within me, or rather, all that was amiable and excellent was drawn out. I was as recluse as ever I had been at the convent, but how different was my seclusion. My time was spent in storing my mind with lofty and poetical ideas; in meditating on all that was striking and noble in history or fiction; in studying and tracing all that was sublime and beautiful in nature. I was always a visionary, imaginative being, but now my reveries and imaginings all elevated me to rapture.

I looked up to my master as to a benevolent genius that had opened to me a region of enchantment. I became devotedly attached to him. He was not a native of Genoa, but had been drawn thither by the solicitation of several of the nobility, and had resided there but a few years, for the completion of certain works he had undertaken. His health was delicate, and he had to confide much of the filling up of his designs to the pencils of his scholars. He considered me as particularly happy in delineating the human countenance; in seizing upon characteristic, though fleeting expressions and fixing them powerfully upon my canvas. I was employed continually, therefore, in sketching faces, and often when some particular grace or beauty or expression was wanted in a countenance, it was entrusted to my pencil. My benefactor was fond of bringing me forward; and partly, perhaps, through my actual skill, and partly by his partial praises, I began to be noted for the expression of my countenances.

Among the various works which he had undertaken, was an historical piece for one of the palaces of Genoa, in which were to be introduced the likenesses of several of the family. Among these was one entrusted to my pencil. It was that of a young girl, who as yet was in a convent for her education. She came out for the purpose of sitting for the picture. I first saw her in an apartment of one of the sumptuous palaces of Genoa. She stood before a casement that looked out upon the bay, a stream of vernal sunshine fell upon her, and shed a kind of glory round her as it lit up the rich crimson chamber. She was but sixteen years of age—and oh, how lovely! The scene broke upon me like a mere vision of spring and youth and beauty. I could have fallen down and worshipped her. She was like one of those fictions of poets and painters, when they would express the *beau ideal* that haunts their minds with shapes of indescribable perfection.

I was permitted to sketch her countenance in various positions, and I Fondly protracted the study that was undoing me. The more I gazed on her the more I became enamoured; there was something almost painful in my intense admiration. I was but nineteen years of age; shy, diffident, and inexperienced. I was treated with attention and encouragement, for my youth and my enthusiasm in my art had won favor for me; and I am inclined to think that there was something in my air and manner that inspired interest and respect. Still the kindness with which I was treated could not dispel the embarrassment into which my own imagination threw me when in presence of this lovely being. It elevated her into something almost more than mortal. She seemed too exquisite for earthly use; too delicate and exalted for human attainment. As I sat tracing her charms on my canvas, with my eyes occasionally riveted on her features, I drank in delicious poison that made me giddy. My heart alternately gushed with tenderness, and ached with despair. Now I became more than ever sensible of the violent fires that had lain dormant at the bottom of my soul. You who are born in a more temperate climate and under a cooler sky, have little idea of the violence of passion in our southern bosoms.

A few days finished my task; Bianca returned to her convent, but her image remained indelibly impressed upon my heart. It dwelt on my imagination; it became my pervading idea of beauty. It had an effect even upon my pencil; I became noted for my felicity in depicting female loveliness; it was but because I multiplied the image of Bianca. I soothed, and yet fed my fancy, by introducing her in all the productions of my master. I have stood with delight in one of the chapels of the Annunciata, and heard the crowd extol the seraphic beauty of a saint which I had painted; I have seen them bow down in adoration before the painting: they were bowing before the loveliness of Bianca.

I existed in this kind of dream, I might almost say delirium, for upwards of a year. Such is the tenacity of my imagination that the image which was formed in it continued in all its power and freshness. Indeed, I was a solitary, meditative being, much given to reverie, and apt to foster ideas which had once taken strong possession of me. I was roused from this fond, melancholy, delicious dream by the death of my worthy benefactor. I cannot describe the pangs his death occasioned me. It left me alone and almost broken-hearted. He bequeathed to me his little property; which, from the liberality of his disposition and his expensive style of living, was indeed but small; and he most particularly recommended me, in dying, to the protection of a nobleman who had been his patron.

The latter was a man who passed for munificent. He was a lover and an encourager of the arts, and evidently wished to be thought so. He fancied he saw in me indications of future excellence; my pencil had already attracted attention; he took me at once under his protection; seeing that I was overwhelmed with grief, and incapable of exerting myself in the mansion of my late benefactor, he invited me to sojourn for a time in a villa which he possessed on the border of the sea, in the picturesque neighborhood of Sestri de Ponenti.

I found at the villa the Count's only son, Filippo: he was nearly of my age, prepossessing in his appearance, and fascinating in his manners; he attached himself to me, and seemed to court my good opinion. I thought there was something of profession in his kindness, and of caprice in his disposition; but I had nothing else near me to attach myself to, and my heart felt the need of something to repose itself upon. His education had been neglected; he looked upon me as his superior in mental powers and acquirements, and tacitly acknowledged my superiority. I felt that I was his equal in birth, and that gave an independence to my manner which had its effect. The caprice and tyranny I saw sometimes exercised on others, over whom he had power, were never manifested towards me. We became intimate friends, and frequent companions. Still I loved to be alone, and to indulge in the reveries of my own imagination, among the beautiful scenery by which I was surrounded.

The villa stood in the midst of ornamented grounds, finely decorated With statues and fountains, and laid out into groves and alleys and shady bowers. It commanded a wide view of the Mediterranean, and the picturesque Ligurian coast. Every thing was assembled here that could gratify the taste or agreeably occupy the mind. Soothed by the tranquillity of this elegant retreat, the turbulence of my feelings gradually subsided, and, blending with the romantic spell that still reigned over my imagination, produced a soft voluptuous melancholy.

I had not been long under the roof of the Count, when our solitude was enlivened by another inhabitant. It was a daughter of a relation of the Count, who had lately died in reduced circumstances, bequeathing this only child to his protection. I had heard much of her beauty from Filippo, but my fancy had become so engrossed by one idea of beauty as not to admit of any other. We were in the central saloon of the villa when she arrived. She was still in mourning, and approached, leaning on the Count's arm. As they ascended the marble portico, I was struck by the elegance of her figure and movement, by the grace with which the *mezzaro*, the bewitching veil of Genoa, was folded about her slender form.

They entered. Heavens! what was my surprise when I beheld Bianca before me. It was herself; pale with grief; but still more matured in loveliness than when I had last beheld her. The time that had elapsed had developed the graces of her person; and the sorrow she had undergone had diffused over her countenance an irresistible tenderness.

She blushed and trembled at seeing me, and tears rushed into her eyes, for she remembered in whose company she had been accustomed to behold me. For my part, I cannot express what were my emotions. By degrees I overcame the extreme shyness that had formerly paralyzed me in her presence. We were drawn together by sympathy of situation. We had each lost our best friend in the world; we were each, in some measure thrown upon the kindness of others. When I came to know her intellectually, all my ideal picturings of her were confirmed. Her newness to the world, her delightful susceptibility to every thing beautiful and agreeable in nature, reminded me of my own emotions when first I escaped from the convent. Her rectitude of thinking delighted my judgment; the sweetness of her nature wrapped itself around my heart; and then her young and tender and budding loveliness, sent a delicious madness to my brain.

I gazed upon her with a kind of idolatry, as something more than mortal; and I felt humiliated at the idea of my comparative unworthiness. Yet she was mortal; and one of mortality's most susceptible and loving compounds; for she loved me!

WASHINGTON IRVING

How first I discovered the transporting truth I cannot recollect; I believe it stole upon me by degrees, as a wonder past hope or belief. We were both at such a tender and loving age; in constant intercourse with each other; mingling in the same elegant pursuits; for music, poetry, and painting were our mutual delights, and we were almost separated from society, among lovely and romantic scenery! Is it strange that two young hearts thus brought together should readily twine round each other?

Oh, gods! what a dream—a transient dream! of unalloyed delight then passed over my soul! Then it was that the world around me was indeed a paradise, for I had a woman—lovely, delicious woman, to share it with me. How often have I rambled over the picturesque shores of Sestri, or climbed its wild mountains, with the coast gemmed with villas, and the blue sea far below me, and the slender Pharo of Genoa on its romantic promontory in the distance; and as I sustained the faltering steps of Bianca, have thought there could no unhappiness enter into so beautiful a world. Why, oh, why is this budding season of life and love so transient—why is this rosy cloud of love that sheds such a glow over the morning of our days so prone to brew up into the whirlwind and the storm!

I was the first to awaken from this blissful delirium of the affections. I had gained Bianca's heart: what was I to do with it? I had no wealth nor prospects to entitle me to her hand. Was I to take advantage of her ignorance of the world, of her confiding affection, and draw her down to my own poverty? Was this requiting the hospitality of the Count?— was this requiting the love of Bianca?

Now first I began to feel that even successful love may have its bitterness. A corroding care gathered about my heart. I moved about the palace like a guilty being. I felt as if I had abused its hospitality— as if I were a thief within its walls. I could no longer look with unembarrassed mien in the countenance of the Count. I accused myself of perfidy to him, and I thought he read it in my looks, and began to distrust and despise me. His manner had always been ostentatious and condescending, it now appeared cold and haughty. Filippo, too, became reserved and distant; or at least I suspected him to be so. Heavens!— was this mere coinage of my brain: was I to become suspicious of all the world?—a poor surmising wretch; watching looks and gestures; and torturing myself with misconstructions. Or if true—was I to remain beneath a roof where I was merely tolerated, and linger there on sufferance? "This is not to be endured!" exclaimed I; "I will tear myself from this state of self-abasement; I will break through this fascination and fly—Fly?—whither?—from the world?—for where is the world when I leave Bianca behind me?"

My spirit was naturally proud, and swelled within me at the idea of being looked upon with contumely. Many times I was on the point of declaring my family and rank, and asserting my equality, in the presence of Bianca, when I thought her relatives assumed an air of superiority. But the feeling was transient. I considered myself discarded and contemned by my family; and had solemnly vowed never to own relationship to them, until they themselves should claim it.

The struggle of my mind preyed upon my happiness and my health. It seemed as if the uncertainty of being loved would be less intolerable than thus to be assured of it, and yet not dare to enjoy the conviction. I was no longer the enraptured admirer of Bianca; I no longer hung in ecstasy on the tones of her voice, nor drank in with insatiate gaze the beauty of her countenance. Her very smiles ceased to delight me, for I felt culpable in having won them.

She could not but be sensible of the change in me, and inquired the cause with her usual frankness and simplicity. I could not evade the inquiry, for my heart was full to aching. I told her all the conflict of my soul; my devouring passion, my bitter self-upbraiding. "Yes!" said I, "I am unworthy of you. I am an offcast from my family—a wanderer—a nameless, homeless wanderer, with nothing but poverty for my portion, and yet I have dared to love you—have dared to aspire to your love!"

My agitation moved her to tears; but she saw nothing in my situation so hopeless as I had depicted it. Brought up in a convent, she knew nothing of the world, its wants, its cares;—and, indeed, what woman is a worldly casuist in matters of the heart!—Nay, more—she kindled into a sweet enthusiasm when she spoke of my fortunes and myself. We had dwelt together on the works of the famous masters. I had related to her their histories; the high reputation, the influence, the magnificence to which they had attained;—the companions of princes, the favorites of kings, the pride and boast of nations. All this she applied to me. Her love saw nothing in their greatest productions that I was not able to achieve; and when I saw the lovely creature glow with fervor, and her whole countenance radiant with the visions of my glory, which seemed breaking upon her, I was snatched up for the moment into the heaven of her own imagination.

WASHINGTON IRVING

I am dwelling too long upon this part of my story; yet I cannot help Lingering over a period of my life, on which, with all its cares and conflicts, I look back with fondness; for as yet my soul was unstained by a crime. I do not know what might have been the result of this struggle between pride, delicacy, and passion, had I not read in a Neapolitan gazette an account of the sudden death of my brother. It was accompanied by an earnest inquiry for intelligence concerning me, and a prayer, should this notice meet my eye, that I would hasten to Naples, to comfort an infirm and afflicted father.

I was naturally of an affectionate disposition; but my brother had never been as a brother to me; I had long considered myself as disconnected from him, and his death caused me but little emotion. The thoughts of my father, infirm and suffering, touched me, however, to the quick; and when I thought of him, that lofty, magnificent being, now bowed down and desolate, and suing to me for comfort, all my resentment for past neglect was subdued, and a glow of filial affection was awakened within me.

The predominant feeling, however, that overpowered all others was transport at the sudden change in my whole fortunes. A home—a name—a rank—wealth awaited me; and love painted a still more rapturous prospect in the distance. I hastened to Bianca, and threw myself at her feet. "Oh, Bianca," exclaimed I, "at length I can claim you for my own. I am no longer a nameless adventurer, a neglected, rejected outcast. Look—read, behold the tidings that restore me to my name and to myself!"

I will not dwell on the scene that ensued. Bianca rejoiced in the reverse of my situation, because she saw it lightened my heart of a load of care; for her own part she had loved me for myself, and had never doubted that my own merits would command both fame and fortune.

I now felt all my native pride buoyant within me; I no longer walked with my eyes bent to the dust; hope elevated them to the skies; my soul was lit up with fresh fires, and beamed from my countenance.

I wished to impart the change in my circumstances to the Count; to let him know who and what I was, and to make formal proposals for the hand of Bianca; but the Count was absent on a distant estate. I opened my whole soul to Filippo. Now first I told him of my passion; of the doubts and fears that had distracted me, and of the tidings that had suddenly dispelled them. He overwhelmed me with congratulations and with the warmest expressions of sympathy. I embraced him in the fullness of my heart. I felt compunctious for having suspected him of coldness, and asked him forgiveness for having ever doubted his friendship.

Nothing is so warm, and enthusiastic as a sudden expansion of the heart between young men. Filippo entered into our concerns with the most eager interest. He was our confidant and counsellor. It was determined that I should hasten at once to Naples to re-establish myself in my father's affections and my paternal home, and the moment the reconciliation was effected and my father's consent insured, I should return and demand Bianca of the Count. Filippo engaged to secure his father's acquiescence; indeed, he undertook to watch over our interests, and was the channel through which we were to correspond.

My parting with Bianca was tender—delicious—agonizing.

It was in a little pavilion of the garden which had been one of our favorite resorts. How often and often did I return to have one more adieu—to have her look once more on me in speechless emotion—to enjoy once more the rapturous sight of those tears streaming down her lovely cheeks—to seize once more on that delicate hand, the frankly accorded pledge of love, and cover it with tears and kisses! Heavens! There is a delight even in the parting agony of two lovers worth a thousand tame pleasures of the world. I have her at this moment before my eyes—at the window of the pavilion, putting aside the vines that clustered about the casement—her light form beaming forth in virgin white—her countenance all tears and smiles—sending a thousand and a thousand adieus after me, as, hesitating, in a delirium of fondness and agitation, I faltered my way down the avenue.

As the bark bore me out of the harbor of Genoa, how eagerly my eyes Stretched along the coast of Sestri, till it discerned the villa gleaming from among trees at the foot of the mountain. As long as day lasted, I gazed and gazed upon it, till it lessened and lessened to a mere white speck in the distance; and still my intense and fixed gaze discerned it, when all other objects of the coast had blended into indistinct confusion, or were lost in the evening gloom.

On arriving at Naples, I hastened to my paternal home. My heart yearned for the long-withheld blessing of a father's love. As I entered the proud portal of the ancestral palace, my emotions were so great that I could not speak. No one knew me. The servants gazed at me with curiosity and surprise. A few years of intellectual elevation and development had made a prodigious change in the poor fugitive stripling from the convent. Still that no one should know me in my rightful home was overpowering. I felt like the prodigal son returned. I was a stranger in the house of my father. I burst into tears, and wept aloud. When I made myself known, however, all was changed. I who had once been almost repulsed from its walls, and forced to fly as an exile, was welcomed back with acclamation, with servility. One of the servants hastened to prepare my father for my reception; my eagerness to receive the paternal embrace was so great that I could not await his return; but hurried after him.

What a spectacle met my eyes as I entered the chamber! My father, whom I had left in the pride of vigorous age, whose noble and majestic bearing had so awed my young imagination, was bowed down and withered into decrepitude. A paralysis had ravaged his stately form, and left it a shaking ruin. He sat propped up in his chair, with pale, relaxed visage and glassy, wandering eye. His intellects had evidently shared in the ravage of his frame. The servant was endeavoring to make him comprehend the visitor that was at hand. I tottered up to him and sunk at his feet. All his past coldness and neglect were forgotten in his present sufferings. I remembered only that he was my parent, and that I had deserted him. I clasped his knees; my voice was almost stifled with convulsive sobs. "Pardon—pardon—oh my father!" was all that I could utter. His apprehension seemed slowly to return to him. He gazed at me for some moments with a vague, inquiring look; a convulsive tremor quivered about his lips; he feebly extended a shaking hand, laid it upon my head, and burst into an infantine flow of tears.

From that moment he would scarcely spare me from his sight. I appeared the only object that his heart responded to in the world; all else was as a blank to him. He had almost lost the powers of speech, and the reasoning faculty seemed at an end. He was mute and passive; excepting that fits of child-like weeping would sometimes come over him without any immediate cause. If I left the room at any time, his eye was incessantly fixed on the door till my return, and on my entrance there was another gush of tears.

To talk with him of my concerns, in this ruined state of mind, would have been worse than useless; to have left him, for ever so short a time, would have been cruel, unnatural. Here then was a new trial for my affections. I wrote to Bianca an account of my return and of my actual situation; painting in colors vivid, for they were true, the torments I suffered at our being thus separated; for to the youthful lover every day of absence is an age of love lost. I enclosed the letter in one to Filippo, who was the channel of our correspondence. I received a reply from him full of friendship and sympathy; from Bianca full of assurances of affection and constancy.

Week after week, month after month elapsed, without making any change in my circumstances. The vital flame, which had seemed nearly extinct when first I met my father, kept fluttering on without any apparent diminution. I watched him constantly, faithfully—I had almost said patiently. I knew that his death alone would set me free; yet I never at any moment wished it. I felt too glad to be able to make any atonement for past disobedience; and, denied as I had been all endearments of relationship in my early days, my heart yearned towards a father, who, in his age and helplessness, had thrown himself entirely on me for comfort. My passion for Bianca gained daily more force from absence; by constant meditation it wore itself a deeper and deeper channel. I made no new friends nor acquaintances; sought none of the pleasures of Naples which my rank and fortune threw open to me. Mine was a heart that confined itself to few objects, but dwelt upon those with the intenser passion. To sit by my father, and administer to his wants, and to meditate on Bianca in the silence of his chamber, was my constant habit. Sometimes I amused myself with my pencil in portraying the image that was ever present to my imagination. I transferred to canvas every look and smile of hers that dwelt in my heart. I showed them to my father in hopes of awakening an interest in his bosom for the mere shadow of my love; but he was too far sunk in intellect to take any more than a child-like notice of them.

When I received a letter from Bianca it was a new source of solitary luxury. Her letters, it is true, were less and less frequent, but they were always full of assurances of unabated affection. They breathed not the frank and innocent warmth with which she expressed herself in conversation, but I accounted for it from the embarrassment which inexperienced minds have often to express themselves upon paper. Filippo assured me of her unaltered constancy. They both lamented in the strongest terms our continued separation, though they did justice to the filial feeling that kept me by my father's side.

Nearly eighteen months elapsed in this protracted exile. To me they were so many ages. Ardent and impetuous by nature, I scarcely know how I should have supported so long an absence, had I not felt assured that the faith of Bianca was equal to my own. At length my father died.

Life went from him almost imperceptibly. I hung over him in mute affliction, and watched the expiring spasms of nature. His last faltering accents whispered repeatedly a blessing on me—alas! how has it been fulfilled!

When I had paid due honors to his remains, and laid them in the tomb of our ancestors, I arranged briefly my affairs; put them in a posture to be easily at my command from a distance, and embarked once more, with a bounding heart, for Genoa.

Our voyage was propitious, and oh! what was my rapture when first, in the dawn of morning, I saw the shadowy summits of the Apennines rising almost like clouds above the horizon. The sweet breath of summer just moved us over the long wavering billows that were rolling us on towards Genoa. By degrees the coast of Sestri rose like a sweet creation of enchantment from the silver bosom of the deep. I behold the line of villages and palaces studding its borders. My eye reverted to a well-known point, and at length, from the confusion of distant objects, it singled out the villa which contained Bianca. It was a mere speck in the landscape, but glimmering from afar, the polar star of my heart.

Again I gazed at it for a livelong summer's day; but oh how different the emotions between departure and return. It now kept growing and growing, instead of lessening on my sight. My heart seemed to dilate with it. I looked at it through a telescope. I gradually defined one feature after another. The balconies of the central saloon where first I met Bianca beneath its roof; the terrace where we so often had passed the delightful summer evenings; the awning that shaded her chamber window—I almost fancied I saw her form beneath it. Could she but know her lover was in the bark whose white sail now gleamed on the sunny bosom of the sea! My fond impatience increased as we neared the coast. The ship seemed to lag lazily over the billows; I could almost have sprung into the sea and swam to the desired shore.

The shadows of evening gradually shrouded the scene, but the moon arose in all her fullness and beauty and shed the tender light so dear to lovers, over the romantic coast of Sestri. My whole soul was bathed in unutterable tenderness. I anticipated the heavenly evenings I should pass in wandering with Bianca by the light of that blessed moon.

It was late at night before we entered the harbor. As early next morning as I could get released from the formalities of landing I threw myself on horseback and hastened to the villa. As I galloped round the rocky promontory on which stands the Faro, and saw the coast of Sestri opening upon me, a thousand anxieties and doubts suddenly sprang up in my bosom. There is something fearful in returning to those we love, while yet uncertain what ills or changes absence may have effected. The turbulence of my agitation shook my very frame. I spurred my horse to redoubled speed; he was covered with foam when we both arrived panting at the gateway that opened to the grounds around the villa. I left my horse at a cottage and walked through the grounds, that I might regain tranquillity for the approaching interview. I chid myself for having suffered mere doubts and surmises thus suddenly to overcome me; but I was always prone to be carried away by these gusts of the feelings.

On entering the garden everything bore the same look as when I had left it; and this unchanged aspect of things reassured me. There were the alleys in which I had so often walked with Bianca; the same shades under which we had so often sat during the noontide. There were the same flowers of which she was fond; and which appeared still to be under the ministry of her hand. Everything around looked and breathed of Bianca; hope and joy flushed in my bosom at every step. I passed a little bower in which we had often sat and read together. A book and a glove lay on the bench. It was Bianca's glove; it was a volume of the Metestasio I had given her. The glove lay in my favorite passage. I clasped them to my heart. "All is safe!" exclaimed I, with rapture, "she loves me! she is still my own!"

I bounded lightly along the avenue down which I had faltered so slowly at my departure. I beheld her favorite pavilion which had witnessed our parting scene. The window was open, with the same vine clambering about it, precisely as when she waved and wept me an adieu. Oh! how transporting was the contrast in my situation. As I passed near the pavilion, I heard the tones of a female voice. They thrilled through me with an appeal to my heart not to be mistaken. Before I could think, I *felt* they were Bianca's. For an instant I paused, overpowered with agitation. I feared to break in suddenly upon her. I softly ascended the steps of the pavilion. The door was open. I saw Bianca seated at a table; her back was towards me; she was warbling a soft melancholy air, and was occupied in drawing. A glance sufficed to show me that she was copying one of my own paintings. I gazed on her for a moment in a delicious tumult of emotions. She paused in her singing; a heavy sigh, almost a sob followed. I could no longer contain myself. "Bianca!" exclaimed I, in a half smothered voice. She started at the sound; brushed back the ringlets that hung clustering about her face; darted a glance at me; uttered a piercing shriek and would have fallen to the earth, had I not caught her in my arms.

"Bianca! my own Bianca!" exclaimed I, folding her to my bosom; my voice stifled in sobs of convulsive joy. She lay in my arms without sense or motion. Alarmed at the effects of my own precipitation, I scarce knew what to do. I tried by a thousand endearing words to call her back to consciousness. She slowly recovered, and half opening her eyes— "where am I?" murmured she faintly. "Here," exclaimed I, pressing her to my bosom. "Here! close to the heart that adores you; in the arms of your faithful Ottavio!"

"Oh no! no! no!" shrieked she, starting into sudden life and terror— "away! away! leave me! leave me!"

She tore herself from my arms; rushed to a corner of the saloon, and covered her face with her hands, as if the very sight of me were baleful. I was thunderstruck—I could not believe my senses. I followed her, trembling, confounded. I endeavored to take her hand, but she shrunk from my very touch with horror.

"Good heavens, Bianca," exclaimed I, "what is the meaning of this? Is this my reception after so long an absence? Is this the love you professed for me?"

At the mention of love, a shuddering ran through her. She turned to me a face wild with anguish. "No more of that! no more of that!" gasped she—"talk not to me of love—I—I—am married!"

I reeled as if I had received a mortal blow. A sickness struck to my very heart. I caught at a window frame for support. For a moment or two, everything was chaos around me. When I recovered, I beheld Bianca lying on a sofa; her face buried in a pillow, and sobbing convulsively. Indignation at her fickleness for a moment overpowered every other feeling.

"Faithless—perjured—" cried I, striding across the room. But another glance at that beautiful being in distress, checked all my wrath. Anger could not dwell together with her idea in my soul.

"Oh, Bianca," exclaimed I, in anguish, "could I have dreamt of this; could I have suspected you would have been false to me?"

She raised her face all streaming with tears, all disordered with emotion, and gave me one appealing look—"False to you!—they told me you were dead!"

"What," said I, "in spite of our constant correspondence?"

She gazed wildly at me—"correspondence!—what correspondence?"

"Have you not repeatedly received and replied to my letters?"

She clasped her hands with solemnity and fervor—"As I hope for mercy, never!"

A horrible surmise shot through my brain—"Who told you I was dead?"

"It was reported that the ship in which you embarked for Naples perished at sea."

"But who told you the report?"

She paused for an instant, and trembled—

"Filippo!"

"May the God of heaven curse him!" cried I, extending my clinched fists aloft.

"Oh do not curse him—do not curse him!" exclaimed she—"He is—he is—my husband!"

This was all that was wanting to unfold the perfidy that had been practised upon me. My blood boiled like liquid fire in my veins. I gasped with rage too great for utterance. I remained for a time bewildered by the whirl of horrible thoughts that rushed through my mind. The poor victim of deception before me thought it was with her I was incensed. She faintly murmured forth her exculpation. I will not dwell upon it. I saw in it more than she meant to reveal. I saw with a glance how both of us had been betrayed. "'Tis well!" muttered I to myself in smothered accents of concentrated fury. "He shall account to me for this!"

Bianca overhead me. New terror flashed in her countenance. "For mercy's sake do not meet him—say nothing of what has passed—for my sake say nothing to him—I only shall be the sufferer!"

A new suspicion darted across my mind—"What!" exclaimed I—"do you then *fear* him—is he *unkind* to you—tell me," reiterated I, grasping her hand and looking her eagerly in the face—"tell me—*dares* he to use you harshly!"

"No! no! no!" cried she faltering and embarrassed; but the glance at her face had told me volumes. I saw in her pallid and wasted features; in the prompt terror and subdued agony of her eye a whole history of a mind broken down by tyranny. Great God! and was this beauteous flower snatched from me to be thus trampled upon? The idea roused me to madness. I clinched my teeth and my hands; I foamed at the mouth; every passion seemed to have resolved itself into the fury that like a lava boiled within my heart. Bianca shrunk from me in speechless affright.

As I strode by the window my eye darted down the alley. Fatal moment! I beheld Filippo at a distance! My brain was in a delirium—I sprang from the pavilion, and was before him with the quickness of lightning. He saw me as I came rushing upon him—he turned pale, looked wildly to right and left, as if he would have fled, and trembling drew his sword.

"Wretch!" cried I, "well may you draw your weapon!"

I spake not another word—I snatched forth a stiletto, put by the sword which trembled in his hand, and buried my poniard in his bosom. He fell with the blow, but my rage was unsated. I sprang upon him with the blood-thirsty feeling of a tiger; redoubled my blows; mangled him in my frenzy, grasped him by the throat, until with reiterated wounds and strangling convulsions he expired in my grasp. I remained glaring on the countenance, horrible in death, that seemed to stare back with its protruded eyes upon me. Piercing shrieks roused me from my delirium. I looked round and beheld Bianca flying distractedly towards us. My brain whirled. I waited not to meet her, but fled from the scene of horror. I fled forth from the garden like another Cain, a hell within my bosom, and a curse upon my head. I fled without knowing whither—almost without knowing why—my only idea was to get farther and farther from the horrors I had left behind; as if I could throw space between myself and my conscience. I fled to the Apennines, and wandered for days and days among their savage heights. How I existed I cannot tell— what rocks and precipices I braved, and how I braved them, I know not. I kept on and on—trying to outtravel the curse that clung to me. Alas, the shrieks of Bianca rung for ever in my ear. The horrible countenance of my victim was for ever before my eyes. "The blood of Filippo cried to me from the ground." Rocks, trees, and torrents all resounded with my crime.

Then it was I felt how much more insupportable is the anguish of remorse than every other mental pang. Oh! could I but have cast off this crime that festered in my heart; could I but have regained the innocence that reigned in my breast as I entered the garden at Sestri; could I but have restored my victim to life, I felt as if I could look on with transport even though Bianca were in his arms.

By degrees this frenzied fever of remorse settled into a permanent malady of the mind. Into one of the most horrible that ever poor wretch was cursed with. Wherever I went, the countenance of him I had slain appeared to follow me. Wherever I turned my head I beheld it behind me, hideous with the contortions of the dying moment. I have tried in every way to escape from this horrible phantom; but in vain. I know not whether it is an illusion of the mind, the consequence of my dismal education at the convent, or whether a phantom really sent by heaven to punish me; but there it ever is—at all times—in all places—nor has time nor habit had any effect in familiarizing me with its terrors. I have travelled from place to place, plunged into amusements—tried dissipation and distraction of every kind—all—all in vain.

I once had recourse to my pencil as a desperate experiment. I painted an exact resemblance of this phantom face. I placed it before me in hopes that by constantly contemplating the copy I might diminish the effect of the original. But I only doubled instead of diminishing the misery.

Such is the curse that has clung to my footsteps—that has made my life a burthen—but the thoughts of death, terrible. God knows what I have suffered. What days and days, and nights and nights, of sleepless torment. What a never-dying worm has preyed upon my heart; what an unquenchable fire has burned within my brain. He knows the wrongs that wrought upon my poor weak nature; that converted the tenderest of affections into the deadliest of fury. He knows best whether a frail erring creature has expiated by long-enduring torture and measureless remorse, the crime of a moment of madness. Often, often have I prostrated myself in the dust, and implored that he would give me a sign of his forgiveness, and let me die.—

Thus far had I written some time since. I had meant to leave this record of misery and crime with you, to be read when I should be no more. My prayer to heaven has at length been heard. You were witness to my emotions last evening at the performance of the Miserere; when the vaulted temple resounded with the words of atonement and redemption. I heard a voice speaking to me from the midst of the music; I heard it rising above the pealing of the organ and the voices of the choir; it spoke to me in tones of celestial melody; it promised mercy and forgiveness, but demanded from me full expiation. I go to make it. Tomorrow I shall be on my way to Genoa to surrender myself to justice. You who have pitied my sufferings; who have poured the balm of sympathy into my wounds, do not shrink from my memory with abhorrence now that you know my story. Recollect, when you read of my crime I shall have atoned for it with my blood!

When the Baronet had finished, there was an universal desire expressed to see the painting of this frightful visage. After much

WASHINGTON IRVING

entreaty the Baronet consented, on condition that they should only visit it one by one. He called his housekeeper and gave her charge to conduct the gentlemen singly to the chamber. They all returned varying in their stories: some affected in one way, some in another; some more, some less; but all agreeing that there was a certain something about the painting that had a very odd effect upon the feelings.

I stood in a deep bow window with the Baronet, and could not help expressing my wonder. "After all," said I, "there are certain mysteries in our nature, certain inscrutable impulses and influences, that warrant one in being superstitious. Who can account for so many persons of different characters being thus strangely affected by a mere painting?"

"And especially when not one of them has seen it!" said the Baronet with a smile.

"How?" exclaimed I, "not seen it?"

"Not one of them?" replied he, laying his finger on his lips in sign of secrecy. "I saw that some of them were in a bantering vein, and I did not choose that the memento of the poor Italian should be made a jest of. So I gave the housekeeper a hint to show them all to a different chamber!"

Thus end the Stories of the Nervous Gentleman.

PART SECOND

BUCKTHORNE AND HIS FRIENDS

"'Tis a very good world that we live in,
To lend, or to spend, or to give in;
But to beg, or to borrow, or get a man's own,
'Tis the very worst world, sir, that ever was known."

—Lines from an Inn Window

Literary Life

Among the great variety of characters which fall in a traveller's way, I became acquainted during my sojourn in London, with an eccentric personage of the name of Buckthorne. He was a literary man, had lived much in the metropolis, and had acquired a great deal of curious, though unprofitable knowledge concerning it. He was a great observer of character, and could give the natural history of every odd animal that presented itself in this great wilderness of men. Finding me very curious about literary life and literary characters, he took much pains to gratify my curiosity.

"The literary world of England," said he to me one day, "is made up of a number of little fraternities, each existing merely for itself, and thinking the rest of the world created only to look on and admire. It may be resembled to the firmament, consisting of a number of systems, each composed of its own central sun with its revolving train of moons and satellites, all acting in the most harmonious concord; but the comparison fails in part, inasmuch as the literary world has no general concord. Each system acts independently of the rest, and indeed considers all other stars as mere exhalations and transient meteors, beaming for awhile with false fires, but doomed soon to fall and be forgotten; while its own luminaries are the lights of the universe, destined to increase in splendor and to shine steadily on to immortality."

"And pray," said I, "how is a man to get a peep into one of these systems you talk of? I presume an intercourse with authors is a kind of intellectual exchange, where one must bring his commodities to barter, and always give a *quid pro quo*."

"Pooh, pooh—how you mistake," said Buckthorne, smiling; "you must never think to become popular among wits by shining. They go into society to shine themselves, not to admire the brilliancy of others. I thought as you do when I first cultivated the society of men of letters, and never went to a blue-stocking coterie without studying my part beforehand as diligently as an actor. The consequence was, I soon got the name of an intolerable proser, and should in a little while have been completely excommunicated had I not changed my plan of operations. From thenceforth I became a most assiduous listener, or if ever I were eloquent, it was tête-a-tête with an author in praise of his own works, or what is nearly as acceptable, in disparagement of the works of his contemporaries. If ever he spoke favorably of the productions of some particular friend, I ventured boldly to dissent from him, and to prove that his friend was a blockhead; and much as people say of the pertinacity and irritability of authors, I never found one to take offence at my contradictions. No, no, sir, authors are particularly candid in admitting the faults of their friends.

"Indeed, I was extremely sparing of my remarks on all modern works, excepting to make sarcastic observations on the most distinguished writers of the day. I never ventured to praise an author that had not been dead at least half a century; and even then I was rather cautious; for you must know that many old writers have been enlisted under the banners of different sects, and their merits have become as complete topics of party prejudice and dispute, as the merits of living statesmen and politicians. Nay, there have been whole periods of literature absolutely *taboo'd*, to use a South Sea phrase. It is, for example, as much as a man's reputation is worth, in some circles, to say a word in praise of any writers of the reign of Charles the Second, or even of Queen Anne; they being all declared to be Frenchmen in disguise."

"And pray, then," said I, "when am I to know that I am on safe grounds; being totally unacquainted with the literary landmarks and the boundary lines of fashionable taste?"

"Oh," replied he, there is fortunately one tract of literature that forms a kind of neutral ground, on which all the literary world meet amicably; lay down their weapons and even run riot in their excess of good humor, and this is, the reigns of Elizabeth and James. Here you may praise away at a venture; here it is 'cut and come again,' and the more obscure the author, and the more quaint and crabbed his style, the more your admiration will smack of the real relish of the connoisseur; whose taste, like that of an epicure, is always for game that has an antiquated flavor.

"But," continued he, "as you seem anxious to know something of literary society I will take an opportunity to introduce you to some coterie, where the talents of the day are assembled. I cannot promise you, however, that they will be of the first order. Somehow or other, our great geniuses are not gregarious, they do not go in flocks, but fly singly in general society. They prefer mingling, like common men, with the multitude; and are apt to carry nothing of the author about them but the reputation. It is only the inferior orders that herd together, acquire strength and importance by their confederacies, and bear all the distinctive characteristics of their species."

A Literary Dinner

A few days after this conversation with Mr. Buckthorne, he called upon me, and took me with him to a regular literary dinner. It was given by a great bookseller, or rather a company of booksellers, whose firm surpassed in length even that of Shadrach, Meschach, and Abednego.

I was surprised to find between twenty and thirty guests assembled, most of whom I had never seen before. Buckthorne explained this to me by informing me that this was a "business dinner," or kind of field day, which the house gave about twice a year to its authors. It is true, they did occasionally give snug dinners to three or four literary men at a time, but then these were generally select authors; favorites of the public; such as had arrived at their sixth and seventh editions. "There are," said he, "certain geographical boundaries in the land of literature, and you may judge tolerably well of an author's popularity, by the wine his bookseller gives him. An author crosses the port line about the third edition and gets into claret, but when he has reached the sixth and seventh, he may revel in champagne and burgundy."

"And pray," said I, "how far may these gentlemen have reached that I see around me; are any of these claret drinkers?"

"Not exactly, not exactly. You find at these great dinners the common steady run of authors, one, two, edition men—or if any others are invited they are aware that it is a kind of republican meeting—You understand me—a meeting of the republic of letters, and that they must expect nothing but plain substantial fare."

These hints enabled me to comprehend more fully the arrangement of the table. The two ends were occupied by two partners of the house. And the host seemed to have adopted Addison's ideas as to the literary precedence of his guests. A popular poet had the post of honor, opposite to whom was a hot-pressed traveller in quarto, with plates. A grave-looking antiquarian, who had produced several solid works, which were much quoted and little read, was treated with great respect, and seated next to a neat, dressy gentleman in black, who had written a thin, genteel, hot-pressed octavo on political economy that was getting into fashion. Several three-volume duodecimo men of fair currency were placed about the centre of the table; while the lower end was taken up with small poets, translators, and authors, who had not as yet risen into much notice.

The conversation during dinner was by fits and starts; breaking out here and there in various parts of the table in small flashes, and ending in smoke. The poet, who had the confidence of a man on good terms with the world and independent of his bookseller, was very gay and brilliant, and said many clever things, which set the partner next him, in a roar, and delighted all the company. The other partner, however, maintained his sedateness, and kept carving on, with the air of a thorough man of business, intent upon the occupation of the moment. His gravity was explained to me by my friend Buckthorne. He informed me that the concerns of the house were admirably distributed among the partners. "Thus, for instance," said he, "the grave gentleman is the carving partner who attends to the joints, and the other is the laughing partner who attends to the jokes."

The general conversation was chiefly carried on at the upper end of the table; as the authors there seemed to possess the greatest courage of the tongue. As to the crew at the lower end, if they did not make much figure in talking, they did in eating. Never was there a more determined, inveterate, thoroughly-sustained attack on the trencher, than by this phalanx of masticators. When the cloth was removed, and the wine began to circulate, they grew very merry and jocose among themselves. Their jokes, however, if by chance any of them reached the upper end of the table, seldom produced much effect. Even the laughing partner did not seem to think it necessary to honor them with a smile; which my neighbour Buckthorne accounted for, by informing me that there was a certain degree of popularity to be obtained, before a bookseller could afford to laugh at an author's jokes.

Among this crew of questionable gentlemen thus seated below the salt, my eye singled out one in particular. He was rather shabbily dressed; though he had evidently made the most of a rusty black coat, and wore his shirt-frill plaited and puffed out voluminously at the bosom. His face was dusky, but florid—perhaps a little too florid, particularly about the nose, though the rosy hue gave the greater lustre to a twinkling black eye. He had a little the look of a boon companion, with that dash of the poor devil in it which gives an inexpressibly mellow tone to a man's humor. I had seldom seen a face of richer promise; but never was promise so ill kept. He said nothing; ate and drank with the keen appetite of a gazetteer, and scarcely stopped to laugh even at the good jokes from the upper end of the table. I inquired who he was. Buckthorne looked at him attentively. "Gad," said he, "I have seen that face before, but where I cannot recollect. He cannot be an author of any note. I suppose some writer of sermons or grinder of foreign travels."

After dinner we retired to another room to take tea and coffee, where we were re-enforced by a cloud of inferior guests. Authors of small volumes in boards, and pamphlets stitched in blue paper. These had not as yet arrived to the importance of a dinner invitation, but were invited occasionally to pass the evening "in a friendly way." They were very respectful to the partners, and indeed seemed to stand a little in awe of them; but they paid very devoted court to the lady of the house, and were extravagantly fond of the children. I looked round for the poor devil author in the rusty black coat and magnificent frill, but he had disappeared immediately after leaving the table; having a dread, no doubt, of the glaring light of a drawing-room. Finding nothing farther to interest my attention, I took my departure as soon as coffee had been served, leaving the port and the thin, genteel, hot-pressed, octavo gentlemen, masters of the field.

The Club of Queer Fellows

I think it was but the very next evening that in coming out of Covent Garden Theatre with my eccentric friend Buckthorne, he proposed to give me another peep at life and character. Finding me willing for any research of the kind, he took me through a variety of the narrow courts and lanes about Covent Garden, until we stopped before a tavern from which we heard the bursts of merriment of a jovial party. There would be a loud peal of laughter, then an interval, then another peal; as if a prime wag were telling a story. After a little while there was a song, and at the close of each stanza a hearty roar and a vehement thumping on the table.

"This is the place," whispered Buckthorne. "It is the 'Club of Queer Fellows.' A great resort of the small wits, third-rate actors, and newspaper critics of the theatres. Any one can go in on paying a shilling at the bar for the use of the club."

We entered, therefore, without ceremony, and took our seats at a lone table in a dusky corner of the room. The club was assembled round a table, on which stood beverages of various kinds, according to the taste of the individual. The members were a set of queer fellows indeed; but what was my surprise on recognizing in the prime wit of the meeting the poor devil author whom I had remarked at the booksellers' dinner for his promising face and his complete taciturnity. Matters, however, were entirely changed with him. There he was a mere cypher: here he was lord of the ascendant; the choice spirit, the dominant genius. He sat at the head of the table with his hat on, and an eye beaming even more luminously than his nose. He had a quiz and a fillip for every one, and a good thing on every occasion. Nothing could be said or done without eliciting a spark from him; and I solemnly declare I have heard much worse wit even from noblemen. His jokes, it must be confessed, were rather wet, but they suited the circle in which he presided. The company were in that maudlin mood when a little wit goes a great way. Every time he opened his lips there was sure to be a roar, and sometimes before he had time to speak.

We were fortunate enough to enter in time for a glee composed by him expressly for the club, and which he sang with two boon companions, who would have been worthy subjects for Hogarth's pencil. As they were each provided with a written copy, I was enabled to procure the reading of it.

Merrily, merrily push round the glass,
And merrily troll the glee,
For he who won't drink till he wink is an ass,
So neighbor I drink to thee.
Merrily, merrily puddle thy nose,
Until it right rosy shall be;
For a jolly red nose, I speak under the rose,
Is a sign of good company.

We waited until the party broke up, and no one but the wit remained. He sat at the table with his legs stretched under it, and wide apart; his hands in his breeches pockets; his head drooped upon his breast; and gazing with lack-lustre countenance on an empty tankard. His gayety was gone, his fire completely quenched.

My companion approached and startled him from his fit of brown study, introducing himself on the strength of their having dined together at the booksellers'.

"By the way," said he, "it seems to me I have seen you before; your face is surely the face of an old acquaintance, though for the life of me I cannot tell where I have known you."

"Very likely," said he with a smile; "many of my old friends have forgotten me. Though, to tell the truth, my memory in this instance is as bad as your own. If, however, it will assist your recollection in any way, my name is Thomas Dribble, at your service."

"What, Tom Dribble, who was at old Birchell's school in Warwickshire?"

"The same," said the other, coolly.

"Why, then we are old schoolmates, though it's no wonder you don't recollect me. I was your junior by several years; don't you recollect little Jack Buckthorne?"

Here then ensued a scene of school-fellow recognition; and a world of talk about old school times and school pranks. Mr. Dribble ended by observing, with a heavy sigh, "that times were sadly changed since those days."

"Faith, Mr. Dribble," said I, "you seem quite a different man here from what you were at dinner. I had no idea that you had so much stuff in you. There you were all silence; but here you absolutely keep the table in a roar."

"Ah, my dear sir," replied he, with a shake of the head and a shrug of the shoulder, "I'm a mere glow-worm. I never shine by daylight.

Besides, it's a hard thing for a poor devil of an author to shine at the table of a rich bookseller. Who do you think would laugh at any thing I could say, when I had some of the current wits of the day about me? But here, though a poor devil, I am among still poorer devils than myself; men who look up to me as a man of letters and a bel esprit, and all my jokes pass as sterling gold from the mint."

"You surely do yourself injustice, sir," said I; "I have certainly heard more good things from you this evening than from any of those beaux esprits by whom you appear to have been so daunted."

"Ah, sir! but they have luck on their side; they are in the fashion—there's nothing like being in the fashion. A man that has once got his character up for a wit, is always sure of a laugh, say what he may. He may utter as much nonsense as he pleases, and all will pass current. No one stops to question the coin of a rich man; but a poor devil cannot pass off either a joke or a guinea, without its being examined on both sides. Wit and coin are always doubted with a threadbare coat.

"For my part," continued he, giving his hat a twitch a little more on one side, "for my part, I hate your fine dinners; there's nothing, sir, like the freedom of a chop-house. I'd rather, any time, have my steak and tankard among my own set, than drink claret and eat venison with your cursed civil, elegant company, who never laugh at a good joke from a poor devil, for fear of its being vulgar. A good joke grows in a wet soil; it flourishes in low places, but withers on your d—d high, dry grounds. I once kept high company, sir, until I nearly ruined myself; I grew so dull, and vapid, and genteel. Nothing saved me but being arrested by my landlady and thrown into prison; where a course of catch-clubs, eight-penny ale, and poor-devil company, manured my mind and brought it back to itself again."

As it was now growing late we parted for the evening; though I felt anxious to know more of this practical philosopher. I was glad, therefore, when Buckthorne proposed to have another meeting to talk over old school times, and inquired his school-mate's address. The latter seemed at first a little shy of naming his lodgings; but suddenly assuming an air of hardihood—"Green Arbour court, sir," exclaimed he—"number—in Green Arbour court. You must know the place. Classic ground, sir! classic ground! It was there Goldsmith wrote his Vicar of Wakefield. I always like to live in literary haunts."

I was amused with this whimsical apology for shabby quarters. On our Way homewards Buckthorne assured me that this Dribble had been the prime wit and great wag of the school in their boyish days, and one of those unlucky urchins denominated bright geniuses. As he perceived me curious respecting his old school-mate, he promised to take me with him, in his proposed visit to Green Arbour court.

A few mornings afterwards he called upon me, and we set forth on our expedition. He led me through a variety of singular alleys, and courts, and blind passages; for he appeared to be profoundly versed in all the intricate geography of the metropolis. At length we came out upon Fleet Market, and traversing it, turned up a narrow street to the bottom of a long steep flight of stone steps, named Break-neck Stairs. These, he told me, led up to Green Arbour court, and that down them poor Goldsmith might many a time have risked his neck. When we entered the court, I could not but smile to think in what out-of-the-way corners genius produces her bantlings! And the muses, those capricious dames, who, forsooth, so often refuse to visit palaces, and deny a single smile to votaries in splendid studies and gilded drawing-rooms,—what holes and burrows will they frequent to lavish their favors on some ragged disciple!

This Green Arbour court I found to be a small square of tall and Miserable houses, the very intestines of which seemed turned inside out, to judge from the old garments and frippery that fluttered from every window. It appeared to be a region of washerwomen, and lines were stretched about the little square, on which clothes were dangling to dry. Just as we entered the square, a scuffle took place between two viragos about a disputed right to a washtub, and immediately the whole community was in a hubbub. Heads in mob caps popped out of every window, and such a clamor of tongues ensued that I was fain to stop my ears. Every Amazon took part with one or other of the disputants, and brandished her arms dripping with soapsuds, and fired away from her window as from the embrazure of a fortress; while the swarms of children nestled and cradled in every procreant chamber of this hive, waking with the noise, set up their shrill pipes to swell the general concert.

Poor Goldsmith! what a time must he have had of it, with his quiet Disposition and nervous habits, penned up in this den of noise and vulgarity. How strange that while every sight and sound was sufficient to embitter the heart and fill it with misanthropy, his pen should be dropping the honey of Hybla. Yet it is more than probable that he drew many of his inimitable pictures of low life from the scenes which surrounded him in this abode. The circumstance of Mrs. Tibbs being obliged to wash her husband's two shirts in a neighbor's house, who refused to lend her washtub, may have been no sport of fancy, but a fact passing under his own eye. His landlady may have sat for the picture, and Beau Tibbs' scanty wardrobe have been a facsimile of his own.

It was with some difficulty that we found our way to Dribble's lodgings. They were up two pair of stairs, in a room that looked upon the court, and when we entered he was seated on the edge of his bed, writing at a broken table. He received us, however, with a free, open, poor devil air, that was irresistible. It is true he did at first appear slightly confused; buttoned up his waistcoat a little higher and tucked in a stray frill of linen. But he recollected himself in an instant; gave a half swagger, half leer, as he stepped forth to receive us; drew a three-legged stool for Mr. Buckthorne; pointed me to a lumbering old damask chair that looked like a dethroned monarch in exile, and bade us welcome to his garret.

We soon got engaged in conversation. Buckthorne and he had much to say about early school scenes; and as nothing opens a man's heart more than recollections of the kind, we soon drew from him a brief outline of his literary career.

The Poor Devil Author

I began life unluckily by being the wag and bright fellow at school; and I had the farther misfortune of becoming the great genius of my native village. My father was a country attorney, and intended that I should succeed him in business; but I had too much genius to study, and he was too fond of my genius to force it into the traces. So I fell into bad company and took to bad habits. Do not mistake me. I mean that I fell into the company of village literati and village blues, and took to writing village poetry.

It was quite the fashion in the village to be literary. We had a little knot of choice spirits who assembled frequently together, formed ourselves into a Literary, Scientific, and Philosophical Society, and fancied ourselves the most learned philos in existence. Every one had a great character assigned him, suggested by some casual habit or affectation. One heavy fellow drank an enormous quantity of tea; rolled in his armchair, talked sententiously, pronounced dogmatically, and was considered a second Dr. Johnson; another, who happened to be a curate, uttered coarse jokes, wrote doggerel rhymes, and was the Swift of our association. Thus we had also our Popes and Goldsmiths and Addisons, and a blue-stocking lady, whose drawing-room we frequented, who corresponded about nothing with all the world, and wrote letters with the stiffness and formality of a printed book, was cried up as another Mrs. Montagu. I was, by common consent, the juvenile prodigy, the poetical youth, the great genius, the pride and hope of the village, through whom it was to become one day as celebrated as Stratford-on-Avon.

My father died and left me his blessing and his business. His blessing brought no money into my pocket; and as to his business it soon deserted me: for I was busy writing poetry, and could not attend to law; and my clients, though they had great respect for my talents, had no faith in a poetical attorney.

I lost my business therefore, spent my money, and finished my poem. It was the Pleasures of Melancholy, and was cried up to the skies by the whole circle. The Pleasures of Imagination, the Pleasures of Hope, and the Pleasures of Memory, though each had placed its author in the first rank of poets, were blank prose in comparison. Our Mrs. Montagu would cry over it from beginning to end. It was pronounced by all the members of the Literary, Scientific, and Philosophical Society the greatest poem of the age, and all anticipated the noise it would make in the great world. There was not a doubt but the London booksellers would be mad after it, and the only fear of my friends was, that I would make a sacrifice by selling it too cheap.

Every time they talked the matter over they increased the price. They reckoned up the great sums given for the poems of certain popular writers, and determined that mine was worth more than all put together, and ought to be paid for accordingly. For my part, I was modest in my expectations, and determined that I would be satisfied with a thousand guineas. So I put my poem in my pocket and set off for London.

My journey was joyous. My heart was light as my purse, and my head full of anticipations of fame and fortune. With what swelling pride did I cast my eyes upon old London from the heights of Highgate. I was like a general looking down upon a place he expects to conquer. The great metropolis lay stretched before me, buried under a home-made cloud of murky smoke, that wrapped it from the brightness of a sunny day, and formed for it a kind of artificial bad weather. At the outskirts of the city, away to the west, the smoke gradually decreased until all was clear and sunny, and the view stretched uninterrupted to the blue line of the Kentish Hills.

My eye turned fondly to where the mighty cupola of St. Paul's swelled Dimly through this misty chaos, and I pictured to myself the solemn realm of learning that lies about its base. How soon should the Pleasures of Melancholy throw this world of booksellers and printers into a bustle of business and delight! How soon should I hear my name repeated by printers' devils throughout Pater Noster Row, and Angel Court, and Ave Maria Lane, until Amen corner should echo back the sound!

Arrived in town, I repaired at once to the most fashionable publisher. Every new author patronizes him of course. In fact, it had been determined in the village circle that he should be the fortunate man. I cannot tell you how vaingloriously I walked the streets; my head was in the clouds. I felt the airs of heaven playing about it, and fancied it already encircled by a halo of literary glory.

As I passed by the windows of bookshops, I anticipated the time when my work would be shining among the hotpressed wonders of the day; and my face, scratched on copper, or cut in wood, figuring in fellowship with those of Scott and Byron and Moore.

WASHINGTON IRVING

When I applied at the publisher's house there was something in the loftiness of my air, and the dinginess of my dress, that struck the clerks with reverence. They doubtless took me for some person of consequence, probably a digger of Greek roots, or a penetrator of pyramids. A proud man in a dirty shirt is always an imposing character in the world of letters; one must feel intellectually secure before he can venture to dress shabbily; none but a great scholar or a great genius dares to be dirty; so I was ushered at once to the sanctum sanctorum of this high priest of Minerva.

The publishing of books is a very different affair now-a-days from what it was in the time of Bernard Lintot. I found the publisher a fashionably-dressed man, in an elegant drawing-room, furnished with sofas and portraits of celebrated authors, and cases of splendidly bound books. He was writing letters at an elegant table. This was transacting business in style. The place seemed suited to the magnificent publications that issued from it. I rejoiced at the choice I had made of a publisher, for I always liked to encourage men of taste and spirit.

I stepped up to the table with the lofty poetical port that I had Been accustomed to maintain in our village circle; though I threw in it something of a patronizing air, such as one feels when about to make a man's fortune. The publisher paused with his pen in his hand, and seemed waiting in mute suspense to know what was to be announced by so singular an apparition.

I put him at his ease in a moment, for I felt that I had but to come, see, and conquer. I made known my name, and the name of my poem; produced my precious roll of blotted manuscript, laid it on the table with an emphasis, and told him at once, to save time and come directly to the point, the price was one thousand guineas.

I had given him no time to speak, nor did he seem so inclined. He Continued looking at me for a moment with an air of whimsical perplexity; scanned me from head to foot; looked down at the manuscript, then up again at me, then pointed to a chair; and whistling softly to himself, went on writing his letter.

I sat for some time waiting his reply, supposing he was making up his mind; but he only paused occasionally to take a fresh dip of ink; to stroke his chin or the tip of his nose, and then resumed his writing. It was evident his mind was intently occupied upon some other subject; but I had no idea that any other subject should be attended to and my poem lie unnoticed on the table. I had supposed that every thing would make way for the Pleasures of Melancholy.

My gorge at length rose within me. I took up my manuscript; thrust it into my pocket, and walked out of the room: making some noise as I went, to let my departure be heard. The publisher, however, was too much busied in minor concerns to notice it. I was suffered to walk down-stairs without being called back. I sallied forth into the street, but no clerk was sent after me, nor did the publisher call after me from the drawing-room window. I have been told since, that he considered me either a madman or a fool. I leave you to judge how much he was in the wrong in his opinion.

When I turned the corner my crest fell. I cooled down in my pride and my expectations, and reduced my terms with the next bookseller to whom I applied. I had no better success: nor with a third: nor with a fourth. I then desired the booksellers to make an offer themselves; but the deuce an offer would they make. They told me poetry was a mere drug; everybody wrote poetry; the market was overstocked with it. And then, they said, the title of my poem was not taking: that pleasures of all kinds were worn threadbare; nothing but horrors did now-a-days, and even these were almost worn out. Tales of pirates, robbers, and bloody Turks might answer tolerably well; but then they must come from some established well-known name, or the public would not look at them.

At last I offered to leave my poem with a bookseller to read it and judge for himself. "Why, really, my dear Mr.—a—a—I forget your name," said he, cutting an eye at my rusty coat and shabby gaiters, "really, sir, we are so pressed with business just now, and have so many manuscripts on hand to read, that we have not time to look at any new production, but if you can call again in a week or two, or say the middle of next month, we may be able to look over your writings and give you an answer. Don't forget, the month after next—good morning, sir—happy to see you any time you are passing this way"—so saying he bowed me out in the civilest way imaginable. In short, sir, instead of an eager competition to secure my poem I could not even get it read! In the mean time I was harassed by letters from my friends, wanting to know when the work was to appear; who was to be my publisher; but above all things warning me not to let it go too cheap.

There was but one alternative left. I determined to publish the poem myself; and to have my triumph over the booksellers, when it should become the fashion of the day. I accordingly published the Pleasures of Melancholy and ruined myself. Excepting the copies sent to the reviews, and to my friends in the country, not one, I believe, ever left the bookseller's warehouse. The printer's bill drained my purse, and the only notice that was taken of my work was contained in the advertisements paid for by myself.

I could have borne all this, and have attributed it as usual to the mismanagement of the publisher, or the want of taste in the public: and could have made the usual appeal to posterity, but my village friends would not let me rest in quiet. They were picturing me to themselves feasting with the great, communing with the literary, and in the high course of fortune and renown. Every little while, some one came to me with a letter of introduction from the village circle, recommending him to my attentions, and requesting that I would make him known in society; with a hint that an introduction to the house of a celebrated literary nobleman would be extremely agreeable.

I determined, therefore, to change my lodgings, drop my correspondence, and disappear altogether from the view of my village admirers. Besides, I was anxious to make one more poetic attempt. I was by no means disheartened by the failure of my first. My poem was evidently too didactic. The public was wise enough. It no longer read for instruction. "They want horrors, do they?" said I, "I'faith, then they shall have enough of them." So I looked out for some quiet retired place, where I might be out of reach of my friends, and have leisure to cook up some delectable dish of poetical "hell-broth."

I had some difficulty in finding a place to my mind, when chance threw me in the way Of Canonbury Castle. It is an ancient brick tower, hard by "merry Islington;" the remains of a hunting-seat of Queen Elizabeth, where she took the pleasures of the country, when the neighborhood was all woodland. What gave it particular interest in my eyes, was the circumstance that it had been the residence of a poet. It was here Goldsmith resided when he wrote his Deserted Village. I was shown the very apartment. It was a relique of the original style of the castle, with pannelled wainscots and gothic windows. I was pleased with its air of antiquity, and with its having been the residence of poor Goldy.

"Goldsmith was a pretty poet," said I to myself, "a very pretty poet; though rather of the old school. He did not think and feel so strongly as is the fashion now-a-days; but had he lived in these times of hot hearts and hot heads, he would have written quite differently."

In a few days I was quietly established in my new quarters; my books all arranged, my writing desk placed by a window looking out into the field; and I felt as snug as Robinson Crusoe, when he had finished his bower. For several days I enjoyed all the novelty of change and the charms which grace a new lodgings before one has found out their defects. I rambled about the fields where I fancied Goldsmith had rambled. I explored merry Islington; ate my solitary dinner at the Black Bull, which according to tradition was a country seat of Sir Walter Raleigh, and would sit and sip my wine and muse on old times in a quaint old room, where many a council had been held.

All this did very well for a few days: I was stimulated by novelty; inspired by the associations awakened in my mind by these curious haunts, and began to think I felt the spirit of composition stirring within me; but Sunday came, and with it the whole city world, swarming about Canonbury Castle. I could not open my window but I was stunned with shouts and noises from the cricket ground. The late quiet road beneath my window was alive with the tread of feet and clack of tongues; and to complete my misery, I found that my quiet retreat was absolutely a "show house!" the tower and its contents being shown to strangers at sixpence a head.

There was a perpetual tramping up-stairs of citizens and their families, to look about the country from the top of the tower, and to take a peep at the city through the telescope, to try if they could discern their own chimneys. And then, in the midst of a vein of thought, or a moment of inspiration, I was interrupted, and all my ideas put to flight, by my intolerable landlady's tapping at the door, and asking me, if I would "jist please to let a lady and gentleman come in to take a look at Mr. Goldsmith's room."

If you know anything what an author's study is, and what an author is himself, you must know that there was no standing this. I put a positive interdict on my room's being exhibited; but then it was shown when I was absent, and my papers put in confusion; and on returning home one day, I absolutely found a cursed tradesman and his daughters gaping over my manuscripts; and my landlady in a panic at my appearance. I tried to make out a little longer by taking the key in my pocket, but it would not do. I overheard mine hostess one day telling some of her customers on the stairs that the room was occupied by an author, who was always in a tantrum if interrupted; and I immediately perceived, by a slight noise at the door, that they were peeping at me through the key-hole. By the head of Apollo, but this was quite too much! with all my eagerness for fame, and my ambition of the stare of the million, I had no idea of being exhibited by retail, at sixpence a head, and that through a key-hole. So I bade adieu to Canonbury Castle, merry Islington, and the haunts of poor Goldsmith, without having advanced a single line in my labors.

My next quarters were at a small white-washed cottage, which stands not far from Hempstead, just on the brow of a hill, looking over Chalk farm, and Camden town, remarkable for the rival houses of Mother Red Cap and Mother Black Cap; and so across Cruckskull common to the distant city.

The cottage is in no wise remarkable in itself; but I regarded it with reverence, for it had been the asylum of a persecuted author. Hither poor Steele had retreated and lain perdue when persecuted by creditors and bailiffs; those immemorial plagues of authors and free-spirited gentlemen; and here he had written many numbers of the Spectator. It was from hence, too, that he had despatched those little notes to his lady, so full of affection and whimsicality; in which the fond husband, the careless gentleman, and the shifting spendthrift, were so oddly blended. I thought, as I first eyed the window, of his apartment, that I could sit within it and write volumes.

No such thing! It was haymaking season, and, as ill luck would have it, immediately opposite the cottage was a little alehouse with the sign of the load of hay. Whether it was there in Steele's time or not I cannot say; but it set all attempt at conception or inspiration at defiance. It was the resort of all the Irish haymakers who mow the broad fields in the neighborhood; and of drovers and teamsters who travel that road. Here would they gather in the endless summer twilight, or by the light of the harvest moon, and sit round a table at the door; and tipple, and laugh, and quarrel, and fight, and sing drowsy songs, and dawdle away the hours until the deep solemn notes of St. Paul's clock would warn the varlets home.

In the day-time I was still less able to write. It was broad summer. The haymakers were at work in the fields, and the perfume of the new-mown hay brought with it the recollection of my native fields. So instead of remaining in my room to write, I went wandering about Primrose Hill and Hempstead Heights and Shepherd's Field, and all those Arcadian scenes so celebrated by London bards. I cannot tell you how many delicious hours I have passed lying on the cocks of new-mown hay, on the pleasant slopes of some of those hills, inhaling the fragrance of the fields, while the summer fly buzzed above me, or the grasshopper leaped into my bosom, and how I have gazed with half-shut eye upon the smoky mass of London, and listened to the distant sound of its population, and pitied the poor sons of earth toiling in its bowels, like Gnomes in "the dark gold mine."

People may say what they please about Cockney pastorals; but after all, there is a vast deal of rural beauty about the western vicinity of London; and any one that has looked down upon the valley of Westend, with its soft bosom of green pasturage, lying open to the south, and dotted with cattle; the steeple of Hempstead rising among rich groves on the brow of the hill, and the learned height of Harrow in the distance; will confess that never has he seen a more absolutely rural landscape in the vicinity of a great metropolis.

Still, however, I found myself not a whit the better off for my frequent change of lodgings; and I began to discover that in literature, as in trade, the old proverb holds good, "a rolling stone gathers no moss."

The tranquil beauty of the country played the very vengeance with me. I could not mount my fancy into the termagant vein. I could not conceive, amidst the smiling landscape, a scene of blood and murder; and the smug citizens in breeches and gaiters, put all ideas of heroes and bandits out of my brain. I could think of nothing but dulcet subjects. "The pleasures of spring"—"the pleasures of solitude"—"the pleasures of tranquillity"—"the pleasures of sentiment"—nothing but pleasures; and I had the painful experience of "the pleasures of melancholy" too strongly in my recollection to be beguiled by them.

Chance at length befriended me. I had frequently in my ramblings loitered about Hempstead Hill; which is a kind of Parnassus of the metropolis. At such times I occasionally took my dinner at Jack Straw's Castle. It is a country inn so named. The very spot where that notorious rebel and his followers held their council of war. It is a favorite resort of citizens when rurally inclined, as it commands fine fresh air and a good view of the city.

I sat one day in the public room of this inn, ruminating over a beefsteak and a pint of port, when my imagination kindled up with ancient and heroic images. I had long wanted a theme and a hero; both suddenly broke upon my mind; I determined to write a poem on the history of Jack Straw. I was so full of my subject that I was fearful of being anticipated. I wondered that none of the poets of the day, in their researches after ruffian heroes, had ever thought of Jack Straw. I went to work pell-mell, blotted several sheets of paper with choice floating

WASHINGTON IRVING

thoughts, and battles, and descriptions, to be ready at a moment's warning. In a few days' time I sketched out the skeleton of my poem, and nothing was wanting but to give it flesh and blood. I used to take my manuscript and stroll about Caen Wood, and read aloud; and would dine at the castle, by way of keeping up the vein of thought.

I was taking a meal there, one day, at a rather late hour, in the public room. There was no other company but one man, who sat enjoying his pint of port at a window, and noticing the passers-by. He was dressed in a green shooting coat. His countenance was strongly marked. He had a hooked nose, a romantic eye, excepting that it had something of a squint; and altogether, as I thought, a poetical style of head. I was quite taken with the man, for you must know I am a little of a physiognomist: I set him down at once for either a poet or a philosopher.

As I like to make new acquaintances, considering every man a volume of human nature, I soon fell into conversation with the stranger, who, I was pleased to find, was by no means difficult of access. After I had dined, I joined him at the window, and we became so sociable that I proposed a bottle of wine together; to which he most cheerfully assented.

I was too full of my poem to keep long quiet on the subject, and began to talk about the origin of the tavern, and the history of Jack Straw. I found my new acquaintance to be perfectly at home on the topic, and to jump exactly with my humor in every respect. I became elevated by the wine and the conversation. In the fullness of an author's feelings, I told him of my projected poem, and repeated some passages; and he was in raptures. He was evidently of a strong poetical turn.

"Sir," said he, filling my glass at the same time, "our poets don't look at home. I don't see why we need go out of old England for robbers and rebels to write about. I like your Jack Straw, sir. He's a home-made hero. I like him, sir. I like him exceedingly. He's English to the back bone, damme. Give me honest old England, after all; them's my sentiments, sir!"

"I honor your sentiments," cried I zealously. "They are exactly my own. An English ruffian for poetry is as good a ruffian for poetry as any in Italy or Germany, or the Archipelago; but it is hard to make our poets think so."

"More shame for them!" replied the man in green. "What a plague would they have?" What have we to do with their Archipelagos of Italy and Germany? Haven't we heaths and commons and high-ways on our own little island? Aye, and stout fellows to pad the hoof over them too? Come, sir, my service to you—I agree with you perfectly."

"Poets in old times had right notions on this subject," continued I; "witness the fine old ballads about Robin Hood, Allen A'Dale, and other staunch blades of yore."

"Right, sir, right," interrupted he. "Robin Hood! He was the lad to cry stand! to a man, and never flinch."

"Ah, sir," said I, "they had famous bands of robbers in the good old times. Those were glorious poetical days. The merry crew of Sherwood Forest, who led such a roving picturesque life, 'under the greenwood tree.' I have often wished to visit their haunts, and tread the scenes of the exploits of Friar Tuck, and Clym of the Clough, and Sir William of Coudeslie."

"Nay, sir," said the gentleman in green, "we have had several very pretty gangs since their day. Those gallant dogs that kept about the great heaths in the neighborhood of London; about Bagshot, and Hounslow, and Black Heath, for instance—come, sir, my service to you. You don't drink."

"I suppose," said I, emptying my glass—"I suppose you have heard of the famous Turpin, who was born in this very village of Hempstead, and who used to lurk with his gang in Epping Forest, about a hundred years since."

"Have I?" cried he—"to be sure I have! A hearty old blade that; sound as pitch. Old Turpentine!—as we used to call him. A famous fine fellow, sir."

"Well, sir," continued I, "I have visited Waltham Abbey, and Chinkford Church, merely from the stories I heard, when a boy, of his exploits there, and I have searched Epping Forest for the cavern where he used to conceal himself. You must know," added I, "that I am a sort of amateur of highwaymen. They were dashing, daring fellows; the last apologies that we had for the knight errants of yore. Ah, sir! the country has been sinking gradually into tameness and commonplace. We are losing the old English spirit. The bold knights of the post have all dwindled down into lurking footpads and sneaking pick-pockets. There's no such thing as a dashing gentlemanlike robbery committed now-a-days on the king's highway. A man may roll from one end of England to the other in a drowsy coach or jingling post-chaise without any other adventure than that of being occasionally overturned, sleeping in damp sheets, or having an ill-cooked dinner.

"We hear no more of public coaches being stopped and robbed by a well-mounted gang of resolute fellows with pistols in their hands and crapes over their faces. What a pretty poetical incident was it for example in domestic life, for a family carriage, on its way to a country seat, to be attacked about dusk; the old gentleman eased of his purse and watch, the ladies of their necklaces and ear-rings, by a politely-spoken highwayman on a blood mare, who afterwards leaped the hedge and galloped across the country, to the admiration of Miss Carolina the daughter, who would write a long and romantic account of The adventure to her friend Miss Juliana in town. Ah, sir! we meet with nothing of such incidents now-a-days."

"That, sir,"—said my companion, taking advantage of a pause, when I stopped to recover breath and to take a glass of wine, which he had just poured out—"that, sir, craving your pardon, is not owing to any want of old English pluck. It is the effect of this cursed system of banking. People do not travel with bags of gold as they did formerly. They have post notes and drafts on bankers. To rob a coach is like catching a crow; where you have nothing but carrion flesh and feathers for your pains. But a coach in old times, sir, was as rich as a Spanish galleon. It turned out the yellow boys bravely; and a private carriage was a cool hundred or two at least."

I cannot express how much I was delighted with the sallies of my new acquaintance. He told me that he often frequented the castle, and would be glad to know more of me; and I promised myself many a pleasant afternoon with him, when I should read him my poem, as it proceeded, and benefit by his remarks; for it was evident he had the true poetical feeling.

"Come, sir!" said he, pushing the bottle, "Damme, I like you!—You're a man after my own heart; I'm cursed slow in making new acquaintances in general. One must stand on the reserve, you know. But when I meet with a man of your kidney, damme my heart jumps at once to him. Them's my sentiments, sir. Come, sir, here's Jack Straw's health! I presume one can drink it now-a-days without treason!"

"With all my heart," said I gayly, "and Dick Turpin's into the bargain!"

"Ah, sir," said the man in green, "those are the kind of men for poetry. The Newgate kalendar, sir! the Newgate kalendar is your only reading! There's the place to look for bold deeds and dashing fellows."

We were so much pleased with each other that we sat until a late hour. I insisted on paying the bill, for both my purse and my heart were full; and I agreed that he should pay the score at our next meeting. As the coaches had all gone that run between Hempstead and London he had to return on foot, He was so delighted with the idea of my poem that he could talk of nothing else. He made me repeat such passages as I could remember, and though I did it in a very mangled manner, having a wretched memory, yet he was in raptures.

Every now and then he would break out with some scrap which he would Misquote most terribly, but would rub his hands and exclaim, "By Jupiter, that's fine! that's noble! Damme, sir, if I can conceive how you hit upon such ideas!"

I must confess I did not always relish his misquotations, which sometimes made absolute nonsense of the passages; but what author stands upon trifles when he is praised? Never had I spent a more delightful evening. I did not perceive how the time flew. I could not bear to separate, but continued walking on, arm in arm with him past my lodgings, through Camden town, and across Crackscull Common, talking the whole way about my poem.

When we were half-way across the common he interrupted me in the midst of a quotation by telling me that this had been a famous place for footpads, and was still occasionally infested by them; and that a man had recently been shot there in attempting to defend himself.

"The more fool he!" cried I. "A man is an idiot to risk life, or even limb, to save a paltry purse of money. It's quite a different case from that of a duel, where one's honor is concerned. For my part," added I, "I should never think of making resistance against one of those desperadoes."

"Say you so?" cried my friend in green, turning suddenly upon me, and putting a pistol to my breast, "Why, then have at you, my lad!— come, disburse! empty! unsack!"

In a word, I found that the muse had played me another of her tricks, and had betrayed me into the hands of a footpad. There was no time to parley; he made me turn my pockets inside out; and hearing the sound of distant footsteps, he made one fell swoop upon purse, watch, and all, gave me a thwack over my unlucky pate that laid me sprawling on the ground; and scampered away with his booty.

I saw no more of my friend in green until a year or two afterwards; when I caught a sight of his poetical countenance among a crew of scapegraces, heavily ironed, who were on the way for transportation. He recognized me at once, tipped me an impudent wink, and asked me how I came on with the history of Jack Straw's castle.

WASHINGTON IRVING

The catastrophe at Crackscull Common put an end to my summer's campaign. I was cured of my poetical enthusiasm for rebels, robbers, and highwaymen. I was put out of conceit of my subject, and what was worse, I was lightened of my purse, in which was almost every farthing I had in the world. So I abandoned Sir Richard Steele's cottage in despair, and crept into less celebrated, though no less poetical and airy lodgings in a garret in town.

I see you are growing weary, so I will not detain you with any more of my luckless attempts to get astride of Pegasus. Still I could not consent to give up the trial and abandon those dreams of renown in which I had indulged. How should I ever be able to look the literary circle of my native village in the face, if I were so completely to falsify their predictions. For some time longer, therefore, I continued to write for fame, and of course was the most miserable dog in existence, besides being in continual risk of starvation.

I have many a time strolled sorrowfully along, with a sad heart and an empty stomach, about five o'clock, and looked wistfully down the areas in the west end of the town; and seen through the kitchen windows the fires gleaming, and the joints of meat turning on the spits and dripping with gravy; and the cook maids beating up puddings, or trussing turkeys, and have felt for the moment that if I could but have the run of one of those kitchens, Apollo and the muses might have the hungry heights of Parnassus for me. Oh, sir! talk of meditations among the tombs—they are nothing so melancholy as the meditations of a poor devil without penny in pouch, along a line of kitchen windows towards dinner-time.

At length, when almost reduced to famine and despair, the idea all at once entered my head, that perhaps I was not so clever a fellow as the village and myself had supposed. It was the salvation of me. The moment the idea popped into my brain, it brought conviction and comfort with it. I awoke as from a dream. I gave up immortal fame to those who could live on air; took to writing for mere bread, and have ever since led a very tolerable life of it. There is no man of letters so much at his ease, sir, as he that has no character to gain or lose. I had to train myself to it a little, however, and to clip my wings short at first, or they would have carried me up into poetry in spite of myself. So I determined to begin by the opposite extreme, and abandoning the higher regions of the craft, I came plump down to the lowest, and turned creeper.

"Creeper," interrupted I, "and pray what is that?" Oh, sir! I see you are ignorant of the language of the craft; a creeper is one who furnishes the newspapers with paragraphs at so much a line, one that goes about in quest of misfortunes; attends the Bow-street office; the courts of justice and every other den of mischief and iniquity. We are paid at the rate of a penny a line, and as we can sell the same paragraph to almost every paper, we sometimes pick up a very decent day's work. Now and then the muse is unkind, or the day uncommonly quiet, and then we rather starve; and sometimes the unconscionable editors will clip our paragraphs when they are a little too rhetorical, and snip off twopence or threepence at a go. I have many a time had my pot of porter snipped off of my dinner in this way; and have had to dine with dry lips. However, I cannot complain. I rose gradually in the lower ranks of the craft, and am now, I think, in the most comfortable region of literature.

"And pray," said I, "what may you be at present!" "At present," said he, "I am a regular job writer, and turn my hand to anything. I work up the writings of others at so much a sheet; turn off translations; write second-rate articles to fill up reviews and magazines; compile travels and voyages, and furnish theatrical criticisms for the newspapers. All this authorship, you perceive, is anonymous; it gives no reputation, except among the trade, where I am considered an author of all work, and am always sure of employ. That's the only reputation I want. I sleep soundly, without dread of duns or critics, and leave immortal fame to those that choose to fret and fight about it. Take my word for it, the only happy author in this world is he who is below the care of reputation."

The preceding anecdotes of Buckthorne's early schoolmate, and a variety of peculiarities which I had remarked in himself, gave me a strong curiosity to know something of his own history. There was a dash of careless good humor about him that pleased me exceedingly, and at times a whimsical tinge of melancholy ran through his humor that gave it an additional relish. He had evidently been a little chilled and buffeted by fortune, without being soured thereby, as some fruits become mellower and sweeter, from having been bruised or frost-bitten. He smiled when I expressed my desire. "I have no great story," said he, "to relate. A mere tissue of errors and follies. But, such as it is, you shall have one epoch of it, by which you may judge of the rest." And so, without any farther prelude, he gave me the following anecdotes of his early adventures.

Buckthorne, or The Young Man
of Great Expectations

I was born to very little property, but to great expectations; which is perhaps one of the most unlucky fortunes that a man can be born to. My father was a country gentleman, the last of a very ancient and honorable, but decayed family, and resided in an old hunting lodge in Warwickshire. He was a keen sportsman and lived to the extent of his moderate income, so that I had little to expect from that quarter; but then I had a rich uncle by the mother's side, a penurious, accumulating curmudgeon, who it was confidently expected would make me his heir; because he was an old bachelor; because I was named after him, and because he hated all the world except myself.

He was, in fact, an inveterate hater, a miser even in misanthropy, and hoarded up a grudge as he did a guinea. Thus, though my mother was an only sister, he had never forgiven her marriage with my father, against whom he had a cold, still, immovable pique, which had lain at the bottom of his heart, like a stone in a well, ever since they had been school boys together. My mother, however, considered me as the intermediate being that was to bring every thing again into harmony, for she looked upon me as a prodigy—God bless her. My heart overflows whenever I recall her tenderness: she was the most excellent, the most indulgent of mothers. I was her only child; it was a pity she had no more, for she had fondness of heart enough to have spoiled a dozen!

I was sent, at an early age, to a public school, sorely against my mother's wishes, but my father insisted that it was the only way to make boys hardy. The school was kept by a conscientious prig of the ancient system, who did his duty by the boys intrusted to his care; that is to say, we were flogged soundly when we did not get our lessons. We were put into classes and thus flogged on in droves along the highways of knowledge, in the same manner as cattle are driven to market, where those that are heavy in gait or short in leg have to suffer for the superior alertness or longer limbs of their companions.

For my part, I confess it with shame, I was an incorrigible laggard. I have always had the poetical feeling, that is to say, I have always been an idle fellow and prone to play the vagabond. I used to get away from my books and school whenever I could, and ramble about the fields. I was surrounded by seductions for such a temperament. The school-house was an old-fashioned, white-washed mansion of wood and plaister, standing on the skirts of a beautiful village. Close by it was the venerable church with a tall Gothic spire. Before it spread a lovely green valley, with a little stream glistening along through willow groves; while a line of blue hills that bounded the landscape gave rise to many a summer day dream as to the fairy land that lay beyond.

In spite of all the scourgings I suffered at that school to make me love my book, I cannot but look back upon the place with fondness. Indeed, I considered this frequent flagellation as the common lot of humanity, and the regular mode in which scholars were made. My kind mother used to lament over my details of the sore trials I underwent in the cause of learning; but my father turned a deaf ear to her expostulations. He had been flogged through school himself, and swore there was no other way of making a man of parts; though, let me speak it with all due reverence, my father was but an indifferent illustration of his own theory, for he was considered a grievous blockhead.

My poetical temperament evinced itself at a very early period. The Village church was attended every Sunday by a neighboring squire—the lord of the manor, whose park stretched quite to the village, and whose spacious country seat seemed to take the church under its protection. Indeed, you would have thought the church had been consecrated to him instead of to the Deity. The parish clerk bowed low before him, and the vergers humbled themselves into the dust in his presence. He always entered a little late and with some stir, striking his cane emphatically on the ground; swaying his hat in his hand, and looking loftily to the right and left, as he walked slowly up the aisle, and the parson, who always ate his Sunday dinner with him, never commenced service until he appeared. He sat with his family in a large pew gorgeously lined, humbling himself devoutly on velvet cushions, and reading lessons of meekness and lowliness of spirit out of splendid gold and morocco prayer-books. Whenever the parson spoke of the difficulty of the rich man's entering the kingdom of heaven, the eyes of the congregation would turn towards the "grand pew," and I thought the squire seemed pleased with the application.

The pomp of this pew and the aristocratical air of the family struck My imagination wonderfully, and I fell desperately in love with a little daughter of the squire's about twelve years of age. This freak of fancy made me more truant from my studies than ever. I used to stroll about the squire's park, and would lurk near the house to catch glimpses of this little damsel at the windows, or playing about the lawns, or walking out with her governess.

I had not enterprise or impudence enough to venture from my concealment; indeed, I felt like an arrant poacher, until I read one or two of Ovid's Metamorphoses, when I pictured myself as some sylvan deity, and she a coy wood nymph of whom I was in pursuit. There is something extremely delicious in these early awakenings of the tender passion. I can feel, even at this moment, the thrilling of my boyish bosom, whenever by chance I caught a glimpse of her white frock fluttering among the shrubbery. I now began to read poetry. I carried about in my bosom a volume of Waller, which I had purloined from my mother's library; and I applied to my little fair one all the compliments lavished upon Sacharissa.

At length I danced with her at a school ball. I was so awkward a booby, that I dared scarcely speak to her; I was filled with awe and embarrassment in her presence; but I was so inspired that my poetical temperament for the first time broke out in verse; and I fabricated some glowing lines, in which I be-rhymed the little lady under the favorite name of Sacharissa. I slipped the verses, trembling and blushing, into her hand the next Sunday as she came out of church. The little prude handed them to her mamma; the mamma handed them to the squire, the squire, who had no soul for poetry, sent them in dudgeon to the school-master; and the school-master, with a barbarity worthy of the dark ages, gave me a sound and peculiarly humiliating flogging for thus trespassing upon Parnassus.

This was a sad outset for a votary of the muse. It ought to have cured me of my passion for poetry; but it only confirmed it, for I felt the spirit of a martyr rising within me. What was as well, perhaps, it cured me of my passion for the young lady; for I felt so indignant at the ignominious horsing I had incurred in celebrating her charms, that I could not hold up my head in church.

Fortunately for my wounded sensibility, the midsummer holydays came on, and I returned home. My mother, as usual, inquired into all my school concerns, my little pleasures, and cares, and sorrows; for boyhood has its share of the one as well as of the others. I told her all, and she was indignant at the treatment I had experienced. She fired up at the arrogance of the squire, and the prudery of the daughter; and as to the school-master, she wondered where was the use of having school-masters, and why boys could not remain at home and be educated by tutors, under the eye of their mothers. She asked to see the verses I had written, and she was delighted with them; for to confess the truth, she had a pretty taste in poetry. She even showed to them to the parson's wife, who protested they were charming, and the parson's three daughters insisted on each having a copy of them.

All this was exceedingly balsamic, and I was still more consoled and encouraged, when the young ladies, who were the blue-stockings of the neighborhood, and had read Dr. Johnson's lives quite through, assured my mother that great geniuses never studied, but were always idle; upon which I began to surmise that I was myself something out of the common run. My father, however, was of a very different opinion, for when my mother, in the pride of her heart, showed him my copy of verses, he threw them out of the window, asking her "if she meant to make a ballad monger of the boy." But he was a careless, common-thinking man, and I cannot say that I ever loved him much; my mother absorbed all my filial affection.

I used occasionally, during holydays, to be sent on short visits to the uncle, who was to make me his heir; they thought it would keep me in his mind, and render him fond of me. He was a withered, anxious-looking old fellow, and lived in a desolate old country seat, which he suffered to go to ruin from absolute niggardliness. He kept but one man-servant, who had lived, or rather starved, with him for years. No woman was allowed to sleep in the house. A daughter of the old servant lived by the gate, in what had been a porter's lodge, and was permitted to come into the house about an hour each day, to make the beds, and cook a morsel of provisions.

The park that surrounded the house was all run wild; the trees grown out of shape; the fish-ponds stagnant; the urns and statues fallen from their pedestals and buried among the rank grass. The hares and pheasants were so little molested, except by poachers, that they bred in great abundance, and sported about the rough lawns and weedy avenues. To guard the premises and frighten off robbers, of whom he was somewhat apprehensive, and visitors, whom he held in almost equal awe, my uncle kept two or three blood-hounds, who were always prowling round the house, and were the dread of the neighboring peasantry. They were gaunt and half-starved, seemed ready to devour one from mere hunger, and were an effectual check on any stranger's approach to this wizard castle.

Such was my uncle's house, which I used to visit now and then during The holydays. I was, as I have before said, the old man's favorite; that is to say, he did not hate me so much as he did the rest of the world. I had been apprised of his character, and cautioned to cultivate his good-will; but I was too young and careless to be a courtier; and indeed have never been sufficiently studious of my interests to let them govern my feelings. However, we seemed to jog on very well together; and as my visits cost him almost nothing, they did not seem to be very unwelcome. I brought with me my gun and fishing-rod, and half supplied the table from the park and the fishponds.

Our meals were solitary and unsocial. My uncle rarely spoke; he pointed for whatever he wanted, and the servant perfectly understood him. Indeed, his man John, or Iron John, as he was called in the neighborhood, was a counterpart of his master. He was a tall, bony old fellow, with a dry wig that seemed made of cow's tail, and a face as tough as though it had been made of bull's hide. He was generally clad in a long, patched livery coat, taken out of the wardrobe of the house; and which bagged loosely about him, having evidently belonged to some corpulent predecessor, in the more plenteous days of the mansion. From long habits of taciturnity, the hinges of his jaws seemed to have grown absolutely rusty, and it cost him as much effort to set them ajar, and to let out a tolerable sentence, as it would have done to set open the iron gates of a park, and let out the family carriage that was dropping to pieces in the coach-house.

I cannot say, however, but that I was for some time amused with my uncle's peculiarities. Even the very desolateness of the establishment had something in it that hit my fancy. When the weather was fine I used to amuse myself, in a solitary way, by rambling about the park, and coursing like a colt across its lawns. The hares and pheasants seemed to stare with surprise, to see a human being walking these forbidden grounds by day-light. Sometimes I amused myself by jerking stones, or shooting at birds with a bow and arrows; for to have used a gun would have been treason. Now and then my path was crossed by a little red-headed, ragged-tailed urchin, the son of the woman at the lodge, who ran wild about the premises. I tried to draw him into familiarity, and to make a companion of him; but he seemed to have imbibed the strange, unsocial character of every thing around him; and always kept aloof; so I considered him as another Orson, and amused myself with shooting at him with my bow and arrows, and he would hold up his breeches with one hand, and scamper away like a deer.

There was something in all this loneliness and wildness strangely pleasing to me. The great stables, empty and weather-broken, with the names of favorite horses over the vacant stalls; the windows bricked and boarded up; the broken roofs, garrisoned by rooks and jackdaws; all had a singularly forlorn appearance: one would have concluded the house to be totally uninhabited, were it not for a little thread of blue smoke, which now and then curled up like a corkscrew, from the centre of one of the wide chimneys, when my uncle's starveling meal was cooking.

My uncle's room was in a remote corner of the building, strongly secured and generally locked. I was never admitted into this strong-hold, where the old man would remain for the greater part of the time, drawn up like a veteran spider in the citadel of his web. The rest of the mansion, however, was open to me, and I sauntered about it unconstrained. The damp and rain which beat in through the broken windows, crumbled the paper from the walls; mouldered the pictures, and gradually destroyed the furniture. I loved to rove about the wide, waste chambers in bad weather, and listen to the howling of the wind, and the banging about of the doors and window-shutters. I pleased myself with the idea how completely, when I came to the estate, I would renovate all things, and make the old building ring with merriment, till it was astonished at its own jocundity.

The chamber which I occupied on these visits was the same that had been my mother's, when a girl. There was still the toilet-table of her own adorning; the landscapes of her own drawing. She had never seen it since her marriage, but would often ask me if every thing was still the same. All was just the same; for I loved that chamber on her account, and had taken pains to put every thing in order, and to mend all the flaws in the windows with my own hands. I anticipated the time when I should once more welcome her to the house of her fathers, and restore her to this little nestling-place of her childhood.

At length my evil genius, or, what perhaps is the same thing, the muse, inspired me with the notion of rhyming again. My uncle, who never went to church, used on Sundays to read chapters out of the Bible; and Iron John, the woman from the lodge, and myself, were his congregation. It seemed to be all one to him what he read, so long as it was something from the Bible: sometimes, therefore, it would be the Song of Solomon; and this withered anatomy would read about being "stayed with flagons and comforted with apples, for he was sick of love." Sometimes he would hobble, with spectacle on nose, through whole chapters of hard Hebrew names in Deuteronomy; at which the poor woman would sigh and groan as if wonderfully moved. His favorite book, however, was "The Pilgrim's Progress;" and when he came to that part which treats of Doubting Castle and Giant Despair, I thought invariably of him and his desolate old country seat. So much did the idea amuse me, that I took to scribbling about it under the trees in the park; and in a few days had made some progress in a poem, in which I had given a description of the place, under the name of Doubting Castle, and personified my uncle as Giant Despair.

I lost my poem somewhere about the house, and I soon suspected that my uncle had found it; as he harshly intimated to me that I could return home, and that I need not come and see him again until he should send for me.

Just about this time my mother died.—I cannot dwell upon this circumstance; my heart, careless and wayworn as it is, gushes with the recollection. Her death was an event that perhaps gave a turn to all my after fortunes. With her died all that made home attractive, for my father was harsh, as I have before said, and had never treated me with kindness. Not that he exerted any unusual severity towards me, but it was his way. I do not complain of him. In fact, I have never been of a complaining disposition. I seem born to be buffeted by friends and fortune, and nature has made me a careless endurer of buffetings.

I now, however, began to grow very impatient of remaining at school, to be flogged for things that I did not like. I longed for variety, especially now that I had not my uncle's to resort to, by way of diversifying the dullness of school with the dreariness of his country seat. I was now turned of sixteen; tall for my age, and full of idle fancies. I had a roving, inextinguishable desire to see different kinds of life, and different orders of society; and this vagrant humor had been fostered in me by Tom Dribble, the prime wag and great genius of the school, who had all the rambling propensities of a poet.

I used to set at my desk in the school, on a fine summer's day, and instead of studying the book which lay open before me, my eye was gazing through the window on the green fields and blue hills. How I envied the happy groups seated on the tops of stage-coaches, chatting, and joking, and laughing, as they were whirled by the school-house, on their way to the metropolis. Even the wagoners trudging along beside their ponderous teams, and traversing the kingdom, from one end to the other, were objects of envy to me. I fancied to myself what adventures they must experience, and what odd scenes of life they must witness. All this was doubtless the poetical temperament working within me, and tempting me forth into a world of its own creation, which I mistook for the world of real life.

While my mother lived, this strange propensity to roam was counteracted by the stronger attractions of home, and by the powerful ties of affection, which drew me to her side; but now that she was gone, the attractions had ceased; the ties were severed. I had no longer an anchorage ground for my heart; but was at the mercy of every vagrant impulse. Nothing but the narrow allowance on which my father kept me, and the consequent penury of my purse, prevented me from mounting the top of a stage-coach and launching myself adrift on the great ocean of life.

Just about this time the village was agitated for a day or two, by the passing through of several caravans, containing wild beasts, and other spectacles for a great fair annually held at a neighboring town.

I had never seen a fair of any consequence, and my curiosity was Powerfully awakened by this bustle of preparation. I gazed with respect and wonder at the vagrant personages who accompanied these caravans. I loitered about the village inn, listening with curiosity and delight to the slang talk and cant jokes of the showmen and their followers; and I felt an eager desire to witness this fair, which my fancy decked out as something wonderfully fine.

A holyday afternoon presented, when I could be absent from the school from noon until evening. A wagon was going from the village to the fair. I could not resist the temptation, nor the eloquence of Tom Dribble, who was a truant to the very heart's core. We hired seats, and set off full of boyish expectation. I promised myself that I would but take a peep at the land of promise, and hasten back again before my absence should be noticed.

Heavens! how happy I was on arriving at the fair! How I was enchanted with the world of fun and pageantry around me! The humors of Punch; the feats of the equestrians; the magical tricks of the conjurors! But what principally caught my attention was—an itinerant theatre; where a tragedy, pantomime, and farce were all acted in the course of half an hour, and more of the dramatis personae murdered, than at either Drury Lane or Covent Garden in a whole evening. I have since seen many a play performed by the best actors in the world, but never have I derived half the delight from any that I did from this first representation.

　　　　　　　　WASHINGTON IRVING

There was a ferocious tyrant in a skull cap like an inverted porringer, and a dress of red baize, magnificently embroidered with gilt leather; with his face so be-whiskered and his eyebrows so knit and expanded with burnt cork, that he made my heart quake within me as he stamped about the little stage. I was enraptured too with the surpassing beauty of a distressed damsel, in faded pink silk, and dirty white muslin, whom he held in cruel captivity by way of gaining her affections; and who wept and wrung her hands and flourished a ragged pocket handkerchief from the top of an impregnable tower, of the size of a band-box.

Even after I had come out from the play, I could not tear myself from the vicinity of the theatre; but lingered, gazing, and wondering, and laughing at the dramatis personae, as they performed their antics, or danced upon a stage in front of the booth, to decoy a new set of spectators.

I was so bewildered by the scene, and so lost in the crowd of sensations that kept swarming upon me that I was like one entranced. I lost my companion Tom Dribble, in a tumult and scuffle that took place near one of the shows, but I was too much occupied in mind to think long about him. I strolled about until dark, when the fair was lighted up, and a new scene of magic opened upon me. The illumination of the tents and booths; the brilliant effect of the stages decorated with lamps, with dramatic groups flaunting about them in gaudy dresses, contrasted splendidly with the surrounding darkness; while the uproar of drums, trumpets, fiddles, hautboys, and cymbals, mingled with the harangues of the showmen, the squeaking of Punch, and the shouts and laughter of the crowd, all united to complete my giddy distraction.

Time flew without my perceiving it. When I came to myself and thought of the school, I hastened to return. I inquired for the wagon in which I had come: it had been gone for hours. I asked the time: it was almost midnight! A sudden quaking seized me. How was I to get back to school? I was too weary to make the journey on foot, and I knew not where to apply for a conveyance. Even if I should find one, could I venture to disturb the school-house long after midnight? to arouse that sleeping lion, the usher, in the very midst of his night's rest? The idea was too dreadful for a delinquent school-boy. All the horrors of return rushed upon me—my absence must long before this have been remarked—and absent for a whole night? A deed of darkness not easily to be expiated. The rod of the pedagogue budded forth into tenfold terrors before my affrighted fancy. I pictured to myself punishment and humiliation in every variety of form; and my heart sickened at the picture. Alas! how often are the petty ills of boyhood as painful to our tender natures, as are the sterner evils of manhood to our robuster minds.

I wandered about among the booths, and I might have derived a lesson from my actual feelings, how much the charms of this world depend upon ourselves; for I no longer saw anything gay or delightful in the revelry around me. At length I lay down, wearied and perplexed, behind one of the large tents, and covering myself with the margin of the tent cloth to keep off the night chill, I soon fell fast asleep.

I had not slept long, when I was awakened by the noise of merriment within an adjoining booth. It was the itinerant theatre, rudely constructed of boards and canvas. I peeped through an aperture, and saw the whole dramatis personae, tragedy, comedy, pantomime, all refreshing themselves after the final dismissal of their auditors. They were merry and gamesome, and made their flimsy theatre ring with laughter. I was astonished to see the tragedy tyrant in red baize and fierce whiskers, who had made my heart quake as he strutted about the boards, now transformed into a fat, good humored fellow; the beaming porringer laid aside from his brow, and his jolly face washed from all the terrors of burnt cork. I was delighted, too, to see the distressed damsel in faded silk and dirty muslin, who had trembled under his tyranny, and afflicted me so much by her sorrows, now seated familiarly on his knee, and quaffing from the same tankard. Harlequin lay asleep on one of the benches; and monks, satyrs, and Vestal virgins were grouped together, laughing outrageously at a broad story told by an unhappy count, who had been barbarously murdered in the tragedy. This was, indeed, novelty to me. It was a peep into another planet. I gazed and listened with intense curiosity and enjoyment. They had a thousand odd stories and jokes about the events of the day, and burlesque descriptions and mimickings of the spectators who had been admiring them. Their conversation was full of allusions to their adventures at different places, where they had exhibited; the characters they had met with in different villages; and the ludicrous difficulties in which they had occasionally been involved. All past cares and troubles were now turned by these thoughtless beings into matter of merriment; and made to contribute to the gayety of the moment. They had been moving from fair to fair about the kingdom, and were the next morning to set out on their way to London.

My resolution was taken. I crept from my nest, and scrambled through a hedge into a neighboring field, where I went to work to make a tatterdemalion of myself. I tore my clothes; soiled them with dirt; begrimed my face and hands; and, crawling near one of the booths, purloined an old hat, and left my new one in its place. It was an honest theft, and I hope may not hereafter rise up in judgment against me.

I now ventured to the scene of merrymaking, and, presenting myself before the dramatic corps, offered myself as a volunteer. I felt terribly agitated and abashed, for "never before stood I in such a presence." I had addressed myself to the manager of the company. He was a fat man, dressed in dirty white; with a red sash fringed with tinsel, swathed round his body. His face was smeared with paint, and a majestic plume towered from an old spangled black bonnet. He was the Jupiter tonans of this Olympus, and was surrounded by the interior gods and goddesses of his court. He sat on the end of a bench, by a table, with one arm akimbo and the other extended to the handle of a tankard, which he had slowly set down from his lips as he surveyed me from head to foot. It was a moment of awful scrutiny, and I fancied the groups around all watching us in silent suspense, and waiting for the imperial nod.

He questioned me as to who I was; what were my qualifications; and what terms I expected. I passed myself off for a discharged servant from a gentleman's family; and as, happily, one does not require a special recommendation to get admitted into bad company, the questions on that head were easily satisfied. As to my accomplishments, I would spout a little poetry, and knew several scenes of plays, which I had learnt at school exhibitions. I could dance—, that was enough; no further questions were asked me as to accomplishments; it was the very thing they wanted; and, as I asked no wages, but merely meat and drink, and safe conduct about the world, a bargain was struck in a moment.

Behold me, therefore transformed of a sudden from a gentleman student to a dancing buffoon; for such, in fact, was the character in which I made my debut. I was one of those who formed the groups in the dramas, and were principally, employed on the stage in front of the booth, to attract company. I was equipped as a satyr, in a dress of drab frize that fitted to my shape; with a great laughing mask, ornamented with huge ears and short horns. I was pleased with the disguise, because it kept me from the danger of being discovered, whilst we were in that part of the country; and, as I had merely to dance and make antics, the character was favorable to a debutant, being almost on a par with Simon Snug's part of the Lion, which required nothing but roaring.

I cannot tell you how happy I was at this sudden change in my situation. I felt no degradation, for I had seen too little of society to be thoughtful about the differences of rank; and a boy of sixteen is seldom aristocratical. I had given up no friend; for there seemed to be no one in the world that cared for me, now my poor mother was dead. I had given up no pleasure; for my pleasure was to ramble about and indulge the flow of a poetical imagination; and I now enjoyed it in perfection. There is no life so truly poetical as that of a dancing buffoon.

It may be said that all this argued grovelling inclinations. I do not think so; not that I mean to vindicate myself in any great degree; I know too well what a whimsical compound I am. But in this instance I was seduced by no love of low company, nor disposition to indulge in low vices. I have always despised the brutally vulgar; and I have always had a disgust at vice, whether in high or low life. I was governed merely by a sudden and thoughtless impulse. I had no idea of resorting to this profession as a mode of life; or of attaching myself to these people, as my future class of society. I thought merely of a temporary gratification of my curiosity, and an indulgence of my humors. I had already a strong relish for the peculiarities of character and the varieties of situation, and I have always been fond of the comedy of life, and desirous of seeing it through all its shifting scenes.

In mingling, therefore, among mountebanks and buffoons I was protected by the very vivacity of imagination which had led me among them. I moved about enveloped, as it were, in a protecting delusion, which my fancy spread around me. I assimilated to these people only as they struck me poetically; their whimsical ways and a certain picturesqueness in their mode of life entertained me; but I was neither amused nor corrupted by their vices. In short, I mingled among them, as Prince Hal did among his graceless associates, merely to gratify my humor.

I did not investigate my motives in this manner, at the time, for I was too careless and thoughtless to reason about the matter; but I do so now, when I look back with trembling to think of the ordeal to which I unthinkingly exposed myself, and the manner in which I passed through it. Nothing, I am convinced, but the poetical temperament, that hurried me into the scrape, brought me out of it without my becoming an arrant vagabond.

WASHINGTON IRVING

Full of the enjoyment of the moment, giddy with the wildness of animal spirits, so rapturous in a boy, I capered, I danced, I played a thousand fantastic tricks about the stage, in the villages in which we exhibited; and I was universally pronounced the most agreeable monster that had ever been seen in those parts. My disappearance from school had awakened my father's anxiety; for I one day heard a description of myself cried before the very booth in which I was exhibiting; with the offer of a reward for any intelligence of me. I had no great scruple about letting my father suffer a little uneasiness on my account; it would punish him for past indifference, and would make him value me the more when he found me again. I have wondered that some of my comrades did not recognize in me the stray sheep that was cried; but they were all, no doubt, occupied by their own concerns. They were all laboring seriously in their antic vocations, for folly was a mere trade with the most of them, and they often grinned and capered with heavy hearts. With me, on the contrary, it was all real. I acted *con amore*, and rattled and laughed from the irrepressible gayety of my spirits. It is true that, now and then, I started and looked grave on receiving a sudden thwack from the wooden sword of Harlequin, in the course of my gambols; as it brought to mind the birch of my school-master. But I soon got accustomed to it; and bore all the cuffing, and kicking, and tumbling about, that form the practical wit of your itinerant pantomime, with a good humor that made me a prodigious favorite.

The country campaign of the troupe was soon at an end, and we set off for the metropolis, to perform at the fairs which are held in its vicinity. The greater part of our theatrical property was sent on direct, to be in a state of preparation for the opening of the fairs; while a detachment of the company travelled slowly on, foraging among the villages. I was amused with the desultory, hap-hazard kind of life we led; here today, and gone tomorrow. Sometimes revelling in ale-houses; sometimes feasting under hedges in the green fields. When audiences were crowded and business profitable, we fared well, and when otherwise, we fared scantily, and consoled ourselves with anticipations of the next day's success.

At length the increasing frequency of coaches hurrying past us, covered with passengers; the increasing number of carriages, carts, wagons, gigs, droves of cattle and flocks of sheep, all thronging the road; the snug country boxes with trim flower gardens twelve feet square, and their trees twelve feet high, all powdered with dust; and the innumerable seminaries for young ladies and gentlemen, situated along the road, for the benefit of country air and rural retirement; all these insignia announced that the mighty London was at hand. The hurry, and the crowd, and the bustle, and the noise, and the dust, increased as we proceeded, until I saw the great cloud of smoke hanging in the air, like a canopy of state, over this queen of cities.

In this way, then, did I enter the metropolis; a strolling vagabond; on the top of a caravan with a crew of vagabonds about me; but I was as happy as a prince, for, like Prince Hal, I felt myself superior to my situation, and knew that I could at any time cast it off and emerge into my proper sphere.

How my eyes sparkled as we passed Hyde-park corner, and I saw splendid equipages rolling by, with powdered footmen behind, in rich liveries, and fine nosegays, and gold-headed canes; and with lovely women within, so sumptuously dressed and so surpassingly fair. I was always extremely sensible to female beauty; and here I saw it in all its fascination; for, whatever may be said of "beauty unadorned," there is something almost awful in female loveliness decked out in jewelled state. The swan-like neck encircled with diamonds; the raven locks, clustered with pearls; the ruby glowing on the snowy bosom, are objects that I could never contemplate without emotion; and a dazzling white arm clasped with bracelets, and taper transparent fingers laden with sparkling rings, are to me irresistible. My very eyes ached as I gazed at the high and courtly beauty that passed before me. It surpassed all that my imagination had conceived of the sex. I shrunk, for a moment, into shame at the company in which I was placed, and repined at the vast distance that seemed to intervene between me and these magnificent beings.

I forbear to give a detail of the happy life which I led about the skirts of the metropolis, playing at the various fairs, held there during the latter part of spring and the beginning of summer. This continual change from place to place, and scene to scene, fed my imagination with novelties, and kept my spirits in a perpetual state of excitement.

As I was tall of my age I aspired, at one time, to play heroes in tragedy; but after two or three trials, I was pronounced, by the manager, totally unfit for the line; and our first tragic actress, who was a large woman, and held a small hero in abhorrence, confirmed his decision.

The fact is, I had attempted to give point to language which had no point, and nature to scenes which had no nature. They said I did not fill out my characters; and they were right. The characters had all been prepared for a different sort of man. Our tragedy hero was a round, robustious fellow, with an amazing voice; who stamped and slapped his breast until his wig shook again; and who roared and bellowed out his bombast, until every phrase swelled upon the ear like the sound of a kettle-drum. I might as well have attempted to fill out his clothes as his characters. When we had a dialogue together, I was nothing before him, with my slender voice and discriminating manner. I might as well have attempted to parry a cudgel with a small sword. If he found me in any way gaining ground upon him, he would take refuge in his mighty voice, and throw his tones like peals of thunder at me, until they were drowned in the still louder thunders of applause from the audience.

To tell the truth, I suspect that I was not shown fair play, and that there was management at the bottom; for without vanity, I think I was a better actor than he. As I had not embarked in the vagabond line through ambition, I did not repine at lack of preferment; but I was grieved to find that a vagrant life was not without its cares and anxieties, and that jealousies, intrigues, and mad ambition were to be found even among vagabonds.

Indeed, as I become more familiar with my situation, and the delusions of fancy began to fade away, I discovered that my associates were not the happy careless creatures I had at first imagined them. They were jealous of each other's talents; they quarrelled about parts, the same as the actors on the grand theatres; they quarrelled about dresses; and there was one robe of yellow silk, trimmed with red, and a head-dress of three rumpled ostrich feathers, which were continually setting the ladies of the company by the ears. Even those who had attained the highest honors were not more happy than the rest; for Mr. Flimsey himself, our first tragedian, and apparently a jovial, good-humored fellow, confessed to me one day, in the fullness of his heart, that he was a miserable man. He had a brother-in-law, a relative by marriage, though not by blood, who was manager of a theatre in a small country town. And this same brother, ("a little more than kin, but less than kind,") looked down upon him, and treated him with contumely, because forsooth he was but a strolling player. I tried to console him with the thoughts of the vast applause he daily received, but it was all in vain. He declared that it gave him no delight, and that he should never be a happy man until the name of Flimsey rivalled the name of Crimp.

How little do those before the scenes know of what passes behind; how little can they judge, from the countenances of actors, of what is passing in their hearts. I have known two lovers quarrel like cats behind the scenes, who were, the moment after, ready to fly into each other's embraces. And I have dreaded, when our Belvidera was to take her farewell kiss of her Jaffier, lest she should bite a piece out of his cheek. Our tragedian was a rough joker off the stage; our prime clown the most peevish mortal living. The latter used to go about snapping and snarling, with a broad laugh painted on his countenance; and I can assure you that, whatever may be said of the gravity of a monkey, or the melancholy of a gibed cat, there is no more melancholy creature in existence than a mountebank off duty.

The only thing in which all parties agreed was to backbite the manager, and cabal against his regulations. This, however, I have since discovered to be a common trait of human nature, and to take place in all communities. It would seem to be the main business of man to repine at government. In all situations of life into which I have looked, I have found mankind divided into two grand parties;—those who ride and those who are ridden. The great struggle of life seems to be which shall keep in the saddle. This, it appears to me, is the fundamental principle of politics, whether in great or little life. However, I do not mean to moralize; but one cannot always sink the philosopher.

Well, then, to return to myself. It was determined, as I said, that I was not fit for tragedy, and unluckily, as my study was bad, having a very poor memory, I was pronounced unfit for comedy also: besides, the line of young gentlemen was already engrossed by an actor with whom I could not pretend to enter into competition, he having filled it for almost half a century. I came down again therefore to pantomime. In consequence, however, of the good offices of the manager's lady, who had taken a liking to me, I was promoted from the part of the satyr to that of the lover; and with my face patched and painted, a huge cravat of paper, a steeple-crowned hat, and dangling, long-skirted, sky-blue coat, was metamorphosed into the lover of Columbine. My part did not call for much of the tender and sentimental. I had merely to pursue the fugitive fair one; to have a door now and then slammed in my face; to run my head occasionally against a post; to tumble and roll about with Pantaloon and the clown; and to endure the hearty thwacks of Harlequin's wooden sword.

As ill luck would have it, my poetical temperament began to ferment within me, and to work out new troubles. The inflammatory air of a great metropolis added to the rural scenes in which the fairs were held; such as Greenwich Park; Epping Forest; and the lovely valley of the West End, had a powerful effect upon me. While in Greenwich Park I was witness to the old holiday games of running down hill; and kissing in the ring; and then the firmament of blooming faces and blue eyes that would be turned towards me as I was playing antics on the stage; all these set my young blood, and my poetical vein, in full flow. In short, I played my character to the life, and became desperately enamored of Columbine. She was a trim, well-made, tempting girl, with a rougish, dimpling face, and fine chestnut hair clustering all about it. The moment I got fairly smitten, there was an end to all playing. I was such a creature of fancy and feeling that I could not put on a pretended, when I was powerfully affected by a real emotion. I could not sport with a fiction that came so near to the fact. I became too natural in my acting to succeed. And then, what a situation for a lover! I was a mere stripling, and she played with my passion; for girls soon grow more adroit and knowing in these than your awkward youngsters. What agonies had I to suffer. Every time that she danced in front of the booth and made such liberal displays of her charms, I was in torment. To complete my misery, I had a real rival in Harlequin; an active, vigorous, knowing varlet of six-and-twenty. What had a raw, inexperienced youngster like me to hope from such a competition?

I had still, however, some advantages in my favor. In spite of my change of life, I retained that indescribable something which always distinguishes the gentleman; that something which dwells in a man's air and deportment, and not in his clothes; and which it is as difficult for a gentleman to put off as for a vulgar fellow to put on. The company generally felt it, and used to call me little gentleman Jack. The girl felt it too; and in spite of her predilection for my powerful rival, she liked to flirt with me. This only aggravated my troubles, by increasing my passion, and awakening the jealousy of her parti-colored lover.

Alas! think what I suffered, at being obliged to keep up an ineffectual chase after my Columbine through whole pantomimes; to see her carried off in the vigorous arms of the happy Harlequin; and to be obliged, instead of snatching her from him, to tumble sprawling with Pantaloon and the clown; and bear the infernal and degrading thwacks of my rival's weapon of lath; which, may heaven confound him! (excuse my passion) the villain laid on with a malicious good-will; nay, I could absolutely hear him chuckle and laugh beneath his accursed mask—I beg pardon for growing a little warm in my narration. I wish to be cool, but these recollections will sometimes agitate me. I have heard and read of many desperate and deplorable situations of lovers; but none, I think, in which true love was ever exposed to so severe and peculiar a trial.

This could not last long. Flesh and blood, at least such flesh and blood as mine, could not bear it. I had repeated heartburnings and quarrels with my rival, in which he treated me with the mortifying forbearance of a man towards a child. Had he quarrelled outright with me, I could have stomached it; at least I should have known what part to take; but to be humored and treated as a child in the presence of my mistress, when I felt all the bantam spirit of a little man swelling within me—gods, it was insufferable!

At length we were exhibiting one day at West End fair, which was at that time a very fashionable resort, and often beleaguered by gay equipages from town. Among the spectators that filled the front row of our little canvas theatre one afternoon, when I had to figure in a pantomime, was a party of young ladies from a boarding-school, with their governess. Guess my confusion, when, in the midst of my antics, I beheld among the number my quondam flame; her whom I had berhymed at school; her for whose charms I had smarted so severely; tho cruel Sacharissa! What was worse, I fancied she recollected me; and was repeating the story of my humiliating flagellation, for I saw her whispering her companions and her governess. I lost all consciousness of the part I was acting, and of the place where I was. I felt shrunk to nothing, and could have crept into a rat-hole—unluckily, none was open to receive me. Before I could recover from my confusion, I was tumbled over by Pantaloon and the clown; and I felt the sword of Harlequin making vigorous assaults, in a manner most degrading to my dignity.

Heaven and earth! was I again to suffer martyrdom in this ignominious manner, in the knowledge, and even before the very eyes of this most beautiful, but most disdainful of fair ones? All my long-smothered wrath broke out at once; the dormant feelings of the gentleman arose within me; stung to the quick by intolerable mortification, I sprang on my feet in an instant; leaped upon Harlequin like a young tiger; tore off his mask; buffeted him in the face, and soon shed more blood on the stage than had been spilt upon it during a whole tragic campaign of battles and murders.

As soon as Harlequin recovered from his surprise he returned my assault with interest. I was nothing in his hands. I was game to be sure, for I was a gentleman; but he had the clownish advantages of bone and muscle. I felt as if I could have fought even unto the death; and I was likely to do so; for he was, according to the vulgar phrase, "putting my head into Chancery," when the gentle Columbine flew to my assistance. God bless the women; they are always on the side of the weak and the oppressed.

The battle now became general; the dramatis personae ranged on either side. The manager interfered in vain. In vain were his spangled black bonnet and towering white feathers seen whisking about, and nodding, and bobbing, in the thickest of the fight. Warriors, ladies, priests, satyrs, kings, queens, gods and goddesses, all joined pell-mell in the fray. Never, since the conflict under the walls of Troy, had there been such a chance medley warfare of combatants, human and divine. The audience applauded, the ladies shrieked and fled from the theatre, and a scene of discord ensued that baffles all description.

Nothing but the interference of the peace officers restored some degree of order. The havoc, however, that had been made among dresses and decorations put an end to all farther acting for that day. The battle over, the next thing was to inquire why it was begun; a common question among politicians, after a bloody and unprofitable war; and one not always easy to be answered. It was soon traced to me, and my unaccountable transport of passion, which they could only attribute to my having run *a muck*. The manager was judge and jury, and plaintiff in the bargain, and in such cases justice is always speedily administered. He came out of the fight as sublime a wreck as the Santissìma Trinidada. His gallant plumes, which once towered aloft, were drooping about his ears. His robe of state hung in ribbands from his back, and but ill concealed the ravages he had suffered in the rear. He had received kicks and cuffs from all sides, during the tumult; for every one took the opportunity of slyly gratifying some lurking grudge on his fat carcass. He was a discreet man, and did not choose to declare war with all his company; so he swore all those kicks and cuffs had been given by me, and I let him enjoy the opinion. Some wounds he bore, however, which were the incontestible traces of a woman's warfare. His sleek rosy cheek was scored by trickling furrows, which were ascribed to the nails of my intrepid and devoted Columbine. The ire of the monarch was not to be appeased. He had suffered in his person, and he had suffered in his purse; his dignity too had been insulted, and that went for something; for dignity is always more irascible the more petty the potentate. He wreaked his wrath upon the beginners of the affray, and Columbine and myself were discharged, at once, from the company.

Figure me, then, to yourself, a stripling of little more than sixteen; a gentleman by birth; a vagabond by trade; turned adrift upon the world; making the best of my way through the crowd of West End fair; my mountebank dress fluttering in rags about me; the weeping Columbine hanging upon my arm, in splendid, but tattered finery; the tears coursing one by one down her face; carrying off the red paint in torrents, and literally "preying upon her damask cheek."

The crowd made way for us as we passed and hooted in our rear. I felt the ridicule of my situation, but had too much gallantry to desert this fair one, who had sacrificed everything for me. Having wandered through the fair, we emerged, like another Adam and Eve, into unknown regions, and "had the world before us where to choose." Never was a more disconsolate pair seen in the soft valley of West End. The luckless Columbine cast back many a lingering look at the fair, which seemed to put on a more than usual splendor; its tents, and booths, and parti-colored groups, all brightening in the sunshine, and gleaming among the trees; and its gay flags and streamers playing and fluttering in the light summer airs. With a heavy sigh she would lean on my arm and proceed. I had no hope or consolation to give her; but she had linked herself to my fortunes, and she was too much of a woman to desert me.

Pensive and silent, then, we traversed the beautiful fields that lie behind Hempstead, and wandered on, until the fiddle, and the hautboy, and the shout, and the laugh, were swallowed up in the deep sound of the big bass drum, and even that died away into a distant rumble. We passed along the pleasant sequestered walk of Nightingale lane. For a pair of lovers what scene could be more propitious?—But such a pair of lovers! Not a nightingale sang to soothe us: the very gypsies who were encamped there during the fair, made no offer to tell the fortunes of such an ill-omened couple, whose fortunes, I suppose, they thought too legibly written to need an interpreter; and the gypsey children crawled into their cabins and peeped out fearfully at us as we went by. For a moment I paused, and was almost tempted to turn gypsey, but the poetical feeling for the present was fully satisfied, and I passed on. Thus we travelled, and travelled, like a prince and princess in nursery chronicle, until we had traversed a part of Hempstead Heath and arrived in the vicinity of Jack Straw's castle.

WASHINGTON IRVING

Here, wearied and dispirited, we seated ourselves on the margin of the hill, hard by the very mile-stone where Whittington of yore heard the Bow bells ring out the presage of his future greatness. Alas! no bell rung in invitation to us, as we looked disconsolately upon the distant city. Old London seemed to wrap itself up unsociably in its mantle of brown smoke, and to offer no encouragement to such a couple of tatterdemalions.

For once, at least, the usual course of the pantomime was reversed. Harlequin was jilted, and the lover had earned off Columbine in good earnest. But what was I to do with her? I had never contemplated such a dilemma; and I now felt that even a fortunate lover may be embarrassed by his good fortune. I really knew not what was to become of me; for I had still the boyish fear of returning home; standing in awe of the stern temper of my father, and dreading the ready arm of the pedagogue. And even if I were to venture home, what was I to do with Columbine? I could not take her in my hand, and throw myself on my knees, and crave his forgiveness and his blessing according to dramatic usage. The very dogs would have chased such a draggle-tailed beauty from the grounds.

In the midst of my doleful dumps, some one tapped me on the shoulder, and looking up I saw a couple of rough sturdy fellows standing behind me. Not knowing what to expect I jumped on my legs, and was preparing again to make battle; but I was tripped up and secured in a twinkling.

"Come, come, young master," said one of the fellows in a gruff, but good-humored tone, "don't let's have any of your tantrums; one would have thought that you had had swing enough for this bout. Come, it's high time to leave off harlequinading, and go home to your father."

In fact I had a couple of Bow street officers hold of me. The cruel Sacharissa had proclaimed who I was, and that a reward had been offered throughout the country for any tidings of me; and they had seen a description of me that had been forwarded to the police office in town. Those harpies, therefore, for the mere sake of filthy lucre, were resolved to deliver me over into the hands of my father and the clutches of my pedagogue.

It was in vain that I swore I would not leave my faithful and Afflicted Columbine. It was in vain that I tore myself from their grasp, and flew to her; and vowed to protect her; and wiped the tears from her cheek, and with them a whole blush that might have vied with the carnation for brilliancy. My persecutors were inflexible; they even seemed to exult in our distress; and to enjoy this theatrical display of dirt, and finery, and tribulation. I was carried off in despair, leaving my Columbine destitute in the wide world; but many a look of agony did I cast back at her, as she stood gazing piteously after me from the brink of Hempstead Hill; so forlorn, so fine, so ragged, so bedraggled, yet so beautiful.

Thus ended my first peep into the world. I returned home, rich in good-for-nothing experience, and dreading the reward I was to receive for my improvement. My reception, however, was quite different from what I had expected. My father had a spice of the devil in him, and did not seem to like me the worse for my freak, which he termed "sowing my wild oats." He happened to have several of his sporting friends to dine with him the very day of my return; they made me tell some of my adventures, and laughed heartily at them. One old fellow, with an outrageously red nose, took to me hugely. I heard him whisper to my father that I was a lad of mettle, and might make something clever; to which my father replied that "I had good points, but was an ill-broken whelp, and required a great deal of the whip." Perhaps this very conversation raised me a little in his esteem, for I found the red-nosed old gentleman was a veteran fox-hunter of the neighborhood, for whose opinion my father had vast deference. Indeed, I believe he would have pardoned anything in me more readily than poetry; which he called a cursed, sneaking, puling, housekeeping employment, the bane of all true manhood. He swore it was unworthy of a youngster of my expectations, who was one day to have so great an estate, and would he able to keep horses and hounds and hire poets to write songs for him into the bargain.

I had now satisfied, for a time, my roving propensity. I had exhausted the poetical feeling. I had been heartily buffeted out of my love for theatrical display. I felt humiliated by my exposure, and was willing to hide my head anywhere for a season; so that I might be out of the way of the ridicule of the world; for I found folks not altogether so indulgent abroad as they were at my father's table. I could not stay at home; the house was intolerably doleful now that my mother was no longer there to cherish me. Every thing around spoke mournfully of her. The little flower-garden in which she delighted was all in disorder and overrun with weeds. I attempted, for a day or two, to arrange it, but my heart grew heavier and heavier as I labored. Every little broken-down flower that I had seen her rear so tenderly, seemed to plead in mute eloquence to my feelings. There was a favorite honeysuckle which I had seen her often training with assiduity, and had heard her say it should be the pride of her garden. I found it grovelling along the ground, tangled and wild, and twining round every worthless weed, and it struck me as an emblem of myself: a mere scatterling, running to waste and uselessness. I could work no longer in the garden.

My father sent me to pay a visit to my uncle, by way of keeping the old gentleman in mind of me. I was received, as usual, without any expression of discontent; which we always considered equivalent to a hearty welcome. Whether he had ever heard of my strolling freak or not I could not discover; he and his man were both so taciturn. I spent a day or two roaming about the dreary mansion and neglected park; and felt at one time, I believe, a touch of poetry, for I was tempted to drown myself in a fish-pond; I rebuked the evil spirit, however, and it left me. I found the same red-headed boy running wild about the park, but I felt in no humor to hunt him at present. On the contrary, I tried to coax him to me, and to make friends with him, but the young savage was untameable.

When I returned from my uncle's I remained at home for some time, for my father was disposed, he said, to make a man of me. He took me out hunting with him, and I became a great favorite of the red-nosed squire, because I rode at everything; never refused the boldest leap, and was always sure to be in at the death. I used often however, to offend my father at hunting dinners, by taking the wrong side in politics. My father was amazingly ignorant—so ignorant, in fact, as not to know that he knew nothing. He was staunch, however, to church and king, and full of old-fashioned prejudices. Now, I had picked up a little knowledge in politics and religion, during my rambles with the strollers, and found myself capable of setting him right as to many of his antiquated notions. I felt it my duty to do so; we were apt, therefore, to differ occasionally in the political discussions that sometimes arose at these hunting dinners.

I was at that age when a man knows least and is most vain of his knowledge; and when he is extremely tenacious in defending his opinion upon subjects about which he knows nothing. My father was a hard man for any one to argue with, for he never knew when he was refuted. I sometimes posed him a little, but then he had one argument that always settled the question; he would threaten to knock me down. I believe he at last grew tired of me, because I both out-talked and outrode him. The red-nosed squire, too, got out of conceit of me, because in the heat of the chase, I rode over him one day as he and his horse lay sprawling in the dirt. My father, therefore, thought it high time to send me to college; and accordingly to Trinity College at Oxford was I sent.

I had lost my habits of study while at home; and I was not likely to find them again at college. I found that study was not the fashion at college, and that a lad of spirit only ate his terms; and grew wise by dint of knife and fork. I was always prone to follow the fashions of the company into which I fell; so I threw by my books, and became a man of spirit. As my father made me a tolerable allowance, notwithstanding the narrowness of his income, having an eye always to my great expectations, I was enabled to appear to advantage among my fellow-students. I cultivated all kinds of sports and exercises. I was one of the most expert oarsmen that rowed on the Isis. I boxed and fenced. I was a keen huntsman, and my chambers in college were always decorated with whips of all kinds, spurs, foils, and boxing gloves. A pair of leather breeches would seem to be throwing one leg out of the half-open drawers, and empty bottles lumbered the bottom of every closet.

I soon grew tired of this, and relapsed into my vein of mere poetical indulgence. I was charmed with Oxford, for it was full of poetry to me. I thought I should never grow tired of wandering about its courts and cloisters; and visiting the different college halls. I used to love to get in places surrounded by the colleges, where all modern buildings were screened from the sight; and to walk about them in twilight, and see the professors and students sweeping along in the dusk in their caps and gowns. There was complete delusion in the scene. It seemed to transport me among the edifices and the people of old times. It was a great luxury, too, for me to attend the evening service in the new college chapel, and to hear the fine organ and the choir swelling an anthem in that solemn building; where painting and music and architecture seem to combine their grandest effects.

I became a loiterer, also, about the Bodleian library, and a great dipper into books; but too idle to follow any course of study or vein of research. One of my favorite haunts was the beautiful walk, bordered by lofty elms, along the Isis, under the old gray walls of Magdalen College, which goes by the name of Addison's Walk; and was his resort when a student at the college. I used to take a volume of poetry in my hand, and stroll up and down this walk for hours.

My father came to see me at college. He asked me how I came on with my studies; and what kind of hunting there was in the neighborhood. He examined my sporting apparatus; wanted to know if any of the professors were fox-hunters; and whether they were generally good shots; for he suspected this reading so much was rather hurtful to the sight. Such was the only person to whom I was responsible for my improvement: is it matter of wonder, therefore, that I became a confirmed idler?

I do not know how it is, but I cannot be idle long without getting in love. I became deeply smitten with a shopkeeper's daughter in the high street; who in fact was the admiration of many of the students. I wrote several sonnets in praise of her, and spent half of my pocket-money at the shop, in buying articles which I did not want, that I might have an opportunity of speaking to her. Her father, a severe-looking old gentleman, with bright silver buckles and a crisp, curled wig, kept a strict guard on her; as the fathers generally do upon their daughters in Oxford; and well they may. I tried to get into his good graces, and to be sociable with him; but in vain. I said several good things in his shop, but he never laughed; he had no relish for wit and humor. He was one of those dry old gentlemen who keep youngsters at bay. He had already brought up two or three daughters, and was experienced in the ways of students.

He was as knowing and wary as a gray old badger that has often been hunted. To see him on Sunday, so stiff and starched in his demeanor; so precise in his dress; with his daughter under his arm, and his ivory-headed cane in his hand, was enough to deter all graceless youngsters from approaching.

I managed, however, in spite of his vigilance, to have several Conversations with the daughter, as I cheapened articles in the shop. I made terrible long bargains, and examined the articles over and over, before I purchased. In the meantime, I would convey a sonnet or an acrostic under cover of a piece of cambric, or slipped into a pair of stockings; I would whisper soft nonsense into her ear as I haggled about the price; and would squeeze her hand tenderly as I received my halfpence of change, in a bit of whity-brown paper. Let this serve as a hint to all haberdashers, who have pretty daughters for shop-girls, and young students for customers. I do not know whether my words and looks were very eloquent; but my poetry was irresistible; for, to tell the truth, the girl had some literary taste, and was seldom without a book from the circulating library.

By the divine power of poetry, therefore, which is irresistible with the lovely sex, did I subdue the heart of this fair little haberdasher. We carried on a sentimental correspondence for a time across the counter, and I supplied her with rhyme by the stockingful. At length I prevailed on her to grant me an assignation. But how was it to be effected? Her father kept her always under his eye; she never walked out alone; and the house was locked up the moment that the shop was shut. All these difficulties served but to give zest to the adventure. I proposed that the assignation should be in her own chamber, into which I would climb at night. The plan was irresistible. A cruel father, a secret lover, and a clandestine meeting! All the little girl's studies from the circulating library seemed about to be realised. But what had I in view in making this assignation? Indeed I know not. I had no evil intentions; nor can I say that I had any good ones. I liked the girl, and wanted to have an opportunity of seeing more of her; and the assignation was made, as I have done many things else, heedlessly and without forethought. I asked myself a few questions of the kind, after all my arrangements were made; but the answers were very unsatisfactory. "Am I to ruin this poor thoughtless girl?" said I to myself. "No!" was the prompt and indignant answer. "Am I to run away with her?" "Whither—and to what purpose?" "Well, then, am I to marry her!"—"Pah! a man of my expectations marry a shopkeeper's daughter!" "What, then, am I to do with her?" "Hum—why.—Let me get into her chamber first, and then consider"—and so the self-examination ended.

Well, sir, "come what come might," I stole under cover of the darkness to the dwelling of my dulcinea. All was quiet. At the concerted signal her window was gently opened. It was just above the projecting bow-window of her father's shop, which assisted me in mounting. The house was low, and I was enabled to scale the fortress with tolerable ease. I clambered with a beating heart; I reached the casement; I hoisted my body half into the chamber and was welcomed, not by the embraces of my expecting fair one, but by the grasp of the crabbed-looking old father in the crisp curled wig.

I extricated myself from his clutches and endeavored to make my retreat; but I was confounded by his cries of thieves! and robbers! I was bothered, too, by his Sunday cane; which was amazingly busy about my head as I descended; and against which my hat was but a poor protection. Never before had I an idea of the activity of an old man's arm, and hardness of the knob of an ivory-headed cane. In my hurry

WASHINGTON IRVING

and confusion I missed my footing, and fell sprawling on the pavement. I was immediately surrounded by myrmidons, who I doubt not were on the watch for me. Indeed, I was in no situation to escape, for I had sprained my ankle in the fall, and could not stand. I was seized as a housebreaker; and to exonerate myself from a greater crime I had to accuse myself of a less. I made known who I was, and why I came there. Alas! the varlets knew it already, and were only amusing themselves at my expense. My perfidious muse had been playing me one of her slippery tricks. The old curmudgeon of a father had found my sonnets and acrostics hid away in holes and corners of his shop; he had no taste for poetry like his daughter, and had instituted a rigorous though silent observation. He had moused upon our letters; detected the ladder of ropes, and prepared everything for my reception. Thus was I ever doomed to be led into scrapes by the muse. Let no man henceforth carry on a secret amour in poetry.

The old man's ire was in some measure appeased by the pummelling of my head, and the anguish of my sprain; so he did not put me to death on the spot. He was even humane enough to furnish a shutter, on which I was carried back to the college like a wounded warrior. The porter was roused to admit me; the college gate was thrown open for my entry; the affair was blazed abroad the next morning, and became the joke of the college from the buttery to the hall.

I had leisure to repent during several weeks' confinement by my sprain, which I passed in translating Boethius' Consolations of Philosophy. I received a most tender and ill-spelled letter from my mistress, who had been sent to a relation in Coventry. She protested her innocence of my misfortunes, and vowed to be true to me "till death." I took no notice of the letter, for I was cured, for the present, both of love and poetry. Women, however, are more constant in their attachments than men, whatever philosophers may say to the contrary. I am assured that she actually remained faithful to her vow for several months; but she had to deal with a cruel father whose heart was as hard as the knob of his cane. He was not to be touched by tears or poetry; but absolutely compelled her to marry a reputable young tradesman; who made her a happy woman in spite of herself, and of all the rules of romance; and what is more, the mother of several children. They are at this very day a thriving couple and keep a snug corner shop, just opposite the figure of Peeping Tom at Coventry.

I will not fatigue you by any more details of my studies at Oxford, though they were not always as severe as these; nor did I always pay as dear for my lessons. People may say what they please, a studious life has its charms, and there are many places more gloomy than the cloisters of a university.

To be brief, then, I lived on in my usual miscellaneous manner, gradually getting a knowledge of good and evil, until I had attained my twenty-first year. I had scarcely come of age when I heard of the sudden death of my father. The shock was severe, for though he had never treated me with kindness, still he was my father, and at his death I felt myself alone in the world.

I returned home to act as chief mourner at his funeral. It was attended by many of the sportsmen of the country; for he was an important member of their fraternity. According to his request his favorite hunter was led after the hearse. The red-nosed fox-hunter, who had taken a little too much wine at the house, made a maudlin eulogy of the deceased, and wished to give the view halloo over the grave; but he was rebuked by the rest of the company. They all shook me kindly by the hand, said many consolatory things to me, and invited me to become a member of the hunt in my father's place.

When I found myself alone in my paternal home, a crowd of gloomy feelings came thronging upon me. It was a place that always seemed to sober me, and bring me to reflection. Now, especially, it looked so deserted and melancholy; the furniture displaced about the room; the chairs in groups, as their departed occupants had sat, either in whispering tête-à-têtes, or gossiping clusters; the bottles and decanters and wine-glasses, half emptied, and scattered about the tables—all dreary traces of a funeral festival. I entered the little breakfasting room. There were my father's whip and spurs hanging by the fire-place, and his favorite pointer lying on the hearth-rug. The poor animal came fondling about me, and licked my hand, though he had never before noticed me; and then he looked round the room, and whined, and wagged his tail slightly, and gazed wistfully in my face. I felt the full force of the appeal. "Poor Dash!" said I, "we are both alone in the world, with nobody to care for us, and we'll take care of one another." The dog never quitted me afterwards.

I could not go into my mother's room: my heart swelled when I passed within sight of the door. Her portrait hung in the parlor, just over the place where she used to sit. As I cast my eyes on it I thought it looked at me with tenderness, and I burst into tears. My heart had long been seared by living in public schools, and buffeting about among strangers who cared nothing for me; but the recollection of a mother's tenderness was overcoming.

I was not of an age or a temperament to be long depressed. There was a reaction in my system that always brought me up again at every pressure; and indeed my spirits were most buoyant after a temporary prostration. I settled the concerns of the estate as soon as possible; realized my property, which was not very considerable, but which appeared a vast deal to me, having a poetical eye that magnified everything; and finding myself, at the end of a few months, free of all farther business or restraint, I determined to go to London and enjoy myself. Why should not I?—I was young, animated, joyous; had plenty of funds for present pleasures, and my uncle's estate in the perspective. Let those mope at college and pore over books, thought I, who have their way to make in the world; it would be ridiculous drudgery in a youth of my expectations.

Well, sir, away to London I rattled in a tandem, determined to take the town gaily. I passed through several of the villages where I had played the jack-pudding a few years before; and I visited the scenes of many of my adventures and follies, merely from that feeling of melancholy pleasure which we have in stepping again into the footprints of foregone existence, even when they have passed among weeds and briars. I made a circuit in the latter part of my journey, so as to take in West End and Hempstead, the scenes of my last dramatic exploit, and of the battle royal of the booth. As I drove along the ridge of Hempstead Hill, by Jack Straw's castle, I paused at the spot where Columbine and I had sat down so disconsolately in our ragged finery, and looked dubiously upon London. I almost expected to see her again, standing on the hill's brink, "like Niobe all tears;"—mournful as Babylon in ruins!

"Poor Columbine!" said I, with a heavy sigh, "thou wert a gallant, generous girl—a true woman, faithful to the distressed, and ready to sacrifice thyself in the cause of worthless man!"

I tried to whistle off the recollection of her; for there was always Something of self-reproach with it. I drove gayly along the road, enjoying the stare of hostlers and stable-boys as I managed my horses knowingly down the steep street of Hempstead; when, just at the skirts of the village, one of the traces of my leader came loose. I pulled up; and as the animal was restive and my servant a bungler, I called for assistance to the robustious master of a snug ale-house, who stood at his door with a tankard in his hand. He came readily to assist me, followed by his wife, with her bosom half open, a child in her arms, and two more at her heels. I stared for a moment as if doubting my eyes. I could not be mistaken; in the fat, beer-blown landlord of the ale-house I recognized my old rival Harlequin, and in his slattern spouse, the once trim and dimpling Columbine.

The change of my looks, from youth to manhood, and the change of my circumstances, prevented them from recognizing me. They could not suspect, in the dashing young buck, fashionably dressed, and driving his own equipage, their former comrade, the painted beau, with old peaked hat and long, flimsy, sky-blue coat. My heart yearned with kindness towards Columbine, and I was glad to see her establishment a thriving one. As soon as the harness was adjusted, I tossed a small purse of gold into her ample bosom; and then, pretending give my horses a hearty cut of the whip, I made the lash curl with a whistling about the sleek sides of ancient Harlequin. The horses dashed off like lightning, and I was whirled out of sight, before either of the parties could get over their surprise at my liberal donations. I have always considered this as one of the greatest proofs of my poetical genius. It was distributing poetical justice in perfection.

I now entered London *en cavalier*, and became a blood upon town. I took fashionable lodgings in the West End; employed the first tailor; frequented the regular lounges; gambled a little; lost my money good-humoredly, and gained a number of fashionable good-for-nothing acquaintances. Had I had more industry and ambition in my nature, I might have worked my way to the very height of fashion, as I saw many laborious gentlemen doing around me. But it is a toilsome, an anxious, and an unhappy life; there are few beings so sleepless and miserable as your cultivators of fashionable smiles.

I was quite content with that kind of society which forms the frontiers of fashion, and may be easily taken possession of. I found it a light, easy, productive soil. I had but to go about and sow visiting cards, and I reaped a whole harvest of invitations. Indeed, my figure and address were by no means against me. It was whispered, too, among the young ladies, that I was prodigiously clever, and wrote poetry; and the old ladies had ascertained that I was a young gentleman of good family, handsome fortune, and "great expectations."

I now was carried away by the hurry of gay life, so intoxicating to a young man; and which a man of poetical temperament enjoys so highly on his first tasting of it. That rapid variety of sensations; that whirl of brilliant objects; that succession of pungent pleasures. I had no time for thought; I only felt. I never attempted to write poetry; my poetry seemed all to go off by transpiration. I lived poetry; it was all a poetical dream to me. A mere sensualist knows nothing of the delights of a splendid metropolis. He lives in a round of animal gratifications and heartless habits. But to a young man of poetical feelings it is an ideal world; a scene of enchantment and delusion; his imagination is in perpetual excitement, and gives a spiritual zest to every pleasure.

A season of town life somewhat sobered me of my intoxication; or rather I was rendered more serious by one of my old complaints—I fell in love. It was with a very pretty, though a very haughty fair one, who had come to London under the care of an old maiden aunt, to enjoy the pleasures of a winter in town, and to get married. There was not a doubt of her commanding a choice of lovers; for she had long been the belle of a little cathedral town; and one of the prebendaries had absolutely celebrated her beauty in a copy of Latin verses.

I paid my court to her, and was favorably received both by her and her aunt. Nay, I had a marked preference shown me over the younger son of a needy baronet, and a captain of dragoons on half pay. I did not absolutely take the field in form, for I was determined not to be precipitate; but I drove my equipage frequently through the street in which she lived, and was always sure to see her at the window, generally with a book in her hand. I resumed my knack at rhyming, and sent her a long copy of verses; anonymously to be sure; but she knew my handwriting. They displayed, however, the most delightful ignorance on the subject. The young lady showed them to me; wondered who they could be written by; and declared there was nothing in this world she loved so much as poetry: while the maiden aunt would put her pinching spectacles on her nose, and read them, with blunders in sense and sound, that were excruciating to an author's ears; protesting there was nothing equal to them in the whole elegant extracts.

The fashionable season closed without my adventuring to make a declaration, though. I certainly had encouragement. I was not perfectly sure that I had effected a lodgment in the young lady's heart; and, to tell the truth, the aunt overdid her part, and was a little too extravagant in her liking of me. I knew that maiden aunts were not apt to be captivated by the mere personal merits of their nieces' admirers, and I wanted to ascertain how much of all this favor I owed to my driving an equipage and having great expectations.

I had received many hints how charming their native town was during the summer months; what pleasant society they had; and what beautiful drives about the neighborhood. They had not, therefore, returned home long, before I made my appearance in dashing style, driving down the principal street. It is an easy thing to put a little quiet cathedral town in a buzz. The very next morning I was seen at prayers, seated in the pew of the reigning belle. All the congregation was in a flutter. The prebends eyed me from their stalls; questions were whispered about the aisles after service, "who is he?" and "what is he?" and the replies were as usual—"A young gentleman of good family and fortune, and great expectations."

I was pleased with the peculiarities of a cathedral town, where I found I was a personage of some consequence. I was quite a brilliant acquisition to the young ladies of the cathedral circle, who were glad to have a beau that was not in a black coat and clerical wig.

You must know that there was a vast distinction between the classes of society of the town. As it was a place of some trade, there were many wealthy inhabitants among the commercial and manufacturing classes, who lived in style and gave many entertainments. Nothing of trade, however, was admitted into the cathedral circle—faugh! the thing could not be thought of. The cathedral circle, therefore, was apt to be very select, very dignified, and very dull. They had evening parties, at which the old ladies played cards with the prebends, and the young ladies sat and looked on, and shifted from one chair to another about the room, until it was time to go home.

It was difficult to get up a ball, from the want of partners, the Cathedral circle being very deficient in dancers; and on those occasions, there was an occasional drafting among the dancing men of the other circle, who, however, were generally regarded with great reserve and condescension by the gentlemen in powdered wigs. Several of the young ladies assured me, in confidence, that they had often looked with a wistful eye at the gayety of the other circle, where there was such plenty of young beaux, and where they all seemed to enjoy themselves so merrily; but that it would be degradation to think of descending from their sphere.

I admired the degree of old-fashioned ceremony and superannuated courtesy that prevailed in this little place. The bowings and courtseyings that would take place about the cathedral porch after morning service, where knots of old gentlemen and ladies would collect together to ask after each other's health, and settle the card party for the evening. The little presents of fruits and delicacies, and the thousand petty messages that would pass from house to house; for in a tranquil community like this, living entirely at ease, and having little to do, little duties and little civilities and little amusements, fill up the day. I have smiled, as I looked from my window on a quiet street near the cathedral, in the middle of a warm summer day, to see a corpulent powdered footman in rich livery, carrying a small tart on a large silver salver. A dainty titbit, sent, no doubt, by some worthy old dowager, to top off the dinner of her favorite prebend.

Nothing could be more delectable, also, than the breaking up of one of their evening card parties. Such shaking of hands such mobbing up in cloaks and tippets! There were two or three old sedan chairs that did the duty of the whole place; though the greater part made their exit in clogs and pattens, with a footman or waiting-maid carrying a lanthorn in advance; and at a certain hour of the night the clank of pattens and the gleam of these jack lanthorns, here and there, about the quiet little town, gave notice that the cathedral card party had dissolved, and the luminaries were severally seeking their homes. To such a community, therefore, or at least to the female part of it, the accession of a gay, dashing young beau was a matter of some importance. The old ladies eyed me with complacency through their spectacles, and the young ladies pronounced me divine. Everybody received me favorably, excepting the gentleman who had written the Latin verses on the belle.—Not that he was jealous of my success with the lady, for he had no pretensions to her; but he heard my verses praised wherever he went, and he could not endure a rival with the muse.

I was thus carrying every thing before me. I was the Adonis of the Cathedral circle; when one evening there was a public ball which was attended likewise by the gentry of the neighborhood. I took great pains with my toilet on the occasion, and I had never looked better. I had determined that night to make my grand assault on the heart of the young lady, to batter it with all my forces, and the next morning to demand a surrender in due form.

I entered the ball-room amidst a buzz and flutter, which generally took place among the young ladies on my appearance. I was in fine spirits; for to tell the truth, I had exhilarated myself by a cheerful glass of wine on the occasion. I talked, and rattled, and said a thousand silly things, slap-dash, with all the confidence of a man sure of his auditors; and every thing had its effect.

In the midst of my triumph I observed a little knot gathering together in the upper part of the room. By degrees it increased. A tittering broke out there; and glances were cast round at me, and then there would be fresh tittering. Some of the young ladies would hurry away to distant parts of the room, and whisper to their friends; wherever they went there was still this tittering and glancing at me. I did not know what to make of all this. I looked at myself from head to foot; and peeped at my back in a glass, to see if any thing was odd about my person; any awkward exposure; any whimsical tag hanging out—no—every thing was right. I was a perfect picture.

I determined that it must be some choice saying of mine, that was handled about in this knot of merry beauties, and I determined to enjoy one of my good things in the rebound.

I stepped gently, therefore, up the room, smiling at every one as I passed, who I must say all smiled and tittered in return. I approached the group, smirking and perking my chin, like a man who is full of pleasant feeling, and sure of being well received. The cluster of little belles opened as I advanced.

Heavens and earth! whom should I perceive in the midst of them, but my early and tormenting flame, the everlasting Sacharissa! She was grown up, it is true, into the full beauty of womanhood, but showed by the provoking merriment of her countenance, that she perfectly recollected me, and the ridiculous flagellations of which she had twice been the cause.

I saw at once the exterminating cloud of ridicule that was bursting over me. My crest fell. The flame of love went suddenly out in my bosom; or was extinguished by overwhelming shame. How I got down the room I know not; I fancied every one tittering at me. Just as I reached the door, I caught a glance of my mistress and her aunt, listening to the whispers of my poetic rival; the old lady raising her hands and eyes, and the face of the young one lighted up with scorn ineffable. I paused to see no more; but made two steps from the top of the stairs to the bottom. The next morning, before sunrise, I beat a retreat; and did not feel the blushes cool from my tingling cheeks until I had lost sight of the old towers of the cathedral.

I now returned to town thoughtful and crestfallen. My money was nearly spent, for I had lived freely and without calculation. The dream of love was over, and the reign of pleasure at an end. I determined to retrench while I had yet a trifle left; so selling my equipage and

WASHINGTON IRVING

horses for half their value, I quietly put the money in my pocket and turned pedestrian. I had not a doubt that, with my great expectations, I could at any time raise funds, either on usury or by borrowing; but I was principled against both one and the other; and resolved, by strict economy, to make my slender purse hold out, until my uncle should give up the ghost; or rather, the estate.

I stayed at home, therefore, and read, and would have written; but I had already suffered too much from my poetical productions, which had generally involved me in some ridiculous scrape. I gradually acquired a rusty look, and had a straightened, money-borrowing air, upon which the world began to shy me. I have never felt disposed to quarrel with the world for its conduct. It has always used me well. When I have been flush, and gay, and disposed for society, it has caressed me; and when I have been pinched, and reduced, and wished to be alone, why, it has left me alone, and what more could a man desire?—Take my word for it, this world is a more obliging world than people generally represent it.

Well, sir, in the midst of my retrenchment, my retirement, and my studiousness, I received news that my uncle was dangerously ill. I hastened on the wings of an heir's affection to receive his dying breath and his last testament. I found him attended by his faithful valet, old Iron John; by the woman who occasionally worked about the house; and by the foxy-headed boy, young Orson, whom I had occasionally hunted about the park.

Iron John gasped a kind of asthmatical salutation as I entered the room, and received me with something almost like a smile of welcome. The woman sat blubbering at the foot of the bed; and the foxy-headed Orson, who had now grown to be a lubberly lout, stood gazing in stupid vacancy at a distance.

My uncle lay stretched upon his back. The chamber was without a fire, or any of the comforts of a sick-room. The cobwebs flaunted from the ceiling. The tester was covered with dust, and the curtains were tattered. From underneath the bed peeped out one end of his strong box. Against the wainscot were suspended rusty blunderbusses, horse pistols, and a cut-and-thrust sword, with which he had fortified his room to defend his life and treasure. He had employed no physician during his illness, and from the scanty relics lying on the table, seemed almost to have denied himself the assistance of a cook.

When I entered the room he was lying motionless; with his eyes fixed and his mouth open; at the first look I thought him a corpse.

The noise of my entrance made him turn his head. At the sight of me a ghastly smile came over his face, and his glazing eye gleamed with satisfaction. It was the only smile he had ever given me, and it went to my heart. "Poor old man!" thought I, "why would you not let me love you?—Why would you force me to leave you thus desolate, when I see that my presence has the power to cheer you?"

"Nephew," said he, after several efforts, and in a low gasping voice— "I am glad you are come. I shall now die with satisfaction. Look," said he, raising his withered hand and pointing—"look—in that box on the table you will find that I have not forgotten you."

I pressed his hand to my heart, and the tears stood in my eyes. I sat down by his bed-side, and watched him, but he never spoke again. My presence, however, gave him evident satisfaction—for every now and then, as he looked at me, a vague smile would come over his visage, and he would feebly point to the sealed box on the table. As the day wore away, his life seemed to wear away with it. Towards sunset, his hand sunk on the bed and lay motionless; his eyes grew glazed; his mouth remained open, and thus he gradually died.

I could not but feel shocked at this absolute extinction of my kindred. I dropped a tear of real sorrow over this strange old man, who had thus reserved his smile of kindness to his deathbed; like an evening sun after a gloomy day, just shining out to set in darkness. Leaving the corpse in charge of the domestics, I retired for the night.

It was a rough night. The winds seemed as if singing my uncle's requiem about the mansion; and the bloodhounds howled without as if they knew of the death of their old master. Iron John almost grudged me the tallow candle to burn in my apartment and light up its dreariness; so accustomed had he been to starveling economy. I could not sleep. The recollection of my uncle's dying scene and the dreary sounds about the house, affected my mind. These, however, were succeeded by plans for the future, and I lay awake the greater part of the night, indulging the poetical anticipation, how soon I would make these old walls ring with cheerful life, and restore the hospitality of my mother's ancestors.

My uncle's funeral was decent, but private, I knew there was nobody That respected his memory; and I was determined that none should be summoned to sneer over his funeral wines, and make merry at his grave. He was buried in the church of the neighboring village, though it was not the burying place of his race; but he had expressly enjoined that he should not be buried with his family; he had quarrelled with the most of them when living, and he carried his resentments even into the grave.

I defrayed the expenses of the funeral out of my own purse, that I might have done with the undertakers at once, and clear the ill-omened birds from the premises. I invited the parson of the parish, and the lawyer from the village to attend at the house the next morning and hear the reading of the will. I treated them to an excellent breakfast, a profusion that had not been seen at the house for many a year. As soon as the breakfast things were removed, I summoned Iron John, the woman, and the boy, for I was particular of having every one present and proceeding regularly. The box was placed on the table. All was silence. I broke the seal; raised the lid; and beheld—not the will, but my accursed poem of Doubting Castle and Giant Despair!

Could any mortal have conceived that this old withered man; so taciturn, and apparently lost to feeling, could have treasured up for years the thoughtless pleasantry of a boy, to punish him with such cruel ingenuity? I could now account for his dying smile, the only one he had ever given me. He had been a grave man all his life; it was strange that he should die in the enjoyment of a joke; and it was hard that that joke should be at my expense.

The lawyer and the parson seemed at a loss to comprehend the matter. "Here must be some mistake," said the lawyer, "there is no will here."

"Oh," said Iron John, creaking forth his rusty jaws, "if it is a will you are looking for, I believe I can find one."

He retired with the same singular smile with which he had greeted me on my arrival, and which I now apprehended boded me no good. In a little while he returned with a will perfect at all points, properly signed and sealed and witnessed; worded with horrible correctness; in which he left large legacies to Iron John and his daughter, and the residue of his fortune to the foxy-headed boy; who, to my utter astonishment, was his son by this very woman; he having married her privately; and, as I verily believe, for no other purpose than to have an heir, and so baulk my father and his issue of the inheritance. There was one little proviso, in which he mentioned that having discovered his nephew to have a pretty turn for poetry, he presumed he had no occasion for wealth; he recommended him, however, to the patronage of his heir; and requested that he might have a garret, rent free, in Doubting Castle.

Mr. Buckthorne had paused at the death of his uncle, and the downfall of his great expectations, which formed, as he said, an epoch in his history; and it was not until some little time afterwards, and in a very sober mood, that he resumed his particolored narrative.

After leaving the domains of my defunct uncle, said he, when the gate Closed between me and what was once to have been mine, I felt thrust out naked into the world, and completely abandoned to fortune. What was to become of me? I had been brought up to nothing but expectations, and they had all been disappointed. I had no relations to look to for counsel or assistance. The world seemed all to have died away from me. Wave after wave of relationship had ebbed off, and I was left a mere hulk upon the strand. I am not apt to be greatly cast down, but at this, time I felt sadly disheartened. I could not realize my situation, nor form a conjecture how I was to get forward.

I was now to endeavor to make money. The idea was new and strange to me. It was like being asked to discover the philosopher's stone. I had never thought about money, other than to put my hand into my pocket and find it, or if there were none there, to wait until a new supply came from home. I had considered life as a mere space of time to be filled up with enjoyments; but to have it portioned out into long hours and days of toil, merely that I might gain bread to give me strength to toil on; to labor but for the purpose of perpetuating a life of labor was new and appalling to me. This may appear a very simple matter to some, but it will be understood by every unlucky wight in my predicament, who has had the misfortune of being born to great expectations.

I passed several days in rambling about the scenes of my boyhood; partly because I absolutely did not know what to do with myself, and partly because I did not know that I should ever see them again. I clung to them as one clings to a wreck, though he knows he must eventually cast himself loose and swim for his life. I sat down on a hill within sight of my paternal home, but I did not venture to approach it, for I felt compunction at the thoughtlessness with which I had dissipated my patrimony. But was I to blame, when I had the rich possessions of my curmudgeon of an uncle in expectation?

The new possessor of the place was making great alterations. The house was almost rebuilt. The trees which stood about it were cut down; my mother's flower-garden was thrown into a lawn; all was undergoing a change. I turned my back upon it with a sigh, and rambled to another part of the country.

How thoughtful a little adversity makes one. As I came in sight of the school-house where I had so often been flogged in the cause of wisdom, you would hardly have recognized the truant boy who but a few years since had eloped so heedlessly from its walls. I leaned over the paling of the playground, and watched the scholars at their games, and looked to see if there might not be some urchin among them, like I was once, full of gay dreams about life and the world. The play-ground seemed smaller than when I used to sport about it. The house and park, too, of the neighboring squire, the father of the cruel Sacharissa, had shrunk in size and diminished in magnificence. The distant hills no longer appeared so far off, and, alas! no longer awakened ideas of a fairy land beyond.

As I was rambling pensively through a neighboring meadow, in which I had many a time gathered primroses, I met the very pedagogue who had been the tyrant and dread of my boyhood. I had sometimes vowed to myself, when suffering under his rod, that I would have my revenge if ever I met him when I had grown to be a man. The time had come; but I had no disposition to keep my vow. The few years which had matured me into a vigorous man had shrunk him into decrepitude. He appeared to have had a paralytic stroke. I looked at him, and wondered that this poor helpless mortal could have been an object of terror to me! That I should have watched with anxiety the glance of that failing eye, or dreaded the power of that trembling hand! He tottered feebly along the path, and had some difficulty in getting over a stile. I ran and assisted him. He looked at me with surprise, but did not recognize me, and made a low bow of humility and thanks. I had no disposition to make myself known, for I felt that I had nothing to boast of. The pains he had taken and the pains he had inflicted had been equally useless. His repeated predictions were fully verified, and I felt that little Jack Buckthorne, the idle boy, had grown up to be a very good-for-nothing man.

This is all very comfortless detail; but as I have told you of my follies, it is meet that I show you how for once I was schooled for them.

The most thoughtless of mortals will some time or other have this day of gloom, when he will be compelled to reflect. I felt on this occasion as if I had a kind of penance to perform, and I made a pilgrimage in expiation of my past levity.

Having passed a night at Leamington, I set off by a private path which leads up a hill, through a grove, and across quiet fields, until I came to the small village, or rather hamlet of Lenington. I sought the village church. It is an old low edifice of gray stone on the brow of a small hill, looking over fertile fields to where the proud towers of Warwick Castle lifted themselves against the distant horizon. A part of the church-yard is shaded by large trees. Under one of these my mother lay buried. You have, no doubt, thought me a light, heartless being. I thought myself so—but there are moments of adversity which let us into some feelings of our nature, to which we might otherwise remain perpetual strangers.

I sought my mother's grave. The weeds were already matted over it, and the tombstone was half hid among nettles. I cleared them away and they stung my hands; but I was heedless of the pain, for my heart ached too severely. I sat down on the grave, and read over and over again the epitaph on the stone. It was simple, but it was true. I had written it myself. I had tried to write a poetical epitaph, but in vain; my feelings refused to utter themselves in rhyme. My heart had gradually been filling during my lonely wanderings; it was now charged to the brim and overflowed. I sank upon the grave and buried my face in the tall grass and wept like a child. Yes, I wept in manhood upon the grave, as I had in infancy upon the bosom of my mother. Alas! how little do we appreciate a mother's tenderness while living! How heedless are we in youth, of all her anxieties and kindness. But when she is dead and gone; when the cares and coldness of the world come withering to our hearts; when we find how hard it is to find true sympathy, how few love us for ourselves, how few will befriend us in our misfortunes; then it is we think of the mother we have lost. It is true I had always loved my mother, even in my most heedless days; but I felt how inconsiderate and ineffectual had been my love. My heart melted as I retraced the days of infancy, when I was led by a mother's hand and rocked to sleep in a mother's arms, and was without care or sorrow. "Oh, my mother!" exclaimed I, burying my face again in the grass of the grave—"Oh, that I were once more by your side; sleeping, never to wake again, on the cares and troubles of this world!"

I am not naturally of a morbid temperament, and the violence of my emotion gradually exhausted itself. It was a hearty, honest, natural discharge of griefs which had been slowly accumulating, and gave me wonderful relief. I rose from the grave as if I had been offering up a sacrifice, and I felt as if that sacrifice had been accepted.

I sat down again on the grass, and plucked, one by one, the weeds from her grave; the tears trickled more slowly down my cheeks, and ceased to be bitter. It was a comfort to think that she had died before sorrow and poverty came upon her child, and that all his great expectations were blasted.

I leaned my cheek upon my hand and looked upon the landscape. Its quiet beauty soothed me. The whistle of a peasant from an adjoining field came cheerily to my ear. I seemed to respire hope and comfort with the free air that whispered through the leaves and played lightly with my hair, and dried the tears upon my cheek. A lark, rising from the field before me, and leaving, as it were, a stream of song behind him as he rose, lifted my fancy with him. He hovered in the air just above the place where the towers of Warwick Castle marked the horizon; and seemed as if fluttering with delight at his own melody. "Surely," thought I, "if there were such a thing as transmigration of souls, this might be taken for some poet, let loose from earth, but still revelling in song, and carolling about fair fields and lordly towns."

At this moment the long forgotten feeling of poetry rose within me. A Thought sprung at once into my mind: "I will become an author," said I. "I have hitherto indulged in poetry as a pleasure, and it has brought me nothing but pain. Let me try what it will do, when I cultivate it with devotion as a pursuit."

The resolution, thus suddenly aroused within me, heaved a load from off my heart. I felt a confidence in it from the very place where it was formed. It seemed as though my mother's spirit whispered it to me from her grave. "I will henceforth," said I, "endeavor to be all that she fondly imagined me. I will endeavor to act as if she were witness of my actions. I will endeavor to acquit myself in such manner, that when I revisit her grave there may, at least, be no compunctious bitterness in my tears."

I bowed down and kissed the turf in solemn attestation of my vow. I plucked some primroses that were growing there and laid them next my heart. I left the church-yard with my spirits once more lifted up, and set out a third time for London, in the character of an author.

Here my companion made a pause, and I waited in anxious suspense; hoping to have a whole volume of literary life unfolded to me. He seemed, however, to have sunk into a fit of pensive musing; and when after some time I gently roused him by a question or two as to his literary career. "No," said he smiling, "over that part of my story I wish to leave a cloud. Let the mysteries of the craft rest sacred for me. Let those who have never adventured into the republic of letters, still look upon it as a fairy land. Let them suppose the author the very being they picture him from his works; I am not the man to mar their illusion. I am not the man to hint, while one is admiring the silken web of Persia, that it has been spun from the entrails of a miserable worm."

"Well," said I, "if you will tell me nothing of your literary history, let me know at least if you have had any farther intelligence from Doubting Castle."

"Willingly," replied he, "though I have but little to communicate."

The Booby Squire

A long time elapsed, said Buckthorne, without my receiving any accounts of my cousin and his estate. Indeed, I felt so much soreness on the subject, that I wished, if possible, to shut it from my thoughts. At length chance took me into that part of the country, and I could not refrain from making some inquiries.

I learnt that my cousin had grown up ignorant, self-willed, and clownish. His ignorance and clownishness had prevented his mingling with the neighboring gentry. In spite of his great fortune he had been unsuccessful in an attempt to gain the hand of the daughter of the parson, and had at length shrunk into the limits of such society as a mere man of wealth can gather in a country neighborhood.

He kept horses and hounds and a roaring table, at which were collected the loose livers of the country round, and the shabby gentlemen of a village in the vicinity. When he could get no other company he would smoke and drink with his own servants, who in their turns fleeced and despised him. Still, with all this apparent prodigality, he had a leaven of the old man in him, which showed that he was his true-born son. He lived far within his income, was vulgar in his expenses, and penurious on many points on which a gentleman would be extravagant. His house servants were obliged occasionally to work on the estate, and part of the pleasure grounds were ploughed up and devoted to husbandry.

His table, though plentiful, was coarse; his liquors strong and bad; and more ale and whiskey were expended in his establishment than generous wine. He was loud and arrogant at his own table, and exacted a rich man's homage from his vulgar and obsequious guests.

As to Iron John, his old grandfather, he had grown impatient of the tight hand his own grandson kept over him, and quarrelled with him soon after he came to the estate. The old man had retired to a neighboring village where he lived on the legacy of his late master, in a small cottage, and was as seldom seen out of it as a rat out of his hole in daylight.

The cub, like Caliban, seemed to have an instinctive attachment to his mother. She resided with him; but, from long habit, she acted more as servant than as mistress of the mansion; for she toiled in all the domestic drudgery, and was oftener in the kitchen than the parlor. Such was the information which I collected of my rival cousin, who had so unexpectedly elbowed me out of all my expectations.

I now felt an irresistible hankering to pay a visit to this scene of my boyhood; and to get a peep at the odd kind of life that was passing within the mansion of my maternal ancestors. I determined to do so in disguise. My booby cousin had never seen enough of me to be very familiar with my countenance, and a few years make great difference between youth and manhood. I understood he was a breeder of cattle and proud of his stock. I dressed myself, therefore, as a substantial farmer, and with the assistance of a red scratch that came low down on my forehead, made a complete change in my physiognomy.

It was past three o'clock when I arrived at the gate of the park, and Was admitted by an old woman, who was washing in a dilapidated building which had once been a porter's lodge. I advanced up the remains of a noble avenue, many of the trees of which had been cut down and sold for timber. The grounds were in scarcely better keeping than during my uncle's lifetime. The grass was overgrown with weeds, and the trees wanted pruning and clearing of dead branches. Cattle were grazing about the lawns, and ducks and geese swimming in the fishponds.

The road to the house bore very few traces of carriage wheels, as my cousin received few visitors but such as came on foot or on horseback, and never used a carriage himself. Once, indeed, as I was told, he had had the old family carriage drawn out from among the dust and cobwebs of the coachhouse and furbished up, and had drove, with his mother, to the village church to take formal possession of the family pew; but there was such hooting and laughing after them as they passed through the village, and such giggling and bantering about the church door, that the pageant had never made a reappearance.

As I approached the house, a legion of whelps sallied out barking at me, accompanied by the low howling, rather than barking, of two old worn-out bloodhounds, which I recognized for the ancient life-guards of my uncle. The house had still a neglected, random appearance, though much altered for the better since my last visit. Several of the windows were broken and patched up with boards; and others had been bricked up to save taxes. I observed smoke, however, rising from the chimneys; a phenomenon rarely witnessed in the ancient establishment. On passing that part of the house where the dining-room was situated, I heard the sound of boisterous merriment; where three or four voices were talking at once, and oaths and laughter were horribly mingled.

The uproar of the dogs had brought a servant to the door, a tall, hard-fisted country clown, with a livery coat put over the under-garments of a ploughman. I requested to see the master of the house, but was told he was at dinner with some "gemmen" of the neighborhood. I made known my business and sent in to know if I might talk with the master about his cattle; for I felt a great desire to have a peep at him at his orgies. Word was returned that he was engaged with company, and could not attend to business, but that if I would "step in and take a drink of something, I was heartily welcome." I accordingly entered the hall, where whips and hats of all kinds and shapes were lying on an oaken table, two or three clownish servants were lounging about; everything had a look of confusion and carelessness.

The apartments through which I passed had the same air of departed gentility and sluttish housekeeping. The once rich curtains were faded and dusty; the furniture greased and tarnished. On entering the dining-room I found a number of odd, vulgar-looking, rustic gentlemen seated round a table, on which were bottles, decanters, tankards, pipes, and tobacco. Several dogs were lying about the room, or sitting and watching their masters, and one was gnawing a bone under a side-table.

The master of the feast sat at the head of the board. He was greatly altered. He had grown thick-set and rather gummy, with a fiery, foxy head of hair. There was a singular mixture of foolishness, arrogance, and conceit in his countenance. He was dressed in a vulgarly fine style, with leather breeches, a red waistcoat, and green coat, and was evidently, like his guests, a little flushed with drinking. The whole company stared at me with a whimsical muggy look, like men whose senses were a little obfuscated by beer rather than wine.

My cousin, (God forgive me! the appellation sticks in my throat,) my cousin invited me with awkward civility, or, as he intended it, condescension, to sit to the table and drink. We talked, as usual, about the weather, the crops, politics, and hard times. My cousin was a loud politician, and evidently accustomed to talk without contradiction at his own table. He was amazingly loyal, and talked of standing by the throne to the last guinea, "as every gentleman of fortune should do." The village exciseman, who was half asleep, could just exclaim, "very true," to every thing he said.

The conversation turned upon cattle; he boasted of his breed, his mode of managing it, and of the general management of his estate. This unluckily drew on a history of the place and of the family. He spoke of my late uncle with the greatest irreverence, which I could easily forgive. He mentioned my name, and my blood began to boil. He described my frequent visits to my uncle when I was a lad, and I found the varlet, even at that time, imp as he was, had known that he was to inherit the estate.

He described the scene of my uncle's death, and the opening of the will, with a degree of coarse humor that I had not expected from him, and, vexed as I was, I could not help joining in the laugh, for I have always relished a joke, even though made at my own expense. He went on to speak of my various pursuits; my strolling freak, and that somewhat nettled me. At length he talked of my parents. He ridiculed my father: I stomached even that, though with great difficulty. He mentioned my mother with a sneer—and in an instant he lay sprawling at my feet.

Here a scene of tumult succeeded. The table was nearly overturned. Bottles, glasses, and tankards, rolled crashing and clattering about the floor. The company seized hold of both of us to keep us from doing farther mischief. I struggled to get loose, for I was boiling with fury. My cousin defied me to strip and fight him on the lawn. I agreed; for I felt the strength of a giant in me, and I longed to pummel him soundly.

Away then we were borne. A ring was formed. I had a second assigned me in true boxing style. My cousin, as he advanced to fight, said something about his generosity in showing me such fair play, when I had made such an unprovoked attack upon him at his own table.

"Stop there!" cried I, in a rage—"unprovoked!—know that I am John Buckthorne, and you have insulted the memory of my mother."

The lout was suddenly struck by what I said. He drew back and reflected for a moment.

"Nay, damn it," said he, "that's too much—that's clear another thing. I've a mother myself, and no one shall speak ill of her, bad as she is."

He paused again. Nature seemed to have a rough struggle in his rude bosom.

"Damn it, cousin," cried he, "I'm sorry for what I said. Thou'st served me right in knocking me down, and I like thee the better for it. Here's my hand. Come and live with me, and damme but the best room in the house, and the best horse in the stable, shall be at thy service."

I declare to you I was strongly moved at this instance of nature breaking her way through such a lump of flesh. I forgave the fellow in a moment all his crimes of having been born in wedlock and inheriting my estate. I shook the hand he offered me, to convince him that I bore him no ill will; and then making my way through the gaping crowd of toad-eaters, bade adieu to my uncle's domains forever. This is the last I have seen or heard of my cousin, or of the domestic concerns of Doubting Castle.

The Strolling Manager

As I was walking one morning with Buckthorne, near one of the Principal theaters, he directed my attention to a group of those equivocal beings that may often be seen hovering about the stage-doors of theaters. They were marvellously ill-favored in their attire, their coats buttoned up to their chins; yet they wore their hats smartly on one side, and had a certain knowing, dirty-gentlemanlike air, which is common to the subalterns of the drama. Buckthorne knew them well by early experience.

These, said he, are the ghosts of departed kings and heroes; fellows who sway sceptres and truncheons; command kingdoms and armies; and after giving way realms and treasures over night, have scarce a shilling to pay for a breakfast in the morning. Yet they have the true vagabond abhorrence of all useful and industrious employment; and they have their pleasures too: one of which is to lounge in this way in the sunshine, at the stage-door, during rehearsals, and make hackneyed theatrical jokes on all passers-by.

Nothing is more traditional and legitimate than the stage. Old scenery, old clothes, old sentiments, old ranting, and old jokes, are handed down from generation to generation; and will probably continue to be so, until time shall be no more. Every hanger-on of a theater becomes a wag by inheritance, and flourishes about at tap-rooms and six-penny clubs, with the property jokes of the green-room.

While amusing ourselves with reconnoitring this group, we noticed one in particular who appeared to be the oracle. He was a weather-beaten veteran, a little bronzed by time and beer, who had no doubt, grown gray in the parts of robbers, cardinals, Roman senators, and walking noblemen.

"There's something in the set of that hat, and the turn of that physiognomy, that is extremely familiar to me," said Buckthorne. He looked a little closer. "I cannot be mistaken," added he, "that must be my old brother of the truncheon, Flimsey, the tragic hero of the strolling company."

It was he in fact. The poor fellow showed evident signs that times went hard with him; he was so finely and shabbily dressed. His coat was somewhat threadbare, and of the Lord Townly cut; single-breasted, and scarcely capable of meeting in front of his body; which, from long intimacy, had acquired the symmetry and robustness of a beer-barrel. He wore a pair of dingy white stockinet pantaloons, which had much ado to reach his waistcoat; a great quantity of dirty cravat; and a pair of old russet-colored tragedy boots.

When his companions had dispersed, Buckthorne drew him aside and made Himself known to him. The tragic veteran could scarcely recognize him, or believe that he was really his quondam associate "little gentleman Jack." Buckthorne invited him to a neighboring coffee-house to talk over old times; and in the course of a little while we were put in possession of his history in brief.

He had continued to act the heroes in the strolling company for some time after Buckthorne had left it, or rather had been driven from it so abruptly. At length the manager died, and the troop was thrown into confusion. Every one aspired to the crown; every one was for taking the lead; and the manager's widow, although a tragedy queen, and a brimstone to boot, pronounced it utterly impossible to keep any control over such a set of tempestuous rascallions.

Upon this hint I spoke, said Flimsey—I stepped forward, and offered my services in the most effectual way. They were accepted. In a week's time I married the widow and succeeded to the throne. "The funeral baked meats did coldly furnish forth the marriage table," as Hamlet says. But the ghost of my predecessor never haunted me; and I inherited crowns, sceptres, bowls, daggers, and all the stage trappings and trumpery, not omitting the widow, without the least molestation.

I now led a flourishing life of it; for our company was pretty strong And attractive, and as my wife and I took the heavy parts of tragedy, it was a great saving to the treasury. We carried off the palm from all the rival shows at country fairs; and I assure you we have even drawn full houses, and being applauded by the critics at Bartlemy fair itself, though we had Astley's troupe, the Irish giant, and "the death of Nelson" in wax-work to contend against.

I soon began to experience, however, the cares of command. I discovered that there were cabals breaking out in the company, headed by the clown, who you may recollect was a terribly peevish, fractious fellow, and always in ill-humor. I had a great mind to turn him off at once, but I could not do without him, for there was not a droller scoundrel on the stage. His very shape was comic, for he had to turn his back upon the audience and all the ladies were ready to die with laughing. He felt his importance, and took advantage of it. He would keep the audience in a continual roar, and then come behind the scenes and fret and fume and play the very devil. I excused a great deal in him, however, knowing that comic actors are a little prone to this infirmity of temper.

I had another trouble of a nearer and dearer nature to struggle with; which was, the affection of my wife. As ill luck would have it, she took it into her head to be very fond of me, and became intolerably jealous. I could not keep a pretty girl in the company, and hardly dared embrace an ugly one, even when my part required it. I have known her to reduce a fine lady to tatters, "to very rags," as Hamlet says, in an instant, and destroy one of the very best dresses in the wardrobe; merely because she saw me kiss her at the side scenes;—though I give you my honor it was done merely by way of rehearsal.

This was doubly annoying, because I have a natural liking to pretty faces, and wish to have them about me; and because they are indispensable to the success of a company at a fair, where one has to vie with so many rival theatres. But when once a jealous wife gets a freak in her head there's no use in talking of interest or anything else. Egad, sirs, I have more than once trembled when, during a fit of her tantrums, she was playing high tragedy, and flourishing her tin dagger on the stage, lest she should give way to her humor, and stab some fancied rival in good earnest.

I went on better, however, than could be expected, considering the weakness of my flesh and the violence of my rib. I had not a much worse time of it than old Jupiter, whose spouse was continually ferreting out some new intrigue and making the heavens almost too hot to hold him.

At length, as luck would have it, we were performing at a country fair, when I understood the theatre of a neighboring town to be vacant. I had always been desirous to be enrolled in a settled company, and the height of my desire was to get on a par with a brother-in-law, who was manager of a regular theatre, and who had looked down upon me. Here was an opportunity not to be neglected. I concluded an agreement with the proprietors, and in a few days opened the theatre with great eclát.

Behold me now at the summit of my ambition, "the high top-gallant of my joy," as Thomas says. No longer a chieftain of a wandering tribe, but the monarch of a legitimate throne—and entitled to call even the great potentates of Covent Garden and Drury Lane cousin.

You no doubt think my happiness complete. Alas, sir! I was one of the Most uncomfortable dogs living. No one knows, who has not tried, the miseries of a manager; but above all, of a country management—no one can conceive the contentions and quarrels within doors, the oppressions and vexations from without.

I was pestered with the bloods and loungers of a country town, who infested my green-room, and played the mischief among my actresses. But there was no shaking them off. It would have been ruin to affront them; for, though troublesome friends, they would have been dangerous enemies. Then there were the village critics and village amateurs, who were continually tormenting me with advice, and getting into a passion if I would not take it:—especially the village doctor and the village attorney; who had both been to London occasionally, and knew what acting should be.

I had also to manage as arrant a crew of scapegraces as were ever collected together within the walls of a theatre. I had been obliged to combine my original troupe with some of the former troupe of the theatre, who were favorites with the public. Here was a mixture that produced perpetual ferment. They were all the time either fighting or frolicking with each other, and I scarcely knew which mood was least troublesome. If they quarrelled, everything went wrong; and if they were friends, they were continually playing off some confounded prank upon each other, or upon me; for I had unhappily acquired among them the character of an easy, good natured fellow, the worst character that a manager can possess.

Their waggery at times drove me almost crazy; for there is nothing so Vexatious as the hackneyed tricks and hoaxes and pleasantries of a veteran band of theatrical vagabonds. I relished them well enough, it is true, while I was merely one of the company, but as manager I found them detestable. They were incessantly bringing some disgrace upon the theatre by their tavern frolics, and their pranks about the country town. All my lectures upon the importance of keeping up the dignity of the profession, and the respectability of the company were in vain. The villains could not sympathize with the delicate feelings of a man in station. They even trifled with the seriousness of stage business. I have had the whole piece interrupted, and a crowded audience of at least twenty-five pounds kept waiting, because the actors had hid away the breeches of Rosalind, and have known Hamlet stalk solemnly on to deliver his soliloquy, with a dish-clout pinned to his skirts. Such are the baleful consequences of a manager's getting a character for good nature.

I was intolerably annoyed, too, by the great actors who came down *starring*, as it is called, from London. Of all baneful influences, keep me from that of a London star. A first-rate actress going the rounds of the country theatres, is as bad as a blazing comet, whisking about the heavens, and shaking fire, and plagues, and discords from its tail.

The moment one of these "heavenly bodies" appeared on my horizon, I was sure to be in hot water. My theatre was overrun by provincial dandies, copper-washed counterfeits of Bond street loungers; who are always proud to be in the train of an actress from town, and anxious to be thought on exceeding good terms with her. It was really a relief to me when some random young nobleman would come in pursuit of the bait, and awe all this small fry to a distance. I have always felt myself more at ease with a nobleman than with the dandy of a country town.

And then the injuries I suffered in my personal dignity and my managerial authority from the visits of these great London actors. Sir, I was no longer master of myself or my throne. I was hectored and lectured in my own green-room, and made an absolute nincompoop on my own stage. There is no tyrant so absolute and capricious as a London star at a country theatre.

I dreaded the sight of all of them; and yet if I did not engage them, I was sure of having the public clamorous against me. They drew full houses, and appeared to be making my fortune; but they swallowed up all the profits by their insatiable demands. They were absolute tapeworms to my little theatre; the more it took in, the poorer it grew. They were sure to leave me with an exhausted public, empty benches, and a score or two of affronts to settle among the townsfolk, in consequence of misunderstandings about the taking of places.

But the worst thing I had to undergo in my managerial career was patronage. Oh, sir, of all things deliver me from the patronage of the great people of a country town. It was my ruin. You must know that this town, though small, was filled with feuds, and parties, and great folks; being a busy little trading and manufacturing town. The mischief was that their greatness was of a kind not to be settled by reference to the court calendar, or college of heraldry. It was therefore the most quarrelsome kind of greatness in existence. You smile, sir, but let me tell you there are no feuds more furious than the frontier feuds, which take place on these "debatable lands" of gentility. The most violent dispute that I ever knew in high life, was one that occurred at a country town, on a question of precedence between the ladies of a manufacturer of pins and a manufacturer of needles.

At the town where I was situated there were perpetual altercations of the kind. The head manufacturer's lady, for instance, was at daggers drawings with the head shopkeeper's, and both were too rich and had too many friends to be treated lightly. The doctor's and lawyer's ladies held their heads still higher; but they in their turn were kept in check by the wife of a country banker, who kept her own carriage; while a masculine widow of cracked character, and second-hand fashion, who lived in a large house, and was in some way related to nobility, looked down upon them all. She had been exiled from the great world, but here she ruled absolute. To be sure her manners were not over-elegant, nor her fortune over-large; but then, sir, her blood—oh, her blood carried it all hollow, there was no withstanding a woman with such blood in her veins.

After all, she had frequent battles for precedence at balls and assemblies, with some of the sturdy dames of the neighborhood, who stood upon their wealth and their reputations; but then she had two dashing daughters, who dressed as fine as dragons, and had as high blood as their mother, and seconded her in everything. So they carried their point with high heads, and every body hated, abused, and stood in awe of the Fantadlins.

Such was the state of the fashionable world in this self-important little town. Unluckily I was not as well acquainted with its politics as I should have been. I had found myself a stranger and in great perplexities during my first season; I determined, therefore, to put myself under the patronage of some powerful name, and thus to take the field with the prejudices of the public in my favor. I cast round my thoughts for the purpose, and in an evil hour they fell upon Mrs. Fantadlin. No one seemed to me to have a more absolute sway in the world of fashion. I had always noticed that her party slammed the box door the loudest at the theatre; had most beaux attending on them; and talked and laughed loudest during the performance; and then the Miss Fantadlins wore always more feathers and flowers than any other ladies; and used quizzing glasses incessantly. The first evening of my theatre's reopening, therefore, was announced in flaring capitals on the play bills, "under the patronage of the Honorable Mrs. Fantadlin,"

Sir, the whole community flew to arms! The banker's wife felt her Dignity grievously insulted at not having the preference; her husband being high bailiff, and the richest man in the place. She immediately issued invitations for a large party, for the night of the performance, and asked many a lady to it whom she never had noticed before. The fashionable world had long groaned under the tyranny of the Fantadlins, and were glad to make a common cause against this new instance of assumption.—Presume to patronize the theatre! insufferable! Those, too, who had never before been noticed by the banker's lady, were ready to enlist in any quarrel, for the honor of her acquaintance. All minor feuds were therefore forgotten. The doctor's lady and the lawyer's lady met together; and the manufacturer's lady and the shopkeeper's lady kissed each other, and all, headed by the banker's lady, voted the theatre a *bore*, and determined to encourage nothing but the Indian Jugglers, and Mr. Walker's Eidonianeon.

Alas for poor Pillgarlick! I little knew the mischief that was brewing against me. My box book remained blank. The evening arrived, but no audience. The music struck up to a tolerable pit and gallery, but no fashionables! I peeped anxiously from behind the curtain, but the time passed away; the play was retarded until pit and gallery became furious; and I had to raise the curtain, and play my greatest part in tragedy to "a beggarly account of empty boxes."

It is true the Fantadlins came late, as was their custom, and entered like a tempest, with a flutter of feathers and red shawls; but they were evidently disconcerted at finding they had no one to admire and envy them, and were enraged at this glaring defection of their fashionable followers. All the beau-monde were engaged at the banker's lady's rout. They remained for some time in solitary and uncomfortable state, and though they had the theatre almost to themselves, yet, for the first time, they talked in whispers. They left the house at the end of the first piece, and I never saw them afterwards.

Such was the rock on which I split. I never got over the patronage of the Fantadlin family. It became the vogue to abuse the theatre and declare the performers shocking. An equestrian troupe opened a circus in the town about the same time, and rose on my ruins. My house was deserted; my actors grew discontented because they were ill paid; my door became a hammering-place for every bailiff in the county; and my wife became more and more shrewish and tormenting, the more I wanted comfort.

The establishment now became a scene of confusion and peculation. I Was considered a ruined man, and of course fair game for every one to pluck at, as every one plunders a sinking ship. Day after day some of the troupe deserted, and like deserting soldiers, carried off their arms and accoutrements with them. In this manner my wardrobe took legs and walked away; my finery strolled all over the country; my swords and daggers glittered in every barn; until at last my tailor made "one fell swoop," and carried off three dress coats, half a dozen doublets, and nineteen pair of flesh-colored pantaloons.

This was the "be all and the end all" of my fortune. I no longer hesitated what to do. Egad, thought I, since stealing is the order of the day, I'll steal too. So I secretly gathered together the jewels of my wardrobe; packed up a hero's dress in a handkerchief, slung it on the end of a tragedy sword, and quietly stole off at dead of night—"the bell then beating one,"—leaving my queen and kingdom to the mercy of my rebellious subjects, and my merciless foes, the bum-bailiffs.

Such, sir, was the "end of all my greatness." I was heartily cured of All passion for governing, and returned once more into the ranks. I had for some time the usual run of an actor's life. I played in various country theatres, at fairs, and in barns; sometimes hard pushed; sometimes flush, until on one occasion I came within an ace of making my fortune, and becoming one of the wonders of the age.

I was playing the part of Richard the Third in a country barn, and Absolutely "out-Heroding Herod." An agent of one of the great London theatres was present. He was on the lookout for something that might be got up as a prodigy. The theatre, it seems, was in desperate condition—nothing but a miracle could save it. He pitched upon me for that miracle. I had a remarkable bluster in my style, and swagger in my gait, and having taken to drink a little during my troubles, my voice was somewhat cracked; so that it seemed like two voices run into one. The thought struck the agent to bring me out as a theatrical wonder; as the restorer of natural and legitimate acting; as the only one who could understand and act Shakespeare rightly. He waited upon me the next morning, and opened his plan. I shrunk from it with becoming modesty; for well as I thought of myself, I felt myself unworthy of such praise.

"'Sblood, man!" said he, "no praise at all. You don't imagine that I think you all this. I only want the public to think so. Nothing so easy as gulling the public if you only set up a prodigy. You need not try to act well, you must only act furiously. No matter what you do, or how you act, so that it be but odd and strange. We will have all the pit packed, and the newspapers hired. Whatever you do different from famous actors, it shall be insisted that you are right and they were wrong. If you rant, it shall be pure passion; if you are vulgar, it shall be a touch of nature. Every one shall be prepared to fall into raptures, and shout and yell, at certain points which you shall make. If you do but escape pelting the first night, your fortune and the fortune of the theatre is made."

I set off for London, therefore, full of new hopes. I was to be the restorer of Shakespeare and nature, and the legitimate drama; my very swagger was to be heroic, and my cracked voice the standard of elocution. Alas, sir! my usual luck attended me. Before I arrived in the metropolis, a rival wonder had appeared. A woman who could dance the slack rope, and run up a cord from the stage to the gallery with fire-works all round her. She was seized on by the management with avidity; she was the saving of the great national theatre for the season. Nothing was talked of but Madame Saqui's fire-works and flame-colored pantaloons; and nature, Shakespeare, the legitimate drama, and poor Pillgarlick were completely left in the lurch.

However, as the manager was in honor bound to provide for me, he kept his word. It had been a turn-up of a die whether I should be Alexander the Great or Alexander the copper-smith; the latter carried it. I could not be put at the head of the drama, so I was put at the tail. In other words, I was enrolled among the number of what are called useful men; who, let me tell you, are the only comfortable actors on the stage. We are safe from hisses and below the hope of applause. We fear not the success of rivals, nor dread the critic's pen. So long as we get the words of our parts, and they are not often many, it is all we care for. We have our own merriment, our own friends, and our own admirers; for every actor has his friends and admirers, from the highest to the lowest. The first-rate actor dines with the noble amateur, and entertains a fashionable table with scraps and songs and theatrical slip-slop. The second-rate actors have their second-rate friends and admirers, with whom they likewise spout tragedy and talk slip-slop; and so down even to us; who have our friends and admirers among spruce clerks and aspiring apprentices, who treat us to a dinner now and then, and enjoy at tenth hand the same scraps and songs and slip-slop that have been served up by our more fortunate brethren at the tables of the great.

I now, for the first time in my theatrical life, knew what true pleasure is. I have known enough of notoriety to pity the poor devils who are called favorites of the public. I would rather be a kitten in the arms of a spoiled child, to be one moment petted and pampered, and the next moment thumped over the head with the spoon. I smile, too, to see our leading actors, fretting themselves with envy and jealousy about a trumpery renown, questionable in its quality and uncertain in its duration. I laugh, too, though of course in my sleeve, at the bustle and importance and trouble and perplexities of our manager, who is harassing himself to death in the hopeless effort to please every body.

I have found among my fellow subalterns two or three quondam managers, who, like myself, have wielded the sceptres of country theatres; and we have many a sly joke together at the expense of the manager and the public. Sometimes, too, we meet like deposed and exiled kings, talk over the events of our respective reigns; moralize over a tankard of ale, and laugh at the humbug of the great and little world; which, I take it, is the very essence of practical philosophy.

Thus end the anecdotes of Buckthorne and his friends. A few mornings after our hearing the history of the ex-manager, he bounced into my room before I was out of bed.

"Give me joy! give me joy!" said he, rubbing his hands with the utmost glee, "my great expectations are realized!"

I stared at him with a look of wonder and inquiry. "My booby cousin is dead!" cried he, "may he rest in peace! He nearly broke his neck in a fall from his horse in a fox-chase. By good luck he lived long enough to make his will. He has made me his heir, partly out of an odd feeling of retributive justice, and partly because, as he says, none of his own family or friends know how to enjoy such an estate. I'm off to the country to take possession. I've done with authorship.—That for the critics!" said he, snapping his fingers. "Come down to Doubting Castle when I get settled, and egad! I'll give you a rouse." So saying he shook me heartily by the hand and bounded off in high spirits.

A long time elapsed before I heard from him again. Indeed, it was but a short time since that I received a letter written in the happiest of moods. He was getting the estate into fine order, everything went to his wishes, and what was more, he was married to Sacharissa: who, it seems, had always entertained an ardent though secret attachment for him, which he fortunately discovered just after coming to his estate.

"I find," said he, "you are a little given to the sin of authorship which I renounce. If the anecdotes I have given you of my story are of any interest, you may make use of them; but come down to Doubting Castle and see how we live, and I'll give you my whole London life over a social glass; and a rattling history it shall be about authors and reviewers."

IF EVER I VISIT DOUBTING Castle, and get the history he promises, the Public shall be sure to hear of it.

PART THIRD

THE ITALIAN BANDITTI

The Inn at Terracina

C rack! crack! crack! crack! crack!

"Here comes the estafette from Naples," said mine host of the inn at Terracina, "bring out the relay."

The estafette came as usual galloping up the road, brandishing over his head a short-handled whip, with a long knotted lash; every smack of which made a report like a pistol. He was a tight square-set young fellow, in the customary uniform—a smart blue coat, ornamented with facings and gold lace, but so short behind as to reach scarcely below his waistband, and cocked up not unlike the tail of a wren. A cocked hat, edged with gold lace; a pair of stiff riding boots; but instead of the usual leathern breeches he had a fragment of a pair of drawers that scarcely furnished an apology for modesty to hide behind.

The estafette galloped up to the door and jumped from his horse.

"A glass of rosolio, a fresh horse, and a pair of breeches," said he, "and quickly—I am behind my time, and must be off."

"San Genaro!" replied the host, "why, where hast thou left thy garment?"

"Among the robbers between this and Fondi."

"What! rob an estafette! I never heard of such folly. What could they hope to get from thee?"

"My leather breeches!" replied the estafette. "They were bran new, and shone like gold, and hit the fancy of the captain."

"Well, these fellows grow worse and worse. To meddle with an estafette! And that merely for the sake of a pair of leather breeches!"

The robbing of a government messenger seemed to strike the host with More astonishment than any other enormity that had taken place on the road; and indeed it was the first time so wanton an outrage had been committed; the robbers generally taking care not to meddle with any thing belonging to government.

The estafette was by this time equipped; for he had not lost an instant in making his preparations while talking. The relay was ready: the rosolio tossed off. He grasped the reins and the stirrup.

"Were there many robbers in the band?" said a handsome, dark young man, stepping forward from the door of the inn.

"As formidable a band as ever I saw," said the estafette, springing into the saddle.

"Are they cruel to travellers?" said a beautiful young Venetian lady, who had been hanging on the gentleman's arm.

"Cruel, signora!" echoed the estafette, giving a glance at the lady as he put spurs to his horse. "*Corpo del Bacco!* they stiletto all the men, and as to the women—"

Crack! crack! crack! crack! crack!—the last words were drowned in the smacking of the whip, and away galloped the estafette along the road to the Pontine marshes.

"Holy Virgin!" exclaimed the fair Venetian, "what will become of us!"

The inn of Terracina stands just outside of the walls of the old town of that name, on the frontiers of the Roman territory. A little, lazy, Italian town, the inhabitants of which, apparently heedless and listless, are said to be little better than the brigands which surround them, and indeed are half of them supposed to be in some way or other connected with the robbers. A vast, rocky height rises perpendicularly above it, with the ruins of the castle of Theodoric the Goth, crowning its summit; before it spreads the wide bosom of the Mediterranean, that sea without flux or reflux. There seems an idle pause in every thing about this place. The port is without a sail, excepting that once in a while a solitary felucca may be seen, disgorging its holy cargo of baccala, the meagre provision for the Quaresima or Lent. The naked watch towers, rising here and there along the coast, speak of pirates and corsairs which hover about these shores: while the low huts, as stations for soldiers, which dot the distant road, as it winds through an olive grove, intimate that in the ascent there is danger for the traveller and facility for the bandit.

Indeed, it is between this town and Fondi that the road to Naples is Mostly infested by banditti. It winds among rocky and solitary places, where the robbers are enabled to see the traveller from a distance from the brows of hills or impending precipices, and to lie in wait for him, at the lonely and difficult passes.

At the time that the estafette made this sudden appearance, almost in *cuerpo*, the audacity of the robbers had risen to an unparalleled height. They had their spies and emissaries in every town, village, and osteria, to give them notice of the quality and movements of travellers. They did not scruple to send messages into the country towns and villas, demanding certain sums of money, or articles of dress and luxury; with menaces of vengeance in case of refusal. They had plundered carriages; carried people of rank and fortune into the mountains and obliged them to write for heavy ransoms; and had committed outrages on females who had fallen in their power.

The police exerted its rigor in vain. The brigands were too numerous And powerful for a weak police. They were countenanced and cherished by several of the villages; and though now and then the limbs of malefactors hung blackening in the trees near which they had committed some atrocity; or their heads stuck upon posts in iron cages made some dreary part of the road still more dreary, still they seemed to strike dismay into no bosom but that of the traveller.

The dark, handsome young man; and the Venetian lady, whom I have mentioned, had arrived early that afternoon in a private carriage, drawn by mules and attended by a single servant. They had been recently married, were spending the honeymoon in travelling through these delicious countries, and were on their way to visit a rich aunt of the young lady's at Naples.

The lady was young, and tender and timid. The stories she had heard along the road had filled her with apprehension, not more for herself than for her husband; for though she had been married almost a month, she still loved him almost to idolatry. When she reached Terracina the rumors of the road had increased to an alarming magnitude; and the sight of two robbers' skulls grinning in iron cages on each side of the old gateway of the town brought her to a pause. Her husband had tried in vain to reassure her. They had lingered all the afternoon at the inn, until it was too late to think of starting that evening, and the parting words of the estafette completed her affright.

"Let us return to Rome," said she, putting her arm within her husband's, and drawing towards him as if for protection—"let us return to Rome and give up this visit to Naples."

"And give up the visit to your aunt, too," said the husband.

"Nay—what is my aunt in comparison with your safety," said she, looking up tenderly in his face.

There was something in her tone and manner that showed she really was Thinking more of her husband's safety at that moment than of her own; and being recently married, and a match of pure affection, too, it is very possible that she was. At least her husband thought so. Indeed, any one who has heard the sweet, musical tone of a Venetian voice, and the melting tenderness of a Venetian phrase, and felt the soft witchery of a Venetian eye, would not wonder at the husband's believing whatever they professed.

He clasped the white hand that had been laid within his, put his arm round her slender waist, and drawing her fondly to his bosom—"This night at least," said he, "we'll pass at Terracina."

Crack! crack! crack! crack! crack!

Another apparition of the road attracted the attention of mine host and his guests. From the road across the Pontine marshes, a carriage drawn by half a dozen horses, came driving at a furious pace—the postillions smacking their whips like mad, as is the case when conscious of the greatness or the munificence of their fare. It was a landaulet, with a servant mounted on the dickey. The compact, highly finished, yet proudly simple construction of the carriage; the quantity of neat, well-arranged trunks and conveniences; the loads of box coats and upper benjamins on the dickey—and the fresh, burly, gruff-looking face at the window, proclaimed at once that it was the equipage of an Englishman.

"Fresh horses to Fondi," said the Englishman, as the landlord came bowing to the carriage door.

"Would not his Excellenza alight and take some refreshment?"

"No—he did not mean to eat until he got to Fondi!"

"But the horses will be some time in getting ready—"

"Ah.—that's always the case—nothing but delay in this cursed country."

"If his Excellenza would only walk into the house—"

"No, no, no!—I tell you no!—I want nothing but horses, and as quick as possible. John! see that the horses are got ready, and don't let us be kept here an hour or two. Tell him if we're delayed over the time, I'll lodge a complaint with the postmaster."

John touched his hat, and set off to obey his master's orders, with the taciturn obedience of an English servant. He was a ruddy, round-faced fellow, with hair cropped close; a short coat, drab breeches, and long gaiters; and appeared to have almost as much contempt as his master for everything around him.

In the mean time the Englishman got out of the carriage and walked up and down before the inn, with his hands in his pockets: taking no notice of the crowd of idlers who were gazing at him and his equipage. He was tall, stout, and well made; dressed with neatness and precision, wore a travelling-cap of the color of gingerbread, and had rather an unhappy expression about the corners of his mouth; partly from not having yet made his dinner, and partly from not having been able to get on at a greater rate than seven miles an hour. Not that he had any other cause for haste than an Englishman's usual hurry to get to the end of a journey; or, to use the regular phrase, "to get on."

After some time the servant returned from the stable with as sour a look as his master.

"Are the horses ready, John?"

"No, sir—I never saw such a place. There's no getting anything done. I think your honor had better step into the house and get something to eat; it will be a long while before we get to Fundy."

"D—n the house—it's a mere trick—I'll not eat anything, just to spite them," said the Englishman, still more crusty at the prospect of being so long without his dinner.

"They say your honor's very wrong," said John, "to set off at this late hour. The road's full of highwaymen."

"Mere tales to get custom."

"The estafette which passed us was stopped by a whole gang," said John, increasing his emphasis with each additional piece of information.

"I don't believe a word of it."

"They robbed him of his breeches," said John, giving at the same time a hitch to his own waist-band.

"All humbug!"

Here the dark, handsome young man stepped forward and addressing the Englishman very politely in broken English, invited him to partake of a repast he was about to make. "Thank'ee," said the Englishman, thrusting his hands deeper into his pockets, and casting a slight side glance of suspicion at the young man, as if he thought from his civility he must have a design upon his purse.

"We shall be most happy if you will do us that favor," said the lady, in her soft Venetian dialect. There was a sweetness in her accents that was most persuasive. The Englishman cast a look upon her countenance; her beauty was still more eloquent. His features instantly relaxed. He made an attempt at a civil bow. "With great pleasure, signora," said he.

In short, the eagerness to "get on" was suddenly slackened; the determination to famish himself as far as Fondi by way of punishing the landlord was abandoned; John chose the best apartment in the inn for his master's reception, and preparations were made to remain there until morning.

The carriage was unpacked of such of its contents as were indispensable for the night. There was the usual parade of trunks and writing-desks, and portfolios, and dressing-boxes, and those other oppressive conveniences which burden a comfortable man. The observant loiterers about the inn door, wrapped up in great dirt-colored cloaks, with only a hawk's eye uncovered, made many remarks to each other on this quantity of luggage that seemed enough for an army. And the domestics of the inn talked with wonder of the splendid dressing-case, with its gold and silver furniture that was spread out on the toilette table, and the bag of gold that chinked as it was taken out of the trunk. The strange "Milor's" wealth, and the treasures he carried about him, were the talk, that evening, over all Terracina.

The Englishman took some time to make his ablutions and arrange his dress for table, and after considerable labor and effort in putting himself at his ease, made his appearance, with stiff white cravat, his clothes free from the least speck of dust, and adjusted with precision. He made a formal bow on entering, which no doubt he meant to be cordial, but which any one else would have considered cool, and took his seat.

The supper, as it was termed by the Italian, or dinner, as the Englishman called it, was now served. Heaven and earth, and the waters under the earth, had been moved to furnish it, for there were birds of the air and beasts of the earth and fish of the sea. The Englishman's servant, too, had turned the kitchen topsy-turvy in his zeal to cook his master a beefsteak; and made his appearance loaded with ketchup, and soy, and Cayenne pepper, and Harvey sauce, and a bottle of port wine, from that warehouse, the carriage, in which his master seemed desirous of carrying England about the world with him. Every thing, however, according to the Englishman, was execrable. The tureen of soup was a black sea, with livers and limbs and fragments of all kinds of birds and beasts, floating like wrecks about it. A meagre winged animal, which my host called a delicate chicken, was too delicate for his stomach, for it had evidently died of a consumption. The macaroni was smoked. The beefsteak was tough buffalo's flesh, and the countenance of mine host confirmed the assertion. Nothing seemed to hit his palate but a dish of stewed eels, of which he ate with great relish, but had nearly refunded them when told that they were vipers, caught among the rocks of Terracina, and esteemed a great delicacy.

In short, the Englishman ate and growled, and ate and growled, like a cat eating in company, pronouncing himself poisoned by every dish, yet eating on in defiance of death and the doctor. The Venetian lady, not accustomed to English travellers, almost repented having persuaded him to the meal; for though very gracious to her, he was so crusty to all the world beside, that she stood in awe of him. There is nothing, however, that conquers John Bull's crustiness sooner than eating, whatever may be the cookery; and nothing brings him into good humor with his company sooner than eating together; the Englishman, therefore, had not half finished his repast and his bottle, before he began to think the Venetian a very tolerable fellow for a foreigner, and his wife almost handsome enough to be an Englishwoman.

In the course of the repast the tales of robbers which harassed the mind of the fair Venetian, were brought into discussion. The landlord and the waiter served up such a number of them as they served up the dishes, that they almost frightened away the poor lady's appetite. Among these was the story of the school of Terracina, still fresh in every mind, where the students were carried up the mountains by the banditti, in hopes of ransom, and one of them massacred, to bring the parents to terms for the others. There was a story also of a gentleman of Rome, who delayed remitting the ransom demanded for his son, detained by the banditti, and received one of his son's ears in a letter with information that the other would be remitted to him soon, if the money were not forthcoming, and that in this way he would receive the boy by instalments until he came to terms.

The fair Venetian shuddered as she heard these tales. The landlord, like a true story-teller, doubled the dose when he saw how it operated. He was just proceeding to relate the misfortunes of a great English lord and his family, when the Englishman, tired of his volubility, testily interrupted him, and pronounced these accounts mere traveller's tales, or the exaggerations of peasants and innkeepers. The landlord was indignant at the doubt levelled at his stories, and the innuendo levelled at his cloth; he cited half a dozen stories still more terrible, to corroborate those he had already told.

"I don't believe a word of them," said the Englishman.

"But the robbers had been tried and executed."

"All a farce!"

"But their heads were stuck up along the road."

"Old skulls accumulated during a century."

The landlord muttered to himself as he went out at the door, "San Genaro, come sono singolari questi Inglesi."

A fresh hubbub outside of the inn announced the arrival of more travellers; and from the variety of voices, or rather clamors, the clattering of horses' hoofs, the rattling of wheels, and the general uproar both within and without, the arrival seemed to be numerous. It was, in fact, the procaccio, and its convoy—a kind of caravan of merchandise, that sets out on stated days, under an escort of soldiery to protect it from the robbers. Travellers avail themselves of the occasion, and many carriages accompany the procaccio. It was a long time before either landlord or waiter returned, being hurried away by the tempest of new custom. When mine host appeared, there was a smile of triumph on his countenance.—"Perhaps," said he, as he cleared away the table, "perhaps the signor has not heard of what has happened."

"What?" said the Englishman, drily.

"Oh, the procaccio has arrived, and has brought accounts of fresh exploits of the robbers, signor."

"Pish!"

"There's more news of the English Milor and his family," said the host, emphatically.

"An English lord.-What English lord?"

"Milor Popkin."

"Lord Popkin? I never heard of such a title!"

"*O Sicuro*—a great nobleman that passed through here lately with his Milady and daughters—a magnifico—one of the grand councillors of London—un almanno."

"Almanno—almanno?—tut! he means alderman."

"Sicuro, aldermanno Popkin, and the principezza Popkin, and the signorina Popkin!" said mine host, triumphantly. He would now have entered into a full detail, but was thwarted by the Englishman, who seemed determined not to credit or indulge him in his stories. An Italian tongue, however, is not easily checked: that of mine host continued to run on with increasing volubility as he conveyed the fragments of the repast out of the room, and the last that could be distinguished of his voice, as it died away along the corridor, was the constant recurrence of the favorite word Popkin—Popkin—Popkin—pop—pop—pop.

The arrival of the procaccio had indeed filled the house with stories as it had with guests. The Englishman and his companions walked out after supper into the great hall, or common room of the inn, which runs through the centre building; a gloomy, dirty-looking apartment, with tables placed in various parts of it, at which some of the travellers were seated in groups, while others strolled about in famished impatience for their evening's meal. As the procaccio was a kind of caravan of travellers, there were people of every class and country, who had come in all kinds of vehicles; and though they kept in some measure in separate parties, yet the being united under one common escort had jumbled them into companionship on the road. Their formidable number and the formidable guard that accompanied them, had prevented any molestation from the banditti; but every carriage had its tale of wonder, and one vied with another in the recital. Not one but had seen groups of robbers peering over the rocks; or their guns peeping out from among the bushes, or had been reconnoitred by some suspicious-looking fellow with scowling eye, who disappeared on seeing the guard.

The fair Venetian listened to all these stories with that eager curiosity with which we seek to pamper any feeling of alarm. Even the Englishman began to feel interested in the subject, and desirous of gaining more correct information than these mere flying reports.

He mingled in one of the groups which appeared to be the most respectable, and which was assembled round a tall, thin person, with long Roman nose, a high forehead, and lively prominent eye, beaming from under a green velvet travelling-cap with gold tassel. He was holding forth with all the fluency of a man who talks well and likes to exert his talent. He was of Rome; a surgeon by profession, a poet by choice, and one who was something of an improvvisatore. He soon gave the Englishman abundance of information respecting the banditti.

"The fact is," said he, "that many of the people in the villages among the mountains are robbers, or rather the robbers find perfect asylum among them. They range over a vast extent of wild impracticable country, along the chain of Apennines, bordering on different states; they know all the difficult passes, the short cuts and strong-holds. They are secure of the good-will of the poor and peaceful inhabitants of those regions, whom they never disturb, and whom they often enrich. Indeed, they are looked upon as a sort of illegitimate heroes among the mountain villages, and some of the frontier towns, where they dispose of their plunder. From these mountains they keep a look-out upon the plains and valleys, and meditate their descents."

"The road to Fondi, which you are about to travel, is one of the places most noted for their exploits. It is overlooked from some distance by little hamlets, perched upon heights. From hence, the brigands, like hawks in their nests, keep on the watch for such travellers as are likely to afford either booty or ransom. The windings of the road enable them to see carriages long before they pass, so that they have time to get to some advantageous lurking-place from whence to pounce upon their prey."

"But why does not the police interfere and root them out?" said the Englishman.

"The police is too weak and the banditti are too strong," replied the improvvisatore. "To root them out would be a more difficult task than you imagine. They are connected and identified with the people of the villages and the peasantry generally; the numerous bands have an understanding with each other, and with people of various conditions in all parts of the country. They know all that is going on; a *gens d'armes* cannot stir without their being aware of it. They have their spies and emissaries in every direction; they lurk about towns, villages, inns,— mingle in every crowd, pervade every place of resort. I should not be surprised," said he, "if some one should be supervising us at this moment."

The fair Venetian looked round fearfully and turned pale.

"One peculiarity of the Italian banditti" continued the improvvisatore, "is that they wear a kind of uniform, or rather costume, which designates their profession. This is probably done to take away from its skulking lawless character, and to give it something of a military air in the eyes of the common people; or perhaps to catch by outward dash and show the fancies of the young men of the villages. These dresses or costumes are often rich and fanciful. Some wear jackets and breeches of bright colors, richly embroidered; broad belts of cloth; or sashes of silk net; broad, high-crowned hats, decorated with feathers of variously-colored ribbands, and silk nets for the hair.

"Many of the robbers are peasants who follow ordinary occupations in the villages for a part of the year, and take to the mountains for the rest. Some only go out for a season, as it were, on a hunting expedition, and then resume the dress and habits of common life. Many of the young men of the villages take to this kind of life occasionally from a mere love of adventure, the wild wandering spirit of youth and the contagion of bad example; but it is remarked that they can never after brook a long continuance in settled life. They get fond of the unbounded freedom and rude license they enjoy; and there is something in this wild mountain life checquered by adventure and peril, that is wonderfully fascinating, independent of the gratification of cupidity by the plunder of the wealthy traveller."

Here the improvvisatore was interrupted by a lively Neapolitan lawyer. "Your mention of the younger robbers," said he, "puts me in mind of an adventure of a learned doctor, a friend of mine, which happened in this very neighborhood."

A wish was of course expressed to hear the adventure of the doctor by all except the improvvisatore, who, being fond of talking and of hearing himself talk, and accustomed moreover to harangue without interruption, looked rather annoyed at being checked when in full career.

The Neapolitan, however, took no notice of his chagrin, but related The following anecdote.

The Adventure of the
Little Antiquary

M y friend the doctor was a thorough antiquary: a little, rusty, musty Old fellow, always groping among ruins. He relished a building as you Englishmen relish a cheese, the more mouldy and crumbling it was, the more it was to his taste. A shell of an old nameless temple, or the cracked walls of a broken-down amphitheatre, would throw him into raptures; and he took more delight in these crusts and cheese parings of antiquity than in the best-conditioned, modern edifice.

He had taken a maggot into his brain at one time to hunt after the Ancient cities of the Pelasgi which are said to exist to this day among the mountains of the Abruzzi; but the condition of which is strangely unknown to the antiquaries. It is said that he had made a great many valuable notes and memorandums on the subject, which he always carried about with him, either for the purpose of frequent reference, or because he feared the precious documents might fall into the hands of brother antiquaries. He had therefore a large pocket behind, in which he carried them, banging against his rear as he walked.

Be this as it may; happening to pass a few days at Terracina, in the course of his researches, he one day mounted the rocky cliffs which overhang the town, to visit the castle of Theodoric. He was groping about these ruins, towards the hour of sunset, buried in his reflections,— his wits no doubt wool-gathering among the Goths and Romans, when he heard footsteps behind him.

He turned and beheld five or six young fellows, of rough, saucy demeanor, clad in a singular manner, half peasant, half huntsman, with fusils in their hands. Their whole appearance and carriage left him in no doubt into what company he had fallen.

The doctor was a feeble little man poor, in look and poorer in purse. He had but little money in his pocket; but he had certain valuables, such as an old silver watch, thick as a turnip, with figures on it large enough for a clock, and a set of seals at the end of a steel chain, that dangled half down to his knees; all which were of precious esteem, being family reliques. He had also a seal ring, a veritable antique intaglio, that covered half his knuckles; but what he most valued was, the precious treatise on the Pelasgian cities, which, he would gladly have given all the money in his pocket to have had safe at the bottom of his trunk in Terracina.

However, he plucked up a stout heart; at least as stout a heart as he could, seeing that he was but a puny little man at the hest of times. So he wished the hunters a "buon giorno." They returned his salutation, giving the old gentleman a sociable slap on the back that made his heart leap into his throat.

They fell into conversation, and walked for some time together among The heights, the doctor wishing them all the while at the bottom of the crater of Vesuvius. At length they came to a small osteria on the mountain, where they proposed to enter and have a cup of wine together. The doctor consented; though he would as soon have been invited to drink hemlock.

One of the gang remained sentinel at the door; the others swaggered into the house; stood their fusils in a corner of the room; and each drawing a pistol or stiletto out of his belt, laid it, with some emphasis, on the table. They now called lustily for wine; drew benches round the table, and hailing the doctor as though he had been a boon companion of long standing, insisted upon his sitting down and making merry. He complied with forced grimace, but with fear and trembling; sitting on the edge of his bench; supping down heartburn with every drop of liquor; eyeing ruefully the black muzzled pistols, and cold, naked stilettos. They pushed the bottle bravely, and plied him vigorously; sang, laughed, told excellent stories of robberies and combats, and the little doctor was fain to laugh at these cut-throat pleasantries, though his heart was dying away at the very bottom of his bosom.

By their own account they were young men from the villages, who had Recently taken up this line of life in the mere wild caprice of youth. They talked of their exploits as a sportsman talks of his amusements. To shoot down a traveller seemed of little more consequence to them than to shoot a hare. They spoke with rapture of the glorious roving life they led; free as birds; here today, gone tomorrow; ranging the forests, climbing the rocks, scouring the valleys; the world their own wherever they could lay hold of it; full purses, merry companions; pretty women.—The little antiquary got fuddled with their talk and their wine, for they did not spare bumpers. He half forgot his fears, his seal ring, and his family watch; even the treatise on the Pelasgian cities which was warming under him, for a time faded from his memory, in the glowing picture which they drew. He declares that he no longer wonders at the prevalence of this robber mania among the mountains; for he felt at the time, that had he been a young man and a strong man, and had there been no danger of the galleys in the background, he should have been half tempted himself to turn bandit.

At length the fearful hour of separating arrived. The doctor was suddenly called to himself and his fears, by seeing the robbers resume their weapons. He now quaked for his valuables, and above all for his antiquarian treatise. He endeavored, however, to look cool and unconcerned; and drew from out of his deep pocket a long, lank, leathern purse, far gone in consumption, at the bottom of which a few coin chinked with the trembling of his hand.

The chief of the party observed this movement; and laying his hand upon the antiquary's shoulder—"Harkee! Signor Dottore!" said he, "we have drank together as friends and comrades, let us part as such. We understand you; we know who and what you are; for we know who every body is that sleeps at Terracina, or that puts foot upon the road. You are a rich man, but you carry all your wealth in your head. We can't get at it, and we should not know what to do with it, if we could. I see you are uneasy about your ring; but don't worry your mind; it is not worth taking; you think it an antique, but it's a counterfeit—a mere sham."

Here the doctor would have put in a word, for his antiquarian pride was touched.

"Nay, nay," continued the other, "we've no time to dispute about it. Value it as you please. Come, you are a brave little old signor—one more cup of wine and we'll pay the reckoning. No compliments—I insist on it. So—now make the best of your way back to Terracina; it's growing late—buono viaggio!—and harkee, take care how you wander among these mountains."

They shouldered their fusils, sprang gaily up the rocks, and the little doctor hobbled back to Terracina, rejoicing that the robbers had let his seal ring, his watch, and his treatise escape unmolested, though rather nettled that they should have pronounced his veritable intaglio a counterfeit.

The improvvisatore had shown many symptoms of impatience during this recital. He saw his theme in danger of being taken out of his hands by a rival story-teller, which to an able talker is always a serious grievance; it was also in danger of being taken away by a Neapolitan, and that was still more vexatious; as the members of the different Italian states have an incessant jealousy of each other in all things, great and small. He took advantage of the first pause of the Neapolitan to catch hold again of the thread of the conversation.

"As I was saying," resumed he, "the prevalence of these banditti is so extensive; their power so combined and interwoven with other ranks of society—"

"For that matter," said the Neapolitan, "I have heard that your government has had some understanding with these gentry, or at least winked at them."

"My government?" said the Roman, impatiently.

"Aye—they say that Cardinal Gonsalvi—"

"Hush!" said the Roman, holding up his finger, and rolling his large eyes about the room.

"Nay-I only repeat what I heard commonly rumored in Rome," replied the other, sturdily. "It was whispered that the Cardinal had been up to the mountain, and had an interview with some of the chiefs. And I have been told that when honest people have been kicking their heels in the Cardinal's anti-chamber, waiting by the hour for admittance, one of these stiletto-looking fellows has elbowed his way through the crowd, and entered without ceremony into the Cardinal's presence.

"I know," replied the Roman, "that there have been such reports; and it is not impossible that government may have made use of these men at particular periods, such as at the time of your abortive revolution, when your carbonari were so busy with their machinations all over the country. The information that men like these could collect, who were familiar, not merely with all the recesses and secret places of the mountains, but also with all the dark and dangerous recesses of society, and knew all that was plotting in the world of mischief; the utility of such instruments in the hands of government was too obvious to be overlooked, and Cardinal Gonsalvi as a politic statesman, may, perhaps, have made use of them; for it is well known the robbers, with all their atrocities, are respectful towards the church, and devout in their religion."

"Religion!—religion?" echoed the Englishman.

"Yes—religion!" repeated the improvvisatore. "Scarce one of them but will cross himself and say his prayers when he hears in his mountain fastness the matin or the *ave maria* bells sounding from the valleys. They will often confess themselves to the village priests, to obtain absolution; and occasionally visit the village churches to pray at some favorite shrine. I recollect an instance in point: I was one evening in the village of Frescati, which lies below the mountains of Abruzzi. The people, as usual in fine evenings in our Italian towns and villages, were standing about in groups in the public square, conversing and amusing themselves. I observed a tall, muscular fellow, wrapped in a great mantle, passing across the square, but skulking along in the dark, as if avoiding notice. The people, too, seemed to draw back as he passed. It was whispered to me that he was a notorious bandit."

"But why was he not immediately seized?" said the Englishman.

"Because it was nobody's business; because nobody wished to incur the vengeance of his comrades; because there were not sufficient *gens d'armes* near to insure security against the numbers of desperadoes he might have at hand; because the *gens d'armes* might not have received particular instructions with respect to him, and might not feel disposed to engage in the hazardous conflict without compulsion. In short, I might give you a thousand reasons, rising out of the state of our government and manners, not one of which after all might appear satisfactory."

The Englishman shrugged his shoulders with an air of contempt.

"I have been told," added the Roman, rather quickly, "that even in your metropolis of London, notorious thieves, well known to the police as such, walk the streets at noon-day, in search of their prey, and are not molested unless caught in the very act of robbery."

The Englishman gave another shrug, but with a different expression.

"Well, sir, I fixed my eye on this daring wolf thus prowling through the fold, and saw him enter a church. I was curious to witness his devotions. You know our spacious, magnificent churches. The one in which he entered was vast and shrouded in the dusk of evening. At the extremity of the long aisles a couple of tapers feebly glimmered on the grand altar. In one of the side chapels was a votive candle placed before the image of a saint. Before this image the robber had prostrated himself. His mantle partly falling off from his shoulders as he knelt, revealed a form of Herculean strength; a stiletto and pistol glittered in his belt, and the light falling on his countenance showed features not unhandsome, but strongly and fiercely charactered. As he prayed he became vehemently agitated; his lips quivered; sighs and murmurs, almost groans burst from him; he beat his breast with violence, then clasped his hands and wrung them convulsively as he extended them towards the image. Never had I seen such a terrific picture of remorse. I felt fearful of being discovered by him, and withdrew. Shortly after I saw him issue from the church wrapped in his mantle; he recrossed the square, and no doubt returned to his mountain with disburthened conscience, ready to incur a fresh arrear of crime."

WASHINGTON IRVING

The conversation was here taken up by two other travellers, recently arrived, Mr. Hobbs and Mr. Dobbs, a linen-draper and a green-grocer, just returning from a tour in Greece and the Holy Land: and who were full of the story of Alderman Popkins. They were astonished that the robbers should dare to molest a man of his importance on 'change; he being an eminent dry-salter of Throgmorton street, and a magistrate to boot.

In fact, the story of the Popkins family was but too true; it was attested by too many present to be for a moment doubted; and from the contradictory and concordant testimony of half a score, all eager to relate it, the company were enabled to make out all the particulars.

The Adventure of the Popkins Family

I t was but a few days before that the carriage of Alderman Popkins had driven up to the inn of Terracina. Those who have seen an English family carriage on the continent, must know the sensation it produces. It is an epitome of England; a little morsel of the old island rolling about the world—every thing so compact, so snug, so finished and fitting. The wheels that roll on patent axles without rattling; the body that hangs so well on its springs, yielding to every motion, yet proof against every shock. The ruddy faces gaping out of the windows; sometimes of a portly old citizen, sometimes of a voluminous dowager, and sometimes of a fine fresh hoyden, just from boarding school. And then the dickeys loaded with well-dressed servants, beef-fed and bluff; looking down from their heights with contempt on all the world around; profoundly ignorant of the country and the people, and devoutly certain that every thing not English must be wrong.

Such was the carriage of Alderman Popkins, as it made its appearance at Terracina. The courier who had preceded it, to order horses, and who was a Neapolitan, had given a magnificent account of the riches and greatness of his master, blundering with all an Italian's splendor of imagination about the alderman's titles and dignities; the host had added his usual share of exaggeration, so that by the time the alderman drove up to the door, he was Milor—Magnifico—Principe—the Lord knows what!

The alderman was advised to take an escort to Fondi and Itri, but he refused. It was as much as a man's life was worth, he said, to stop him on the king's highway; he would complain of it to the ambassador at Naples; he would make a national affair of it. The principezza Popkins, a fresh, motherly dame, seemed perfectly secure in the protection of her husband, so omnipotent a man in the city. The signorini Popkins, two fine bouncing girls, looked to their brother Tom, who had taken lessons in boxing; and as to the dandy himself, he was sure no scaramouch of an Italian robber would dare to meddle with an Englishman. The landlord shrugged his shoulders and turned out the palms of his hands with a true Italian grimace, and the carriage of Milor Popkins rolled on.

They passed through several very suspicious places without any molestation. The Misses Popkins, who were very romantic, and had learnt to draw in water colors, were enchanted with the savage scenery

WASHINGTON IRVING

around; it was so like what they had read in Mrs. Radcliffe's romances, they should like of all things to make sketches. At length, the carriage arrived at a place where the road wound up a long hill. Mrs. Popkins had sunk into a sleep; the young ladies were reading the last works of Sir Walter Scott and Lord Byron, and the dandy was hectoring the postilions from the coach box. The Alderman got out, as he said, to stretch his legs up the hill. It was a long winding ascent, and obliged him every now and then to stop and blow and wipe his forehead with many a pish! and phew! being rather pursy and short of wind. As the carriage, however, was far behind him, and toiling slowly under the weight of so many well-stuffed trunks and well-stuffed travellers, he had plenty of time to walk at leisure.

On a jutting point of rock that overhung the road nearly at the summit of the hill, just where the route began again to descend, he saw a solitary man seated, who appeared to be tending goats. Alderman Popkins was one of your shrewd travellers that always like to be picking up small information along the road, so he thought he'd just scramble up to the honest man, and have a little talk with him by way of learning the news and getting a lesson in Italian. As he drew near to the peasant he did not half like his looks. He was partly reclining on the rocks wrapped in the usual long mantle, which, with his slouched hat, only left a part of a swarthy visage, with a keen black eye, a beetle brow, and a fierce moustache to be seen. He had whistled several times to his dog which was roving about the side of the hill. As the Alderman approached he rose and greeted him. When standing erect he seemed almost gigantic, at least in the eyes of Alderman Popkins; who, however, being a short man, might be deceived.

The latter would gladly now have been back in the carriage, or even on 'change in London, for he was by no means well pleased with his company. However, he determined to put the best face on matters, and was beginning a conversation about the state of the weather, the baddishness of the crops, and the price of goats in that part of the country, when he heard a violent screaming. He ran to the edge of the rock, and, looking over, saw away down the road his carriage surrounded by robbers. One held down the fat footman, another had the dandy by his starched cravat, with a pistol to his head; one was rummaging a portmanteau, another rummaging the principezza's pockets, while the two Misses Popkins were screaming from each window of the carriage, and their waiting maid squalling from the dickey.

Alderman Popkins felt all the fury of the parent and the magistrate Roused within him. He grasped his cane and was on the point of scrambling down the rocks, either to assault the robbers or to read the riot act, when he was suddenly grasped by the arm. It was by his friend the goatherd, whose cloak, falling partly off, discovered a belt stuck full of pistols and stilettos. In short, he found himself in the clutches of the captain of the band, who had stationed himself on the rock to look out for travellers and to give notice to his men.

A sad ransacking took place. Trunks were turned inside out, and all the finery and the frippery of the Popkins family scattered about the road. Such a chaos of Venice beads and Roman mosaics; and Paris bonnets of the young ladies, mingled with the alderman's night-caps and lamb's wool stockings, and the dandy's hair-brushes, stays, and starched cravats.

The gentlemen were eased of their purses and their watches; the ladies of their jewels, and the whole party were on the point of being carried up into the mountain, when fortunately the appearance of soldiery at a distance obliged the robbers to make off with the spoils they had secured, and leave the Popkins family to gather together the remnants of their effects, and make the best of their way to Fondi.

When safe arrived, the alderman made a terrible blustering at the inn; threatened to complain to the ambassador at Naples, and was ready to shake his cane at the whole country. The dandy had many stories to tell of his scuffles with the brigands, who overpowered him merely by numbers. As to the Misses Popkins, they were quite delighted with the adventure, and were occupied the whole evening in writing it in their journals. They declared the captain of the band to be a most romantic-looking man; they dared to say some unfortunate lover, or exiled nobleman: and several of the band to be very handsome young men—"quite picturesque!"

"In verity," said mine host of Terracina, "they say the captain of the band is *un galant uomo*."

"A gallant man!" said the Englishman. "I'd have your gallant man hang'd like a dog!"

"To dare to meddle with Englishmen!" said Mr. Hobbs.

"And such a family as the Popkinses!" said Mr. Dobbs.

"They ought to come upon the country for damages!" said Mr. Hobbs.

"Our ambassador should make a complaint to the government of Naples," said Mr. Dobbs.

"They should be requested to drive these rascals out of the country," said Hobbs.

"If they did not, we should declare war against them!" said Dobbs.

The Englishman was a little wearied by this story, and by the ultra zeal of his countrymen, and was glad when a summons to their supper relieved him from a crowd of travellers. He walked out with his Venetian friends and a young Frenchman of an interesting demeanor, who had become sociable with them in the course of the conversation. They directed their steps toward the sea, which was lit up by the rising moon. The Venetian, out of politeness, left his beautiful wife to be escorted by the Englishman. The latter, however, either from shyness or reserve, did not avail himself of the civility, but walked on without offering his arm. The fair Venetian, with all her devotion to her husband, was a little nettled at a want of gallantry to which her charms had rendered her unaccustomed, and took the proffered arm of the Frenchman with a pretty air of pique, which, however, was entirely lost upon the phlegmatic delinquent.

Not far distant from the inn they came to where there was a body of soldiers on the beach, encircling and guarding a number of galley slaves, who were permitted to refresh themselves in the evening breeze, and to sport and roll upon the sand.

"It was difficult," the Frenchman observed, "to conceive a more frightful mass of crime than was here collected. The parricide, the fratricide, the infanticide, who had first fled from justice and turned mountain bandit, and then, by betraying his brother desperadoes, had bought a commutation of punishment, and the privilege of wallowing on the shore for an hour a day, with this wretched crew of miscreants!"

The remark of the Frenchman had a strong effect upon the company, particularly upon the Venetian lady, who shuddered as she cast a timid look at this horde of wretches at their evening relaxation. "They seemed," she said, "like so many serpents, wreathing and twisting together."

The Frenchman now adverted to the stories they had been listening to at the inn, adding, that if they had any further curiosity on the subject, he could recount an adventure which happened to himself among the robbers and which might give them some idea of the habits and manners of those beings. There was an air of modesty and frankness about the Frenchman which had gained the good-will of the whole party, not even excepting the Englishman. They all gladly accepted his proposition; and as they strolled slowly up and down the seashore, he related the following adventure.

The Painter's Adventure

I am an historical painter by profession, and resided for some time in the family of a foreign prince, at his villa, about fifteen miles from Rome, among some of the most interesting scenery of Italy. It is situated on the heights of ancient Tusculum. In its neighborhood are the ruins of the villas of Cicero, Sulla, Lucullus, Rufinus, and other illustrious Romans, who sought refuge here occasionally, from their toils, in the bosom of a soft and luxurious repose. From the midst of delightful bowers, refreshed by the pure mountain breeze, the eye looks over a romantic landscape full of poetical and historical associations. The Albanian mountains, Tivoli, once the favorite residence of Horace and Maecenas; the vast deserted Campagna with the Tiber running through it, and St. Peter's dome swelling in the midst, the monument—as it were, over the grave of ancient Rome.

I assisted the prince in the researches he was making among the classic ruins of his vicinity. His exertions were highly successful. Many wrecks of admirable statues and fragments of exquisite sculpture were dug up; monuments of the taste and magnificence that reigned in the ancient Tusculan abodes. He had studded his villa and its grounds with statues, relievos, vases, and sarcophagi; thus retrieved from the bosom of the earth.

The mode of life pursued at the villa was delightfully serene, diversified by interesting occupations and elegant leisure. Every one passed the day according to his pleasure or occupation; and we all assembled in a cheerful dinner party at sunset. It was on the fourth of November, a beautiful serene day, that we had assembled in the saloon at the sound of the first dinner-bell. The family were surprised at the absence of the prince's confessor. They waited for him in vain, and at length placed themselves at table. They first attributed his absence to his having prolonged his customary walk; and the first part of the dinner passed without any uneasiness. When the dessert was served, however, without his making his appearance, they began to feel anxious. They feared he might have been taken ill in some alley of the woods; or, that he might have fallen into the hands of robbers. At the interval of a small valley rose the mountains of the Abruzzi, the strong-hold of banditti. Indeed, the neighborhood had, for some time, been infested by them; and Barbone, a notorious bandit chief, had often been met prowling about the solitudes of Tusculum. The daring enterprises of these ruffians were well known; the objects of their cupidity or vengeance were insecure even in palaces. As yet they had respected the possessions of the prince; but the idea of such dangerous spirits hovering about the neighbourhood was sufficient to occasion alarm.

The fears of the company increased as evening closed in. The prince ordered out forest guards, and domestics with flambeaux to search for the confessor. They had not departed long, when a slight noise was heard in the corridor of the ground floor. The family were dining on the first floor, and the remaining domestics were occupied in attendance. There was no one on the ground floor at this moment but the house keeper, the laundress, and three field laborers, who were resting themselves, and conversing with the women.

I heard the noise from below, and presuming it to be occasioned by the return of the absentee, I left the table, and hastened down stairs, eager to gain intelligence that might relieve the anxiety of the prince and princess. I had scarcely reached the last step, when I beheld before me a man dressed as a bandit; a carbine in his hand, and a stiletto and pistols in his belt. His countenance had a mingled expression of ferocity and trepidation. He sprang upon me, and exclaimed exultingly, "Ecco il principe!"

I saw at once into what hands I had fallen, but endeavored to summon up coolness and presence of mind. A glance towards the lower end of the corridor showed me several ruffians, clothed and armed in the same manner with the one who had seized me. They were guarding the two females and the field laborers. The robber, who held me firmly by the collar, demanded repeatedly whether or not I were the prince. His object evidently was to carry off the prince, and extort an immense ransom. He was enraged at receiving none but vague replies; for I felt the importance of misleading him.

A sudden thought struck me how I might extricate myself from his clutches. I was unarmed, it is true, but I was vigorous. His companions were at a distance. By a sudden exertion I might wrest myself from him and spring up the staircase, whither he would not dare to follow me singly. The idea was put in execution as soon as conceived. The ruffian's throat was bare: with my right hand I seized him by it, just between the mastoides; with my left hand I grasped the arm which held the carbine. The suddenness of my attack took him completely unawares; and the strangling nature of my grasp paralyzed him. He choked and faltered.

I felt his hand relaxing its hold, and was on the point of jerking myself away and darting up the staircase before he could recover himself, when I was suddenly seized by some one from behind.

I had to let go my grasp. The bandit, once more released, fell upon me with fury, and gave me several blows with the butt end of his carbine, one of which wounded me severely in the forehead, and covered me with blood. He took advantage of my being stunned to rifle me of my watch and whatever valuables I had about my person.

When I recovered from the effects of the blow, I heard the voice of the chief of the banditti, who exclaimed "Quello e il principe, siamo contente, audiamo!" (It is the prince, enough, let us be off.) The band immediately closed round me and dragged me out of the palace, bearing off the three laborers likewise.

I had no hat on, and the blood was flowing from my wound; I managed to staunch it, however, with my pocket-handkerchief, which I bound round my forehead. The captain of the band conducted me in triumph, supposing me to be the prince. We had gone some distance before he learnt his mistake from one of the laborers. His rage was terrible. It was too late to return to the villa and endeavor to retrieve his error, for by this time the alarm must have been given, and every one in arms. He darted at me a furious look; swore I had deceived him, and caused him to miss his fortune; and told me to prepare for death. The rest of the robbers were equally furious. I saw their hands upon their poinards; and I knew that death was seldom an empty menace with these ruffians.

The laborers saw the peril into which their information had betrayed me, and eagerly assured the captain that I was a man for whom the prince would pay a great ransom. This produced a pause. For my part, I cannot say that I had been much dismayed by their menaces. I mean not to make any boast of courage; but I have been so schooled to hardship during the late revolutions, and have beheld death around me in so many perilous and disastrous scenes that I have become, in some measure callous to its terrors. The frequent hazard of life makes a man at length as reckless of it as a gambler of his money. To their threat of death, I replied: "That the sooner it was executed, the better." This reply seemed to astonish the captain, and the prospect of ransom held out by the laborers, had, no doubt, a still greater effect on him. He considered for a moment; assumed a calmer manner, and made a sign to his companions, who had remained waiting for my death warrant. "Forward," said he, "we will see about this matter by and bye."

We descended rapidly towards the road of la Molara, which leads to Rocca Priori. In the midst of this road is a solitary inn. The captain ordered the troop to halt at the distance of a pistol shot from it; and enjoined profound silence. He then approached the threshold alone with noiseless steps. He examined the outside of the door very narrowly, and then returning precipitately, made a sign for the troop to continue its march in silence. It has since been ascertained that this was one of those infamous inns which are the secret resorts of banditti. The innkeeper had an understanding with the captain, as he most probably had with the chiefs of the different bands. When any of the patroles and gens d'armes were quartered at his house, the brigands were warned of it by a preconcerted signal on the door; when there was no such signal, they might enter with safety and be sure of welcome. Many an isolated inn among the lonely parts of the Roman territories, and especially on the skirts of the mountains, have the same dangerous and suspicious character. They are places where the banditti gather information; where they concert their plans, and where the unwary traveller, remote from hearing or assistance, is sometimes betrayed to the stiletto of the midnight murderer.

After pursuing our road a little farther, we struck off towards the Woody mountains which envelope Rocca Priori. Our march was long and painful, with many circuits and windings; at length we clambered a steep ascent, covered with a thick forest, and when we had reached the centre, I was told to seat myself on the earth. No sooner had I done so, than at a sign from their chief, the robbers surrounded me, and spreading their great cloaks from one to the other, formed a kind of pavilion of mantles, to which their bodies might be said to seem as columns. The captain then struck a light, and a flambeau was lit immediately. The mantles were extended to prevent the light of the flambeau from being seen through the forest. Anxious as was my situation, I could not look round upon this screen of dusky drapery, relieved by the bright colors of the robbers' under-dresses, the gleaming of their weapons, and the variety of strong-marked countenances, lit up by the flambeau, without admiring the picturesque effect of the scene. It was quite theatrical.

The captain now held an ink-horn, and giving me pen and paper, ordered me to write what he should dictate. I obeyed. It was a demand, couched in the style of robber eloquence, "that the prince should send three thousand dollars for my ransom, or that my death should be the consequence of a refusal."

I knew enough of the desperate character of these beings to feel assured this was not an idle menace. Their only mode of insuring attention to their demands, is to make the infliction of the penalty inevitable. I saw at once, however, that the demand was preposterous, and made in improper language.

I told the captain so, and assured him, that so extravagant a sum would never be granted; that I was neither friend or relative of the prince, but a mere artist, employed to execute certain paintings. That I had nothing to offer as a ransom but the price of my labors; if this were not sufficient, my life was at their disposal: it was a thing on which I sat but little value.

I was the more hardy in my reply, because I saw that coolness and hardihood had an effect upon the robbers. It is true, as I finished speaking the captain laid his hand upon his stiletto, but he restrained himself, and snatching the letter, folded it, and ordered me, in a peremptory tone, to address it to the prince. He then despatched one of the laborers with it to Tusculum, who promised to return with all possible speed.

The robbers now prepared themselves for sleep, and I was told that I might do the same. They spread their great cloaks on the ground, and lay down around me. One was stationed at a little distance to keep watch, and was relieved every two hours. The strangeness and wildness of this mountain bivouac, among lawless beings whose hands seemed ever ready to grasp the stiletto, and with whom life was so trivial and insecure, was enough to banish repose. The coldness of the earth and of the dew, however, had a still greater effect than mental causes in disturbing my rest. The airs wafted to these mountains from the distant Mediterranean diffused a great chilliness as the night advanced. An expedient suggested itself. I called one of my fellow prisoners, the laborers, and made him lie down beside me. Whenever one of my limbs became chilled I approached it to the robust limb of my neighbor, and borrowed some of his warmth. In this way I was able to obtain a little sleep.

Day at length dawned, and I was roused from my slumber by the voice of the chieftain. He desired me to rise and follow him. I obeyed. On considering his physiognomy attentively, it appeared a little softened. He even assisted me in scrambling up the steep forest among rocks and brambles. Habit had made him a vigorous mountaineer; but I found it excessively toilsome to climb those rugged heights. We arrived at length at the summit of the mountain.

Here it was that I felt all the enthusiasm of my art suddenly awakened; and I forgot, in an instant, all perils and fatigues at this magnificent view of the sunrise in the midst of the mountains of Abruzzi. It was on these heights that Hannibal first pitched his camp, and pointed out Rome to his followers. The eye embraces a vast extent of country. The minor height of Tusculum, with its villas, and its sacred ruins, lie below; the Sabine hills and the Albanian mountains stretch on either hand, and beyond Tusculum and Frescati spreads out the immense Campagna, with its line of tombs, and here and there a broken aqueduct stretching across it, and the towers and domes of the eternal city in the midst.

Fancy this scene lit up by the glories of a rising sun, and bursting upon my sight, as I looked forth from among the majestic forests of the Abruzzi. Fancy, too, the savage foreground, made still more savage by groups of the banditti, armed and dressed in their wild, picturesque manner, and you will not wonder that the enthusiasm of a painter for a moment overpowered all his other feelings.

The banditti were astonished at my admiration of a scene which familiarity had made so common in their eyes. I took advantage of their halting at this spot, drew forth a quire of drawing-paper, and began to sketch the features of the landscape. The height, on which I was seated, was wild and solitary, separated from the ridge of Tusculum by a valley nearly three miles wide; though the distance appeared less from the purity of the atmosphere. This height was one of the favorite retreats of the banditti, commanding a look-out over the country; while, at the same time, it was covered with forests, and distant from the populous haunts of men.

While I was sketching, my attention was called off for a moment by the cries of birds and the bleatings of sheep. I looked around, but could see nothing of the animals that uttered them. They were repeated, and appeared to come from the summits of the trees. On looking more narrowly, I perceived six of the robbers perched on the tops of oaks, which grew on the breezy crest of the mountain, and commanded an uninterrupted prospect. From hence they were keeping a look-out, like so many vultures; casting their eyes into the depths of the valley below us; communicating; with each other by signs, or holding discourse in sounds, which might be mistaken by the wayfarer for the cries of hawks and crows, or the bleating of the mountain flocks. After they had reconnoitred the neighborhood, and finished their singular discourse, they descended from their airy perch, and returned to their prisoners.

The captain posted three of them at three naked sides of the mountain, while he remained to guard us with what appeared his most trusty companion.

I had my book of sketches in my hand; he requested to see it, and after having run his eye over it, expressed himself convinced of the truth of my assertion, that I was a painter. I thought I saw a gleam of good feeling dawning in him, and determined to avail myself of it. I knew that the worst of men have their good points and their accessible sides, if one would but study them carefully. Indeed, there is a singular mixture in the character of the Italian robber. With reckless ferocity, he often mingles traits of kindness and good humor. He is often not radically bad, but driven to his course of life by some unpremeditated crime, the effect of those sudden bursts of passion to which the Italian temperament is prone. This has compelled him to take to the mountains, or, as it is technically termed among them, "andare in Campagna." He has become a robber by profession; but like a soldier, when not in action, he can lay aside his weapon and his fierceness, and become like other men.

I took occasion from the observations of the captain on my sketchings, to fall into conversation with him. I found him sociable and communicative. By degrees I became completely at my ease with him. I had fancied I perceived about him a degree of self-love, which I determined to make use of. I assumed an air of careless frankness, and told him that, as artist, I pretended to the power of judging of the physiognomy; that I thought I perceived something in his features and demeanor which announced him worthy of higher fortunes. That he was not formed to exercise the profession to which he had abandoned himself; that he had talents and qualities fitted for a nobler sphere of action; that he had but to change his course of life, and in a legitimate career, the same courage and endowments which now made him an object of terror, would ensure him the applause and admiration of society.

I had not mistaken my man. My discourse both touched and excited him. He seized my hand, pressed it, and replied with strong emotion, "You have guessed the truth; you have judged me rightly." He remained for a moment silent; then with a kind of effort he resumed. "I will tell you some particulars of my life, and you will perceive that it was the oppression of others, rather than my own crimes, that drove me to the mountains. I sought to serve my fellow-men, and they have persecuted me from among them." We seated ourselves on the grass, and the robber gave me the following anecdotes of his history.

The Story of the Bandit Chieftain

I am a native of the village of Prossedi. My father was easy enough In circumstances, and we lived peaceably and independently, cultivating our fields. All went on well with us until a new chief of the sbirri was sent to our village to take command of the police. He was an arbitrary fellow, prying into every thing, and practising all sorts of vexations and oppressions in the discharge of his office.

I was at that time eighteen years of age, and had a natural love of justice and good neighborhood. I had also a little education, and knew something of history, so as to be able to judge a little of men and their actions. All this inspired me with hatred for this paltry despot. My own family, also, became the object of his suspicion or dislike, and felt more than once the arbitrary abuse of his power. These things worked together on my mind, and I gasped after vengeance. My character was always ardent and energetic; and acted upon by my love of justice, determined me by one blow to rid the country of the tyrant.

Full of my project I rose one morning before peep of day, and concealing a stiletto under my waistcoat—here you see it!—(and he drew forth a long keen poniard)—I lay in wait for him in the outskirts of the village. I knew all his haunts, and his habit of making his rounds and prowling about like a wolf, in the gray of the morning; at length I met him, and attacked him with fury. He was armed, but I took him unawares, and was full of youth and vigor. I gave him repeated blows to make sure work, and laid him lifeless at my feet.

When I was satisfied that I had done for him, I returned with all haste to the village, but had the ill-luck to meet two of the sbirri as I entered it. They accosted me and asked if I had seen their chief. I assumed an air of tranquillity, and told them I had not. They continued on their way, and, within a few hours, brought back the dead body to Prossedi. Their suspicions of me being already awakened, I was arrested and thrown into prison. Here I lay several weeks, when the prince, who was Seigneur of Prossedi, directed judicial proceedings against me. I was brought to trial, and a witness was produced who pretended to have seen me not far from the bleeding body, and flying with precipitation, so I was condemned to the galleys for thirty years.

"Curse on such laws," vociferated the bandit, foaming with rage; "curse on such a government, and ten thousand curses on the prince who caused me to be adjudged so rigorously, while so many other Roman princes harbor and protect assassins a thousand times more culpable. What had I done but what was inspired by a love of justice and my country? Why was my act more culpable than that of Brutus, when he sacrificed Caesar to the cause of liberty and justice?"

There was something at once both lofty and ludicrous in the rhapsody of this robber chief, thus associating himself with one of the great names of antiquity. It showed, however, that he had at least the merit of knowing the remarkable facts in the history of his country. He became more calm, and resumed his narrative.

I was conducted to Civita Vecchia in fetters. My heart was burning with rage. I had been married scarce six months to a woman whom I passionately loved, and who was pregnant. My family was in despair. For a long time I made unsuccessful efforts to break my chain. At length I found a morsel of iron which I hid carefully, endeavored with a pointed flint to fashion it into a kind of file. I occupied myself in this work during the night-time, and when it was finished, I made out, after a long time, to sever one of the rings of my chain. My flight was successful.

I wandered for several weeks in the mountains which surround Prossedi, and found means to inform my wife of the place where I was concealed. She came often to see me. I had determined to put myself at the head of an armed band. She endeavored for a long time to dissuade me; but finding my resolution fixed, she at length united in my project of vengeance, and brought me, herself, my poniard.

By her means I communicated with several brave fellows of the Neighboring villages, who I knew to be ready to take to the mountains, and only panting for an opportunity to exercise their daring spirits. We soon formed a combination, procured arms, and we have had ample opportunities of revenging ourselves for the wrongs and injuries which most of us have suffered. Every thing has succeeded with us until now, and had it not been for our blunder in mistaking you for the prince, our fortunes would have been made.

Here the robber concluded his story. He had talked himself into companionship, and assured me he no longer bore me any grudge for the error of which I had been the innocent cause. He even professed a kindness for me, and wished me to remain some time with them. He promised to give me a sight of certain grottos which they occupied beyond Villetri, and whither they resorted during the intervals of their expeditions. He assured me that they led a jovial life there; had plenty of good cheer; slept on beds of moss, and were waited upon by young and beautiful females, whom I might take for models.

I confess I felt my curiosity roused by his descriptions of these grottos and their inhabitants; they realized those scenes in robber-story which I had always looked upon as mere creations of the fancy. I should gladly have accepted his invitation, and paid a visit to those caverns, could I have felt more secure in my company.

I began to find my situation less painful. I had evidently propitiated the good-will of the chieftain, and hoped that he might release me for a moderate ransom. A new alarm, however, awaited me. While the captain was looking out with impatience for the return of the messenger who had been sent to the prince, the sentinel who had been posted on the side of the mountain facing the plain of la Molara, came running towards us with precipitation. "We are betrayed!" exclaimed he. "The police of Frescati are after us. A party of carabiniers have just stopped at the inn below the mountain." Then laying his hand on his stiletto, he swore, with a terrible oath, that if they made the least movement towards the mountains, my life and the lives of my fellow-prisoners should answer for it.

The chieftain resumed all his ferocity of demeanor, and approved of what his companion said; but when the latter had returned to his post, he turned to me with a softened air: "I must act as chief," said he, "and humor my dangerous subalterns. It is a law with us to kill our prisoners rather than suffer them to be rescued; but do not be alarmed. In case we are surprised keep by me; fly with us, and I will consider myself responsible for your life."

There was nothing very consolatory in this arrangement, which would have placed me between two dangers; I scarcely knew, in case of flight, which I should have most to apprehend from, the carbines of the pursuers, or the stilettos of the pursued. I remained silent, however, and endeavored to maintain a look of tranquillity.

For an hour was I kept in this state of peril and anxiety. The robbers, crouching among their leafy coverts, kept an eagle watch upon the carabiniers below, as they loitered about the inn; sometimes lolling about the portal; sometimes disappearing for several minutes, then sallying out, examining their weapons, pointing in different directions and apparently asking questions about the neighborhood; not a movement or gesture was last upon the keen eyes of the brigands. At length we were relieved from our apprehensions. The carabiniers having finished their refreshment, seized their arms, continued along the valley towards the great road, and gradually left the mountain behind them. "I felt almost certain," said the chief, "that they could not be sent after us. They know too well how prisoners have fared in our hands on similar occasions. Our laws in this respect are inflexible, and are necessary for our safety. If we once flinched from them, there would no longer be such thing as a ransom to be procured."

There were no signs yet of the messenger's return. I was preparing to resume my sketching, when the captain drew a quire of paper from his knapsack—"Come," said he, laughing, "you are a painter; take my likeness. The leaves of your portfolio are small; draw it on this." I gladly consented, for it was a study that seldom presents itself to a painter. I recollected that Salvator Rosa in his youth had voluntarily sojourned for a time among the banditti of Calabria, and had filled his mind with the savage scenery and savage associates by which he was surrounded. I seized my pencil with enthusiasm at the thought. I found the captain the most docile of subjects, and after various shifting of positions, I placed him in an attitude to my mind.

Picture to yourself a stern, muscular figure, in fanciful bandit costume, with pistols and poniards in belt, his brawny neck bare, a handkerchief loosely thrown around it, and the two ends in front strung with rings of all kinds, the spoils of travellers; reliques and medals hung on his breast; his hat decorated with various-colored ribbands; his vest and short breeches of bright colors and finely embroidered; his legs in buskins or leggins. Fancy him on a mountain height, among wild rocks and rugged oaks, leaning on his carbine as if meditating some exploit, while far below are beheld villages and villas, the scenes of his maraudings, with the wide Campagna dimly extending in the distance.

The robber was pleased with the sketch, and seemed to admire himself upon paper. I had scarcely finished, when the laborer arrived who had been sent for my ransom. He had reached Tusculum two hours after midnight. He brought me a letter from the prince, who was in bed at the time of his arrival. As I had predicted, he treated the demand as extravagant, but offered five hundred dollars for my ransom. Having no money by him at the moment, he had sent a note for the amount, payable to whomever should conduct me safe and sound to Rome. I presented the note of hand to the chieftain; he received it with a shrug. "Of what use are notes of hand to us?" said he, "who can we send with you to Rome to receive it? We are all marked men, known and described at every gate and military post, and village church-door. No, we must have gold and silver; let the sum be paid in cash and you shall be restored to liberty."

The captain again placed a sheet of paper before me to communicate His determination to the prince. When I had finished the letter and took the sheet from the quire, I found on the opposite side of it the portrait which I had just been tracing. I was about to tear it off and give it to the chief.

"Hold," said he, "let it go to Rome; let them see what kind of looking fellow I am. Perhaps the prince and his friends may form as good an opinion of me from my face as you have done."

This was said sportively, yet it was evident there was vanity lurking at the bottom. Even this wary, distrustful chief of banditti forgot for a moment his usual foresight and precaution in the common wish to be admired. He never reflected what use might be made of this portrait in his pursuit and conviction.

The letter was folded and directed, and the messenger departed again For Tusculum. It was now eleven o'clock in the morning, and as yet we had eaten nothing. In spite of all my anxiety, I began to feel a craving appetite. I was glad, therefore, to hear the captain talk something of eating. He observed that for three days and nights they had been lurking about among rocks and woods, meditating their expedition to Tusculum, during which all their provisions had been exhausted. He should now take measures to procure a supply. Leaving me, therefore, in the charge of his comrade, in whom he appeared to have implicit confidence, he departed, assuring me, that in less than two hours we should make a good dinner. Where it was to come from was an enigma to me, though it was evident these beings had their secret friends and agents throughout the country.

Indeed, the inhabitants of these mountains and of the valleys which they embosom are a rude, half civilized set. The towns and villages among the forests of the Abruzzi, shut up from the rest of the world, are almost like savage dens. It is wonderful that such rude abodes, so little known and visited, should be embosomed in the midst of one of the most travelled and civilized countries of Europe. Among these regions the robber prowls unmolested; not a mountaineer hesitates to give him secret harbor and assistance. The shepherds, however, who tend their flocks among the mountains, are the favorite emissaries of the robbers, when they would send messages down to the valleys either for ransom or supplies. The shepherds of the Abruzzi are as wild as the scenes they frequent. They are clad in a rude garb of black or brown sheep-skin; they have high conical hats, and coarse sandals of cloth bound round their legs with thongs, similar to those worn by the robbers. They carry long staffs, on which as they lean they form picturesque objects in the lonely landscape, and they are followed by their ever-constant companion, the dog. They are a curious, questioning set, glad at any time to relieve the monotony of their solitude by the conversation of the passerby, and the dog will lend an attentive ear, and put on as sagacious and inquisitive a look as his master.

But I am wandering from my story. I was now left alone with one of the robbers, the confidential companion of the chief. He was the youngest and most vigorous of the band, and though his countenance had something of that dissolute fierceness which seems natural to this desperate, lawless mode of life, yet there were traits of manly beauty about it. As an artist I could not but admire it. I had remarked in him an air of abstraction and reverie, and at times a movement of inward suffering and impatience. He now sat on the ground; his elbows on his knees, his head resting between his clenched fists, and his eyes fixed on the earth with an expression of sad and bitter rumination. I had grown familiar with him from repeated conversations, and had found him superior in mind to the rest of the band. I was anxious to seize every opportunity of sounding the feelings of these singular beings. I fancied I read in the countenance of this one traces of self-condemnation and remorse; and the ease with which I had drawn forth the confidence of the chieftain encouraged me to hope the same with his followers.

After a little preliminary conversation, I ventured to ask him if he did not feel regret at having abandoned his family and taken to this dangerous profession. "I feel," replied he, "but one regret, and that will end only with my life;" as he said this he pressed his clenched fists upon his bosom, drew his breath through his set teeth, and added with deep emotion, "I have something within here that stifles me; it is like a burning iron consuming my very heart. I could tell you a miserable story, but not now—another time."—He relapsed into his former position, and sat with his head between his hands, muttering to himself in broken exclamations, and what appeared at times to be curses and maledictions. I saw he was not in a mood to be disturbed, so I left him to himself. In a little time the exhaustion of his feelings, and probably the fatigues he had undergone in this expedition, began to produce drowsiness. He struggled with it for a time, but the warmth and sultriness of mid-day made it irresistible, and he at length stretched himself upon the herbage and fell asleep.

I now beheld a chance of escape within my reach. My guard lay before me at my mercy. His vigorous limbs relaxed by sleep; his bosom open for the blow; his carbine slipped from his nerveless grasp, and lying by his side; his stiletto half out of the pocket in which it was usually carried. But two of his comrades were in sight, and those at a considerable distance, on the edge of the mountain; their backs turned to us, and their attention occupied in keeping a look-out upon the plain. Through a strip of intervening forest, and at the foot of a steep descent, I beheld the village of Rocca Priori. To have secured the carbine of the sleeping brigand, to have seized upon his poniard and have plunged it in his heart, would have been the work of an instant. Should he die without noise, I might dart through the forest and down to Rocca Priori before my flight might be discovered. In case of alarm, I should still have a fair start of the robbers, and a chance of getting beyond the reach of their shot.

Here then was an opportunity for both escape and vengeance; perilous, indeed, but powerfully tempting. Had my situation been more critical I could not have resisted it. I reflected, however, for a moment. The attempt, if successful, would be followed by the sacrifice of my two fellow prisoners, who were sleeping profoundly, and could not be awakened in time to escape. The laborer who had gone after the ransom might also fall a victim to the rage of the robbers, without the money which he brought being saved. Besides, the conduct of the chief towards me made me feel certain of speedy deliverance. These reflections overcame the first powerful impulse, and I calmed the turbulent agitation which it had awakened.

I again took out my materials for drawing, and amused myself with sketching the magnificent prospect. It was now about noon, and every thing seemed sunk into repose, like the bandit that lay sleeping before me. The noon-tide stillness that reigned over these mountains, the vast landscape below, gleaming with distant towns and dotted with various habitations and signs of life, yet all so silent, had a powerful effect upon my mind. The intermediate valleys, too, that lie among mountains have a peculiar air of solitude. Few sounds are heard at mid-day to break the quiet of the scene. Sometimes the whistle of a solitary muleteer, lagging with his lazy animal along the road that winds through the centre of the valley; sometimes the faint piping of a shepherd's reed from the side of the mountain, or sometimes the bell of an ass slowly pacing along, followed by a monk with bare feet and bare shining head, and carrying provisions to the convent.

I had continued to sketch for some time among my sleeping companions, when at length I saw the captain of the band approaching, followed by a peasant leading a mule, on which was a well-filled sack. I at first apprehended that this was some new prey fallen into the hands of the robbers, but the contented look of the peasant soon relieved me, and I was rejoiced to hear that it was our promised repast. The brigands now came running from the three sides of the mountain, having the quick scent of vultures. Every one busied himself in unloading the mule and relieving the sack of its contents.

The first thing that made its appearance was an enormous ham of a color and plumpness that would have inspired the pencil of Teniers. It was followed by a large cheese, a bag of boiled chestnuts, a little barrel of wine, and a quantity of good household bread. Everything was arranged on the grass with a degree of symmetry, and the captain presenting me his knife, requested me to help myself. We all seated ourselves round the viands, and nothing was heard for a time but the sound of vigorous mastication, or the gurgling of the barrel of wine as it revolved briskly about the circle. My long fasting and the mountain air and exercise had given me a keen appetite, and never did repast appear to me more excellent or picturesque.

From time to time one of the band was despatched to keep a look-out upon the plain: no enemy was at hand, and the dinner was undisturbed.

The peasant received nearly twice the value of his provisions, and set off down the mountain highly satisfied with his bargain. I felt invigorated by the hearty meal I had made, and notwithstanding that the wound I had received the evening before was painful, yet I could not but feel extremely interested and gratified by the singular scenes continually presented to me. Every thing seemed pictured about these wild beings and their haunts. Their bivouacs, their groups on guard, their indolent noon-tide repose on the mountain brow, their rude repast on the herbage among rocks and trees, every thing presented a study for a painter. But it was towards the approach of evening that I felt the highest enthusiasm awakened.

The setting sun, declining beyond the vast Campagna, shed its rich yellow beams on the woody summits of the Abruzzi. Several mountains crowned with snow shone brilliantly in the distance, contrasting their brightness with others, which, thrown into shade, assumed deep tints of purple and violet. As the evening advanced, the landscape darkened into a sterner character. The immense solitude around; the wild mountains broken into rocks and precipices, intermingled with vast oak, cork, and chestnuts; and the groups of banditti in the foreground, reminded me of those savage scenes of Salvator Rosa.

To beguile the time the captain proposed to his comrades to spread before me their jewels and cameos, as I must doubtless be a judge of such articles, and able to inform them of their nature. He set the example, the others followed it, and in a few moments I saw the grass before me sparkling with jewels and gems that would have delighted the eyes of an antiquary or a fine lady. Among them were several precious jewels and antique intaglios and cameos of great value, the spoils doubtless of travellers of distinction. I found that they were in the habit of selling their booty in the frontier towns. As these in general were thinly and poorly peopled, and little frequented by travellers, they could offer no market for such valuable articles of taste and luxury. I suggested to them the certainty of their readily obtaining great pieces for these gems among the rich strangers with which Rome was thronged.

The impression made upon their greedy minds was immediately apparent. One of the band, a young man, and the least known, requested permission of the captain to depart the following day in disguise for Rome, for the purpose of traffick; promising on the faith of a bandit (a sacred pledge amongst them) to return in two days to any place he might appoint. The captain consented, and a curious scene took place. The robbers crowded round him eagerly, confiding to him such of their jewels as they wished to dispose of, and giving him instructions what to demand. There was bargaining and exchanging and selling of trinkets among themselves, and I beheld my watch, which had a chain and valuable seals, purchased by the young robber merchant of the ruffian who had plundered me, for sixty dollars. I now conceived a faint hope that if it went to Rome, I might somehow or other regain possession of it.

In the mean time day declined, and no messenger returned from Tusculum.

The idea of passing another night in the woods was extremely disheartening; for I began to be satisfied with what I had seen of robber life. The chieftain now ordered his men to follow him, that he might station them at their posts, adding, that if the messenger did not return before night they must shift their quarters to some other place.

I was again left alone with the young bandit who had before guarded me: he had the same gloomy air and haggard eye, with now and then a bitter sardonic smile. I was determined to probe this ulcerated heart, and reminded him of a kind of promise he had given me to tell me the cause of his suffering.

It seemed to me as if these troubled spirits were glad of an opportunity to disburthen themselves; and of having some fresh undiseased mind with which they could communicate. I had hardly made the request but he seated himself by my side, and gave me his story in, as nearly as I can recollect, the following words.

THE STORY OF THE YOUNG ROBBER

I was born at the little town of Frosinone, which lies at the skirts of the Abruzzi. My father had made a little property in trade, and gave me some education, as he intended me for the church, but I had kept gay company too much to relish the cowl, so I grew up a loiterer about the place. I was a heedless fellow, a little quarrelsome on occasions, but good-humored in the main, so I made my way very well for a time, until I fell in love. There lived in our town a surveyor, or land bailiff, of the prince's who had a young daughter, a beautiful girl of sixteen. She was looked upon as something better than the common run of our townsfolk, and kept almost entirely at home. I saw her occasionally, and became madly in love with her, she looked so fresh and tender, and so different to the sunburnt females to whom I had been accustomed.

As my father kept me in money, I always dressed well, and took all Opportunities of showing myself to advantage in the eyes of the little beauty. I used to see her at church; and as I could play a little upon the guitar, I gave her a tune sometimes under her window of an evening; and I tried to have interviews with her in her father's vineyard, not far from the town, where she sometimes walked. She was evidently pleased with me, but she was young and shy, and her Father kept a strict eye upon her, and took alarm at my attentions, for he had a bad opinion of me, and looked for a better match for his daughter. I became furious at the difficulties thrown in my way, having been accustomed always to easy success among the women, being considered one of the smartest young fellows of the place.

Her father brought home a suitor for her; a rich farmer from a neighboring town. The wedding-day was appointed, and preparations were making. I got sight of her at her window, and I thought she looked sadly at me. I determined the match should not take place, cost what it might. I met her intended bridegroom in the market-place, and could not restrain the expression of my rage. A few hot words passed between us, when I drew my stiletto, and stabbed him to the heart. I fled to a neighboring church for refuge; and with a little money I obtained absolution; but I did not dare to venture from my asylum.

At that time our captain was forming his troop. He had known me from boyhood, and hearing of my situation, came to me in secret, and made such offers that I agreed to enlist myself among his followers.

Indeed, I had more than once thought of taking to this mode of life, having known several brave fellows of the mountains, who used to spend their money freely among us youngsters of the town. I accordingly left my asylum late one night, repaired to the appointed place of meeting; took the oaths prescribed, and became one of the troop. We were for some time in a distant part of the mountains, and our wild adventurous kind of life hit my fancy wonderfully, and diverted my thoughts. At length they returned with all their violence to the recollection of Rosetta. The solitude in which I often found myself gave me time to brood over her image, and as I have kept watch at night over our sleeping camp in the mountains, my feelings have been roused almost to a fever.

At length we shifted our ground, and determined to make a descent upon the road between Terracina and Naples. In the course of our expedition, we passed a day or two in the woody mountains which rise above Frosinone. I cannot tell you how I felt when I looked down upon the place, and distinguished the residence of Rosetta. I determined to have an interview with her; but to what purpose? I could not expect that she would quit her home, and accompany me in my hazardous life among the mountains. She had been brought up too tenderly for that; and when I looked upon the women who were associated with some of our troop, I could not have borne the thoughts of her being their companion. All return to my former life was likewise hopeless; for a price was set upon my head. Still I determined to see her; the very hazard and fruitlessness of the thing made me furious to accomplish it.

It is about three weeks since I persuaded our captain to draw down to the vicinity of Frosinone, in hopes of entrapping some of its principal inhabitants, and compelling them to a ransom. We were lying in ambush towards evening, not far from the vineyard of Rosetta's father. I stole quietly from my companions, and drew near to reconnoitre the place of her frequent walks.

How my heart beat when, among the vines, I beheld the gleaming of a white dress! I knew it must be Rosetta's; it being rare for any female of the place to dress in white. I advanced secretly and without noise, until putting aside the vines, I stood suddenly before her. She uttered a piercing shriek, but I seized her in my arms, put my hand upon her mouth and conjured her to be silent. I poured out all the frenzy of my passion; offered to renounce my mode of life, to put my fate in her hands, to fly with her where we might live in safety together. All that I could say, or do, would not pacify her. Instead of love, horror and affright seemed to have taken possession of her breast.—She struggled partly from my grasp, and filled the air with her cries. In an instant the captain and the rest of my companions were around us. I would have given anything at that moment had she been safe out of our hands, and in her father's house. It was too late. The captain pronounced her a prize, and ordered that she should be borne to the mountains. I represented to him that she was my prize, that I had a previous claim to her; and I mentioned my former attachment. He sneered bitterly in reply; observed that brigands had no business with village intrigues, and that, according to the laws of the troop, all spoils of the kind were determined by lot. Love and jealousy were raging in my heart, but I had to choose between obedience and death. I surrendered her to the captain, and we made for the mountains.

She was overcome by affright, and her steps were so feeble and faltering, and it was necessary to support her. I could not endure the idea that my comrades should touch her, and assuming a forced tranquillity, begged that she might be confided to me, as one to whom she was more accustomed. The captain regarded me for a moment with a searching look, but I bore it without flinching, and he consented, I took her in my arms: she was almost senseless. Her head rested on my shoulder, her mouth was near to mine. I felt her breath on my face, and it seemed to fan the flame which devoured me. Oh, God! to have this glowing treasure in my arms, and yet to think it was not mine!

We arrived at the foot of the mountain. I ascended it with difficulty, particularly where the woods were thick; but I would not relinquish my delicious burthen. I reflected with rage, however, that I must soon do so. The thoughts that so delicate a creature must be abandoned to my rude companions, maddened me. I felt tempted, the stiletto in my hand, to cut my way through them all, and bear her off in triumph. I scarcely conceived the idea, before I saw its rashness; but my brain was fevered with the thought that any but myself should enjoy her charms. I endeavored to outstrip my companions by the quickness of my movements; and to get a little distance ahead, in case any favorable opportunity of escape should present. Vain effort! The voice of the captain suddenly ordered a halt. I trembled, but had to obey. The poor girl partly opened a languid eye, but was without strength or motion. I laid her upon the grass. The captain darted on me a terrible look of suspicion, and ordered me to scour the woods with my companions, in search of some shepherd who might be sent to her father's to demand a ransom.

I saw at once the peril. To resist with violence was certain death; but to leave her alone, in the power of the captain!—I spoke out then with a fervor inspired by my passion and my despair. I reminded the captain that I was the first to seize her; that she was my prize, and that my previous attachment for her should make her sacred among my companions. I insisted, therefore, that he should pledge me his word to respect her; otherwise I should refuse obedience to his orders. His only reply was, to cock his carbine; and at the signal my comrades did the same. They laughed with cruelty at my impotent rage. What could I do? I felt the madness of resistance. I was menaced on all hands, and my companions obliged me to follow them. She remained alone with the chief—yes, alone and almost lifeless!—

Here the robber paused in his recital, overpowered by his emotions. Great drops of sweat stood on his forehead; he panted rather than breathed; his brawny bosom rose and fell like the waves of a troubled sea. When he had become a little calm, he continued his recital.

I was not long in finding a shepherd, said he. I ran with the rapidity of a deer, eager, if possible, to get back before what I dreaded might take place. I had left my companions far behind, and I rejoined them before they had reached one-half the distance I had made. I hurried them back to the place where we had left the captain. As we approached, I beheld him seated by the side of Rosetta. His triumphant look, and the desolate condition of the unfortunate girl, left me no doubt of her fate. I know not how I restrained my fury.

It was with extreme difficulty, and by guiding her hand, that she was made to trace a few characters, requesting her father to send three hundred dollars as her ransom. The letter was despatched by the shepherd. When he was gone, the chief turned sternly to me: "You have set an example," said he, "of mutiny and self-will, which if indulged would be ruinous to the troop. Had I treated you as our laws require, this bullet would have been driven through your brain. But you are an old friend; I have borne patiently with your fury and your folly; I have even protected you from a foolish passion that would have unmanned you. As to this girl, the laws of our association must have their course." So saying, he gave his commands, lots were drawn, and the helpless girl was abandoned to the troop.

Here the robber paused again, panting with fury and it was some moments before he could resume his story.

Hell, said he, was raging in my heart. I beheld the impossibility of avenging myself, and I felt that, according to the articles in which we stood bound to one another, the captain was in the right. I rushed with frenzy from the place. I threw myself upon the earth; tore up the grass with my hands, and beat my head, and gnashed my teeth in agony and rage. When at length I returned, I beheld the wretched victim, pale, dishevelled; her dress torn and disordered. An emotion of pity for a moment subdued my fiercer feelings. I bore her to the foot of a tree, and leaned her gently against it. I took my gourd, which was filled with wine, and applying it to her lips, endeavored to make her swallow a little. To what a condition was she recovered! She, whom I had once seen the pride of Frosinone, who but a short time before I had beheld sporting in her father's vineyard, so fresh and beautiful and happy! Her teeth were clenched; her eyes fixed on the ground; her form without motion, and in a state of absolute insensibility. I hung over her in an agony of recollection of all that she had been, and of anguish at what I now beheld her. I darted round a look of horror at my companions, who seemed like so many fiends exulting in the downfall of an angel, and I felt a horror at myself for being their accomplice.

The captain, always suspicious, saw with his usual penetration what was passing within me, and ordered me to go upon the ridge of woods to keep a look-out upon the neighborhood and await the return of the shepherd. I obeyed, of course, stifling the fury that raged within me, though I felt for the moment that he was my most deadly foe.

On my way, however, a ray of reflection came across my mind. I perceived that the captain was but following with strictness the terrible laws to which we had sworn fidelity. That the passion by which I had been blinded might with justice have been fatal to me but for his forbearance; that he had penetrated my soul, and had taken precautions, by sending me out of the way, to prevent my committing any excess in my anger. From that instant I felt that I was capable of pardoning him.

Occupied with these thoughts, I arrived at the foot of the mountain. The country was solitary and secure; and in a short time I beheld the shepherd at a distance crossing the plain. I hastened to meet him. He had obtained nothing. He had found the father plunged in the deepest distress. He had read the letter with violent emotion, and then calming himself with a sudden exertion, he had replied coldly, "My daughter has been dishonored by those wretches; let her be returned without ransom, or let her die!"

I shuddered at this reply. I knew, according to the laws of our troop, her death was inevitable. Our oaths required it. I felt, nevertheless, that, not having been able to have her to myself, I could become her executioner!

The robber again paused with agitation. I sat musing upon his last Frightful words, which proved to what excess the passions may be carried when escaped from all moral restraint. There was a horrible verity in this story that reminded me of some of the tragic fictions of Danté.

We now came to a fatal moment, resumed the bandit. After the report of the shepherd, I returned with him, and the chieftain received from his lips the refusal of the father. At a signal, which we all understood, we followed him some distance from the victim. He there pronounced her sentence of death. Every one stood ready to execute his order; but I interfered. I observed that there was something due to pity, as well as to justice. That I was as ready as any one to approve the implacable law which was to serve as a warning to all those who hesitated to pay the ransoms demanded for our prisoners, but that, though the sacrifice was proper, it ought to be made without cruelty. The night is approaching, continued I; she will soon be wrapped in sleep; let her then be despatched. All that I now claim on the score of former fondness for her is, let me strike the blow. I will do it as surely, but more tenderly than another.

Several raised their voices against my proposition, but the captain Imposed silence on them. He told me I might conduct her into a thicket at some distance, and he relied upon my promise.

I hastened to seize my prey. There was a forlorn kind of triumph at having at length become her exclusive possessor. I bore her off into the thickness of the forest. She remained in the same state of insensibility and stupor. I was thankful that she did not recollect me; for had she once murmured my name, I should have been overcome. She slept at length in the arms of him who was to poniard her. Many were the conflicts I underwent before I could bring myself to strike the blow. My heart had become sore by the recent conflicts it had undergone, and I dreaded lest, by procrastination, some other should become her executioner. When her repose had continued for some time, I separated myself gently from her, that I might not disturb her sleep, and seizing suddenly my poniard, plunged it into her bosom. A painful and concentrated murmur, but without any convulsive movement, accompanied her last sigh. So perished this unfortunate.

He ceased to speak. I sat horror-struck, covering my face with my hands, seeking, as it were, to hide from myself the frightful images he had presented to my mind. I was roused from this silence by the voice of the captain. "You sleep," said he, "and it is time to be off. Come, we must abandon this height, as night is setting in, and the messenger is not returned. I will post some one on the mountain edge, to conduct him to the place where we shall pass the night."

This was no agreeable news to me. I was sick at heart with the dismal story I had heard. I was harassed and fatigued, and the sight of the banditti began to grow insupportable to me.

The captain assembled his comrades. We rapidly descended the forest which we had mounted with so much difficulty in the morning, and soon arrived in what appeared to be a frequented road. The robbers proceeded with great caution, carrying their guns cocked, and looking on every side with wary and suspicious eyes. They were apprehensive of encountering the civic patrole. We left Rocca Priori behind us. There was a fountain near by, and as I was excessively thirsty, I begged permission to stop and drink. The captain himself went, and brought me water in his hat. We pursued our route, when, at the extremity of an alley which crossed the road, I perceived a female on horseback, dressed in white. She was alone. I recollected the fate of the poor girl in the story, and trembled for her safety.

One of the brigands saw her at the same instant, and plunging into the bushes, he ran precipitately in the direction towards her. Stopping on the border of the alley, he put one knee to the ground, presented his carbine ready for menace, or to shoot her horse if she attempted to fly, and in this way awaited her approach. I kept my eyes fixed on her with intense anxiety. I felt tempted to shout, and warn her of her danger, though my own destruction would have been the consequence. It was awful to see this tiger crouching ready for a bound, and the poor innocent victim wandering unconsciously near him. Nothing but a mere chance could save her. To my joy, the chance turned in her favor. She seemed almost accidentally to take an opposite path, which led outside of the wood, where the robber dare not venture. To this casual deviation she owed her safety.

I could not imagine why the captain of the band had ventured to such a distance from the height, on which he had placed the sentinel to watch the return of the messengers. He seemed himself uneasy at the risk to which he exposed himself. His movements were rapid and uneasy; I could scarce keep pace with him. At length, after three hours of what might be termed a forced march, we mounted the extremity of the same woods, the summit of which we had occupied during the day; and I learnt with satisfaction, that we had reached our quarters for the night.

"You must be fatigued," said the chieftain; "but it was necessary to survey the environs, so as not to be surprised during the night. Had we met with the famous civic guard of Rocca Priori you would have seen fine sport." Such was the indefatigable precaution and forethought of this robber chief, who really gave continual evidences of military talent.

The night was magnificent. The moon rising above the horizon in a cloudless sky, faintly lit up the grand features of the mountains, while lights twinkling here and there, like terrestrial stars, in the wide, dusky expanse of the landscape, betrayed the lonely cabins of the shepherds. Exhausted by fatigue, and by the many agitations I had experienced, I prepared to sleep, soothed by the hope of approaching deliverance. The captain ordered his companions to collect some dry moss; he arranged with his own hands a kind of mattress and pillow of it, and gave me his ample mantle as a covering. I could not but feel both surprised and gratified by such unexpected attentions on the part of this benevolent cut-throat: for there is nothing more striking than to find the ordinary charities, which are matters of course in common life, flourishing by the side of such stern and sterile crime. It is like finding the tender flowers and fresh herbage of the valley growing among the rocks and cinders of the volcano.

Before I fell asleep, I had some farther discourse with the captain, who seemed to put great confidence in me. He referred to our previous conversation of the morning; told me he was weary of his hazardous profession; that he had acquired sufficient property, and was anxious to return to the world and lead a peaceful life in the bosom of his family. He wished to know whether it was not in my power to procure him a passport for the United States of America. I applauded his good intentions, and promised to do everything in my power to promote its success. We then parted for the night. I stretched myself upon my couch of moss, which, after my fatigues, felt like a bed of down, and sheltered by the robber's mantle from all humidity, I slept soundly without waking, until the signal to arise.

It was nearly six o'clock, and the day was just dawning. As the place where we had passed the night was too much exposed, we moved up into the thickness of the woods. A fire was kindled. While there was any flame, the mantles were again extended round it; but when nothing remained but glowing cinders, they were lowered, and the robbers seated themselves in a circle.

The scene before me reminded me of some of those described by Homer. There wanted only the victim on the coals, and the sacred knife, to cut off the succulent parts, and distribute them around. My companions might have rivalled the grim warriors of Greece. In place of the noble repasts, however, of Achilles and Agamemnon, I beheld displayed on the grass the remains of the ham which had sustained so vigorous an attack on the preceding evening, accompanied by the reliques of the bread, cheese, and wine.

We had scarcely commenced our frugal breakfast, when I heard again an Imitation of the bleating of sheep, similar to what I had heard the day before. The captain answered it in the same tone. Two men were soon after seen descending from the woody height, where we had passed the preceding evening. On nearer approach, they proved to be the sentinel and the messenger. The captain rose and went to meet them. He made a signal for his comrades to join him. They had a short conference, and then returning to me with eagerness, "Your ransom is paid," said he; "you are free!"

Though I had anticipated deliverance, I cannot tell you what a rush of delight these tidings gave me. I cared not to finish my repast, but prepared to depart. The captain took me by the hand; requested permission to write to me, and begged me not to forget the passport. I replied, that I hoped to be of effectual service to him, and that I relied on his honor to return the prince's note for five hundred dollars, now that the cash was paid. He regarded me for a moment with surprise; then, seeming to recollect himself, "E giusto," said he, "eccoloadio!"[1] He delivered me the note, pressed my hand once more, and we separated. The laborers were permitted to follow me, and we resumed with joy our road towards Tusculum.

The artist ceased to speak; the party continued for a few moments to pace the shore of Terracina in silence. The story they had heard had made a deep impression on them, particularly on the fair Venetian, who had gradually regained her husband's arm. At the part that related to the young girl of Frosinone, she had been violently affected; sobs broke

1. It is just—there it is—adieu!

from her; she clung close to her husband, and as she looked up to him as if for protection, the moon-beams shining on her beautifully fair countenance showed it paler than usual with terror, while tears glittered in her fine dark eyes. "O caro mio!" would she murmur, shuddering at every atrocious circumstance of the story.

"Corragio, mia vita!" was the reply, as the husband gently and fondly tapped the white hand that lay upon his arm.

The Englishman alone preserved his usual phlegm, and the fair Venetian was piqued at it.

She had pardoned him a want of gallantry towards herself, though a sin of omission seldom met with in the gallant climate of Italy, but the quiet coolness which he maintained in matters which so much affected her, and the slow credence which he had given to the stories which had filled her with alarm, were quite vexatious.

"Santa Maria!" said she to husband as they retired for the night, "what insensible beings these English are!"

In the morning all was bustle at the inn at Terracina.

The procaccio had departed at day-break, on its route towards Rome, but the Englishman was yet to start, and the departure of an English equipage is always enough to keep an inn in a bustle. On this occasion there was more than usual stir; for the Englishman having much property about him, and having been convinced of the real danger of the road, had applied to the police and obtained, by dint of liberal pay, an escort of eight dragoons and twelve foot-soldiers, as far as Fondi.

Perhaps, too, there might have been a little ostentation at bottom, from which, with great delicacy be it spoken, English travellers are not always exempt; though to say the truth, he had nothing of it in his manner. He moved about taciturn and reserved as usual, among the gaping crowd in his gingerbread-colored travelling cap, with his hands in his pockets. He gave laconic orders to John as he packed away the thousand and one indispensable conveniencies of the night, double loaded his pistols with great *sang-froid*, and deposited them in the pockets of the carriage, taking no notice of a pair of keen eyes gazing on him from among the herd of loitering idlers. The fair Venetian now came up with a request made in her dulcet tones, that he would permit their carriage to proceed under protection of his escort. The Englishman, who was busy loading another pair of pistols for his servant, and held the ramrod between his teeth, nodded assent as a matter of course, but without lifting up his eyes. The fair Venetian was not accustomed to such indifference. "O Dio!" exclaimed she softly as she retired, "como sono freddi questi Inglesi." At length off they set in gallant style, the eight dragoons prancing in front, the twelve foot-soldiers marching in rear, and carriages moving slowly in the centre to enable the infantry to keep pace with them. They had proceeded but a few hundred yards when it was discovered that some indispensable article had been left behind.

In fact, the Englishman's purse was missing, and John was despatched to the inn to search for it.

This occasioned a little delay, and the carriage of the Venetians drove slowly on. John came back out of breath and out of humor; the purse was not to be found; his master was irritated; he recollected the very place where it lay; the cursed Italian servant had pocketed it. John was again sent back. He returned once more, without the purse, but with the landlord and the whole household at his heels. A thousand exclamations and protestations, accompanied by all sorts of grimaces and contortions. "No purse had been seen—his excellenza must be mistaken."

No—his excellenza was not mistaken; the purse lay on the marble table, under the mirror: a green purse, half full of gold and silver. Again a thousand grimaces and contortions, and vows by San Genario, that no purse of the kind had been seen.

The Englishman became furious. "The waiter had pocketed it. The landlord was a knave. The inn a den of thieves—it was a d——d country—he had been cheated and plundered from one end of it to the other—but he'd have satisfaction—he'd drive right off to the police."

He was on the point of ordering the postilions to turn back, when, on rising, he displaced the cushion of the carriage, and the purse of money fell chinking to the floor.

All the blood in his body seemed to rush into his face. "D—n the purse," said he, as he snatched it up. He dashed a handful of money on the ground before the pale, cringing waiter. "There—be off," cried he; "John, order the postilions to drive on."

Above half an hour had been exhausted in this altercation. The Venetian carriage had loitered along; its passengers looking out from time to time, and expecting the escort every moment to follow. They had gradually turned an angle of the road that shut them out of sight. The little army was again in motion, and made a very picturesque appearance as it wound along at the bottom of the rocks; the morning sunshine beaming upon the weapons of soldiery.

The Englishman lolled back in his carriage, vexed with himself at what had passed, and consequently out of humor with all the world. As this, however, is no uncommon case with gentlemen who travel for their pleasure, it is hardly worthy of remark.

They had wound up from the coast among the hills, and came to a part of the road that admitted of some prospect ahead.

"I see nothing of the lady's carriage, sir," said John, leaning over from the coach box.

"Hang the lady's carriage!" said the Englishman, crustily; "don't plague me about the lady's carriage; must I be continually pestered with strangers?"

John said not another word, for he understood his master's mood. The road grew more wild and lonely; they were slowly proceeding in a foot pace up a hill; the dragoons were some distance ahead, and had just reached the summit of the hill, when they uttered an exclamation, or rather shout, and galloped forward. The Englishman was aroused from his sulky revery. He stretched his head from the carriage, which had attained the brow of the hill. Before him extended a long hollow defile, commanded on one side by rugged, precipitous heights, covered with bushes and scanty forest trees. At some distance he beheld the carriage of the Venitians overturned; a numerous gang of desperadoes were rifling it; the young man and his servant were overpowered and partly stripped, and the lady was in the hands of two of the ruffians.

The Englishman seized his pistols, sprang from his carriage, and called upon John to follow him. In the meantime, as the dragoons came forward, the robbers who were busy with the carriage quitted their spoil, formed themselves in the middle of the road, and taking deliberate aim, fired. One of the dragoons fell, another was wounded, and the whole were for a moment checked and thrown in confusion. The robbers loaded again in an instant. The dragoons had discharged their carbines, but without apparent effect; they received another volley, which, though none fell, threw them again into confusion. The robbers were loading a second time, when they saw the foot soldiers at hand.—"Scampa via!" was the word. They abandoned their prey, and retreated up the rocks; the soldiers after them. They fought from cliff to cliff, and bush to bush, the robbers turning every now and then to fire upon their pursuers; the soldiers scrambling after them, and discharging their muskets whenever they could get a chance. Sometimes a soldier or a robber was shot down, and came tumbling Among the cliffs. The dragoons kept firing from below, whenever a robber came in sight.

The Englishman hastened to the scene of action, and the balls discharged at the dragoons had whistled past him as he advanced. One object, however, engrossed his attention. It was the beautiful Venetian lady in the hands of two of the robbers, who, during the confusion of the fight, carried her shrieking up the mountains. He saw her dress gleaming among the bushes, and he sprang up the rocks to intercept the robbers as they bore off their prey. The ruggedness of the steep and the entanglements of the bushes, delayed and impeded him. He lost sight of the lady, but was still guided by her cries, which grew fainter and fainter. They were off to the left, while the report of muskets showed that the battle was raging to the right.

At length he came upon what appeared to be a rugged footpath, faintly worn in a gully of the rock, and beheld the ruffians at some distance hurrying the lady up the defile. One of them hearing his approach let go his prey, advanced towards him, and levelling the carbine which had been slung on his back, fired. The ball whizzed through the Englishman's hat, and carried with it some of his hair. He returned the fire with one of his pistols, and the robber fell. The other brigand now dropped the lady, and drawing a long pistol from his belt, fired on his adversary with deliberate aim; the ball passed between his left arm and his side, slightly wounding the arm. The Englishman advanced and discharged his remaining pistol, which wounded the robber, but not severely. The brigand drew a stiletto, and rushed upon his adversary, who eluded the blow, receiving merely a slight wound, and defending himself with his pistol, which had a spring bayonet. They closed with one another, and a desperate struggle ensued. The robber was a square-built, thick-set, man, powerful, muscular, and active. The Englishman, though of larger frame and greater strength, was less active and less accustomed to athletic exercises and feats of hardihood, but he showed himself practised and skilled in the art of defence. They were on a craggy height, and the Englishman perceived that his antagonist was striving to press him to the edge.

A side glance showed him also the robber whom he had first wounded, Scrambling up to the assistance of his comrade, stiletto in hand. He had, in fact, attained the summit of the cliff, and the Englishman saw him within a few steps, when he heard suddenly the report of a pistol and the ruffian fell. The shot came from John, who had arrived just in time to save his master.

The remaining robber, exhausted by loss of blood and the violence of the contest, showed signs of faltering. His adversary pursued his advantage; pressed on him, and as his strength relaxed, dashed him headlong from the precipice. He looked after him and saw him lying motionless among the rocks below.

The Englishman now sought the fair Venetian. He found her senseless on the ground. With his servant's assistance he bore her down to the road, where her husband was raving like one distracted.

The occasional discharge of fire-arms along the height showed that a Retreating fight was still kept up by the robbers. The carriage was righted; the baggage was hastily replaced; the Venetian, transported with joy and gratitude, took his lovely and senseless burthen in his arms, and the party resumed their route towards Fondi, escorted by the dragoons, leaving the foot soldiers to ferret out the banditti. While on the way John dressed his master's wounds, which were found not to be serious.

Before arriving at Fondi the fair Venetian had recovered from her swoon, and was made conscious of her safety and of the mode of her deliverance. Her transports were unbounded; and mingled with them were enthusiastic exclamations of gratitude to her deliverer. A thousand times did she reproach herself for having accused him of coldness and insensibility. The moment she saw him she rushed into his arms, and clasped him round the neck with all the vivacity of her nation.

Never was man more embarrassed by the embraces of a fine woman.

"My deliverer! my angel!" exclaimed she.

"Tut! tut!" said the Englishman.

"You are wounded!" shrieked the fair Venetian, as she saw the blood upon his clothes.

"Pooh—nothing at all!"

"O Dio!" exclaimed she, clasping him again round the neck and sobbing on his bosom.

"Pooh!" exclaimed the Englishman, looking somewhat foolish; "this is all nonsense."

PART FOURTH

THE MONEY DIGGERS

(Found Among the Papers of the Late
Diedrich Knickerbocker)

Now I remember those old women's words
Who in my youth would tell me winter's tales;
And speak of spirits and ghosts that glide by night
About the place where treasure had been hid.

—Marlow's Jew of Malta

Hell Gate

About six miles from the renowned city of the Manhattoes, and in that Sound, or arm of the sea, which passes between the main land and Nassau or Long Island, there is a narrow strait, where the current is violently compressed between shouldering promontories, and horribly irritated and perplexed by rocks and shoals. Being at the best of times a very violent, hasty current, its takes these impediments in mighty dudgeon; boiling in whirlpools; brawling and fretting in ripples and breakers; and, in short, indulging in all kinds of wrong-headed paroxysms. At such times, woe to any unlucky vessel that ventures within its clutches.

This termagant humor is said to prevail only at half tides. At low water it is as pacific as any other stream. As the tide rises, it begins to fret; at half tide it rages and roars as if bellowing for more water; but when the tide is full it relapses again into quiet, and for a time seems almost to sleep as soundly as an alderman after dinner. It may be compared to an inveterate hard drinker, who is a peaceable fellow enough when he has no liquor at all, or when he has a skin full, but when half seas over plays the very devil.

This mighty, blustering, bullying little strait was a place of great Difficulty and danger to the Dutch navigators of ancient days; hectoring their tub-built barks in a most unruly style; whirling them about, in a manner to make any but a Dutchman giddy, and not unfrequently stranding them upon rocks and reefs. Whereupon out of sheer spleen they denominated it Hellegat (literally Hell Gut) and solemnly gave it over to the devil. This appellation has since been aptly rendered into English by the name of Hell Gate; and into nonsense by the name of Hurl Gate, according to certain foreign intruders who neither understood Dutch nor English. May St. Nicholas confound them!

From this strait to the city of the Manhattoes the borders of the Sound are greatly diversified; in one part, on the eastern shore of the island of Manhata and opposite Blackwell's Island, being very much broken and indented by rocky nooks, overhung with trees which give them a wild and romantic look.

The flux and reflux of the tide through this part of the Sound is extremely rapid, and the navigation troublesome, by reason of the whirling eddies and counter currents. I speak this from experience, having been much of a navigator of these small seas in my boyhood, and having more than once run the risk of shipwreck and drowning in the course of divers holiday voyages, to which in common with the Dutch urchins I was rather prone.

In the midst of this perilous strait, and hard by a group of rocks called "the Hen and Chickens," there lay in my boyish days the wreck of a vessel which had been entangled in the whirlpools and stranded during a storm. There was some wild story about this being the wreck of a pirate, and of some bloody murder, connected with it, which I cannot now recollect. Indeed, the desolate look of this forlorn hulk, and the fearful place where it lay rotting, were sufficient to awaken strange notions concerning it. A row of timber heads, blackened by time, peered above the surface at high water; but at low tide a considerable part of the hull was bare, and its great ribs or timbers, partly stripped of their planks, looked like the skeleton of some sea monster. There was also the stump of a mast, with a few ropes and blocks swinging about and whistling in the wind, while the sea gull wheeled and screamed around this melancholy carcass.

The stories connected with this wreck made it an object of great awe to my boyish fancy; but in truth the whole neighborhood was full of fable and romance for me, abounding with traditions about pirates, hobgoblins, and buried money. As I grew to more mature years I made many researches after the truth of these strange traditions; for I have always been a curious investigator of the valuable, but obscure branches of the history of my native province. I found infinite difficulty, however, in arriving at any precise information. In seeking to dig up one fact it is incredible the number of fables which I unearthed; for the whole course of the Sound seemed in my younger days to be like the straits of Pylorus of yore, the very region of fiction. I will say nothing of the Devil's Stepping Stones, by which that arch fiend made his retreat from Connecticut to Long Island, seeing that the subject is likely to be learnedly treated by a worthy friend and contemporary historian[1] whom I have furnished with particulars thereof. Neither will I say anything of the black man in a three-cornered hat, seated in the stern of a jolly boat who used to be seen about Hell Gate in stormy weather; and who

---

1. For a very interesting account of the Devil and his Stepping Stones, see the learned memoir read before the New York Historical Society since the death of Mr. Knickerbocker, by his friend, an eminent jurist of the place.

WASHINGTON IRVING

went by the name of the Pirate's Spuke, or Pirate's Ghost, because I never could meet with any person of stanch credibility who professed to have seen this spectrum; unless it were the widow of Manus Conklin, the blacksmith of Frog's Neck, but then, poor woman, she was a little purblind, and might have been mistaken; though they said she saw farther than other folks in the dark. All this, however, was but little satisfactory in regard to the tales of buried money about which I was most curious; and the following was all that I could for a long time collect that had anything like an air of authenticity.

KIDD THE PIRATE

I n old times, just after the territory of the New Netherlands had been wrested from the hands of their High Mightinesses, the Lords States General of Holland, by Charles the Second, and while it was as yet in an unquiet state, the province was a favorite resort of adventurers of all kinds, and particularly of buccaneers. These were piratical rovers of the deep, who made sad work in times of peace among the Spanish settlements and Spanish merchant ships. They took advantage of the easy access to the harbor of the Manhattoes, and of the laxity of its scarcely-organized government, to make it a kind of rendezvous, where they might dispose of their ill-gotten spoils, and concert new depredations. Crews of these desperadoes, the runagates of every country and clime, might be seen swaggering, in open day, about the streets of the little burgh; elbowing its quiet Mynheers; trafficking away their rich outlandish plunder, at half price, to the wary merchant, and then squandering their gains in taverns; drinking, gambling, singing, swearing, shouting, and astounding the neighborhood with sudden brawl and ruffian revelry.

At length the indignation of government was aroused, and it was determined to ferret out this vermin brood from, the colonies. Great consternation took place among the pirates on finding justice in pursuit of them, and their old haunts turned to places of peril. They secreted their money and jewels in lonely out-of-the-way places; buried them about the wild shores of the rivers and sea-coast, and dispersed themselves over the face of the country.

Among the agents employed to hunt them by sea was the renowned Captain Kidd. He had long been a hardy adventurer, a kind of equivocal borderer, half trader, half smuggler, with a tolerable dash of the pickaroon. He had traded for some time among the pirates, lurking about the seas in a little rakish, musquito-built vessel, prying into all kinds of odd places, as busy as a Mother Carey's chicken in a gale of wind.

This nondescript personage was pitched upon by government as the very man to command a vessel fitted out to cruise against the pirates, since he knew all their haunts and lurking-places: acting upon the shrewd old maxim of "setting a rogue to catch a rogue." Kidd accordingly sailed from New York in the Adventure galley, gallantly armed and duly commissioned, and steered his course to the Madeiras, to Bonavista, to Madagascar, and cruised at the entrance of the Red Sea. Instead, however, of making war upon the pirates, he turned pirate himself: captured friend or foe; enriched himself with the spoils of a wealthy Indiaman, manned by Moors, though commanded by an Englishman, and having disposed of his prize, had the hardihood to return to Boston, laden with wealth, with a crew of his comrades at his heels.

His fame had preceded him. The alarm was given of the reappearance of this cut-purse of the ocean. Measures were taken for his arrest; but he had time, it is said, to bury the greater part of his treasures. He even attempted to draw his sword and defend himself when arrested; but was secured and thrown into prison, with several of his followers. They were carried to England in a frigate, where they were tried, condemned, and hanged at Execution Dock. Kidd died hard, for the rope with which he was first tied up broke with his weight, and he tumbled to the ground; he was tied up a second time, and effectually; from whence arose the story of his having been twice hanged.

Such is the main outline of Kidd's history; but it has given birth to an innumerable progeny of traditions. The circumstance of his having buried great treasures of gold and jewels after returning from his cruising set the brains of all the good people along the coast in a ferment. There were rumors on rumors of great sums found here and there; sometimes in one part of the country, sometimes in another; of trees and rocks bearing mysterious marks; doubtless indicating the spots where treasure lay hidden; of coins found with Moorish characters, the plunder of Kidd's eastern prize, but which the common people took for diabolical or magic inscriptions.

Some reported the spoils to have been buried in solitary unsettled places about Plymouth and Cape Cod; many other parts of the Eastern coast, also, and various places in Long Island Sound, have been gilded by these rumors, and have been ransacked by adventurous money-diggers.

In all the stories of these enterprises the devil played a conspicuous part. Either he was conciliated by ceremonies and invocations, or some bargain or compact was made with him. Still he was sure to play the money-diggers some slippery trick. Some had succeeded so far as to touch the iron chest which contained the treasure, when some baffling circumstance was sure to take place. Either the earth would fall in and fill up the pit or some direful noise or apparition would throw the party into a panic and frighten them from the place; and sometimes the devil himself would appear and bear off the prize from their very grasp; and if they visited the place on the next day, not a trace would be seen of their labors of the preceding night.

Such were the vague rumors which for a long time tantalized without gratifying my curiosity on the interesting subject of these pirate traditions. There is nothing in this world so hard to get at as truth. I sought among my favorite sources of authentic information, the oldest inhabitants, and particularly the old Dutch wives of the province; but though I flatter myself I am better versed than most men in the curious history of my native province, yet for a long time my inquiries were unattended with any substantial result.

At length it happened, one calm day in the latter part of summer, that I was relaxing myself from the toils of severe study by a day's amusement in fishing in those waters which had been the favorite resort of my boyhood. I was in company with several worthy burghers of my native city. Our sport was indifferent; the fish did not bite freely; and we had frequently changed our fishing ground without bettering our luck. We at length anchored close under a ledge of rocky coast, on the eastern side of the island of Manhata. It was a still, warm day. The stream whirled and dimpled by us without a wave or even a ripple, and every thing was so calm and quiet that it was almost startling when the kingfisher would pitch himself from the branch of some dry tree, and after suspending himself for a moment in the air to take his aim, would souse into the smooth water after his prey. While we were lolling in our boat, half drowsy with the warm stillness of the day and the dullness of our sport, one of our party, a worthy alderman, was overtaken by a slumber, and, as he dozed, suffered the sinker of his drop-line to lie upon the bottom of the river. On waking, he found he had caught something of importance, from the weight; on drawing it to the surface, we were much surprised to find a long pistol of very curious and outlandish fashion, which, from its rusted condition, and its stock being worm-eaten and covered with barnacles, appeared to have been a long time under water. The unexpected appearance of this document of warfare occasioned much speculation among my pacific companions. One supposed it to have fallen there during the revolutionary war. Another, from the peculiarity of its fashion, attributed it to the voyagers in the earliest days of the settlement; perchance to the renowned Adrian Block, who explored the Sound and discovered Block Island, since so noted for its cheese. But a third, after regarding it for some time, pronounced it to be of veritable Spanish workmanship.

"I'll warrant," said he, "if this pistol could talk it would tell strange stories of hard fights among the Spanish Dons. I've not a doubt but it's a relique of the buccaneers of old times."

"Like enough," said another of the party. "There was Bradish the pirate, who at the time Lord Bellamont made such a stir after the buccaneers, buried money and jewels somewhere in these parts or on Long-Island; and then there was Captain Kidd—"

"Ah, that Kidd was a daring dog," said an iron-faced Cape Cod whaler. "There's a fine old song about him, all to the tune of:

> *'My name is Robert Kidd,*
> *As I sailed, as I sailed.'*

And it tells how he gained the devil's good graces by burying the Bible:

> *'I had the Bible in my hand,*
> *As I sailed, as I sailed,*
> *And I buried it in the sand,*
> *As I sailed.'*

Egad, if this pistol had belonged to him I should set some store by it out of sheer curiosity. Ah, well, there's an odd story I have heard about one Tom Walker, who, they say, dug up some of Kidd's buried money; and as the fish don't seem to bite at present, I'll tell it to you to pass away time."

The Devil and Tom Walker

A few miles from Boston, in Massachusetts, there is a deep inlet winding several miles into the interior of the country from Charles Bay, and terminating in a thickly-wooded swamp, or morass. On one side of this inlet is a beautiful dark grove; on the opposite side the land rises abruptly from the water's edge, into a high ridge on which grow a few scattered oaks of great age and immense size. It was under one of these gigantic trees, according to old stories, that Kidd the pirate buried his treasure. The inlet allowed a facility to bring the money in a boat secretly and at night to the very foot of the hill. The elevation of the place permitted a good look-out to be kept that no one was at hand, while the remarkable trees formed good landmarks by which the place might easily be found again. The old stories add, moreover, that the devil presided at the hiding of the money, and took it under his guardianship; but this, it is well-known, he always does with buried treasure, particularly when it has been ill gotten. Be that as it may, Kidd never returned to recover his wealth; being shortly after seized at Boston, sent out to England, and there hanged for a pirate.

About the year 1727, just at the time when earthquakes were prevalent in New England, and shook many tall sinners down upon their knees, there lived near this place a meagre miserly fellow of the name of Tom Walker. He had a wife as miserly as himself; they were so miserly that they even conspired to cheat each other. Whatever the woman could lay hands on she hid away; a hen could not cackle but she was on the alert to secure the new-laid egg. Her husband was continually prying about to detect her secret hoards, and many and fierce were the conflicts that took place about what ought to have been common property. They lived in a forlorn-looking house, that stood alone and had an air of starvation. A few straggling savin trees, emblems of sterility, grew near it; no smoke ever curled from its chimney; no traveller stopped at its door. A miserable horse, whose ribs were as articulate as the bars of a gridiron, stalked about a field where a thin carpet of moss, scarcely covering the ragged beds of pudding-stone, tantalized and balked his hunger; and sometimes he would lean his head over the fence, looked piteously at the passer-by, and seem to petition deliverance from this land of famine.

The house and its inmates had altogether a bad name. Tom's wife was a tall termagant, fierce of temper, loud of tongue, and strong of arm. Her voice was often heard in wordy warfare with her husband; and his face sometimes showed signs that their conflicts were not confined to words. No one ventured, however, to interfere between them; the lonely wayfarer shrunk within himself at the horrid clamor and clapper-clawing; eyed the den of discord askance, and hurried on his way, rejoicing, if a bachelor, in his celibacy.

One day that Tom Walker had been to a distant part of the neighborhood, he took what he considered a short cut homewards through the swamp. Like most short cuts, it was an ill-chosen route. The swamp was thickly grown with great gloomy pines and hemlocks, some of them ninety feet high; which made it dark at noon-day, and a retreat for all the owls of the neighborhood. It was full of pits and quagmires, partly covered with weeds and mosses; where the green surface often betrayed the traveller into a gulf of black smothering mud; there were also dark and stagnant pools, the abodes of the tadpole, the bull-frog, and the water-snake, and where trunks of pines and hemlocks lay half drowned, half rotting, looking like alligators, sleeping in the mire.

Tom had long been picking his way cautiously through this treacherous forest; stepping from tuft to tuft of rushes and roots which afforded precarious footholds among deep sloughs; or pacing carefully, like a cat, among the prostrate trunks of trees; startled now and then by the sudden screaming of the bittern, or the quacking of a wild duck, rising on the wing from some solitary pool. At length he arrived at a piece of firm ground, which ran out like a peninsula into the deep bosom of the swamp. It had been one of the strongholds of the Indians during their wars with the first colonists. Here they had thrown up a kind of fort which they had looked upon as almost impregnable, and had used as a place of refuge for their squaws and children. Nothing remained of the Indian fort but a few embankments gradually sinking to the level of the surrounding earth, and already overgrown in part by oaks and other forest trees, the foliage of which formed a contrast to the dark pines and hemlocks of the swamp.

It was late in the dusk of evening that Tom Walker reached the old fort, and he paused there for a while to rest himself. Any one but he would have felt unwilling to linger in this lonely, melancholy place, for the common people had a bad opinion of it from the stories handed down from the time of the Indian wars; when it was asserted that the savages held incantations here and made sacrifices to the evil spirit.

Tom Walker, however, was not a man to be troubled with any fears of the kind.

He reposed himself for some time on the trunk of a fallen hemlock, listening to the boding cry of the tree-toad, and delving with his walking-staff into a mound of black mould at his feet. As he turned up the soil unconsciously, his staff struck against something hard. He raked it out of the vegetable mould, and lo! a cloven skull with an Indian tomahawk buried deep in it, lay before him. The rust on the weapon showed the time that had elapsed since this death blow had been given. It was a dreary memento of the fierce struggle that had taken place in this last foothold of the Indian warriors.

"Humph!" said Tom Walker, as he gave the skull a kick to shake the dirt from it.

"Let that skull alone!" said a gruff voice.

Tom lifted up his eyes and beheld a great black man, seated directly Opposite him on the stump of a tree. He was exceedingly surprised, having neither seen nor heard any one approach, and he was still more perplexed on observing, as well as the gathering gloom would permit, that the stranger was neither negro nor Indian. It is true, he was dressed in a rude, half Indian garb, and had a red belt or sash swathed round his body, but his face was neither black nor copper color, but swarthy and dingy and begrimed with soot, as if he had been accustomed to toil among fires and forges. He had a shock of coarse black hair, that stood out from his head in all directions; and bore an axe on his shoulder.

He scowled for a moment at Tom with a pair of great red eyes.

"What are you doing in my grounds?" said the black man, with a hoarse growling voice.

"Your grounds?" said Tom, with a sneer; "no more your grounds than mine: they belong to Deacon Peabody."

"Deacon Peabody be d——d," said the stranger, "as I flatter myself he will be, if he does not look more to his own sins and less to his neighbor's. Look yonder, and see how Deacon Peabody is faring."

Tom looked in the direction that the stranger pointed, and beheld one of the great trees, fair and flourishing without, but rotten at the core, and saw that it had been nearly hewn through, so that the first high wind was likely to blow it down. On the bark of the tree was scored the name of Deacon Peabody. He now looked round and found most of the tall trees marked with the names of some great men of the colony, and all more or less scored by the axe. The one on which he had been seated, and which had evidently just been hewn down, bore the name of Crowninshield; and he recollected a mighty rich man of that name, who made a vulgar display of wealth, which it was whispered he had acquired by buccaneering.

"He's just ready for burning!" said the black man, with a growl of triumph. "You see I am likely to have a good stock of firewood for winter."

"But what right have you," said Tom, "to cut down Deacon Peabody's timber?"

"The right of prior claim," said the other. "This woodland belonged to me long before one of your white-faced race put foot upon the soil."

"And pray, who are you, if I may be so bold?" said Tom.

"Oh, I go by various names. I am the Wild Huntsman in some countries; the Black Miner in others. In this neighborhood I am known by the name of the Black Woodsman. I am he to whom the red men devoted this spot, and now and then roasted a white man by way of sweet-smelling sacrifice. Since the red men have been exterminated by you white savages, I amuse myself by presiding at the persecutions of quakers and anabaptists; I am the great patron and prompter of slave dealers, and the grand master of the Salem witches."

"The upshot of all which is, that, if I mistake not," said Tom, sturdily, "you are he commonly called Old Scratch."

"The same at your service!" replied the black man, with a half civil nod.

Such was the opening of this interview, according to the old story, though it has almost too familiar an air to be credited. One would think that to meet with such a singular personage in this wild, lonely place, would have shaken any man's nerves; but Tom was a hard-minded fellow, not easily daunted, and he had lived so long with a termagant wife, that he did not even fear the devil.

It is said that after this commencement they had a long and earnest Conversation together, as Tom returned homewards. The black man told him of great sums of money which had been buried by Kidd the pirate, under the oak trees on the high ridge not far from the morass. All these were under his command and protected by his power, so that none could find them but such as propitiated his favor. These he offered to place within Tom Walker's reach, having conceived an especial kindness for him: but they were to be had only on certain conditions. What these conditions were, may easily be surmised, though Tom never disclosed them publicly. They must have been very hard, for he required time to think of them, and he was not a man to stick at trifles where money was in view. When they had reached the edge of the swamp the stranger paused.

"What proof have I that all you have been telling me is true?" said Tom.

"There is my signature," said the black man, pressing his finger on Tom's forehead. So saying, he turned off among the thickets of the swamp, and seemed, as Tom said, to go down, down, down, into the earth, until nothing but his head and shoulders could be seen, and so on until he totally disappeared.

When Tom reached home he found the black print of a finger burnt, as it were, into his forehead, which nothing could obliterate.

The first news his wife had to tell him was the sudden death of Absalom Crowninshield, the rich buccaneer. It was announced in the papers with the usual flourish, that "a great man had fallen in Israel."

Tom recollected the tree which his black friend had just hewn down, and which was ready for burning. "Let the freebooter roast," said Tom, "who cares!" He now felt convinced that all he had heard and seen was no illusion.

He was not prone to let his wife into his confidence; but as this was an uneasy secret, he willingly shared it with her. All her avarice was awakened at the mention of hidden gold, and she urged her husband to comply with the black man's terms and secure what would make them wealthy for life. However Tom might have felt disposed to sell himself to the devil, he was determined not to do so to oblige his wife; so he flatly refused out of the mere spirit of contradiction. Many and bitter were the quarrels they had on the subject, but the more she talked the more resolute was Tom not to be damned to please her. At length she determined to drive the bargain on her own account, and if she succeeded, to keep all the gain to herself.

Being of the same fearless temper as her husband, she sat off for the old Indian fort towards the close of a summer's day. She was many hour's absent. When she came back she was reserved and sullen in her replies. She spoke something of a black man whom she had met about twilight, hewing at the root of a tall tree. He was sulky, however, and would not come to terms; she was to go again with a propitiatory offering, but what it was she forebore to say.

The next evening she sat off again for the swamp, with her apron heavily laden. Tom waited and waited for her, but in vain: midnight came, but she did not make her appearance; morning, noon, night returned, but still she did not come. Tom now grew uneasy for her safety; especially as he found she had carried off in her apron the silver tea pot and spoons and every portable article of value. Another night elapsed, another morning came; but no wife. In a word, she was ever heard of more.

What was her real fate nobody knows, in consequence of so many pretending to know. It is one of those facts that have become confounded by a variety of historians. Some asserted that she lost her way among the tangled mazes of the swamp and sunk into some pit or slough; others, more uncharitable, hinted that she had eloped with the household booty, and made off to some other province; while others assert that the tempter had decoyed her into a dismal quagmire, on top of which her hat was found lying. In confirmation of this, it was said a great black man with an axe on his shoulder was seen late that very evening coming out of the swamp, carrying a bundle tied in a check apron, with an air of surly triumph.

The most current and probable story, however, observes that Tom Walker grew so anxious about the fate of his wife and his property that he sat out at length to seek them both at the Indian fort. During a long summer's afternoon he searched about the gloomy place, but no wife was to be seen. He called her name repeatedly, but she was no where to be heard. The bittern alone responded to his voice, as he flew screaming by; or the bull-frog croaked dolefully from a neighboring pool. At length, it is said, just in the brown hour of twilight, when the owls began to hoot and the bats to flit about, his attention was attracted by the clamor of carrion crows that were hovering about a cypress tree. He looked and beheld a bundle tied in a check apron and hanging in the branches of a tree; with a great vulture perched hard by, as if keeping watch upon it. He leaped with joy, for he recognized his wife's apron, and supposed it to contain the household valuables.

"Let us get hold of the property," said he consolingly to himself, "and we will endeavor to do without the woman."

As he scrambled up the tree the vulture spread its wide wings, and sailed off screaming into the deep shadows of the forest. Tom seized the check apron, but, woful sight! found nothing but a heart and liver tied up in it.

Such, according to the most authentic old story, was all that was to be found of Tom's wife. She had probably attempted to deal with the black man as she had been accustomed to deal with her husband; but though a female scold is generally considered a match for the devil, yet in this instance she appears to have had the worst of it. She must have died game, however: from the part that remained unconquered. Indeed, it is said Tom noticed many prints of cloven feet deeply stamped about the tree, and several handfuls of hair that looked as if they had been plucked from the coarse black shock of the woodsman. Tom knew his wife's prowess by experience. He shrugged his shoulders as he looked at the signs of a fierce clapper-clawing. "Egad," said he to himself, "Old Scratch must have had a tough time of it!"

Tom consoled himself for the loss of his property by the loss of his wife; for he was a little of a philosopher. He even felt something like gratitude towards the black woodsman, who he considered had done him a kindness. He sought, therefore, to cultivate a farther acquaintance with him, but for some time without success; the old black legs played shy, for whatever people may think, he is not always to be had for calling for; he knows how to play his cards when pretty sure of his game.

At length, it is said, when delay had whetted Tom's eagerness to the quick, and prepared him to agree to any thing rather than not gain the promised treasure, he met the black man one evening in his usual woodman dress, with his axe on his shoulder, sauntering along the edge of the swamp, and humming a tune. He affected to receive Tom's advance with great indifference, made brief replies, and went on humming his tune.

By degrees, however, Tom brought him to business, and they began to haggle about the terms on which the former was to have the pirate's treasure. There was one condition which need not be mentioned, being generally understood in all cases where the devil grants favors; but there were others about which, though of less importance, he was inflexibly obstinate. He insisted that the money found through his means should be employed in his service. He proposed, therefore, that Tom should employ it in the black traffic; that is to say, that he should fit out a slave ship. This, however, Tom resolutely refused; he was bad enough, in all conscience; but the devil himself could not tempt him to turn slave dealer.

Finding Tom so squeamish on this point, he did not insist upon it, but proposed instead that he should turn usurer; the devil being extremely anxious for the increase of usurers, looking upon them as his peculiar people.

To this no objections were made, for it was just to Tom's taste.

"You shall open a broker's shop in Boston next month," said the black man.

"I'll do it tomorrow, if you wish," said Tom Walker.

"You shall lend money at two per cent a month."

"Egad, I'll charge four!" replied Tom Walker.

"You shall extort bonds, foreclose mortgages, drive the merchant to bankruptcy—"

"I'll drive him to the d——l," cried Tom Walker, eagerly.

"You are the usurer for my money!" said the black legs, with delight. "When will you want the rhino?"

"This very night."

"Done!" said the devil.

"Done!" said Tom Walker.—So they shook hands and struck a bargain.

A few days' time saw Tom Walker seated behind his desk in a counting house in Boston. His reputation for a ready-moneyed man, who would lend money out for a good consideration, soon spread abroad. Every body remembers the days of Governor Belcher, when money was particularly scarce. It was a time of paper credit. The country had been deluged with government bills; the famous Land Bank had been established; there had been a rage for speculating; the people had run mad with schemes for new settlements; for building cities in the wilderness; land jobbers went about with maps of grants, and townships, and Eldorados, lying nobody knew where, but which every body was ready to purchase. In a word, the great speculating fever which breaks out every now and then in the country, had raged to an alarming degree, and body was dreaming of making sudden fortunes from nothing. As usual, the fever had subsided; the dream had gone off, and the imaginary fortunes with it; the patients were left in doleful plight, and the whole country resounded with the consequent cry of "hard times."

At this propitious time of public distress did Tom Walker set up as a usurer in Boston. His door was soon thronged by customers. The needy and the adventurous; the gambling speculator; the dreaming land jobber; the thriftless tradesman; the merchant with cracked credit; in short, every one driven to raise money by desperate means and desperate sacrifices, hurried to Tom Walker.

Thus Tom was the universal friend of the needy, and he acted like a "friend in need;" that is to say, he always exacted good pay and good security. In proportion to the distress of the applicant was the hardness of his terms. He accumulated bonds and mortgages; gradually squeezed his customers closer and closer; and sent them, at length, dry as a sponge from his door.

In this way he made money hand over hand; became a rich and mighty man, and exalted his cocked hat upon 'change. He built himself, as usual, a vast house, out of ostentation; but left the greater part of it unfinished and unfurnished out of parsimony. He even set up a carriage in the fullness of his vain-glory, though he nearly starved the horses which drew it; and as the ungreased wheels groaned and screeched on the axle trees, you would have thought you heard the souls of the poor debtors he was squeezing.

As Tom waxed old, however, he grew thoughtful. Having secured the good things of this world, he began to feel anxious about those of the next. He thought with regret on the bargain he had made with his black friend, and set his wits to work to cheat him out of the conditions. He became, therefore, all of a sudden, a violent church-goer. He prayed loudly and strenuously as if heaven were to be taken by force of lungs. Indeed, one might always tell when he had sinned most during the week, by the clamor of his Sunday devotion. The quiet Christians who had been modestly and steadfastly travelling Zion-ward, were struck with self-reproach at seeing themselves so suddenly outstripped in their career by this new-made convert. Tom was as rigid in religious, as in money matters; he was a stern supervisor and censurer of his neighbors, and seemed to think every sin entered up to their account became a credit on his own side of the page. He even talked of the expediency of reviving the persecution of quakers and anabaptists. In a word, Tom's zeal became as notorious as his riches.

Still, in spite of all this strenuous attention to forms, Tom had a Lurking dread that the devil, after all, would have his due. That he might not be taken unawares, therefore, it is said he always carried a small Bible in his coat pocket. He had also a great folio Bible on his counting-house desk, and would frequently be found reading it when people called on business; on such occasions he would lay his green spectacles on the book, to mark the place, while he turned round to drive some usurious bargain.

Some say that Tom grew a little crack-brained in his old days, and that fancying his end approaching, he had his horse new shod, saddled and bridled, and buried with his feet uppermost; because he supposed that at the last day the world would be turned upside down; in which case he should find his horse standing ready for mounting, and he was determined at the worst to give his old friend a run for it. This, however, is probably a mere old wives' fable. If he really did take such a precaution it was totally superfluous; at least so says the authentic old legend, which closes his story in the following manner:

On one hot afternoon in the dog days, just as a terrible black thunder-gust was coming up, Tom sat in his counting-house in his white linen cap and India silk morning-gown. He was on the point of foreclosing a mortgage, by which he would complete the ruin of an unlucky land speculator for whom he had professed the greatest friendship. The poor land jobber begged him to grant a few months' indulgence. Tom had grown testy and irritated and refused another day.

"My family will be ruined and brought upon the parish," said the land jobber.

"Charity begins at home," replied Tom, "I must take care of myself in these hard times."

"You have made so much money out of me," said the speculator.

Tom lost his patience and his piety—"The devil take me," said he, "if I have made a farthing!"

Just then there were three loud knocks at the street door. He stepped out to see who was there. A black man was holding a black horse which neighed and stamped with impatience.

"Tom, you're come for!" said the black fellow, gruffly. Tom shrunk back, but too late. He had left his little Bible at the bottom of his coat pocket, and his big Bible on the desk buried under the mortgage he was about to foreclose: never was sinner taken more unawares. The black man whisked him like a child astride the horse and away he galloped in the midst of a thunder-storm. The clerks stuck their pens behind their ears and stared after him from the windows. Away went Tom Walker, dashing down the street; his white cap bobbing up and down; his morning-gown fluttering in the wind, and his steed striking fire out of the pavement at every bound. When the clerks turned to look for the black man he had disappeared.

Tom Walker never returned to foreclose the mortgage. A countryman who lived on the borders of the swamp, reported that in the height of the thunder-gust he had heard a great clattering of hoofs and a howling along the road, and that when he ran to the window he just caught sight of a figure, such as I have described, on a horse that galloped like mad across the fields, over the hills and down into the black hemlock swamp towards the old Indian fort; and that shortly after a thunder-bolt fell in that direction which seemed to set the whole forest in a blaze.

The good people of Boston shook their heads and shrugged their shoulders, but had been so much accustomed to witches and goblins and tricks of the devil in all kinds of shapes from the first settlement of the colony, that they were not so much horror-struck as might have been expected. Trustees were appointed to take charge of Tom's effects. There was nothing, however, to administer upon. On searching his coffers all his bonds and mortgages were found reduced to cinders. In place of gold and silver, his iron chest was filled with chips and shavings; two skeletons lay in his stable instead of his half-starved horses, and the very next day his great house took fire and was burnt to the ground.

Such was the end of Tom Walker and his ill-gotten wealth. Let all griping money-brokers lay this story to heart. The truth of it is not to be doubted. The very hole under the oak trees, from whence he dug Kidd's money, is to be seen to this day; and the neighboring swamp and old Indian fort is often haunted in stormy nights by a figure on horseback, in a morning-gown and white cap, which is doubtless the troubled spirit of the usurer. In fact, the story has resolved itself into a proverb, and is the origin of that popular saying prevalent throughout New-England, of "The Devil and Tom Walker."

Such, as nearly as I can recollect, was the tenor of the tale told by the Cape Cod whaler. There were divers trivial particulars which I have omitted, and which wiled away the morning very pleasantly, until the time of tide favorable for fishing being passed, it was proposed that we should go to land, and refresh ourselves under the trees, until the noontide heat should have abated.

We accordingly landed on a delectable part of the island of Mannahatta, in that shady and embowered tract formerly under dominion of the ancient family of the Hardenbrooks. It was a spot well known to me in the course of the aquatic expeditions of my boyhood. Not far from where we landed, was an old Dutch family vault, in the side of a bank, which had been an object of great awe and fable among my schoolboy associates. There were several mouldering coffins within; but what gave it a fearful interest with us, was its being connected in our minds with the pirate wreck which lay among the rocks of Hell Gate. There were also stories of smuggling connected with it, particularly during a time that this retired spot was owned by a noted burgher called

Ready Money Prevost; a man of whom it was whispered that he had many and mysterious dealings with parts beyond seas. All these things, however, had been jumbled together in our minds in that vague way in which such things are mingled up in the tales of boyhood.

While I was musing upon these matters my companions had spread a repast, from the contents of our well-stored pannier, and we solaced ourselves during the warm sunny hours of mid-day under the shade of a broad chestnut, on the cool grassy carpet that swept down to the water's edge. While lolling on the grass I summoned up the dusky recollections of my boyhood respecting this place, and repeated them like the imperfectly remembered traces of a dream, for the entertainment of my companions. When I had finished, a worthy old burgher, John Josse Vandermoere, the same who once related to me the adventures of Dolph Heyliger, broke silence and observed, that he recollected a story about money-digging which occurred in this very neighborhood. As we knew him to be one of the most authentic narrators of the province we begged him to let us have the particulars, and accordingly, while we refreshed ourselves with a clean long pipe of Blase Moore's tobacco, the authentic John Josse Vandermoere related the following tale.

Wolfert Webber; or, Golden Dreams

In the year of grace one thousand seven hundred and—blank—for I do not remember the precise date; however, it was somewhere in the early part of the last century, there lived in the ancient city of the Manhattoes a worthy burgher, Wolfert Webber by name. He was descended from old Cobus Webber of the Brille in Holland, one of the original settlers, famous for introducing the cultivation of cabbages, and who came over to the province during the protectorship of Oloffe Van Kortlandt, otherwise called the Dreamer. The field in which Cobus Webber first planted himself and his cabbages had remained ever since in the family, who continued in the same line of husbandry, with that praiseworthy perseverance for which our Dutch burghers are noted. The whole family genius, during several generations was devoted to the study and development of this one noble vegetable; and to this concentration of intellect may doubtless be ascribed the prodigious size and renown to which the Webber cabbages attained.

The Webber dynasty continued in uninterrupted succession; and never did a line give more unquestionable proofs of legitimacy. The eldest son succeeded to the looks, as well as the territory of his sire; and had the portraits of this line of tranquil potentates been taken, they would have presented a row of heads marvellously resembling in shape and magnitude the vegetables over which they reigned.

The seat of government continued unchanged in the family mansion:—a Dutch-built house, with a front, or rather gable-end of yellow brick, tapering to a point, with the customary iron weathercock at the top. Every thing about the building bore the air of long-settled ease and security. Flights of martins peopled the little coops nailed against the walls, and swallows built their nests under the eaves; and every one knows that these house-loving birds bring good luck to the dwelling where they take up their abode. In a bright sunny morning in early summer, it was delectable to hear their cheerful notes, as they sported about in the pure, sweet air, chirping forth, as it were, the greatness and prosperity of the Webbers.

Thus quietly and comfortably did this excellent family vegetate under the shade of a mighty button-wood tree, which by little and little grew so great as entirely to overshadow their palace. The city gradually spread its suburbs round their domain. Houses sprung up to interrupt their prospects. The rural lanes in the vicinity began to grow into the bustle and populousness of streets; in short, with all the habits of rustic life they began to find themselves the inhabitants of a city.

Still, however, they maintained their hereditary character, and Hereditary possessions, with all the tenacity of petty German princes in the midst of the Empire. Wolfert was the last of the line, and succeeded to the patriarchal bench at the door, under the family tree, and swayed the sceptre of his fathers, a kind of rural potentate in the midst of a metropolis.

To share the cares and sweets of sovereignty, he had taken unto himself a help-mate, one of that excellent kind called stirring women; that is to say, she was one of those notable little housewives who are always busy when there is nothing to do. Her activity however, took one particular direction; her whole life seemed devoted to intense knitting; whether at home or abroad; walking or sitting, her needles were continually in motion, and it is even affirmed that by her unwearied industry she very nearly supplied her household with stockings throughout the year. This worthy couple were blessed with one daughter, who was brought up with great tenderness and care; uncommon pains had been taken with her education, so that she could stitch in every variety of way; make all kinds of pickles and preserves, and mark her own name on a sampler. The influence of her taste was seen also in the family garden, where the ornamental began to mingle with the useful; whole rows of fiery marigolds and splendid hollyhocks bordered the cabbage-beds; and gigantic sunflowers lolled their broad, jolly faces over the fences, seeming to ogle most affectionately the passers-by.

Thus reigned and vegetated Wolfert Webber over his paternal acres, peaceably and contentedly. Not but that, like all other sovereigns, he had his occasional cares and vexations. The growth of his native city sometimes caused him annoyance. His little territory gradually became hemmed in by streets and houses, which intercepted air and sunshine. He was now and then subject to the irruptions of the border population, that infest the streets of a metropolis, who would sometimes make midnight forays into his dominions, and carry off captive whole platoons of his noblest subjects. Vagrant swine would make a descent, too, now and then, when the gate was left open, and lay all waste before them; and mischievous urchins would often decapitate the illustrious sunflowers, the glory of the garden, as they lolled their heads so fondly over the walls. Still all these were petty grievances, which might now and then ruffle the surface of his mind, as a summer breeze will ruffle the surface of a mill-pond; but they could not disturb the deep-seated quiet of his soul. He would seize a trusty staff, that stood behind the door, issue suddenly out, and anoint the back of the aggressor, whether pig or urchin, and then return within doors, marvellously refreshed and tranquillized.

The chief cause of anxiety to honest Wolfert, however, was the growing prosperity of the city. The expenses of living doubled and trebled; but he could not double and treble the magnitude of his cabbages; and the number of competitors prevented the increase of price; thus, therefore, while every one around him grew richer, Wolfert grew poorer, and he could not, for the life of him, perceive how the evil was to be remedied.

This growing care which increased from day to day, had its gradual effect upon our worthy burgher; insomuch, that it at length implanted two or three wrinkles on his brow; things unknown before in the family of the Webbers; and it seemed to pinch up the corners of his cocked hat into an expression of anxiety, totally opposite to the tranquil, broad-brimmed, low-crowned beavers of his illustrious progenitors.

Perhaps even this would not have materially disturbed the serenity of his mind had he had only himself and his wife to care for; but there was his daughter gradually growing to maturity; and all the world knows when daughters begin to ripen no fruit or flower requires so much looking after. I have no talent at describing female charms, else fain would I depict the progress of this little Dutch beauty. How her blue eyes grew deeper and deeper, and her cherry lips redder and redder; and how she ripened and ripened, and rounded and rounded in the opening breath of sixteen summers, until, in her seventeenth spring, she seemed ready to burst out of her bodice like a half-blown rose-bud.

Ah, well-a-day! could I but show her as she was then, tricked out on a Sunday morning in the hereditary finery of the old Dutch clothes-press, of which her mother had confided to her the key. The wedding dress of her grandmother, modernized for use, with sundry ornaments, handed down as heirlooms in the family. Her pale brown hair smoothed with buttermilk in flat waving lines on each side of her fair forehead. The chain of yellow virgin gold, that encircled her neck; the little cross, that just rested at the entrance of a soft valley of happiness, as if it would sanctify the place. The—but pooh!—it is not for an old man like me to be prosing about female beauty: suffice it to say, Amy had attained her seventeenth year. Long since had her sampler exhibited hearts in couples desperately transfixed with arrows, and true lovers' knots worked in deep blue silk; and it was evident she began to languish for some more interesting occupation than the rearing of sunflowers or pickling of cucumbers.

At this critical period of female existence, when the heart within a damsel's bosom, like its emblem, the miniature which hangs without, is apt to be engrossed by a single image, a new visitor began to make his appearance under the roof of Wolfert Webber. This was Dirk Waldron, the only son of a poor widow, but who could boast of more fathers than any lad in the province; for his mother had had four husbands, and this only child, so that though born in her last wedlock, he might fairly claim to be the tardy fruit of a long course of cultivation. This son of four fathers united the merits and the vigor of his sires. If he had not a great family before him, he seemed likely to have a great one after him; for you had only to look at the fresh gamesome youth, to see that he was formed to be the founder of a mighty race.

This youngster gradually became an intimate visitor of the family. He talked little, but he sat long. He filled the father's pipe when it was empty, gathered up the mother's knitting-needle, or ball of worsted when it fell to the ground; stroked the sleek coat of the tortoise-shell cat, and replenished the teapot for the daughter from the bright copper kettle that sung before the fire. All these quiet little offices may seem of trifling import, but when true love is translated into Low Dutch, it is in this way that it eloquently expresses itself. They were not lost upon the Webber family. The winning youngster found marvellous favor in the eyes of the mother; the tortoise-shell cat, albeit the most staid and demure of her kind, gave indubitable signs of approbation of his visits, the tea-kettle seemed to sing out a cheering note of welcome at his approach, and if the sly glances of the daughter might be rightly read, as she sat bridling and dimpling, and sewing by her mother's side, she was not a wit behind Dame Webber, or grimalkin, or the tea-kettle in good-will.

Wolfert alone saw nothing of what was going on. Profoundly wrapt up in meditation on the growth of the city and his cabbages, he sat looking in the fire, and puffing his pipe in silence. One night, however, as the gentle Amy, according to custom, lighted her lover to the outer door, and he, according to custom, took his parting salute, the smack resounded so vigorously through the long, silent entry as to startle even the dull ear of Wolfert. He was slowly roused to a new source of anxiety. It had never entered into his head, that this mere child, who, as it seemed but the other day, had been climbing about his knees, and playing with dolls and baby-houses, could all at once be thinking of love and matrimony. He rubbed his eyes, examined into the fact, and really found that while he had been dreaming of other matters, she had actually grown into a woman, and what was more, had fallen in love. Here were new cares for poor Wolfert. He was a kind father, but he was a prudent man. The young man was a very stirring lad; but then he had neither money or land. Wolfert's ideas all ran in one channel, and he saw no alternative in case of a marriage, but to portion off the young couple with a corner of his cabbage garden, the whole of which was barely sufficient for the support of his family.

Like a prudent father, therefore, he determined to nip this passion in the bud, and forbade the youngster the house, though sorely did it go against his fatherly heart, and many a silent tear did it cause in the bright eye of his daughter. She showed herself, however, a pattern of filial piety and obedience. She never pouted and sulked; she never flew in the face of parental authority; she never fell into a passion, or fell into hysterics, as many romantic novel-read young ladies would do. Not she, indeed! She was none such heroical rebellious trumpery, I warrant ye. On the contrary, she acquiesced like an obedient daughter; shut the street-door in her lover's face, and if ever she did grant him an interview, it was either out of the kitchen window, or over the garden fence.

Wolfert was deeply cogitating these things in his mind, and his brow wrinkled with unusual care, as he wended his way one Saturday afternoon to a rural inn, about two miles from the city. It was a favorite resort of the Dutch part of the community from being always held by a Dutch line of landlords, and retaining an air and relish of the good old times. It was a Dutch-built house, that had probably been a country seat of some opulent burgher in the early time of the settlement. It stood near a point of land, called Corlears Hook, which stretches out into the Sound, and against which the tide, at its flux and reflux, sets with extraordinary rapidity. The venerable and somewhat crazy mansion was distinguished from afar, by a grove of elms and sycamores that seemed to wave a hospitable invitation, while a few weeping willows with their dank, drooping foliage, resembling falling waters, gave an idea of coolness, that rendered it an attractive spot during the heats of summer.

Here, therefore, as I said, resorted many of the old inhabitants of the Manhattoes, where, while some played at the shuffle-board and quoits and ninepins, others smoked a deliberate pipe, and talked over public affairs.

It was on a blustering autumnal afternoon that Wolfert made his visit to the inn. The grove of elms and willows was stripped of its leaves, which whirled in rustling eddies about the fields.

The ninepin alley was deserted, for the premature chilliness of the day had driven the company within doors. As it was Saturday afternoon, the habitual club was in session, composed principally of regular Dutch burghers, though mingled occasionally with persons of various, character and country, as is natural in a place of such motley population.

Beside the fire-place, and in a huge leather-bottomed armchair, sat the dictator of this little world, the venerable Rem, or, as it was pronounced, Ramm Rapelye.

He was a man of Walloon race, and illustrious for the antiquity of his line, his great grandmother having been the first white child born in the province. But he was still more illustrious for his wealth and dignity: he had long filled the noble office of alderman, and was a man to whom the governor himself took off his hat. He had maintained possession of the leathern-bottomed chair from time immemorial; and had gradually waxed in bulk as he sat in his seat of government, until in the course of years he filled its whole magnitude. His word was decisive with his subjects; for he was so rich a man, that he was never expected to support any opinion by argument. The landlord waited on him with peculiar officiousness; not that he paid better than his neighbors, but then the coin of a rich man seems always to be so much more acceptable. The landlord had always a pleasant word and a joke, to insinuate in the ear of the august Ramm. It is true, Ramm never laughed, and, indeed, maintained a mastiff-like gravity, and even surliness of aspect, yet he now and then rewarded mine host with a token of approbation; which, though nothing more nor less than a kind of grunt, yet delighted the landlord more than a broad laugh from a poorer man.

"This will be a rough night for the money-diggers," said mine host, as a gust of wind howled round the house, and rattled at the windows.

"What, are they at their works again?" said an English half-pay captain, with one eye, who was a frequent attendant at the inn.

"Aye, are they," said the landlord, "and well may they be. They've had luck of late. They say a great pot of money has been dug up in the field, just behind Stuyvesant's orchard. Folks think it must have been buried there in old times by Peter Stuyvesant, the Dutch Governor."

"Fudge!" said the one-eyed man of war, as he added a small portion of water to a bottom of brandy.

"Well, you may believe, or not, as you please," said mine host, somewhat nettled; "but every body knows that the old governor buried a great deal of his money at the time of the Dutch troubles, when the English red-coats seized on the province. They say, too, the old gentleman walks; aye, and in the very Same dress that he wears in the picture which hangs up in the family house."

"Fudge!" said the half-pay officer.

"Fudge, if you please!—But didn't Corney Van Zandt see him at midnight, stalking about in the meadow with his wooden leg, and a drawn sword in his hand, that flashed like fire? And what can he be walking for, but because people have been troubling the place where he buried his money in old times?"

Here the landlord was interrupted by several guttural sounds from Ramm Rapelye, betokening that he was laboring with the unusual production of an idea. As he was too great a man to be slighted by a prudent publican, mine host respectfully paused until he should deliver himself. The corpulent frame of this mighty burgher now gave all the symptoms of a volcanic mountain on the point of an eruption. First, there was a certain heaving of the abdomen, not unlike an earthquake; then was emitted a cloud of tobacco smoke from that crater, his mouth; then there was a kind of rattle in the throat, as if the idea were working its way up through a region of phlegm; then there were several disjointed members of a sentence thrown out, ending in a cough; at length his voice forced its way in the slow, but absolute tone of a man who feels the weight of his purse, if not of his ideas; every portion of his speech being marked by a testy puff of tobacco smoke.

"Who talks of old Peter Stuyvesant's walking?—puff—Have people no respect for persons?—puff—puff—Peter Stuyvesant knew better what to do with his money than to bury it—puff—I know the Stuyvesant family—puff—every one of them—puff—not a more respectable family in the province—puff—old standers—puff—warm householders—puff—none of your upstarts—puff—puff—puff.—Don't talk to me of Peter Stuyvesant's walking—puff—puff—puff—puff."

Here the redoubtable Ramm contracted his brow, clasped up his mouth, till it wrinkled at each corner, and redoubled his smoking with such vehemence, that the cloudly volumes soon wreathed round his head, as the smoke envelopes the awful summit of Mount Etna.

A general silence followed the sudden rebuke of this very rich man. The subject, however, was too interesting to be readily abandoned. The conversation soon broke forth again from the lips of Peechy Prauw Van Hook, the chronicler of the club, one of those narrative old men who seem to grow incontinent of words, as they grow old, until their talk flows from them almost involuntarily.

Peechy, who could at any time tell as many stories in an evening as his hearers could digest in a month, now resumed the conversation, by affirming that, to his knowledge, money had at different times been dug up in various parts of the island. The lucky persons who had discovered them had always dreamt of them three times beforehand, and what was worthy of remark, these treasures had never been found but by some descendant of the good old Dutch families, which clearly proved that they had been buried by Dutchmen in the olden time.

"Fiddle-stick with your Dutchmen!" cried the half-pay officer. "The Dutch had nothing to do with them. They were all buried by Kidd, the pirate, and his crew."

Here a key-note was touched that roused the whole company. The name of Captain Kidd was like a talisman in those times, and was associated with a thousand marvellous stories.

The half-pay officer was a man of great weight among the peaceable members of the club, by reason of his military character, and of the gunpowder scenes which, by his own account, he had witnessed.

The golden stories of Kidd, however, were resolutely rivalled by the tales of Peechy Prauw, who, rather than suffer his Dutch progenitors to be eclipsed by a foreign freebooter, enriched every spot in the neighborhood with the hidden wealth of Peter Stuyvesant and his contemporaries.

Not a word of this conversation was lost upon Wolfert Webber. He returned pensively home, full of magnificent ideas of buried riches. The soil of his native island seemed to be turned into gold-dust; and every field teemed with treasure. His head almost reeled at the thought how often he must have heedlessly rambled over places where countless sums lay, scarcely covered by the turf beneath his feet. His mind was in a vertigo with this whirl of new ideas. As he came in sight of the venerable mansion of his forefathers, and the little realm where the Webbers had so long and so contentedly flourished, his gorge rose at the narrowness of his destiny.

"Unlucky Wolfert!" exclaimed he, "others can go to bed and dream themselves into whole mines of wealth; they have but to seize a spade in the morning, and turn up doubloons like potatoes; but thou must dream of hardship, and rise to poverty—must dig thy field from year's end to year's end, and—and yet raise nothing but cabbages!"

Wolfert Webber went to bed with a heavy heart; and it was long before the golden visions that disturbed his brain, permitted him to sink into repose. The same visions, however, extended into his sleeping thoughts, and assumed a more definite form. He dreamt that he had discovered an immense treasure in the centre of his garden. At every stroke of the spade he laid bare a golden ingot; diamond crosses sparkled out of the dust; bags of money turned up their bellies, corpulent with pieces of eight, or venerable doubloons; and chests, wedged close with moidores, ducats, and pistareens, yawned before his ravished eyes, and vomited forth their glittering contents.

Wolfert awoke a poorer man than ever. He had no heart to go about his daily concerns, which appeared so paltry and profitless; but sat all day long in the chimney-corner, picturing to himself ingots and heaps of gold in the fire. The next night his dream was repeated. He was again in his garden, digging, and laying open stores of hidden wealth. There was something very singular in this repetition. He passed another day of reverie, and though it was cleaning-day, and the house, as usual in Dutch households, completely topsy-turvy, yet he sat unmoved amidst the general uproar.

The third night he went to bed with a palpitating heart. He put on his red nightcap, wrong side outwards for good luck. It was deep midnight before his anxious mind could settle itself into sleep. Again the golden dream was repeated, and again he saw his garden teeming with ingots and money-bags.

Wolfert rose the next morning in complete bewilderment. A dream three times repeated was never known to lie; and if so, his fortune was made.

In his agitation he put on his waistcoat with the hind part before, and this was a corroboration of good luck. He no longer doubted that a huge store of money lay buried somewhere in his cabbage-field, coyly waiting to be sought for, and he half repined at having so long been scratching about the surface of the soil, instead of digging to the centre.

He took his seat at the breakfast-table full of these speculations; asked his daughter to put a lump of gold in to his tea, and on handing his wife a plate of slap-jacks, begging her to help herself to a doubloon.

His grand care now was how to secure this immense treasure without it being known. Instead of working regularly in his grounds in the day-time, he now stole from his bed at night, and with spade and pickaxe, went to work to rip up and dig about his paternal acres, from one end to the other. In a little time the whole garden, which had presented such a goodly and regular appearance, with its phalanx of cabbages, like a vegetable army in battle array, was reduced to a scene of devastation, while the relentless Wolfert, with nightcap on head, and lantern and spade in hand, stalked through the slaughtered ranks, the destroying angel of his own vegetable world.

Every morning bore testimony to the ravages of the preceding night in cabbages of all ages and conditions, from the tender sprout to the full-grown head, piteously rooted from their quiet beds like worthless weeds, and left to wither in the sunshine. It was in vain Wolfert's wife remonstrated; it was in vain his darling daughter wept over the destruction of some favorite marygold. "Thou shalt have gold of another guess-sort," he would cry, chucking her under the chin; "thou shalt have a string of crooked ducats for thy wedding-necklace, my child." His family began really to fear that the poor man's wits were diseased. He muttered in his sleep at night of mines of wealth, of pearls and diamonds and bars of gold. In the day-time he was moody and abstracted, and walked about as if in a trance. Dame Webber held frequent councils with all the old women of the neighborhood, not omitting the parish dominie; scarce an hour in the day but a knot of them might be seen wagging their white caps together round her door, while the poor woman made some piteous recital. The daughter, too, was fain to seek for more frequent consolation from the stolen interviews of her favored swain, Dirk Waldron. The delectable little Dutch songs with which she used to dulcify the house grew less and less frequent, and she would forget her sewing and look wistfully in her father's face as he sat pondering by the fireside.

Wolfert caught her eye one day fixed on him thus anxiously, and for a moment was roused from his golden reveries—"Cheer up, my girl," said he, exultingly, "why dost thou droop?—thou shalt hold up thy head one day with the—and the Schenaerhorns, the Van Hornes, and the Van Dams—the patroon himself shall be glad to get thee for his son!"

Amy shook her head at this vain-glorious boast, and was more than ever in doubt of the soundness of the good man's intellect.

In the meantime Wolfert went on digging, but the field was extensive, and as his dream had indicated no precise spot, he had to dig at random. The winter set in before one-tenth of the scene of promise had been explored. The ground became too frozen and the nights too cold for the labors of the spade. No sooner, however, did the returning warmth of spring loosen the soil, and the small frogs begin to pipe in the meadows, but Wolfert resumed his labors with renovated zeal. Still, however, the hours of industry were reversed. Instead of working cheerily all day, planting and setting out his vegetables, he remained thoughtfully idle, until the shades of night summoned him to his secret labors. In this way he continued to dig from night to night, and week to week, and month to month, but not a stiver did he find. On the contrary, the more he digged the poorer he grew. The rich soil of his garden was digged away, and the sand and gravel from beneath were thrown to the surface, until the whole field presented an aspect of sandy barrenness.

In the meantime the seasons gradually rolled on. The little frogs that had piped in the meadows in early spring, croaked as bull-frogs in the brooks during the summer heats, and then sunk into silence. The peach tree budded, blossomed, and bore its fruit. The swallows and martins came, twittered about the roof, built their nests, reared their young, held their congress along the eaves, and then winged their flight in search of another spring. The caterpillar spun its winding-sheet, dangled in it from the great buttonwood tree that shaded the house, turned into a moth, fluttered with the last sunshine of summer, and disappeared; and finally the leaves of the buttonwood tree turned yellow, then brown, then rustled one by one to the ground, and whirling about in little eddies of wind and dust, whispered that winter was at hand.

Wolfert gradually awoke from his dream of wealth as the year declined. He had reared no crop to supply the wants of his household during the sterility of winter. The season was long and severe, and for the first time the family was really straightened in its comforts. By degrees a revulsion of thought took place in Wolfert's mind, common to those whose golden dreams have been disturbed by pinching realities. The idea gradually stole upon him that he should come to want. He already considered himself one of the most unfortunate men in the province, having lost such an incalculable amount of undiscovered treasure, and now, when thousands of pounds had eluded his search, to be perplexed for shillings and pence was cruel in the extreme.

Haggard care gathered about his brow; he went about with a money-seeking air, his eyes bent downwards into the dust, and carrying his hands in his pockets, as men are apt to do when they have nothing else to put into them. He could not even pass the city almshouse without giving it a rueful glance, as if destined to be his future abode.

The strangeness of his conduct and of his looks occasioned much speculation and remark. For a long time he was suspected of being crazy, and then every body pitied him; at length it began to be suspected that he was poor, and then every body avoided him.

The rich old burghers of his acquaintance met him, outside of the door when he called, entertained him hospitably on the threshold, pressed him warmly by the hand on parting, shook their heads as he walked away, with the kind-hearted expression of "poor Wolfert," and turned a corner nimbly, if by chance they saw him approaching as they walked the streets. Even the barber and cobbler of the neighborhood, and a tattered tailor in an alley hard by, three of the poorest and merriest rogues in the world, eyed him with that abundant sympathy which usually attends a lack of means, and there is not a doubt but their pockets would have been at his command, only that they happened to be empty.

Thus every body deserted the Webber mansion, as if poverty were contagious, like the plague; every body but honest Dirk Waldron, who still kept up his stolen visits to the daughter, and indeed seemed to wax more affectionate as the fortunes of his mistress were on the wane.

Many months had elapsed since Wolfert had frequented his old resort, the rural inn. He was taking a long lonely walk one Saturday afternoon, musing over his wants and disappointments, when his feet took instinctively their wonted direction, and on awaking out of a reverie, he found himself before the door of the inn. For some moments he hesitated whether to enter, but his heart yearned for companionship; and where can a ruined man find better companionship than at a tavern, where there is neither sober example nor sober advice to put him out of countenance?

Wolfert found several of the old frequenters of the tavern at their usual posts, and seated in their usual places; but one was missing, the great Ramm Rapelye, who for many years had filled the chair of state. His place was supplied by a stranger, who seemed, however, completely at home in the chair and the tavern. He was rather under-size, but deep-chested, square, and muscular. His broad shoulders, double joints, and bow-knees, gave tokens of prodigious strength. His face was dark and weather-beaten; a deep scar, as if from the slash of a cutlass, had almost divided his nose, and made a gash in his upper lip, through which his teeth shone like a bull-dog's. A mass of iron gray hair gave a grizzly finish to his hard-favored visage. His dress was of an amphibious character. He wore an old hat edged with tarnished lace, and cocked in martial style, on one side of his head; a rusty blue military coat with brass buttons, and a wide pair of short petticoat trousers, or rather breeches, for they were gathered up at the knees. He ordered every body about him with an authoritative air; talked in a brattling voice, that sounded like the crackling of thorns under a pot; damned the landlord and servants with perfect impunity, and was waited upon with greater obsequiousness than had ever been shown to the mighty Ramm himself.

Wolfert's curiosity was awakened to know who and what was this stranger who had thus usurped absolute sway in this ancient domain. He could get nothing, however, but vague information. Peechy Prauw took him aside, into a remote corner of the hall, and there in an under-voice, and with great caution, imparted to him all that he knew on the subject. The inn had been aroused several months before, on a dark stormy night, by repeated long shouts, that seemed like the howlings of a wolf. They came from the water-side; and at length were distinguished to be hailing the house in the seafaring manner. "House-a-hoy!" The landlord turned out with his head-waiter, tapster, hostler, and errand boy—that is to say with his old negro Cuff. On approaching the place from whence the voice proceeded, they found this amphibious-looking personage at the water's edge, quite alone, and seated on a great oaken sea-chest. How he came there, whether he had been set on shore from some boat, or had floated to land on his chest, nobody could tell, for he did not seem disposed to answer questions, and there was something in his looks and manners that put a stop to all questioning. Suffice it to say, he took possession of a corner room of the inn, to which his chest was removed with great difficulty. Here he had remained ever since, keeping about the inn and its vicinity. Sometimes, it is true, he disappeared for one, two, or three days at a time, going and returning without giving any notice or account of his movements. He always appeared to have plenty of money, though often of very strange, outlandish coinage; and he regularly paid his bill every evening before turning in.

He had fitted up his room to his own fancy, having slung a hammock from the ceiling instead of a bed, and decorated the walls with rusty pistols and cutlasses of foreign workmanship. A great part of his time was passed in this room, seated by the window, which commanded a wide view of the Sound, a short old-fashioned pipe in his mouth, a glass of rum toddy at his elbow, and a pocket telescope in his hand, with which he reconnoitred every boat that moved upon the water. Large square-rigged vessels seemed to excite but little attention; but the moment he descried any thing with a shoulder-of-mutton sail, or that a barge, or yawl, or jolly boat hove in sight, up went the telescope, and he examined it with the most scrupulous attention.

All this might have passed without much notice, for in those times the province was so much the resort of adventurers of all characters and climes that any oddity in dress or behavior attracted but little attention. But in a little while this strange sea monster, thus strangely cast up on dry land, began to encroach upon the long-established customs and customers of the place; to interfere in a dictatorial manner in the affairs of the ninepin alley and the bar-room, until in the end he usurped an absolute command over the little inn. It was in vain to attempt to withstand his authority. He was not exactly quarrelsome, but boisterous and peremptory, like one accustomed to tyrannize on a quarter deck; and there was a dare-devil air about every thing he said and did, that inspired a wariness in all bystanders. Even the half-pay officer, so long the hero of the club, was soon silenced by him; and the quiet burghers stared with wonder at seeing their inflammable man of war so readily and quietly extinguished.

And then the tales that he would tell were enough to make a peaceable man's hair stand on end. There was not a sea fight, or marauding or free-booting adventure that had happened within the last twenty years but he seemed perfectly versed in it. He delighted to talk of the exploits of the buccaneers in the West-Indies and on the Spanish Main. How his eyes would glisten as he described the waylaying of treasure ships, the desperate fights, yard arm and yard arm—broadside and broad side—the boarding and capturing of large Spanish galleons! with what chuckling relish would he describe the descent upon some rich Spanish colony; the rifling of a church; the sacking of a convent! You would have thought you heard some gormandizer dilating upon the roasting a savory goose at Michaelmas as he described the roasting of some Spanish Don to make him discover his treasure—a detail given with a minuteness that made every rich old burgher present turn uncomfortably in his chair. All this would be told with infinite glee, as if he considered it an excellent joke; and then he would give such a tyrannical leer in the face of his next neighbor, that the poor man would be fain to laugh out of sheer faint-heartedness. If any one, however, pretended to contradict him in any of his stories he was on fire in an instant. His very cocked hat assumed a momentary fierceness, and seemed to resent the contradiction.—"How the devil should you know as well as I! I tell you it was as I say!" and he would at the same time let slip a broadside of thundering oaths and tremendous sea phrases, such as had never been heard before within those peaceful walls.

Indeed, the worthy burghers began to surmise that he knew more of these stories than mere hearsay. Day after day their conjectures concerning him grew more and more wild and fearful. The strangeness of his manners, the mystery that surrounded him, all made him something incomprehensible in their eyes. He was a kind of monster of the deep to them—he was a merman—he was behemoth—he was leviathan—in short, they knew not what he was.

The domineering spirit of this boisterous sea urchin at length grew quite intolerable. He was no respecter of persons; he contradicted the richest burghers without hesitation; he took possession of the sacred elbow chair, which time out of mind had been the seat of sovereignty of the illustrious Ramm Rapelye. Nay, he even went so far in one of his rough jocular moods, as to slap that mighty burgher on the back, drink his toddy and wink in his face, a thing scarcely to be believed. From this time Ramm Rapelye appeared no more at the inn; his example was followed by several of the most eminent customers, who were too rich to tolerate being bullied out of their opinions, or being obliged to laugh at another man's jokes. The landlord was almost in despair, but he knew not how to get rid of this sea monster and his sea-chest, which seemed to have grown like fixtures, or excrescences on his establishment.

Such was the account whispered cautiously in Wolfert's ear, by the narrator, Peechy Prauw, as he held him by the button in a corner of the hall, casting a wary glance now and then towards the door of the bar-room, lest he should be overheard by the terrible hero of his tale.

Wolfert took his seat in a remote part of the room in silence; impressed with profound awe of this unknown, so versed in freebooting history. It was to him a wonderful instance of the revolutions of mighty empires, to find the venerable Ramm Rapelye thus ousted from the throne; a rugged tarpaulin dictating from his elbow chair, hectoring the patriarchs, and filling this tranquil little realm with brawl and bravado.

WASHINGTON IRVING

The stranger was on this evening in a more than usually communicative mood, and was narrating a number of astounding stories of plunderings and burnings upon the high seas. He dwelt upon them with peculiar relish, heightening the frightful particulars in proportion to their effect on his peaceful auditors. He gave a long swaggering detail of the capture of a Spanish merchantman. She was laying becalmed during a long summer's day, just off from an island which was one of the lurking places of the pirates. They had reconnoitred her with their spy-glasses from the shore, and ascertained her character and force. At night a picked crew of daring fellows set off for her in a whale boat. They approached with muffled oars, as she lay rocking idly with the undulations of the sea and her sails flapping against the masts. They were close under her stern before the guard on deck was aware of their approach. The alarm was given; the pirates threw hand grenades on deck and sprang up the main chains sword in hand.

The crew flew to arms, but in great confusion some were shot down, others took refuge in the tops; others were driven overboard and drowned, while others fought hand to hand from the main deck to the quarter deck, disputing gallantly every inch of ground. There were three Spanish gentlemen on board with their ladies, who made the most desperate resistance; they defended the companion-way, cut down several of their assailants, and fought like very devils, for they were maddened by the shrieks of the ladies from the cabin. One of the Dons was old and soon despatched. The other two kept their ground vigorously, even though the captain of the pirates was among their assailants. Just then there was a shout of victory from the main deck. "The ship is ours!" cried the pirates.

One of the Dons immediately dropped his sword and surrendered; the other, who was a hot-headed youngster, and just married, gave the captain a slash in the face that laid all open. The captain just made out to articulate the words "no quarter."

"And what did they do with their prisoners?" said Peechy Prauw, eagerly.

"Threw them all overboard!" said the merman.

A dead pause followed this reply. Peechy Prauw shrunk quietly back like a man who had unwarily stolen upon the lair of a sleeping lion. The honest burghers cast fearful glances at the deep scar slashed across the visage of the stranger, and moved their chairs a little farther off. The seaman, however, smoked on without moving a muscle, as though he either did not perceive or did not regard the unfavorable effect he had produced upon his hearers.

The half-pay officer was the first to break the silence; for he was Continually tempted to make ineffectual head against this tyrant of the seas, and to regain his lost consequence in the eyes of his ancient companions. He now tried to match the gunpowder tales of the stranger by others equally tremendous. Kidd, as usual, was his hero, concerning whom he had picked up many of the floating traditions of the province. The seaman had always evinced a settled pique against the red-faced warrior. On this occasion he listened with peculiar impatience. He sat with one arm a-kimbo, the other elbow on a table, the hand holding on to the small pipe he was pettishly puffing; his legs crossed, drumming with one foot on the ground and casting every now and then the side glance of a basilisk at the prosing captain. At length the latter spoke of Kidd's having ascended the Hudson with some of his crew, to land his plunder in secrecy.

"Kidd up the Hudson!" burst forth the seaman, with a tremendous oath; "Kidd never was up the Hudson!"

"I tell you he was," said the other. "Aye, and they say he buried a quantity of treasure on the little flat that runs out into the river, called the Devil's Dans Kammer."

"The Devil's Dans Kammer in your teeth!" cried the seaman. "I tell you Kidd never was up the Hudson—what the plague do you know of Kidd and his haunts?"

"What do I know?" echoed the half-pay officer; "why, I was in London at the time of his trial, aye, and I had the pleasure of seeing him hanged at Execution Dock."

"Then, sir, let me tell you that you saw as pretty a fellow hanged as ever trod shoe leather. Aye!" putting his face nearer to that of the officer, "and there was many a coward looked on, that might much better have swung in his stead."

The half-pay officer was silenced; but the indignation thus pent up in his bosom glowed with intense vehemence in his single eye, which kindled like a coal.

Peechy Prauw, who never could remain silent, now took up the word, and in a pacifying tone observed that the gentleman certainly was in the right. Kidd never did bury money up the Hudson, nor indeed in any of those parts, though many affirm the fact. It was Bradish and others of the buccaneers who had buried money, some said in Turtle

Bay, others on Long-Island, others in the neighborhood of Hell Gate. Indeed, added he, I recollect an adventure of Mud Sam, the negro fisherman, many years ago, which some think had something to do with the buccaneers. As we are all friends here, and as it will go no farther, I'll tell it to you.

"Upon a dark night many years ago, as Sam was returning from fishing in Hell Gate—"

Here the story was nipped in the bud by a sudden movement from the unknown, who, laying his iron fist on the table, knuckles downward, with a quiet force that indented the very boards, and looking grimly over his shoulder, with the grin of an angry bear. "Heark'ee, neighbor," said he, with significant nodding of the head, "you'd better let the buccaneers and their money alone—they're not for old men and old women to meddle with. They fought hard for their money, they gave body and soul for it, and wherever it lies buried, depend upon it he must have a tug with the devil who gets it."

This sudden explosion was succeeded by a blank silence throughout the room. Peechy Prauw shrunk within himself, and even the red-faced officer turned pale. Wolfert, who, from a dark corner of the room, had listened with intense eagerness to all this talk about buried treasure, looked with mingled awe and reverence on this bold buccaneer, for such he really suspected him to be. There was a chinking of gold and a sparkling of jewels in all his stories about the Spanish Main that gave a value to every period, and Wolfert would have given any thing for the rummaging of the ponderous sea-chest, which his imagination crammed full of golden chalices and crucifixes and jolly round bags of doubloons.

The dead stillness that had fallen upon the company was at length interrupted by the stranger, who pulled out a prodigious watch of curious and ancient workmanship, and which in Wolferts' eyes had a decidedly Spanish look. On touching a spring it struck ten o'clock; upon which the sailor called for his reckoning, and having paid it out of a handful of outlandish coin, he drank off the remainder of his beverage, and without taking leave of any one, rolled out of the room, muttering to himself as he stamped up-stairs to his chamber.

It was some time before the company could recover from the silence into which they had been thrown. The very footsteps of the stranger, which were heard now and then as he traversed his chamber, inspired awe.

Still the conversation in which they had been engaged was too interesting not to be resumed. A heavy thunder-gust had gathered up unnoticed while they were lost in talk, and the torrents of rain that fell forbade all thoughts of setting off for home until the storm should subside. They drew nearer together, therefore, and entreated the worthy Peechy Prauw to continue the tale which had been so discourteously interrupted. He readily complied, whispering, however, in a tone scarcely above his breath, and drowned occasionally by the rolling of the thunder, and he would pause every now and then, and listen with evident awe, as he heard the heavy footsteps of the stranger pacing overhead.

The following is the purport of his story.

THE ADVENTURE OF SAM,
THE BLACK FISHERMAN

Commonly Denominated Mud Sam

E very body knows Mud Sam, the old negro fisherman who has fished about the Sound for the last twenty or thirty years. Well, it is now many years since that Sam, who was then a young fellow, and worked on the farm of Killian Suydam on Long Island, having finished his work early, was fishing, one still summer evening, just about the neighborhood of Hell Gate. He was in a light skiff, and being well acquainted with the currents and eddies, he had been able to shift his station with the shifting of the tide, from the Hen and Chickens to the Hog's back, and from the Hog's back to the Pot, and from the Pot to the Frying-pan; but in the eagerness of his sport Sam did not see that the tide was rapidly ebbing; until the roaring of the whirlpools and rapids warned him of his danger, and he had some difficulty in shooting his skiff from among the rocks and breakers, and getting to the point of Blackwell's Island. Here he cast anchor for some time, waiting the turn of the tide to enable him to return homewards.

As the night set in it grew blustering and gusty. Dark clouds came bundling up in the west; and now and then a growl of thunder or a flash of lightning told that a summer storm was at hand. Sam pulled over, therefore, under the lee of Manhattan Island, and coasting along came to a snug nook, just under a steep beetling rock, where he fastened his skiff to the root of a tree that shot out from a cleft and spread its broad branches like a canopy over the water. The gust came scouring along; the wind threw up the river in white surges; the rain rattled among the leaves, the thunder bellowed worse than that which is now bellowing, the lightning seemed to lick up the surges of the stream; but Sam, snugly sheltered under rock and tree, lay crouched in his skiff, rocking upon the billows, until he fell asleep. When he awoke all was quiet. The gust had passed away, and only now and then a faint gleam of lightning in the east showed which way it had gone. The night was dark and moonless; and from the state of the tide Sam concluded it was near midnight. He was on the point of making loose his skiff to return homewards, when he saw a light gleaming along the water from a distance, which seemed rapidly approaching. As it drew near he perceived that it came from a lanthorn in the bow of a boat which was gliding along under shadow of the land. It pulled up in a small cove, close to where he was. A man jumped on shore, and searching about with the lanthorn exclaimed, "This is the place—here's the Iron ring." The boat was then made fast, and the man returning on board, assisted his comrades in conveying something heavy on shore. As the light gleamed among them, Sam saw that they were five stout, desperate-looking fellows, in red woollen caps, with a leader in a three-cornered hat, and that some of them were armed with dirks, or long knives, and pistols. They talked low to one another, and occasionally in some outlandish tongue which he could not understand.

On landing they made their way among the bushes, taking turns to relieve each other in lugging their burthen up the rocky bank. Sam's curiosity was now fully aroused, so leaving his skiff he clambered silently up the ridge that overlooked their path. They had stopped to rest for a moment, and the leader was looking about among the bushes with his lanthorn. "Have you brought the spades?" said one. "They are here," replied another, who had them on his shoulder. "We must dig deep, where there will be no risk of discovery," said a third.

A cold chill ran through Sam's veins. He fancied he saw before him a gang of murderers, about to bury their victim. His knees smote together. In his agitation he shook the branch of a tree with which he was supporting himself as he looked over the edge of the cliff.

"What's that?" cried one of the gang. "Some one stirs among the bushes!"

The lanthorn was held up in the direction of the noise. One of the red-caps cocked a pistol, and pointed it towards the very lace where Sam was standing. He stood motionless—breathless; expecting the next moment to be his last. Fortunately, his dingy complexion was in his favor, and made no glare among the leaves.

"'Tis no one," said the man with the lanthorn. "What a plague! you would not fire off your pistol and alarm the country."

The pistol was uncocked; the burthen was resumed, and the party slowly toiled up the bank. Sam watched them as they went; the light sending back fitful gleams through the dripping bushes, and it was not till they were fairly out of sight that he ventured to draw breath freely. He now thought of getting back to his boat, and making his escape out of the reach of such dangerous neighbors; but curiosity was all-powerful with poor Sam. He hesitated and lingered and listened. By and bye he heard the strokes of spades.

"They are digging the grave!" said he to himself; the cold sweat started upon his forehead. Every stroke of a spade, as it sounded through the silent groves, went to his heart; it was evident there was as little noise made as possible; every thing had an air of mystery and secrecy. Sam had a great relish for the horrible—a tale of murder was a treat for him; and he was a constant attendant at executions. He could not, therefore, resist an impulse, in spite of every danger, to steal nearer, and overlook the villains at their work. He crawled along cautiously, therefore, inch by inch; stepping with the utmost care among the dry leaves, lest their rustling should betray him. He came at length to where a steep rock intervened between him and the gang; he saw the light of their lanthorn shining up against the branches of the trees on the other side. Sam slowly and silently clambered up the surface of the rock, and raising his head above its naked edge, beheld the villains immediately below him, and so near that though he dreaded discovery, he dared not withdraw lest the least movement should be heard. In this way he remained, with his round black face peering over the edge of the rock, like the sun just emerging above the edge of the horizon, or the round-cheeked moon on the dial of a clock.

The red-caps had nearly finished their work; the grave was filled up, and they were carefully replacing the turf. This done, they scattered dry leaves over the place. "And now," said the leader, "I defy the devil himself to find it out."

"The murderers!" exclaimed Sam involuntarily.

The whole gang started, and looking up, beheld the round black head of Sam just above them. His white eyes strained half out of their orbits; his white teeth chattering, and his whole visage shining with cold perspiration.

"We're discovered!" cried one.

"Down with him!" cried another.

Sam heard the cocking of a pistol, but did not pause for the report. He scrambled over rock and stone, through bush and briar; rolled down banks like a hedgehog; scrambled up others like a catamount. In every direction he heard some one or other of the gang hemming him in. At length he reached the rocky ridge along the river; one of the red-caps was hard behind him. A steep rock like a wall rose directly in his way; it seemed to cut off all retreat, when he espied the strong cord-like branch of a grape-vine reaching half way down it. He sprang at it with the force of a desperate man, seized it with both hands, and being young and agile, succeeded in swinging himself to the summit of the cliff. Here he stood in full relief against the sky, when the red-cap cocked his pistol and fired. The ball whistled by Sam's head. With the lucky thought of a man in an emergency, he uttered a yell, fell to the ground, and detached at the same time a fragment of the rock, which tumbled with a loud splash into the river.

"I've done his business," said the red-cap, to one or two of his comrades as they arrived panting. "He'll tell no tales, except to the fishes in the river."

His pursuers now turned off to meet their companions. Sam sliding silently down the surface of the rock, let himself quietly into his skiff, cast loose the fastening, and abandoned himself to the rapid current, which in that place runs like a mill-stream, and soon swept him off from the neighborhood. It was not, however, until he had drifted a great distance that he ventured to ply his oars; when he made his skiff dart like an arrow through the strait of Hell Gate, never heeding the danger of Pot, Frying-pan, or Hog's-back itself; nor did he feel himself thoroughly secure until safely nestled in bed in the cockloft of the ancient farm-house of the Suydams.

Here the worthy Peechy paused to take breath and to take a sip of the gossip tankard that stood at his elbow. His auditors remained with open mouths and outstretched necks, gaping like a nest of swallows for an additional mouthful.

"And is that all?" exclaimed the half-pay officer.

"That's all that belongs to the story," said Peechy Prauw.

"And did Sam never find out what was buried by the redcaps?" said Wolfert, eagerly; whose mind was haunted by nothing but ingots and doubloons.

"Not that I know of; he had no time to spare from his work; and to tell the truth, he did not like to run the risk of another race among the rocks. Besides, how should he recollect the spot where the grave had been digged? every thing would look different by daylight. And then, where was the use of looking for a dead body, when there was no chance of hanging the murderers?"

"Aye, but are you sure it was a dead body they buried?" said Wolfert.

"To be sure," cried Peechy Prauw, exultingly. "Does it not haunt in the neighborhood to this very day?"

"Haunts!" exclaimed several of the party, opening their eyes still wider and edging their chairs still closer.

"Aye, haunts," repeated Peechy; "has none of you heard of father red-cap that haunts the old burnt farm-house in the woods, on the border of the Sound, near Hell Gate?"

"Oh, to be sure, I've heard tell of something of the kind, but then I took it for some old wives' fable."

"Old wives' fable or not," said Peechy Prauw, "that farmhouse stands hard by the very spot. It's been unoccupied time out of mind, and stands in a wild, lonely part of the coast; but those who fish in the neighborhood have often heard strange noises there; and lights have been seen about the wood at night; and an old fellow in a red cap has been seen at the windows more than once, which people take to be the ghost of the body that was buried there. Once upon a time three soldiers took shelter in the building for the night, and rummaged it from top to bottom, when they found old father red-cap astride of a cider-barrel in the cellar, with a jug in one hand and a goblet in the other. He offered them a drink out of his goblet, but just as one of the soldiers was putting it to his mouth-Whew! a flash of fire blazed through the cellar, blinded every mother's son of them for several minutes, and when they recovered their eye-sight, jug, goblet, and red-cap had vanished, and nothing but the empty cider-barrel remained."

Here the half-pay officer, who was growing very muzzy and sleepy, and nodding over his liquor, with half-extinguished eye, suddenly gleamed up like an expiring rushlight.

"That's all humbug!" said he, as Peechy finished his last story.

"Well, I don't vouch for the truth of it myself," said Peechy Prauw, "though all the world knows that there's something strange about the house and grounds; but as to the story of Mud Sam, I believe it just as well as if it had happened to myself."

The deep interest taken in this conversation by the company, had made them unconscious of the uproar that prevailed abroad, among the elements, when suddenly they were all electrified by a tremendous clap of thunder. A lumbering crash followed instantaneously that made the building shake to its foundation. All started from their seats, imagining it the shock of an earthquake, or that old father red-cap was coming among them in all his terrors. They listened for a moment, but only heard the rain pelting against the windows, and the wind howling among the trees. The explosion was soon explained by the apparition of an old negro's bald head thrust in at the door, his white goggle eyes contrasting with his jetty poll, which was wet with rain and shone like a bottle. In a jargon but half intelligible he announced that the kitchen chimney had been struck with lightning.

A sullen pause of the storm, which now rose and sunk in gusts, produced a momentary stillness. In this interval the report of a musket was heard, and a long shout, almost like a yell, resounded from the shore. Every one crowded to the window; another musket shot was heard, and another long shout, that mingled wildly with a rising blast of wind. It seemed as if the cry came up from the bosom of the waters; for though incessant flashes of lightning spread a light about the shore, no one was to be seen.

Suddenly the window of the room overhead was opened, and a loud halloo uttered by the mysterious stranger. Several hailings passed from one party to the other, but in a language which none of the company in the bar-room could understand; and presently they heard the window closed, and a great noise overhead as if all the furniture were pulled and hauled about the room. The negro servant was summoned, and shortly after was seen assisting the veteran to lug the ponderous sea-chest down stairs.

The landlord was in amazement. "What, you are not going on the water in such a storm?"

"Storm!" said the other, scornfully, "do you call such a sputter of weather a storm?"

"You'll get drenched to the skin—You'll catch your death!" said Peechy Prauw, affectionately.

"Thunder and lightning!" exclaimed the merman, "don't preach about weather to a man that has cruised in whirlwinds and tornadoes."

The obsequious Peechy was again struck dumb. The voice from the water was again heard in a tone of impatience; the bystanders stared with redoubled awe at this man of storms, which seemed to have come up out of the deep and to be called back to it again. As, with the assistance of the negro, he slowly bore his ponderous sea-chest towards the shore, they eyed it with a superstitious feeling; half doubting whether he were not really about to embark upon it, and launch forth upon the wild waves. They followed him at a distance with a lanthorn.

"Douse the light!" roared the hoarse voice from the water. "No one wants light here!"

"Thunder and lightning!" exclaimed the veteran; "back to the house with you!"

Wolfert and his companions shrunk back is dismay. Still their curiosity would not allow them entirely to withdraw. A long sheet of lightning now flickered across the waves, and discovered a boat, filled with men, just under a rocky point, rising and sinking with the heavy surges, and swashing the water at every heave. It was with difficulty held to the rocks by a boat hook, for the current rushed furiously round the point. The veteran hoisted one end of the lumbering sea-chest on the gunwale of the boat; he seized the handle at the other end to lift it in, when the motion propelled the boat from the shore; the chest slipped off from the gunwale, sunk into the waves, and pulled the veteran headlong after it. A loud shriek was uttered by all on shore, and a volley of execrations by those on board; but boat and man were hurried away by the rushing swiftness of the tide. A pitchy darkness succeeded; Wolfert Webber indeed fancied that He distinguished a cry for help, and that he beheld the drowning man beckoning for assistance; but when the lightning again gleamed along the water all was drear and void. Neither man nor boat was to be seen; nothing but the dashing and weltering of the waves as they hurried past.

The company returned to the tavern, for they could not leave it before the storm should subside. They resumed their seats and gazed on each other with dismay. The whole transaction had not occupied five minutes and not a dozen words had been spoken. When they looked at the oaken chair they could scarcely realize the fact that the strange being who had so lately tenanted it, full of life and Herculean vigor, should already be a corpse. There was the very glass he had just drunk from; there lay the ashes from the pipe which he had smoked as it were with his last breath. As the worthy burghers pondered on these things, they felt a terrible conviction of the uncertainty of human existence, and each felt as if the ground on which he stood was rendered less stable by this awful example.

As, however, the most of the company were possessed of that valuable philosophy which enables a man to bear up with fortitude against the misfortunes of his neighbors, they soon managed to console themselves for the tragic end of the veteran. The landlord was happy that the poor dear man had paid his reckoning before he went.

"He came in a storm, and he went in a storm; he came in the night, and he went in the night; he came nobody knows from whence, and he has gone nobody knows where. For aught I know he has gone to sea once more on his chest and may land to bother some people on the other side of the world! Though it's a thousand pities," added the landlord, "if he has gone to Davy Jones that he had not left his sea-chest behind him."

"The sea-chest! St. Nicholas preserve us!" said Peechy Prauw. "I'd not have had that sea-chest in the house for any money; I'll warrant he'd come racketing after it at nights, and making a haunted house of the inn. And as to his going to sea on his chest, I recollect what happened to Skipper Onderdonk's ship on his voyage from Amsterdam.

"The boatswain died during a storm, so they wrapped him up in a sheet, and put him in his own sea-chest, and threw him overboard; but they neglected in their hurry-skurry to say prayers over him—and the storm raged and roared louder than ever, and they saw the dead man seated in his chest, with his shroud for a sail, coming hard after the ship; and the sea breaking before him in great sprays like fire, and there they kept scudding day after day and night after night, expecting every moment to go to wreck; and every night they saw the dead boatswain in his sea-chest trying to get up with them, and they heard his whistle above the blasts of wind, and he seemed to send great seas mountain high after them, that would have swamped the ship if they had not put up the dead lights. And so it went on till they lost sight of him in the fogs of Newfoundland, and supposed he had veered ship and stood for Dead Man's Isle. So much for burying a man at sea without saying prayers over him."

The thunder-gust which had hitherto detained the company was now at an end. The cuckoo clock in the hall struck midnight; every one pressed to depart, for seldom was such a late hour trespassed on by these quiet burghers. As they sallied forth they found the heavens once more serene. The storm which had lately obscured them had rolled aways and lay piled up in fleecy masses on the horizon, lighted up by the bright crescent of the moon, which looked like a silver lamp hung up in a palace of clouds.

The dismal occurrence of the night, and the dismal narrations they had made, had left a superstitious feeling in every mind. They cast a fearful glance at the spot where the buccaneer had disappeared, almost expecting to see him sailing on his chest in the cool moonshine. The trembling rays glittered along the waters, but all was placid; and the current dimpled over the spot where he had gone down. The party huddled together in a little crowd as they repaired homewards; particularly when they passed a lonely field where a man had been murdered; and he who had farthest to go and had to complete his journey alone, though a veteran sexton, and accustomed, one would think to ghosts and goblins, yet went a long way round, rather than pass by his own church-yard.

Wolfert Webber had now carried home a fresh stock of stories and notions to ruminate upon. His mind was all of a whirl with these freebooting tales; and then these accounts of pots of money and Spanish treasures, buried here and there and every where about the rocks and bays of this wild shore, made him almost dizzy.

"Blessed St. Nicholas!" exclaimed he, half aloud, "is it not possible to come upon one of these golden hoards, and so make one's self rich in a twinkling. How hard that I must go on, delving and delving, day in and day out, merely to make a morsel of bread, when one lucky stroke of a spade might enable me to ride in my carriage for the rest of my life!"

As he turned over in his thoughts all that he had been told of the singular adventure of the black fisherman, his imagination gave a totally different complexion to the tale. He saw in the gang of redcaps nothing but a crew of pirates burying their spoils, and his cupidity was once more awakened by the possibility of at length getting on the traces of some of this lurking wealth. Indeed, his infected fancy tinged every thing with gold. He felt like the greedy inhabitant of Bagdad, when his eye had been greased with the magic ointment of the dervise, that gave him to see all the treasures of the earth. Caskets of buried jewels, chests of ingots, bags of outlandish coins, seemed to court him from their concealments, and supplicate him to relieve them from their untimely graves.

On making private inquiries about the grounds said to be haunted by father red-cap, he was more and more confirmed in his surmise. He learned that the place had several times been visited by experienced money-diggers, who had heard Mud Sam's story, though none of them had met with success. On the contrary, they had always been dogged with ill luck of some kind or other, in consequence, as Wolfert concluded, of their not going to work at the proper time, and with the proper ceremonials. The last attempt had been made by Cobus Quackenbos, who dug for a whole night and met with incredible difficulty, for as fast as he threw one shovel full of earth out of the hole, two were thrown in by invisible hands. He succeeded so far, however, as to uncover an iron chest, when there was a terrible roaring, and ramping, and raging of uncouth figures about the hole, and at length a shower of blows, dealt by invisible cudgels, that fairly belabored him off the forbidden ground.

This Cobus Quackenbos had declared on his death-bed, so that there could not be any doubt of it. He was a man that had devoted many years of his life to money-digging, and it was thought would have ultimately succeeded, had he not died suddenly of a brain fever in the alms-house.

Wolfert Webber was now in a worry of trepidation and impatience; fearful lest some rival adventurer should get a scent of the buried gold. He determined privately to seek out the negro fisherman and get him to serve as guide to the place where he had witnessed the mysterious scene of interment. Sam was easily found; for he was one of those old habitual beings that live about a neighborhood until they wear themselves a place in the public mind, and become, in a manner, public characters. There was not an unlucky urchin about the town that did not know Mud Sam the fisherman, and think that he had a right to play his tricks upon the old negro. Sam was an amphibious kind of animal, something more of a fish than a man; he had led the life of an otter for more than half a century, about the shores of the bay, and the fishing grounds of the Sound. He passed the greater part of his time on and in the water, particularly about Hell Gate; and might have been taken, in bad weather, for one of the hobgoblins that used to haunt that strait. There would he be seen, at all times, and in all weathers; sometimes in his skiff, anchored among the eddies, or prowling, like a shark about some wreck, where the fish are supposed to be most abundant. Sometimes seated on a rock from hour to hour, looming through mist and drizzle, like a solitary heron watching for its prey. He was well acquainted with every hole and corner of the Sound; from the Wallabout to Hell Gate, and from Hell Gate even unto the Devil's Stepping Stones; and it was even affirmed that he knew all the fish in the river by their Christian names.

Wolfert found him at his cabin, which was not much larger than a tolerable dog-house. It was rudely constructed of fragments of wrecks and drift-wood, and built on the rocky shore, at the foot of the old fort, just about what at present forms the point of the Battery. A "most ancient and fish-like smell" pervaded the place. Oars, paddles, and fishing-rods were leaning against the wall of the fort; a net was spread on the sands to dry; a skiff was drawn up on the beach, and at the door of his cabin lay Mud Sam himself, indulging in a true negro's luxury— sleeping in the sunshine.

Many years had passed away since the time of Sam's youthful adventure, and the snows of many a winter had grizzled the knotty wool upon his head. He perfectly recollected the circumstances, however, for he had often been called upon to relate them, though in his version of the story he differed in many points from Peechy Prauw; as is not unfrequently the case with authentic historians. As to the subsequent researches of money-diggers, Sam knew nothing about them; they were matters quite out of his line; neither did the cautious Wolfert care to disturb his thoughts on that point. His only wish was to secure the old fisherman as a pilot to the spot, and this was readily effected. The long time that had intervened since his nocturnal adventure had effaced all Sam's awe of the place, and the promise of a trifling reward roused him at once from his sleep and his sunshine.

The tide was adverse to making the expedition by water, and Wolfert was too impatient to get to the land of promise, to wait for its turning; they set off, therefore, by land. A walk of four or five miles brought them to the edge of a wood, which at that time covered the greater part of the eastern side of the island. It was just beyond the pleasant region of Bloomen-dael. Here they struck into a long lane, straggling among trees and bushes, very much overgrown with weeds and mullein stalks as if but seldom used, and so completely overshadowed as to enjoy but a kind of twilight. Wild vines entangled the trees and flaunted in their faces; brambles and briars caught their clothes as they passed; the garter-snake glided across their path; the spotted toad hopped and waddled before them, and the restless cat-bird mewed at them from every thicket. Had Wolfert Webber been deeply read in romantic legend he might have fancied himself entering upon forbidden, enchanted ground; or that these were some of the guardians set to keep a watch upon buried treasure. As it was, the loneliness of the place, and the wild stories connected with it, had their effect upon his mind.

On reaching the lower end of the lane they found themselves near the shore of the Sound, in a kind of amphitheatre, surrounded by forest tree. The area had once been a grass-plot, but was now shagged with briars and rank weeds. At one end, and just on the river bank, was a ruined building, little better than a heap of rubbish, with a stack of chimneys rising like a solitary tower out of the centre. The current of the Sound rushed along just below it, with wildly-grown trees drooping their branches into its waves.

Wolfert had not a doubt that this was the haunted house of father red-cap, and called to mind the story of Peechy Prauw. The evening was approaching, and the light falling dubiously among these places, gave a melancholy tone to the scene, well calculated to foster any lurking feeling of awe or superstition. The night-hawk, wheeling about in the highest regions of the air, emitted his peevish, boding cry. The woodpecker gave a lonely tap now and then on some hollow tree, and the firebird,[1] as he streamed by them with his deep-red plumage, seemed like some genius flitting about this region of mystery.

They now came to an enclosure that had once been a garden. It extended along the foot of a rocky ridge, but was little better than a wilderness of weeds, with here and there a matted rose-bush, or a peach or plum tree grown wild and ragged, and covered with moss. At the lower end of the garden they passed a kind of vault in the side of the bank, facing the water. It had the look of a root-house. The door, though decayed, was still strong, and appeared to have been recently patched up. Wolfert pushed it open. It gave a harsh grating upon its hinges, and striking against something like a box, a rattling sound ensued, and a skull rolled on the floor. Wolfert drew back shuddering, but was reassured on being informed by Sam that this was a family vault belonging to one of the old Dutch families that owned this estate; an assertion which was corroborated by the sight of coffins of various sizes piled within. Sam had been familiar with all these scenes when a boy, and now knew that he could not be far from the place of which they were in quest.

They now made their way to the water's edge, scrambling along ledges of rocks, and having often to hold by shrubs and grape-vines to avoid slipping into the deep and hurried stream. At length they came to a small cove, or rather indent of the shore. It was protected by steep rocks and overshadowed by a thick copse of oaks and chestnuts, so as to be sheltered and almost concealed. The beach sloped gradually within the cove, but the current swept deep and black and rapid along its jutting points. Sam paused; raised his remnant of a hat, and scratched his grizzled poll for a moment, as he regarded this nook: then suddenly clapping his hands, he stepped exultingly forward, and pointing to a large iron ring, stapled firmly in the rock, just where a broad shelve of stone furnished a commodious landing-place. It was the very spot where the red-caps had landed. Years had changed the more perishable features of the scene; but rock and iron yield slowly to the influence of time. On looking more narrowly, Wolfert remarked three crosses cut in the rock just above the ring, which had no doubt some mysterious signification. Old Sam now readily recognized the overhanging rock

---

1. Orchard Oriole.

under which his skiff had been sheltered during the thunder-gust. To follow up the course which the midnight gang had taken, however, was a harder task. His mind had been so much taken up on that eventful occasion by the persons of the drama, as to pay but little attention to the scenes; and places looked different by night and day. After wandering about for some time, however, they came to an opening among the trees which Sam thought resembled the place. There was a ledge of rock of moderate height like a wall on one side, which Sam thought might be the very ridge from which he overlooked the diggers. Wolfert examined it narrowly, and at length described three crosses similar to those above the iron ring, cut deeply into the face of the rock, but nearly obliterated by the moss that had grown on them. His heart leaped with joy, for he doubted not but they were the private marks of the buccaneers, to denote the places where their treasure lay buried. All now that remained was to ascertain the precise spot; for otherwise he might dig at random without coming upon the spoil, and he has already had enough of such profitless labor. Here, however, Sam was perfectly at a loss, and, indeed, perplexed him by a variety of opinions; for his recollections were all confused. Sometimes he declared it must have been at the foot of a mulberry tree hard by; then it was just beside a great white stone; then it must have been under a small green knoll, a short distance from the ledge of rock: until at length Wolfert became as bewildered as himself.

The shadows of evening were now spreading themselves over the woods, and rock and tree began to mingle together. It was evidently too late to attempt anything farther at present; and, indeed, Wolfert had come unprepared with implements to prosecute his researches. Satisfied, therefore, with having ascertained the place, he took note of all its landmarks, that he might recognize it again, and set out on his return homeward, resolved to prosecute this golden enterprise without delay.

The leading anxiety which had hitherto absorbed every feeling being now in some measure appeased, fancy began to wander, and to conjure up a thousand shapes and chimeras as he returned through this haunted region. Pirates hanging in chains seemed to swing on every tree, and he almost expected to see some Spanish Don, with his throat cut from ear to ear, rising slowly out of the ground, and shaking the ghost of a money-bag.

Their way back lay through the desolate garden, and Wolfert's nerves had arrived at so sensitive a state that the flitting of a bird, the rustling of a leaf, or the falling of a nut was enough to startle him. As they entered the confines of the garden, they caught sight of a figure at a distance advancing slowly up one of the walks and bending under the weight of a burthen. They paused and regarded him attentively. He wore what appeared to be a woollen cap, and still more alarming, of a most sanguinary red. The figure moved slowly on, ascended the bank, and stopped at the very door of the sepulchral vault. Just before entering he looked around. What was the horror of Wolfert when he recognized the grizzly visage of the drowned buccaneer. He uttered an exclamation of horror. The figure slowly raised his iron fist and shook it with a terrible menace. Wolfert did not pause to see more, but hurried off as fast as his legs could carry him, nor was Sam slow in following at his heels, having all his ancient terrors revived. Away, then, did they scramble, through bush and brake, horribly frightened at every bramble that tagged at their skirts, nor did they pause to breathe, until they had blundered their way through this perilous wood and had fairly reached the high-road to the city.

Several days elapsed before Wolfert could summon courage enough to prosecute the enterprise, so much had he been dismayed by the apparition, whether living dead, of the grizzly buccaneer. In the meantime, what a conflict of mind did he suffer! He neglected all his concerns, was moody and restless all day, lost his appetite; wandered in his thoughts and words, and committed a thousand blunders. His rest was broken; and when he fell asleep, the nightmare, in shape of a huge money-bag, sat squatted upon his breast. He babbled about incalculable sums; fancied himself engaged in money digging; threw the bed-clothes right and left, in the idea that he was shovelling among the dirt, groped under the bed in quest of the treasure, and lugged forth, as he supposed, an inestimable pot of gold.

Dame Webber and her daughter were in despair at what they conceived a returning touch of insanity. There are two family oracles, one or other of which Dutch housewives consult in all cases of great doubt and perplexity: the dominie and the doctor. In the present instance they repaired to the doctor. There was at that time a little, dark, mouldy man of medicine famous among the old wives of the Manhattoes for his skill not only in the healing art, but in all matters of strange and mysterious nature. His name was Dr. Knipperhausen, but he was more commonly known by the appellation of the High German doctor.[2] To him did

---

2. The same, no doubt, of whom mention is made in the history of Dolph Heyliger.

WASHINGTON IRVING

the poor women repair for counsel and assistance touching the mental vagaries of Wolfert Webber.

They found the doctor seated in his little study, clad in his dark camblet robe of knowledge, with his black velvet cap, after the manner of Boorhaave, Van Helmont, and other medical sages: a pair of green spectacles set in black horn upon his clubbed nose, and poring over a German folio that seemed to reflect back the darkness of his physiognomy. The doctor listened to their statement of the symptoms of Wolfert's malady with profound attention; but when they came to mention his raving about buried money, the little man pricked up his ears. Alas, poor women! they little knew the aid they had called in.

Dr. Knipperhausen had been half his life engaged in seeking the short cuts to fortune, in quest of which so many a long lifetime is wasted. He had passed some years of his youth in the Harz mountains of Germany, and had derived much valuable instruction from the miners, touching the mode of seeking treasure buried in the earth. He had prosecuted his studies also under a travelling sage who united all the mysteries of medicine with magic and legerdemain. His mind, therefore, had become stored with all kinds of mystic lore: he had dabbled a little in astrology, alchemy, and divination; knew how to detect stolen money, and to tell where springs of water lay hidden; in a word, by the dark nature of his knowledge he had acquired the name of the High German doctor, which is pretty nearly equivalent to that of necromancer. The doctor had often heard rumors of treasure being buried in various parts of the island, and' had long been anxious to get on the traces of it. No sooner were Wolfert's waking and sleeping vagaries confided to him, than he beheld in them the confirmed symptoms of a case of money-digging, and lost no time in probing it to the bottom. Wolfert had long been sorely depressed in mind by the golden secret, and as a family physician is a kind of father confessor, he was glad of the opportunity of unburthening himself. So far from curing, the doctor caught the malady from his patient. The circumstances unfolded to him awakened all his cupidity; he had not a doubt of money being buried somewhere in the neighborhood of the mysterious crosses, and offered to join Wolfert in the search. He informed him that much secrecy and caution must be observed in enterprises of the kind; that money is only to be digged for at night; with certain forms and ceremonies; the burning of drugs; the repeating of mystic words, and above all, that the seekers must be provided with a divining rod, which had the wonderful property of pointing to the very spot on the surface of the earth under which treasure lay hidden. As the doctor had given much of his mind to these matters, he charged himself with all the necessary preparations, and, as the quarter of the moon was propitious, he undertook to have the divining rod ready by a certain night.[3]

Wolfert's heart leaped with joy at having met with so learned and able a coadjutor. Every thing went on secretly, but swimmingly. The doctor had many consultations with his patient, and the good women of the household lauded the comforting effect of his visits. In the meantime, the wonderful divining rod, that great key to nature's secrets, was duly prepared. The doctor had thumbed over all his books of knowledge for the occasion; and Mud Sam was engaged to take them in his skiff to the scene of enterprise; to work with spade and pick-axe in unearthing the treasure; and to freight his bark with the weighty spoils they were certain of finding.

At length the appointed night arrived for this perilous undertaking. Before Wolfert left his home he counselled his wife and daughter to go

---

3. The following note was found appended to this paper in the handwriting of Mr. Knickerbocker. "There has been much written against the divining rod by those light minds who are ever ready to scoff at the mysteries of nature, but I fully join with Dr. Knipperhausen in giving it my faith. I shall not insist upon its efficacy in discovering the concealment of stolen goods, the boundary-stones of fields, the traces of robbers and murderers, or even the existence of subterraneous springs and streams of water; albeit, I think these properties not easily to be discredited; but of its potency in discovering vein of precious metal, and hidden sums of money and jewels, I have not the least doubt. Some said that the rod turned only in the hands of persons who had been born in particular months of the year; hence astrologers had recourse to planetary influence when they would procure a talisman. Others declared that the properties of the rod were either an effect of chance, or the fraud of the holder, or the work of the devil. Thus sayeth the reverend Father Gaspard Schott in his Treatise on Magic. 'Propter haec et similia argumenta audacter ego pronuncio vim conversivam virgulae befurcatae nequaquam naturalem esse, sed vel casa vel fraude virgulam tractantis vel ope diaboli,' etc.

"Georgius Agricula also was of opinion that it was a mere delusion of the devil to inveigle the avaricious and unwary into his clutches, and in his treatise 'de re Metallica,' lays particular stress on the mysterious words pronounced by those persons who employed the divining rod during his time. But I make not a doubt that the divining rod is one of those secrets of natural magic, the mystery of which is to be explained by the sympathies existing between physical things operated upon by the planets, and rendered efficacious by the strong faith of the individual. Let the divining rod be properly gathered at the proper time of the moon, cut into the proper form, used with the necessary ceremonies, and with a perfect faith in its efficacy, and I can confidently recommend it to my fellow-citizens as an infallible means of discovering the various places on the island of the Manhattoes where treasure hath been buried in the olden time. D.K."

to bed, and feel no alarm if he should not return during the night. Like reasonable women, on being told not to feel alarm, they fell immediately into a panic. They saw at once by his manner that something unusual was in agitation; all their fears about the unsettled state of his mind were roused with tenfold force: they hung about him entreating him not to expose himself to the night air, but all in vain. When Wolfert was once mounted on his hobby, it was no easy matter to get him out of the saddle. It was a clear starlight night, when he issued out of the portal of the Webber palace. He wore a large napped hat tied under the chin with a handkerchief of his daughter's, to secure him from the night damp, while Dame Webber threw her long red cloak about his shoulders, and fastened it round his neck.

The doctor had been no less carefully armed and accoutred by his housekeeper, the vigilant Frau Ilsy, and sallied forth in his camblet robe by way of surtout; his black velvet cap under his cocked hat, a thick clasped book under his arm, a basket of drugs and dried herbs in one hand, and in the other the miraculous rod of divination.

The great church clock struck ten as Wolfert and the doctor passed by the church-yard, and the watchman bawled in hoarse voice a long and doleful "All's well!" A deep sleep had already fallen upon this primitive little burgh; nothing disturbed this awful silence, excepting now and then the bark of some profligate night-walking dog, or the serenade of some romantic cat. It is true, Wolfert fancied more than once that he heard the sound of a stealthy footfall at a distance behind them; but it might have been merely the echo of their own steps echoing along the quiet streets. He thought also at one time that he saw a tall figure skulking after them—stopping when they stopped, and moving on as they proceeded; but the dim and uncertain lamp light threw such vague gleams and shadows, that this might all have been mere fancy.

They found the negro fisherman waiting for them, smoking his pipe in the stern of his skiff, which was moored just in front of his little cabin. A pick-axe and spade were lying in the bottom of the boat, with a dark lanthorn, and a stone jug of good Dutch courage, in which honest Sam no doubt, put even more faith than Dr. Knipperhausen in his drugs.

Thus then did these three worthies embark in their cockleshell of a skiff upon this nocturnal expedition, with a wisdom and valor equalled only by the three wise men of Gotham, who went to sea in a bowl. The tide was rising and running rapidly up the Sound. The current bore them along, almost without the aid of an oar. The profile of the town lay all in shadow. Here and there a light feebly glimmered from some sick chamber, or from the cabin window of some vessel at anchor in the stream. Not a cloud obscured the deep starry firmament, the lights of which wavered on the surface of the placid river; and a shooting meteor, streaking its pale course in the very direction they were taking, was interpreted by the doctor into a most propitious omen.

In a little while they glided by the point of Corlears Hook with the rural inn which had been the scene of such night adventures. The family had retired to rest, and the house was dark and still. Wolfert felt a chill pass over him as they passed the point where the buccaneer had disappeared. He pointed it out to Dr. Knipperhausen. While regarding it, they thought they saw a boat actually lurking at the very place; but the shore cast such a shadow over the border of the water that they could discern nothing distinctly. They had not proceeded far when they heard the low sounds of distant oars, as if cautiously pulled. Sam plied his oars with redoubled vigor, and knowing all the eddies and currents of the stream, soon left their followers, if such they were, far astern. In a little while they stretched across Turtle bay and Kip's bay, then shrouded themselves in the deep shadows of the Manhattan shore, and glided swiftly along, secure from observation. At length Sam shot his skiff into a little cove, darkly embowered by trees, and made it fast to the well known iron ring. They now landed, and lighting the lanthorn, gathered their various implements and proceeded slowly through the bushes. Every sound startled them, even that of their footsteps among the dry leaves; and the hooting of a screech owl, from the shattered chimney of father red-cap's ruin, made their blood run cold.

In spite of all Wolfert's caution in taking note of the landmarks, it was some time before they could find the open place among the trees, where the treasure was supposed to be buried. At length they came to the ledge of rock; and on examining its surface by the aid of the lanthorn, Wolfert recognized the three mystic crosses. Their hearts beat quick, for the momentous trial was at hand that was to determine their hopes.

The lanthorn was now held by Wolfert Webber, while the doctor produced the divining rod. It was a forked twig, one end of which was grasped firmly in each hand, while the centre, forming the stem, pointed perpendicularly upwards. The doctor moved this wand about, within a certain distance of the earth, from place to place, but for some time without any effect, while Wolfert kept the light of the lanthorn turned full upon it, and watched it with the most breathless interest. At length the rod began slowly to turn. The doctor grasped it with greater earnestness, his hand trembling with the agitation of his mind. The wand continued slowly to turn, until at length the stem had reversed its position, and pointed perpendicularly downward; and remained pointing to one spot as fixedly as the needle to the pole.

"This is the spot!" said the doctor in an almost inaudible tone.

Wolfert's heart was in his throat.

"Shall I dig?" said Sam, grasping the spade.

"*Pots tousends*, no!" replied the little doctor, hastily. He now ordered his companions to keep close by him and to maintain the most inflexible silence. That certain precautions must be taken, and ceremonies used to prevent the evil spirits which keep about buried treasure from doing them any harm. The doctor then drew a circle round the place, enough to include the whole party. He next gathered dry twigs and leaves, and made a fire, upon which he threw certain drugs and dried herbs which he had brought in his basket. A thick smoke rose, diffusing a potent odor, savoring marvellously of brimstone and assafoetida, which, however grateful it might be to the olfactory nerves of spirits, nearly strangled poor Wolfert, and produced a fit of coughing and wheezing that made the whole grove resound. Doctor Knipperhausen then unclasped the volume which he had brought under his arm, which was printed in red and black characters in German text. While Wolfert held the lanthorn, the doctor, by the aid of his spectacles, read off several forms of conjuration in Latin and German. He then ordered Sam to seize the pick-axe and proceed to work. The close-bound soil gave obstinate signs of not having been disturbed for many a year. After having picked his way through the surface, Sam came to a bed of sand and gravel, which he threw briskly to right and left with the spade.

"Hark!" said Wolfert, who fancied he heard a trampling among the dry leaves, and a rustling through the bushes. Sam paused for a moment, and they listened. No footstep was near. The bat flitted about them in silence; a bird roused from its nest by the light which glared up among the trees, flew circling about the flame. In the profound stillness of the woodland they could distinguish the current rippling along the rocky shore, and the distant murmuring and roaring of Hell Gate.

Sam continued his labors, and had already digged a considerable hole. The doctor stood on the edge, reading formulae every now and then from the black letter volume, or throwing more drugs and herbs upon the fire;

while Wolfert bent anxiously over the pit, watching every stroke of the spade. Any one witnessing the scene thus strangely lighted up by fire, lanthorn, and the reflection of Wolfert's red mantle, might have mistaken the little doctor for some foul magician, busied in his incantations, and the grizzled-headed Sam as some swart goblin, obedient to his commands.

At length the spade of the fisherman struck upon something that sounded hollow. The sound vibrated to Wolfert's heart. He struck his spade again.

"'Tis a chest," said Sam.

"Full of gold, I'll warrant it!" cried Wolfert, clasping his hands with rapture.

Scarcely had he uttered the words when a sound from overhead caught his ear. He cast up his eyes, and lo! by the expiring light of the fire he beheld, just over the disk of the rock, what appeared to be the grim visage of the drowned buccaneer, grinning hideously down upon him.

Wolfert gave a loud cry and let fall the lanthorn. His panic communicated itself to his companions. The negro leaped out of the hole, the doctor dropped his book and basket and began to pray in German. All was horror and confusion. The fire was scattered about, the lanthorn extinguished. In their hurry-skurry they ran against and confounded one another. They fancied a legion of hobgoblins let loose upon them, and that they saw by the fitful gleams of the scattered embers, strange figures in red caps gibbering and ramping around them. The doctor ran one way, Mud Sam another, and Wolfert made for the water side. As he plunged struggling onwards through bush and brake, he heard the tread of some one in pursuit.

He scrambled frantically forward. The footsteps gained upon him. He felt himself grasped by his cloak, when suddenly his pursuer was attacked in turn: a fierce fight and struggle ensued—a pistol was discharged that lit up rock and bush for a period, and showed two figures grappling together—all was then darker than ever. The contest continued—the combatants clenched each other, and panted and groaned, and rolled among the rocks. There was snarling and growling as of a cur, mingled with curses in which Wolfert fancied he could recognize the voice of the buccaneer. He would fain have fled, but he was on the brink of a precipice and could go no farther.

Again the parties were on their feet; again there was a tugging and struggling, as if strength alone could decide the combat, until one was precipitated from the brow of the cliff and sent headlong into the deep stream that whirled below. Wolfert heard the plunge, and a kind of strangling bubbling murmur, but the darkness of the night hid every thing from view, and the swiftness of the current swept every thing instantly out of hearing. One of the combatants was disposed of, but whether friend or foe Wolfert could not tell, nor whether they might not both be foes. He heard the survivor approach and his terror revived. He saw, where the profile of the rocks rose against the horizon, a human form advancing. He could not be mistaken: it must be the buccaneer. Whither should he fly! a precipice was on one side; a murderer on the other. The enemy approached: he was close at hand. Wolfert attempted to let himself down the face of the cliff. His cloak caught in a thorn that grew on the edge. He was jerked from off his feet and held dangling in the air, half choked by the string with which his careful wife had fastened the garment round his neck. Wolfert thought his last moment had arrived; already had he committed his soul to St. Nicholas, when the string broke and he tumbled down the bank, bumping from rock to rock and bush to bush, and leaving the red cloak fluttering like a bloody banner in the air.

It was a long while before Wolfert came to himself. When he opened his eyes the ruddy streaks of the morning were already shooting up the sky. He found himself lying in the bottom of a boat, grievously battered. He attempted to sit up but was too sore and stiff to move. A voice requested him in friendly accents to lie still. He turned his eyes toward the speaker: it was Dirk Waldron. He had dogged the party, at the earnest request of Dame Webber and her daughter, who, with the laudable curiosity of their sex, had pried into the secret consultations of Wolfert and the doctor. Dirk had been completely distanced in following the light skiff of the fisherman, and had just come in time to rescue the poor money-digger from his pursuer.

Thus ended this perilous enterprise. The doctor and Mud Sam severally found their way back to the Manhattoes, each having some dreadful tale of peril to relate. As to poor Wolfert, instead of returning in triumph, laden with bags of gold, he was borne home on a shutter, followed by a rabble route of curious urchins. His wife and daughter saw the dismal pageant from a distance, and alarmed the neighborhood with their cries: they thought the poor man had suddenly settled the great debt of nature in one of his wayward moods. Finding him, however, still living, they had him conveyed speedily to bed, and a jury of old matrons of the neighborhood assembled to determine how he should be doctored. The whole town was in a buzz with the story of the money-diggers. Many repaired to the scene of the previous night's adventures: but though they found the very place of the digging, they discovered nothing that compensated for their trouble. Some say they found the fragments of an oaken chest and an iron pot lid, which savored strongly of hidden money; and that in the old family vault there were traces of holes and boxes, but this is all very dubious.

In fact, the secret of all this story has never to this day been discovered: whether any treasure was ever actually buried at that place, whether, if so, it was carried off at night by those who had buried it; or whether it still remains there under the guardianship of gnomes and spirits until it shall be properly sought for, is all matter of conjecture. For my part I incline to the latter opinion; and make no doubt that great sums lie buried, both there and in many other parts of this island and its neighborhood, ever since the times of the buccaneers and the Dutch colonists; and I would earnestly recommend the search after them to such of my fellow citizens as are not engaged in any other speculations.

There were many conjectures formed, also, as to who and what was the strange man of the seas who had domineered over the little fraternity at Corlears Hook for a time; disappeared so strangely, and reappeared so fearfully. Some supposed him a smuggler stationed at that place to assist his comrades in landing their goods among the rocky coves of the island. Others that he was a buccaneer; one of the ancient comrades either of Kidd or Bradish, returned to convey away treasures formerly hidden in the vicinity. The only circumstance that throws any thing like a vague light over this mysterious matter is a report that prevailed of a strange foreign-built shallop, with the look of a piccaroon, having been seen hovering about the Sound for several days without landing or reporting herself, though boats were seen going to and from her at night: and that she was seen standing out of the mouth of the harbor, in the gray of the dawn after the catastrophe of the money-diggers.

I must not omit to mention another report, also, which I confess is rather apocryphal, of the buccaneer, who was supposed to have been drowned, being seen before daybreak, with a lanthorn in his hand, seated astride his great sea-chest and sailing through Hell Gate, which just then began to roar and bellow with redoubled fury.

While all the gossip world was thus filled with talk and rumor, poor Wolfert lay sick and sorrowful in his bed, bruised in body and sorely beaten down in mind. His wife and daughter did all they could to bind up his wounds both corporal and spiritual. The good old dame never stirred from his bedside, where she sat knitting from morning till night; while his daughter busied herself about him with the fondest care. Nor did they lack assistance from abroad. Whatever may be said of the desertions of friends in distress, they had no complaint of the kind to make. Not an old wife of the neighborhood but abandoned her work to crowd to the mansion of Wolfert Webber, inquire after his health and the particulars of his story. Not one came, moreover, without her little pipkin of pennyroyal, sage, balm, or other herb-tea, delighted at an opportunity of signalizing her kindness and her doctorship. What drenchings did not the poor Wolfert undergo, and all in vain. It was a moving sight to behold him wasting away day by day; growing thinner and thinner and ghastlier and ghastlier, and staring with rueful visage from under an old patchwork counterpane upon the jury of matrons kindly assembled to sigh and groan and look unhappy around him.

Dirk Waldron was the only being that seemed to shed a ray of sunshine into this house of mourning. He came in with cheery look and manly spirit, and tried to reanimate the expiring heart of the poor money-digger, but it was all in vain. Wolfert was completely done over. If any thing was wanting to complete his despair, it was a notice served upon him in the midst of his distress, that the corporation were about to run a new street through the very centre of his cabbage garden. He saw nothing before him but poverty and ruin; his last reliance, the garden of his forefathers, was to be laid waste, and what then was to become of his poor wife and child?

His eyes filled with tears as they followed the dutiful Amy out of the room one morning. Dirk Waldron was seated beside him; Wolfert grasped his hand, pointed after his daughter, and for the first time since his illness broke the silence he had maintained.

"I am going!" said he, shaking his head feebly, "and when I am gone—my poor daughter—"

"Leave her to me, father!" said Dirk, manfully—"I'll take care of her!"

Wolfert looked up in the face of the cheery, strapping youngster, and saw there was none better able to take care of a woman.

"Enough," said he, "she is yours!—and now fetch me a lawyer—let me make my will and die."

The lawyer was brought—a dapper, bustling, round-headed little man, Roorback (or Rollebuck, as it was pronounced) by name. At the sight of him the women broke into loud lamentations, for they looked upon the signing of a will as the signing of a death-warrant. Wolfert made a feeble motion for them to be silent. Poor Amy buried her face and her grief in the bed-curtain. Dame Webber resumed her knitting to hide her distress, which betrayed itself, however, in a pellucid tear, that trickled silently down and hung at the end of her peaked nose; while the cat, the only unconcerned member of the family, played with the good dame's ball of worsted, as it rolled about the floor.

Wolfert lay on his back, his nightcap drawn over his forehead; his eyes closed; his whole visage the picture of death. He begged the lawyer to be brief, for he felt his end approaching, and that he had no time to lose. The lawyer nibbed his pen, spread out his paper, and prepared to write.

"I give and bequeath," said Wolfert, faintly, "my small farm—"

"What—all!" exclaimed the lawyer.

Wolfert half opened his eyes and looked upon the lawyer.

"Yes—all" said he.

"What! all that great patch of land with cabbages and sunflowers, which the corporation is just going to run a main street through?"

"The same," said Wolfert, with a heavy sigh and sinking back upon his pillow.

"I wish him joy that inherits it!" said the little lawyer, chuckling and rubbing his hands involuntarily.

"What do you mean?" said Wolfert, again opening his eyes.

"That he'll be one of the richest men in the place!" cried little Rollebuck.

The expiring Wolfert seemed to step back from the threshold of existence: his eyes again lighted up; he raised himself in his bed, shoved back his red worsted nightcap, and stared broadly at the lawyer.

"You don't say so!" exclaimed he.

"Faith, but I do!" rejoined the other. "Why, when that great field and that piece of meadow come to be laid out in streets, and cut up into snug building lots—why, whoever owns them need not pull off his hat to the patroon!"

"Say you so?" cried Wolfert, half thrusting one leg out of bed, "why, then I think I'll not make my will yet!"

To the surprise of everybody the dying man actually recovered. The vital spark which had glimmered faintly in the socket, received fresh fuel from the oil of gladness, which the little lawyer poured into his soul. It once more burnt up into a flame.

Give physic to the heart, ye who would revive the body of a spirit-broken man! In a few days Wolfert left his room; in a few days more his table was covered with deeds, plans of streets and building lots. Little Rollebuck was constantly with him, his right-hand man and adviser, and instead of making his will, assisted in the more agreeable task of making his fortune. In fact, Wolfert Webber was one of those worthy Dutch burghers of the Manhattoes whose fortunes have been made, in a manner, in spite of themselves; who have tenaciously held on to their hereditary acres, raising turnips and cabbages about the skirts of the city, hardly able to make both ends meet, until the corporation has cruelly driven streets through their abodes, and they have suddenly awakened out of a lethargy, and, to their astonishment, found themselves rich men.

Before many months had elapsed a great bustling street passed through the very centre of the Webber garden, just where Wolfert had dreamed of finding a treasure. His golden dream was accomplished; he did indeed find an unlooked-for source of wealth; for, when his paternal lands were distributed into building lots, and rented out to safe tenants, instead of producing a paltry crop of cabbages, they returned him an abundant crop of rents; insomuch that on quarter day, it was a goodly sight to see his tenants rapping at his door, from morning to night, each with a little round-bellied bag of money, the golden produce of the soil.

The ancient mansion of his forefathers was still kept up, but instead of being a little yellow-fronted Dutch house in a garden, it now stood boldly in the midst of a street, the grand house of the neighborhood; for Wolfert enlarged it with a wing on each side, and a cupola or tea room on top, where he might climb up and smoke his pipe in hot weather; and in the course of time the whole mansion was overrun by the chubby-faced progeny of Amy Webber and Dirk Waldron.

As Wolfert waxed old and rich and corpulent, he also set up a great gingerbread-colored carriage drawn by a pair of black Flanders mares with tails that swept the ground; and to commemorate the origin of his greatness he had for a crest a fullblown cabbage painted on the pannels, with the pithy motto *Alles Kopf* that is to say, ALL HEAD; meaning thereby that he had risen by sheer head-work.

To fill the measure of his greatness, in the fullness of time the renowned Ramm Rapelye slept with his fathers, and Wolfert Webber succeeded to the leathern-bottomed arm-chair in the inn parlor at Corlears Hook; where he long reigned greatly honored and respected, insomuch that he was never known to tell a story without its being believed, nor to utter a joke without its being laughed at.

A Note About the Author

Washington Irving (1783–1859) was an American writer, historian, and diplomat. Irving served as the American ambassador to Spain in the 1840s and was among the first American writers to earn acclaim in Europe. He argued that writing should be considered a legitimate profession and advocated for stronger laws to protect writers against copyright infringement. Irving's love for adventure and drama influenced his work heavily. His most popular works, *Rip Van Winkle* and *The Legend of Sleepy Hollow*, were inspired by his visit to the Catskill mountains. Irving is credited to have perfected the short story form, and inspired generations of American writers.

A Note from the Publisher

Spanning many genres, from non-fiction essays to literature classics to children's books and lyric poetry, Mint Edition books showcase the master works of our time in a modern new package. The text is freshly typeset, is clean and easy to read, and features a new note about the author in each volume. Many books also include exclusive new introductory material. Every book boasts a striking new cover, which makes it as appropriate for collecting as it is for gift giving. Mint Edition books are only printed when a reader orders them, so natural resources are not wasted. We're proud that our books are never manufactured in excess and exist only in the exact quantity they need to be read and enjoyed.

bookfinity™

Discover more of your favorite classics with Bookfinity™.

- Track your reading with custom book lists.
- Get great book recommendations for your personalized Reader Type.
- Add reviews for your favorite books.
- AND MUCH MORE!

Visit **bookfinity.com** and take the fun Reader Type quiz to get started.

Enjoy our classic and modern companion pairings!